I0573097

A PLACE of SAFETY
(Volume Three)
Home Not Home

Kyle Michel Sullivan

KMSCB
Buffalo, NY

Cover design by Emily Jackson
ISBN: 979-8-9923177-2-5

LIBRARY OF CONGRESS CATALOGUING IN PUBLICATION DATA
Sullivan, Kyle Michel (1952-   )
A Place of Safety – Home Not Home / by Kyle Michel Sullivan
Buffalo, NY : KMSCB, 2024 | Summary: Set between 1966 and 1981, Brendan Kinsella just wants to live his life, but he was born and raised in Londonderry, Northern Ireland, and history keeps intruding.
Library of Congress Control Number: 2024922801
(print) ISBN: 979-8-9887577-3-3 (Hardcover; alk. paper)
Historical-Fiction | Narrative Fiction

Acknowledgements

Thanks to Carrie Armstrong for assisting in the editing and proofing of this book.

Thanks to Eamon and Martin Melaugh for allowing me to pick their brains and use their knowledge of the times to keep it as true as possible.

Thanks to CAIN, PRONI and *Derry of the Past* on Facebook for their excellent attention to the period and collection of images and information.

A Place of Safety
(Volume Three)
Home Not Home

Table of Contents

Preparations

I'm leaving Houston.

Finally leaving.

Departing a city I truly despised, with its cold meaning and hidden ways. Ways I'd run up against during my low-key incarceration and probationary time. Ways that had slammed me to the ground, more than once. There would be no sorrow on my part, once I was gone. It seems all I'd done, here, was drift and wait and postpone trying build a new life, thanks in no small part to constraints put on me. Where I could live. With whom I could consort. Even how I might work for my living. It had been an odd situation to be caught in, but everything about my life had been odd, while here.

No...it simply always had been.

I once mentioned all of this to my mate, Jeremy, and he said it was as if I were in a holding pattern. I smiled at the kindness of that description. In truth, I was locked in a prison awaiting notification of my release. And now that it had finally come, I could get on with more than merely existing.

Perhaps.

That was why I chose to travel on April Fools Day. It seemed too bloody appropriate a comment on my life. I had no doubt the fates were now rolling with laughter at me and my foolish notions.

Of course, I could have left a month earlier. Gone through Dublin to hop a train at Connolly Station and ride straight to Derry through Belfast. Well, if the tracks hadn't been blown up, again, by the IRA. But then, even a bus would have worked as well, and straight from the airport.

However, Bobby Sands had begun his hunger strike the first of March, and knowing full well how people in the North of Ireland could be about something so major and symbolic, it seemed best to wait till the daily protests—which would become confrontations with the constables and British Army, and then collapse into riots, and then into accusations traded back and forth and back, again—it was best to wait until they had at least begun to settle into a more orderly routine. Which it now appeared they were doing, if one could trust the nightly news, two local papers and a recent letter from my sister in Toronto. And that was despite three more lads joining in the strike, with Bobby.

A quick snippet from Mairead's last letter confirmed the difficulties.

Maeve tells us how it has become near impossible to get past the Army's checkpoints, so the majority of her shopping stays in the Bogside and Creggan. There's full support of the hunger strikers, of course, and certainty London will back down in the face of it. I hope it's soon. My mother has only once been to see a doctor and she refuses to have to deal with the army's demands and abuse, again. I cannot blame her. When I was there it was trying, and I returned home before the strike began.

Aunt Mari's friend at the Galleria office of American Express had been most sympathetic. She knew my mother was riddled with cancer and *ready to pass away at any moment*, so she had set out to find a plan for the trip that would be as easy as possible.

"And avoid the worst of the unpleasantness," as she put it.

What she'd finally decided upon was flying into New York to change planes for Shannon, and from there a bus to Galway where I would change to another bus, for Derry. The exact same route my aunt had taken, but two months earlier.

That was what she called quick and painless? I had to comment at her cheerful optimism in this itinerary. Which hurt her feelings somewhat and she explained it was the best she could do because of some *stupid little music festival*, in Dublin.

The name of that *stupid little music festival*?

Eurovision.

Fucking *Eurovision*!

It was being hosted in Dublin the first week of April, and the city had lost its goddamned mind. Flight costs were double. Decent hotels impossible to come by. Trains packed. Busses, too. The riots in Belfast and Derry were nothing compared to those rowdy crowds.

So I just knew the fates were howling with laughter at me, for having timed my travel so right. But I couldn't wait any longer; Ma was sinking, according to Maeve.

It was fortunate my mate, Everett, knew the owner of a travel agency in Montrose. That man understood the chaos of Eurovision and told me the simplest way to get back to my city of birth was avoid the Republic altogether. Fly through Gatwick then Glasgow, on British Caledonian. I could go straight from Houston, and while I'd change planes twice, I only had to change airlines once.

Of course, then I had to trust the fates that my bag would follow. There was a certain disdain he offered about Gatwick, as *not being on the level of Heathrow.*

As for Glasgow? Well, enough said about that, thank you very much. He simply suggested I add a change of clothes and any valuables to a backpack I could carry onto the plane.

But I suppose it is the perfect way to return to a home I could no longer call home in an area of the world I was from, but no longer was. If that seems confusing, it's because despite having been born Brendan Kinsella in the city of Derry, I was no longer him...and all who'd known me in that town thought me dead.

Even though I am not.

The life that wasn't mine but now was had once belonged to a lad named Brennan McGabbhinn. Of Letterkenny. In the Republic. A third or fourth cousin to myself, who had died as an infant but was now resurrected, like Lazarus, through me. And according to all, it was set in stone. McGabbhinn was my name to my cousins and those I'd met in Houston. It was the name on my visa, passport, and Green Card. I even had a driving license and health insurance under that name, something my Uncle Sean had demanded to make it look right and complete. In fact, the only proof I had that I am not the person who everyone says I am is my memory—which, according to my medical history, is not really to be trusted.

Of course, the British were not yet convinced I was no longer of this earth. But that was due only to their stubborn bureaucratic insistence that if there was no body to examine, then they needed to speak with this lad named Brendan Kinsella about a bombing he'd been caught in. And that was despite there being no evidence that he had even been there. Still, that need would not vanish until their conditions had been met.

If then.

So all I could do was accept the madness as it was.

To be honest, flying through Gatwick did seem the best way

to travel with as little fanfare as possible. Once in Glasgow, I was to shift to Logan Air's short-hopper to Derry's Airport. And one good thing about my timing was the uproar over the hunger strikes would keep everyone's focus on that, making it less likely anyone would pay much attention to me. At least, I hoped that would be the case.

It was also a much faster routing, though nowhere near as cheap as what American Express had come up with. Still, I had more than enough savings to cover it. I was even assured I could catch some sleep on the long haul across the water, if I wanted. So it was settled, and soon I was to leave for a home that was no longer my home.

Derry.

A city of ghosts. Some of whom I'd known. Some, still living. Some, God only knows what's become of them. In truth, I would have done anything in the world to avoid returning. But familial duty has its demands, and despite what people have said about the once-was-me, I honor my duties. So here I am, set to leave a city I had never existed in, for one I did not long to see, again.

When I'd revealed my plan for departure, Uncle Sean had offered to buy the ticket. Which grated on me. In the past four years I'd found any excuse I could to leave when he entered the room, so he knew full-well I wanted nothing from him. And I knew full-well he was glad to be quit of me.

But he had stupidly made the offer in front of my Aunt Mari, so certain was he that I would refuse. Instead, just to play the maggot, I'd politely thanked him, told him I'd bought the ticket, already, shown him my receipt for the cost, and then sweetly added I'd *be happy to accept reimbursement*. In *cash*, as I had no bank account. He had grown tense and angry, but he was caught. So the next day I had the money, also very deliberately handed over in front of Aunt Mari.

God, it was a petty, childish game we were playing. My uncle presenting himself as a calm, cool, collected businessman who was always on top of things. I grant you, he provided well for a wife, three children and a golden hound, and proud was he of his public image. And to his credit, he rarely drank, despite now owning four bars around the city, and he had struck me only the one time. Physically. To any and all, he would seem to be the perfect husband and father. Especially in comparison to my Da, who looked and acted the part of a drunken brute, to one and all.

But as hard as my father had been with his fists and words, not once could I think of a time where he had verbally threatened harm to any but Ma, Eamonn, or myself. And even then, it was only when he was caught in that sick need for alcohol that made him desperate. Or when someone, in his damaged mind, did wrong by him.

As a child, I'd thought his actions brutal, cruel, and unforgivable. But in comparison to my uncle's, I could almost see a sort of reason behind them. For my father had been torn by secrets and pain from his past, while my aunt's husband had no honest excuse for what he'd done except it suited him.

I sometimes think I should have fought him, openly. Argued with him. Condemned him. Revealed him as the vicious, conniving bastard he truly was. But the all too credible threats he'd made against my younger brother's life held me back. And I was now at the point of thinking of him not even worthy of contempt.

Aunt Mari had noticed our childish game, of course, for little escaped her sharp eyes. But she had not a word to say. In fact, she'd spoken with me little, since my surrender, and then about nothing of true importance. How much she knew of the reasons for it was of no matter. It was she wed to him, not I. It was just to my sorrow that she had chosen husband over blood.

While she was gone to Ma's bedside, any calls home had been to her husband or daughters, not myself. None of which were shared with me. Her return came a week after Bobby Sands began refusing food, so she got to see many of the demonstrations and hear about the brutality of those in power. Those who stupidly thought batons and rubber bullets would put the stupid taigs in their place. She had her husband and myself join her at the kitchen table to fill us in.

She agreed with me about the route through Shannon and the bus. It had proven quite the chore.

"No trouble through Letterkenny," she'd said. "Oh, but the moment we reached the border. My little suitcase was rifled, as if I were carryin' guns or drugs."

"Or cash," said Uncle Sean.

She cast a glare at him, saying, "That they found in my purse, and didn't they make an issue of it?" She was nearly shaking with anger. "Naught but a thousand pounds, and that only to help me one sister have a decent wake and burial."

"It's good you had an American passport," I said.

Aunt Mari nodded. "Those with Irish or British passports did have it worse. Some men were physically searched. And the words used on the women! It would shame Judas. What do the British think they're achievin' with this sort of nonsense?"

"Just reminding the little people of who once ruled the world," I chuckled. "They haven't the strength to admit they're nothing more than a tiny island of minimal significance."

"They're more important than you let on," said Uncle Sean.

"Aren't we all unto ourselves?" I smiled back at him.

"Even with Thatcher runnin' things, now?"

"Just more proof to my point."

He was about to growl at me, but that was when the B-girls had burst through the door—Brandi from Rice University and Bernadette from her last year of high school. At seeing their mother returned, they had instantly begun their interrogation of her, with no care for her jet-lag. So Uncle Sean had simply cast me a glare then carried her bag upstairs.

I'd gone out to have a smoke by the pool and count the minutes until I could leave. And shake my head at the never-ending stupidity of the place I once called home.

I changed my savings into traveler's checks. Pounds sterling, at American Express. All but five-hundred dollars worth; that was English cash. Then I finished the last of my projects. Those I could not sell I donated to Goodwill, who were quite appreciative. Everett let me use his Chrysler to do my carrying. That thing was a beast to drive, but that trunk held everything.

"Another reason to keep it," he'd told me. "I like the room, and if I'm ever homeless, I can sleep in its back seat."

"That'll never happen to you," I'd replied, as I returned the barge to him. He was living in a fourplex on Branard, near the high school, and had wound up being owned by two cats and their litters.

"Never say never," he'd smirked, with a wink. "Besides, I can lay my largest portfolio flat, in it. And since I'm not commuting, the price of gas is nothing."

"Would you like my Montesa to run about?" I'd asked.

"Good God, no. The way people in this town drive? The more metal I have around me, for protection, the better."

I'd laughed, pulled a kitten out of my helmet, handed it to him, and headed off.

Now it was the day before I was set to leave, and I found myself dealing with surprising moments of déjà vu. I was in the same attic space I'd woken in, eight years ago. The morning I first regained control of my lost mind. The gable windows still looked down on a pool and back yard that needed tending, and would long after I'd left. The pool house was just as reclusive. The only difference was, poor old Angus was lounging in the sun beside it, and Aunt Mari's new Aires wagon sat where that old Volvo once had.

It was as if no time had passed since that bloody bomb.

As if none of it had ever happened.

Or mattered.

Yeah, Brendan...would that it were so.

Questions Unanswered

I was packing the last of my things in my duffel bag when I heard someone come up the stairs. They paused for a bit then knocked. The heavy tread had already told me it was Aunt Mari so I said, "It's your house. Come on in."

She entered my room, her face caught in uncertainty. The month she'd stayed with Ma had been hard on her. Neighbors had helped by bringing in groceries and meals, and Maeve had dealt with the checkpoints by making the trek to Altnagelvin for Ma's medicines, as needed, since she knew best how to work past the bastards.

In the three weeks since her return, Aunt Mari had been more quiet than usual. Sometimes, her mind would wander while fixing a meal or rinsing a dish for the washer, then after a moment she'd snap back. If I was around, in any way, she'd cast me a near glance, huff at herself and continue on. At night, she had taken to having more than one beer and, if the weather wasn't too chill or raining, she'd sit at a table by the pool to smoke her cigarettes. She'd shifted to Virginia Slims menthol, as they were milder than the Kools. On those nights, after she'd almost caught me for a chat when I came out to smoke, I avoided her.

Sometimes I'd see her looking up at my window, as if trying to decide to come talk to me like she had before she went over, but she never did. So far as I knew, she never spoke with anyone about anything that might really be troubling her. Just sat and drank and smoked, for an hour, then went inside. So her approaching me, this time, made me wary.

"Just checkin' to make sure ya got all ya need for the journey," she said, almost apologetic, her brogue more in evidence.

She noticed the passport for the me who was not me. She also saw the stack of pound notes; the rest was rolled up in a couple pairs of socks, in my backpack. Not the safest method of transport, but not easily noticed.

"Ya...um, ya changed yer look," she finally mentioned.

I'd had my hair cut close, removed my sideburns, and asked Everett to put in some reddish highlights.

"The less I look as I once did, the better," I replied.

"Bren..." she said, her voice still uncertain, "is that really a concern, now?"

"Since for all anyone knows, I'm dead?"

"No! No. It's only...well...your uncle's settled the State Department down and...and surely they aren't still on about the...the—"

The silence and blinding white and that leg twisting and twirling in the air as it whispered down to land before me and splatter blood over me and—

I froze, my mind a blank. That memory hadn't cut at me in so long, it was like new. My heart was flipping and I had a pair of socks in hand, and I could not understand why. I was already wearing my boots. I noticed my duffel open before me, but I had no idea why it was like that. I had to make myself take in a deep breath and all but force myself to think—

What you see is socks and a bag near full of clothes, so you're packing, Brendan. Packing. Keep at it.

Which I finally managed to make myself do.

Aunt Mari had been talking, but I could not tell you a word she said until she sighed and sat on the edge of the bed to say, "Bren, I should let ya know—when ya see Bernadette, yer mother is...well, it may come as a shock. Try not to show it."

That jolted me into breathing, again; I hadn't realized I'd stopped. "She...does Ma know I'm coming?"

"Mairead let Maeve know all. About Brennan McGabbhinn."

Of course.

"A cousin," she continued. "Who's come to help. I backed her in that story. When I was over. Neither Bernadette nor Maeve were best pleased."

I took in a long breath. So not even my mother and sister were told it was really me. Did they honestly think this would fool either of them for more a minute or two? So what was the purpose of maintaining that lie? Hopes that they might spread the story of *a distant relative's arrival* so the bloody cows would make it truth during their usual craics? It was a weak cover story we were offering up.

I let myself sigh and finished the last of my packing, saying, "Well, that passport's the proof."

"Yes," she murmured. "Sean showed me before he give to ya. Now yer full legal. It was quite a fight, for him..."

So there it was. In my childish way, I'd been clinging to the idea she'd been in the dark about that, at least, but she knew all about it. Which probably meant she'd stood aside and let him threaten death to her own nephew. To my little brother. To force me to remain in this purgatory. Her own blood. Christ. It meant she probably knew a great many other things I'd rather not know she knew.

God, the betrayal I felt at this. The anger.

But I managed to keep my voice cool and even. "As he promised."

"Yes." Still a murmur. "An' when ya return, ya can do as ya like."

That made me pause. Return? Here? Did she honestly think I'd come back to this prison?

"I might move..." whispered from me as—

"I hear Aspen's nice," Rocky was saying, in her soft voice.

Another ghost...

Another memory I'd not had in years. Again, it was hard to breathe. Christ.

"If ya want, ya could, I suppose, but I don't think it would be best for ya. For so...so many reasons."

"You think me too simple to live on my own?" I asked.

"No! Why would you think that?"

Why would I not? It was she who'd made an issue of me being born on the Second of February, telling everyone about America's Woodchuck—no, Groundhog Day, thus labeling me as wary, selfish and stupid. I could remember some of the craic about me, even as a wain.

"Saw his shadow as he was being born so ran back into his darkness."

"Didn't come out till half-seven."

"That must be why he loves the night."

"And why his thoughts are hard to make out."

"All cloaked in silence."

"Off to himself. No friends."

And Ma emphasizing it with, *"Don't make too much out of him. He's just simple."*

And here was Aunt Mari pushing it further.

"That's not what I meant, at all," she continued. It's just...it's just so many other things. Your doctor's here. And insurance for yourself is so expensive and..."

It sounded as if she was leading up to something. Were that the case, I wish she'd just get it the fuck out of the way.

All I murmured was, "If you say so."

She gave a long sigh then asked, "How long do ya think ya'll be there?"

"Depends on Ma." I was impressed with how casual I seemed. I looked at her. "Will you be coming for the wake?"

She shook her head, almost sad. "I've said me good-byes. No need to show off for others."

I let myself chuckle. "Never heard a funeral referred to, like that."

"That's Ireland. People come from far and wide to say lovely things about the dead, and nothin' bad, whether they knew them or not."

I nodded. "I remember, from Da's."

She cast me a sad look. "He was rough with ya, wasn't he?"

"You know full well he was!" I snapped. I took in a deep breath and continued in calmness, "Me and Eamonn. And Ma. Not the girls and the youngest. Kieran timed his birth well; he missed all the man's hate and anger."

"Bren, it's unkind to speak ill of the dead."

I just rolled my eyes and zipped my duffel closed.

"There is...well...there's one thing I should tell ya..." Her voice trailed off.

Despite myself, my voice was sharp as I snapped, "Aunt Mari, I've hardly led what I would call a sheltered existence, so tell me what you need to. No hemming and hawing, as you like to say."

It took her a moment but then she drew in a deep breath and whispered, "Yer father may not have been born a Kinsella."

If she thought I was going to be shocked or horrified or angry, I disappointed her. "*May* not have? Who says so?"

She was quiet for a moment then finally said, "Yer mother."

Of course. Ma and her secrets. Her anger when I went looking into Da's past. Her refusal to acknowledge her brothers. It all rang odd to me, even at the time, and now I was finding my suspicions had some basis in fact. That's probably why I was still so calm in the face of this revelation.

"Kinsella's the name on the registry of my birth. I had to get a copy of it when I sent for...for my passport..."

That I showed to Joanna, not minutes before the world went white and dead...dead...dead...

"If I'm understandin' Bernadette right, yer father took that name when he married her. I think it was from a solicitor she knew. His birth name—it may have been Clark."

"*Understood her right?* What does that mean?"

"She was babblin' on and...well...some of the things she was tellin' me—some of the stories—they didn't make sense so they may have been nothin'. I'm not completely sure Bernadette knew what she was sayin'. Percocet can bother your mind and..." Her voice trailed off.

"What other things did she say?"

"Oh, nonsense. Like claimin' yer brother was blessed by Eamon de Valera, when they weren't even there durin' the man's visit."

That made me turn my full attention to her. "But Eamonn and Mairead were born in Derry, weren't they?"

"That's what I've been told, but—"

"Then where were they?"

"I don't know," she said. "Not really. I was still at the home and they hadn't settled in Nailors, yet."

She leaned her head against her hand, propped on her knee, and sighed. "It's hard to keep track of everything, now. The news about yer father was so off, I just got lost and uncertain an'-an' seein' Bernadette like she is..."

I let myself chuckle. "Well, it might explain why Da's past was that of a ghost. Did she tell you what he did to make him change his name?"

"She never said. But somethin' else. Ya know of yer seven uncles?" I nodded. "Bernadette still swears she and I have no siblings. No brothers. So if any do show to see her, she will become a horror to them. I saw that when Michael and his wife came over, while I was there. A very pleasant man, he is. And his wife is sweet. But to my shock, Bernadette near came off her bed to attack him when he was up in her room, screamin' that since they'd abandoned her and myself, they were no kin to us."

I nodded. "Must be why she never spoke to us of them."

"I've made contact with all seven, now, an' they are aware of the situation. If any do show while yer there, or come to the wake, they'll know ya as Brennan McGabbhinn."

I hesitated before asking, "Did any of them know me Da?"

"No, all had gone across the water long before he came into the picture."

"When did *you* first meet him?"

"At the weddin'."

"In Derry?"

She shook her head. "Magherafelt. I was still held in the home, so Sister Luke accompanied me. It was just us, the married couple, a priest and the man to register it."

"Why did they get married?"

She hesitated then murmured, "To give yer brother a name."

Oh. Well. "Da never told you why he changed his name? Or Ma?"

"He was introduced to me as Kinsella and I had no reason not to believe him, or my sister. Now she's dyin' and-and-and as I said, wasn't in full control of her thoughts. Maeve is of a mind she's only confused."

I nodded and said, "So it may be best to leave it at that."

"Which is why yer the only one I'm tellin' any of this to," she said, weary to the bone.

"Ma never said anything to Mai, when she was there?"

"No, I don't think so. She didn't want to upset her, now she's havin' another set of twins."

"Twins? Jesus, no wonder she's threatening Tur's prized possession."

"Brendan!"

I noticed a pair of black briefs I'd neglected to pack so unzipped my duffel bag to shove them in. Then as I re-zipped it closed, I asked, "So why're *you* telling *me* this? And the night before I leave?"

She eyed me then took in a deep breath. "I wasn't goin' to, but then I began thinkin' an' I...I just thought ya should know what to expect."

What a pile of bollocks, after all she'd told me about her journey there and back. I half-think she wanted me to verify this new information for her, one way or the other, but done it in such a way as to not make it a request. She knew me well enough to figure I'd probably look into it, in my own way. Then she'd find out the truth without ever touching the issue, herself. I had never thought of my aunt as a sneak, until that moment.

I took in a deep breath and let it out before saying, "Well. Now I know. Is there anything else?"

"No." She rose and drew me into a hug.

I made myself hug her back.

"When ya return," she said, "this will be yer home, again. Right?"

"When I return." Said without hesitation.

She nodded and left.

I stood in the middle of the room for I don't know how long, fighting to keep my brain from running wild. Finally, I opened a beer and downed it. I'd have gone for a couple valium, as well, but I'd pulled back from the drugs while working on that Peugeot so had none. Dammit. Though probably for the best. I'd have difficulty enough passing safely into Derry without a drug-addled haze part of the mix. And were I to be arrested for drugs offenses, the falseness of my passport could be easily found out.

It is unwise to tempt fate, Grasshopper.

Which was why I was not going as Brennan McGabbhinn, though I did slip that passport into an inside pocket of my duffel bag, just in case. That was another reason for me to pay my own ticket; so the Houston family wouldn't know what I was doing.

I was traveling as Jeremy Landau.

Shadow Plans

It came up when I was at the last dinner I would attend at Mrs. Glendon's, to let one and all know I was heading home. In honor of my departure, Mrs. Kendall made as fine an Irish stew as ever was and Miss Sauvage dressed the table in true Celtic tradition. Eldon brought books on Ireland and the Irish to use as a centerpiece and Sonja pulled together mugs from the recent St. Patrick's Day for the beer. Everett tried to get hold of some Guinness, but...

"You'd think I was trying to import heroin, the way the FDA freaked out," he said. "Couldn't even find any when I was in New York, and that fucking town was sellin' Lone Star longnecks at five dollars a bottle! Fuckin' LONE Star!"

Instead, we wound up with Grölsch and its swing-top lids, and we had much fun with that.

Jeremy joined us a bit late but in time to eat. "Had to finish up the paperwork for a meeting Sunday night, nine pm. Talking to Peking...whoa, I mean, Pinyin. Ten am, their time."

"You heading over anytime soon?" I asked.

He'd stretched and said, "Maybe the end of May. Already renewed my passport. No more Bicentennial one."

That's when I showed him my supposed passport. Everett joined us and they both eyed it, wary. They were the only two who knew who I truly was, and I trusted them, in full.

"How do you feel about travelin' on this?" Everett asked.

I shrugged. "It's what I got."

"Any problem with a guy from Ireland entering Derry, now?"

Again, I shrugged.

Eldon eyed the passport over Jeremy's Shoulder, saying, "You would be subjected to greater scrutiny. Questioned. Noticed. It is very unfortunate you do not have an American one."

"Or be Jewish, like Jeremy," I'd chuckled.

He laughed. "I'd let you have my old one but it's got *canceled* stamped on it."

Everett hesitated, his mind going fast, and asked him, "When was it good till?"

Jeremy thought for a moment then said, "August."

"Could I look at it? You two look so damn much alike, I'm just wonderin'...well, maybe I could get it off..."

"Why?"

I knew what Everett was up to the second he said it, and I liked the idea but had to be sure about something. "Couldn't that cause a problem? Isn't everything computerized now?"

Eldon said, "They won't care as you leave the country. Only when you return. In England, they check to make certain you are not on a warning list. If all else is correct..."

Jeremy finally caught on to the idea. "He's right. I mean, I had to show it to the airline to prove I had it with me, but it never got checked till I arrived in Hong Kong or Israel."

"First let's make sure I can do anything," said Everett.

Eldon said, "You are considering an action that is rather dangerous and very illegal." But he was almost smiling.

"It could work," Jeremy said, getting caught up in the idea. "I already got my new one. Anyone says anything, I can show it to 'em; tell 'em they screwed up. And if they want to see my old one, I...I shredded it. And if they still get nasty, I call Uncle David and we go with *somebody must've forged a copy*." He seemed to be enjoying the sneakiness of his plan.

"But when Bren returns...?" Eldon asked, wary.

I smiled and said, "I'll use that." Pointing to Brennan's.

He looked at it, looked at me and said, "I think you will need an exit stamp on it." And he gave it back.

"I'll deal with that when I have to," I said, slipping it into my back pocket.

He eyed me, for a moment, then turned back to his stew and spoke not another word. But I did catch a hint of sadness had come to his smile, as if he knew I was not returning. He was another of the few I truly trusted, and still wrote his letters in Gaelic to Rhuari, so I felt he would say nothing.

After the dinner was done and all good-byes said, we three hopped over to Jeremy's apartment and he showed his old passport to me. It had a blue cover with a special seal on the face.

CANCELED was stamped on the page above his photo in bright red. His hair was short and he was clean-shaven, looking very young and quite professional.

And so much like me when I was still alive and hopeful and still unscarred, it felt strange. Unreal.

Everett looked at it for a long, quiet moment, then quietly said to me, "Yes...this could easily be a photo of you."

"Even the B-girls swear we're brothers," I said.

Everett stayed focused on it as he said, "Yeah, just...uh, just cut your hair a bit shorter so it's not as long as this photo and isn't so curly. Put some highlights in. Touch of Lady Clairol. But will it be good for long enough?"

I shrugged. "Mairead says she's fading, then there'll be the wake and family to settle. A month, maybe. Six weeks."

At which time it'll come back to Jere via post.

Everett took in a deep breath and said, "Let me see what I can do with it. I have a solvent...Q-tips..." And his voice trailed off. He walked out the door, still not looking at either of us.

We followed him out to the walkway and watched him head down to his car, so soft and ethereal it's like he was merely a shadow passing by.

"He's been doin' that a lot, lately," Jeremy said. "You know why he was in New York?"

I gave him a shrug. I knew he'd taken his portfolio with him so his plan was clear.

Jeremy nodded. "He wants a job there, is my bet. My fault."

I cast Jeremy a wary look.

He sort of grimaced. "I wasn't gonna tell you, but Tole got into a fight. In Oceanside. And he...uh, he got outed to his commander. Gettin' court-martialed."

That took me by surprise. "Vangie's brother?"

He nodded. "We stayed in touch and-and he's gonna stay here, for a bit. Till he figures out how to tell his dad."

"I can't see Rene or Louise having a problem with him. They got so many sons."

"That's what Vangie says."

So he was still in contact with her and—

She slapped me. Twice. For being a true bastard.

"But you never know," he continued. "She's flyin' to New Orleans, next month, so we'll face 'em down, together."

Christ, thank God I'd not be here. "Do *your* parents know?"

He shook his head.

I let out a long breath. "Well, not to push, but you might want to tell them."

"Why? What d'you mean?"

"Your sister talked to me, once or twice..."

He gave me a comical look of shock. "Rachel had a conversation with a goy-boy? I am shocked."

I nodded. "Jere, you know I never tell on people, but I-I-I think in this case you...you should be aware. She was...well, it's mad, but she was asking how I felt about *incestuous relationships.*"

"What the fuck?"

"It struck me odd, as well, but then...considering she's agreed with the B-girls that you and I are like brothers...and she has mentioned more than once you and I are *such very good friends...*"

I could see the realization wash over him and he gripped the railing. "I'll fuckin' kill her..."

Just for fun I smirked and said, "All I said back was, *Rachel, do I really look the part of a Jew?*"

That made him snort, then laugh and backhand my shoulder. "What the fuck does a Jew look like, bitch? And your dick sure as hell is Jewish. You'll pass. So long as you don't talk with that fuckin' brogue."

I snapped into a Texas twang, "Yor right a-bout tha-yat, little feller. Better if'n Ah talk lahk yeeeew."

"I don't sound like that!"

"Y'ever lissen t' yer-self?"

"Shit, just-just-just don't talk much at all. And when you do, make like you got laryngitis."

I chuckled. "I only told you because I...well, I get the feeling Rachel's planning something dramatic and it might be best if you get out ahead of it."

"Yeah, like tellin' my folks Tole and I're fuckin' each other," he growled.

Which I figured but did not need to have verified, so bluntly.

He sighed. "She's divin' deep into the Torat Moshe and been quotin' the Talmud more. All Zionist shit and righteousness, since Scott got married. Might be movin' to Jerusalem, so thanks. It's just...just..."

He was shaking, a little, and fear was making its way into his face. I nudged him.

"Jere, you're me China. We've both seen the worst. We know what the rest is truly worth. And keep in mind...if things don't go well with any of them, you've always got family with Mrs. Glendon."

He nodded and chuckled. "My oasis of sanity." Then he cast a hard look at me and asked, "*Are* you comin' back?"

I hesitated then shook my head. I didn't dare give voice to it. Instead, I pulled him into a hug, saying, "You can hand my Montesa over to Tole, if you like."

He hugged me harder.

"Gonna miss you," whispered from him, then I stepped back and headed down the stairs. "Lemme know where you settle, Bren."

I didn't look back, just waved my hand as if in agreement.

A couple days later, I got my hair clipped then went to Everett to shift its color closer to Jeremy's. The dyeing took all of two hours, as he'd also had to touch up my goatee. And my eyebrows. Once he was done, to my eyes I was near Jeremy's twin—and looked damn strange to myself.

"This isn't a good look for you," Everett said. "Skin tone's wrong. But by the time you get to the entry desk, they'll be so sick of dealin' with Americans they'll probably just give it a glance, stamp it and tell you to fuck off."

"In true Brit fashion."

He showed me the old passport and damn, he'd done a fine job. You couldn't see a trace of the red ink.

He hesitated then asked, trying to be playful, "What're you givin' me for doin' this?"

I knew what he was hinting at, but all I said was, "I could go to *Rocky Horror* in a gold Speedo and blond wig."

He jolted and smiled, almost sweetly. "You...you'd really do that? Jeremy laughs at me when I ask him to. Of course, that was a couple years ago and..."

"I enjoy it, well enough. Susan Sarandon's got a nice set on her. Of course, I haven't the body of the Rocky actor."

"Don't diss yourself," he laughed, then coughed. "You'd make the perfect Rocky." And coughed, again.

"You need some water?" I asked.

He shook his head. "Touch of bronchitis. So, what're they doin'? Keepin' the rest of your stuff in the pool house or attic?"

"Nothing left to keep."

His expression froze and he looked at me. Hard. Searched my face then pushed me to the wall, grabbed the back of my neck and kissed me long and deep and French in style. Tender but needy.

I let him.

After all these last years of madness, much of which he knew about, this was hardly the time to pretend outrage.

When his lips finally parted from mine, his eyes were filled with hurt. His voice a whisper. "Is...is that how you kissed her?"

I joined his soft tone. "Vangie?" He nodded. "Yes."

"But not..." He brushed his fingers over my left shoulder.

Over *Joanna—*

Kissing me on the Ha'penny Bridge. My shoulder pounding from the tattoo. Her breath laced with spearmint. Holding me close atop the circle fort. Dreaming about forever.

"No." I finally said, barely audible. "It would've put her off, and I'd have done anything to keep that from happening."

He nodded and stepped back. "Like what I just did."

"Have I run screaming down the street, yet? Though if I do catch your bronchitis, I may have to beat the hell out of you."

He stroked a thumb over my left eyebrow. The tenderness of it made my heart ache. "Considering your luck with girls," he half chuckled, "maybe you oughta shift to the wild side."

"With you?"

He laughed to himself, then coughed. "Yeah, right. Right. Me as *Frankenfurter,* you as *Rocky*? No way. I ain't got pumps for that and I'll be damned if I shave off my mustache. No, I...I'll be gone before you're back. Got a job offer. Ad agency."

"New York?" He nodded. "Don't like working freelance?"

"Don't like livin' here," he whispered. "Met some nice guys, there, and...and..."

He was hurting and he'd been such a mate to me, I couldn't help but give him a light kiss, back, then pat his cheek. Like Vangie had done me that last horrible day. Before I'd been the bastard, to her.

Before she'd slapped me.

He reacted to it like a kitten laying into being petted. "Why can't I fall in love with people who'll love me back?"

"I do love you," I said, and meant it.

"But not the way I want," he'd sighed, almost wistful. Still that simple touch seemed to soothe him, so he grinned and said, "So if you're ever in New York, Pug."

"I'll stop in and piss on your hydrant."

He laughed. "Try a tree, instead. They need the water."

I yapped at him in answer, slipped the passport in my back pocket, and we parted with him still laughing.

Two days later, I was dumped at Intercontinental by my Aunt and Uncle and the B-Girls. Not from irritation or anger or pleasure for me to be gone, but because I insisted they not follow me inside.

"I'll not be off for so very long," I lied. "No need to park and waste your time, here, on chit-chat over nothing."

"But it's a long trip," said Brandi.

"And we need to make sure you have everything you need," Bernadette growled.

"There's meal service on the plane," said Aunt Mari, more than a hint of relief on her face, "and he's hardly goin' to darkest Africa."

The girls would have argued further, but Uncle Sean was behind the wheel of the Aries and he snapped, "He said he wants to be alone, so let him go and let's get home 'fore the traffic's bad."

I nodded in agreement with him, so away they went.

A couple hours later, I was bound for Gatwick.

I'd booked a window seat so I could watch the clouds pass. Enjoy the vision of dusk dancing in closer and closer, as if it thought it was being clever in its sneaky manner of taking over the day. I loved how peaceful and soft everything became in the nighttime sky, the stars sharp and brilliant, my true companions once more and—

I looked out my window at Nailors as the gleaming pinpoints of light took over the sky and brought me peace and Father Jack sat next to me, sipping a brandy and casting me furtive glances, pretending to read his missal in a simple room of pale walls and no windows, just a door. He checked his watch then Aunt Mari was signaling for the stewardess and water accompanied a pill and I accepted both, obedient, and turned to watch the clouds and—

Lightning flashed between two huge banks of thick black

cotton. Twisting. Turning. Wicked glimmers of life within them, dancing like the furies and giving meaning to things that could never truly live. Yanking me back to the here and now. I had to chuckle. It seemed the heavens were saying...

You could just not go on from Gatwick. Or even vanish from Glasgow. Mail Jeremy's passport back to him. Hop a ferry to Dublin as Brennan, and the devil with Eurovision. Bus it down to Cobh and find work on a boat or cruise or something, like you once thought. Rejoin your life on your own terms. Live unto yourself, and the devil with those who claim to care for you.

I snorted and my mind growled its response. *You're a bit late, aren't you? Bastard fates. I could've done any of that in Houston.*

But you didn't. Did you?

A simple response to put me back in my place. Because I was now old enough to accept that I'd always just done the minimum needed to get by in my life. Fallen over and over into the pattern of waiting for others to make my decisions for me as I wandered along. I'd not have needed anyone's agreement to move to Aspen; I could have gone on my own. If Uncle Sean was so prone to hiring help *under the table*, I could have found work of the same sort, there. Fixed things there, as well. Made my own way in my own time. I'd shown that while at Mrs. Glendon's. Hell, I could still have gone after Rocky was killed. Instead, I'd waited till my Aunt and Uncle had taken over and made the decisions for me. Like I was a child.

Same for Vangie. To be a bastard to her, like I was? There was no need for that. It accomplished nothing but to spread the pain. For she had been right. It would have been the adult thing to meet with her at the theater, watched the movie, discussed the situation, parted ways and remained friends. Moved on like a man. And my beating might not ever have taken place, once those animals realized we were no longer a couple. Lon would have heard and he might have put an end to it before it began.

But in truth, that was a silly thing to think. It still could have happened. My thought is, Lon's real reason for helping in it was to revenge Matty's death, and me dating his sister was nothing but a means to an end. As for Uncle Sean, he was perfectly happy to let me be punished. He thought I deserved it for being such trouble. Causing him so much expense. Putting his financial trajectory into peril. So if Lon hadn't pushed it, he might have.

Hell, for all I knew, he actually was the one behind it. You never can really know, with people.

On top of it, I had shown myself I was capable of picking up and moving and making my own decisions by leaving and keeping to myself for that year. I'd started to build a life apart from everyone I knew, which I'd liked. And which had worked out well for my Aunt and Uncle. Had I remained in the pool house, I truly believed I'd have been caught out as an illegal alien during one of the FBI's casual visits and returned to the North, for interrogation. That would have been hell for everyone involved.

But by vanishing, I'd provided them a sort of plausible deniability. You'd think my Uncle would have been happy for that instead of using my brother's situation to drag me back close to the family, against my will.

Against my will.

What a silly phrase.

I'd given in to his blackmail with minimal fight, as if I was glad for someone else to make the decision for me, again. I could have told him to fuck off, hopped on my Montesa and just gone wherever. Dared him to kill my brother. He wouldn't have done it. Todd was right; he was a coward, down deep. I halfway wonder if he'd made the threat to see if he could just get rid of me. I don't know. I only know I took the easiest route.

Maybe I truly am simple.

God, when will I stop second-guessing myself so much? I did what I thought was right, at the time, and now it was done so cannot be changed.

Did the stars ever beat themselves up, like that? Of course not. They knew what they were, always high above, shining, gleaming in the night sky and hidden in daytime light. They were constant and steady.

Unlike me.

More lightning danced across distant clouds, as if to argue with the quiet stars. For all the good that did. Not even the slightest dimming of them. Barely any notice.

I chuckled, pulled a portable tape recorder from my backpack and popped in a cassette of Joan Baez. On went my earphones and I whisper-sang to *Farewell, Angelina*

And so I was returning to my home that was not my home. Not because I had to or was forced to or held at the point of a gun to be made to, but because once again it seemed I was drifting down a course in history that had long been decided for me.

Straight to catastrophe, I was sure.

Arrival

Gatwick was almost up to the standards of Intercontinental. Almost. Naturally customs was in the darkest, dingiest part of it. I did like Everett said—kept myself at the back of the line to hand over my entry card and passport, then spouted my one-word responses in a Texas chirp. I had slept on the plane so I was feeling quite good. The ever-weary official had little cause to look hard at anything, so he passed me on.

Fortunately, I was not selected for further investigation, for I'd been so long in the customs line it was a race to catch the Glasgow flight. From there I boarded an odd-shaped propeller craft that reminded me of a sardine's can and was loud, but with few passengers. It flew in low and straight, and despite myself I felt a sense of anticipation as the coast passed beneath us and the dark land rushed up to let us bounce down upon it.

I was on the single-seat side so couldn't catch a look of Derry from the air, not that there'd be much to see; a thick mist was building off the sea. But soon as I stepped off the plane I knew I was home from the bite in the damp air and the soft breeze with the scent of the farms, close by.

It wasn't much of an airport, really; more like a private airfield that was run down, with the terminal built up as an afterthought. I had to go to a table and present my passport, again, even though this was within the UK. Miracle of miracles, my duffel bag appeared in the luggage cart—and was searched for the first time. As was my backpack. The agent found a roll of the traveler's checks, so a pair of soldiers were called over to consider them.

"Papers," one of them snarled, his accent thick with Cockney.

"He's got mah payas-port an' ree-turn ticket," I said, indicating the immigration officer. I'd bought a round trip set for a month later, for appearance's sake. The soldier took it and flipped through every page of Jeremy's travels as if in disbelief while the other thick bastard counted through the checks, frowning. At the same time, the agent continued to dig through my bag as if hoping he might find a package of pot or a hidden bottle of whiskey to confiscate.

The first soldier snarled at me, "Isr'el, 'ong Kong, Dubai, Tokyo? What sor' of business ya do, then?"

"I's workin' in aw-l. Made some money an' now I'm goin' ba-yack for my Master's."

"What brings ya 'ere?"

"We-yell, in Israel they's havin' trouble with the-yem Palestinians, and I'm thinkin' I'll do mah thesis on com-paris-on of British methods of controlin' crowds to the IDF."

"IDF?"

"Israeli Defe-yense Fo-orce."

He nodded.

His compatriot held up the book of checks. "It's twenty-five hundred quid, here."

They hadn't found the other two, yet.

Thick eyed it. "What's it fer?"

"I'm gonna bee he-yer a whole month. Never know what's gonna hayah-pen. I can change 'em back for doll-lars when I get home."

"Where ya stayin'?"

"A fre-yend of mine's got fam-ily hee-yer, so I'm stayin' with the-yem. They're s'posed to be me-etin' me. I already been through customs..." I was laying the accent on thick, but I'd heard from Mairead *Dallas* was showing here so maybe this bastard's fart would have seen the bloody show and accepted it as documentary, not fiction.

It seems he did. The passport was tossed back to the immigration officer or whatever the hell he was and stamped, again, and slapped on my chest. Then my duffel bag was kicked over, totally in shambles. I had to force it closed before I could sling its strap over my shoulder. Between the lumpiness of that and my backpack, I could barely walk upright.

I saw Maeve standing by the entrance, watching everyone who was coming out. She might have been eight years older and much more grown from when I'd left, but I recognized the set of her jaw and sharp eyes. She was also as solid as Aunt Mari, if not yet as round. She cast a look over me then turned back to checking others...until she frowned and looked, again.

Okay, so here we go.

I strode up to her, smiling, and said, "Are you May-eve?"

Her frown deepened. "Mr. McGabbhinn?"

"No, I'm Jeremy Landau. I'm here in Brennan's stead."

She took a step back, wary. "You're not? I—I've been told nothing of this, Mr. Lad-y-ow."

"Landau," I said, "and it's Jeremy, or Jere, if'n yew lahk. Brennan said you'd meet me. He was gonna call you, set it all up."

"Well, he hasn't, as if he had the right to. Treat me like a bloody hotel. I don't know him or you. Is he still comin'?"

"No, ma'am. He's not."

"But I-I-I...the situation is so-so...I mean...well, how'd you even know to approach me? I've never even met this Brennan and you—"

"Oh, I'm a friend of the family, 'specially your cousin, Scott. I know Brandi and Berni, the girls that think they're twi-yns, and your Uncle Sean—well, Mr. Nolan, and your Aunt, Mizz Nolan. She was just here an' showed me some pictures of you."

"And *she* knew you were comin'?" I could see her temper starting to flair.

"Well...yes. I-I-I thought it's all settled. But if'n it ain't, I could get a hotel room till you get a chance to find out if it's all okay."

Maeve huffed and looked around, her Derry manners fighting to take over. "No, no, Mr. Landau..."

"Jeremy."

She nodded. "Jeremy. Yes, yes. Forgive me, you've been on a long journey and-and I've got things set up, so I'll not put you out. I'll call my aunt when we're to home and-and-and I'm sure it's naught but a failure to communicate. It's only...the situation you're comin' into is hardly..."

"Yes, I know all about that, ma'am."

"Please, the *ma'am* has me soundin' like I'm your mother. It's Maeve."

"Maeve. I know your momma's ill, and that is somethin' Brennan wasn't gonna be able to help with, but I will in any way you need. My daddy's a doctor, so I picked a few things up. Bren felt that would make me better suited to provide backup."

"That's very kind of you." She looked harder at me, as if she didn't quite believe a word of my story. Finally she said, "Sorry to stare, but you look so much like someone..."

I nodded. "I'm to-old I could be mistaken for your brother. Brendan, wa'n't it?"

Maeve nodded. "That must be it. I'd swear I see him in you. But it has been years."

"Oh? They don't talk 'bout him much, your aunt an' uncle. It's like he passed on."

"No!" Her voice was sharp. "He-he's just not here, is all."

"Is your brother comin' to pick us up? Roar-ry, wasn't it?"

"Rhuari. No, he can't get across. Hunger strike's set the British too on edge."

"I he-yer everything does that to them."

She looked at me, even harder, then shook her head and eyed my duffel, saying, "Is-is this all of it?" I nodded. "Then come along; we'll hire a taxi."

I have to say it felt good to be near Maeve, again, and would have let her know my truth, but the customs lads were still watching after me, and I saw more British soldiers and constables marching about, armed to the teeth, their eyes filled with warning. No need to raise questions in anyone's mind.

Outside, a little black coffin rolled up, its driver one of those round-faced lads with only his cap and jacket keeping his whiskey-eyes hid. I was about to put my suitcase in the boot—no, we're from America so it's *trunk*. But Maeve guided it to the back seat with us.

"It's better up here." We got in and she told the driver, "Off to Lecky and Fahan; I'll tell you where to go from there."

"Aye, miss," was all he said and we were off at a crawl.

I thought it odd to be going so slow—till we were stopped at a roadblock before we hit Clooney Road and two paras with rifles extended were yelling, "Lights off! Lights off!"

The driver dimmed his headlamps and more paras shot torch lights—*flash*lights into the taxi.

"W'erre ye bound ferr?" snapped one of them in a Burr.

"Clíodhna Place off Abbey Street," said Maeve, calm and cool as ice. Her purse was open and she handed over her identity card without them even asking.

Burr took them and looked at me. "W'erre's yerrs?"

"What's he wa-nt?" I asked, acting dumb and drawling it out.

"Your passport, Jeremy."

I nodded and handed it over. Burr glared at it, confused. "'Merrican, 'err ye?"

"Shore am."

"A rrepor'err, 'err ye?"

"Oh, no. I'm he-yer to research—"

He nodded. "Open yon sack."

Maeve pointed to the duffel and said, "Open your bag, Jeremy."

I did.

Burr saw the mess it was in and shoved his hand through my clothes, anyway, and noticed my NASA cap. He picked it up to look at. "Houston? Herrd o' it, but w'erre th' feck's 'at?"

"Texas."

"An' herre ye come? Fecked up, is 'at? Got ye a drriverr's permit?"

Shite, I hadn't thought about someone asking for that. I covered it with, "No, I le-yeft it at home. Didn't think I'd ne-ed it."

He looked at Jeremy's passport, again, shined his torch on me, then cast a quick look at the driver's identity card and face before tossing ours back at us and waving us on. I dropped the passport and had to dig for it in the darkness.

"Don't put it away," said Maeve. "We'll have a good three stops more like this."

"Good Lo-ord, just to the air-port?"

"To anywhere. To live."

"I'd heard things was gettin' better."

"Compared to how it was. The hunger strike's set us back, some."

"Looks like I'm here just in time for some fu-un."

"If chaos is your idea of it," Maeve snorted, glaring at me as if I were the mad one, but before any more could be said the driver cleared his throat and began to slow down. I forced a smile to my face and turned it on a para who was approaching us, his rifle at the ready, two more of the bastards behind him, their fingers itching to fire as one yelled, "Let's see yer bloody pay-pers," in some nasty British gargle.

Fuckin' shite, I was home all right.

Déjà vu

We had two more stops like that—one getting on the Craigavon, the next getting off before we could head to the Bogside—and it was the same fear and anger and danger at each one. The same slow process of letting you pass in your own town. The same denigration by a mix of the same sorts of soldiers.

Then down this new flyover we went, past the Long Tower to Lecky Road. God, the houses torn down to make it. Generations of families tossed out. In the dark and thick mist, it was as if I'd never been born and raised here. New low apartments. Streets built over. Neighborhoods completely gone. No hint of our old home on Nailors Row. The Walker Monument destroyed. The Free Derry gable once at the end of a line of terrace homes now standing alone. The only recognizable parts of this *new and improved* city were the shadowy tower of St. Eugene's and the big ugly Rossville Flats, all looking weary beyond belief.

We were stopped by yet another roadblock, this one manned by lads in Balaclavas or bandanas to cover themselves. It was the same questions—*Who are ya? What're ya doin' here? Where ya stayin'?* But this time with Derry accents, though one seemed to be from Belfast. These lads were quite impressed with who I claimed to be and started questioning me about the States and what America was like. Sounded like a few were ready to go on the run to get away from the insanity. But the one from Belfast snarled them quiet and sent us on our way.

We finally turned onto Clíodhna and were dropped in front of the same door I'd walked away from more than eight years ago. I got out, pulled my duffel from the cab by its handles—I hadn't even bothered trying to close it after the second checkpoint—and stood there for a moment, taking in how little changed my old home was. Oh, the paint was fresh, the doorstep washed, and the windows completely intact with soft lace curtains visible inside, but it was still a mirror image of my memory. I looked up a street that was tight and dark and quiet and reeked of pain and suffering. A near despair rolled over me in a wave of such depth, I had to face away from Maeve so she'd not see me close to weeping.

Eight years.

Eight bloody fucking years of death and destruction, and it was as if time had frozen still, here...and it tore into me.

"It's here, Jeremy," Maeve said as she pushed her key into the latch. Then she led me inside and Jesus God, the furniture was all the same—settee, tables, comfy chair, shrine to the virgin Mother, fireplace, ratty rug completely untouched if a bit more worn.

The one true difference? Photos in frames now covered the walls—Mairead's wedding to Tur; their family of seven, soon to be nine; a press photo of Eamonn in Long Kesh on the blanket; Rhuari's sweet but simple wedding photo with his lovely, happy Bridie, whose name was the perfect description of her. Next to it was one with their wain.

Other new photos surrounded it—Maeve smiling as a snapshot was taken; Kieran half-scowling, for the same reason; official snaps of each of us at our Confirmation, which included the one and only image of the lad banished across the water...or to a grave, whichever. That brought a crooked grin to my face as I took another glance about the room and...

I heard Maeve take in a sudden breath. I turned to find her glaring at me, scowling.

"I know that smirk," she snapped, low and whispery.

I dropped the twang and said, soft and easy, "Howya, Maeve." Someone was probably upstairs with Ma so wanted to be careful.

Torn between anger, fear, happiness and joy, Maeve crept closer and closer, finally murmuring, "Brendan? It *is* you?"

I nodded.

Anger took over and she growled up to me. "So you've finally come! What the bloody hell is all this!?"

I kept my voice soft as the words tumbled out. "I-I-I think the Brits want to—well, to talk to me about that bombing and I-I-I...well, that means I can't come back under my legal name, now can I? So I-I-I made me as different from who I used to be, as possible, and I-I-I just felt it best to wait till we were someplace safe to let you know this and...and..." And my voice trailed off.

She was still low and scowling. "Did Aunt Mari know?"

"No, and you can't tell her. They set me up to return as Brennan McGabbhinn, but it was too similar so I-I'm using a friend's passport to get by. We look like brothers, me and Jeremy. Everyone says so and...and I stole his old one and used that. It was just better, this way. But we have to keep it quiet. Do you full understand?" And it was an effort to stop my yammering.

Her scowl shifted to a whimper, then she nearly broke down in tears and yanked me into a hug. I held her, just as tight.

"Oh, thank God it's you," she whispered. "Thank God you've come. I was so afraid you were dead."

"Didn't you know I was with Aunt Mari?"

She shook her head. "I kind of thought...but then there was that nonsense story how the British just snatched you, and then no more word. Ever. Then Rhuari—he said, when he heard of this Brennan person, he thought it was really you they meant."

"So you see? See how easy it would've been to work out who I truly am?"

"But we kept it between ourselves."

"Not a word to Ma?"

"No. Ma—she—Ma wouldn't even speak of-of-of it. She said you died in the bombing and they took your body away, but I knew better. No mourning? No funeral? Not even a wake for you?"

All I could say was, "She and I were not on the best of terms."

Still, this sat very wrong with me. Ma lying to my brother and sister? Trying to make them think I was gone from this world, complete? With only Maeve's wary stubbornness to keep her from believing it?

Of course, Mairead knew all that had been done, but her reticence with the information was understandable, with Canada still under the thumb of England. But still...not to let my brother and sister know I was still alive, while she was here? It boiled up emotions within me that I had no time to understand or accept. Instead, I just whispered, "She...she may have said that because the British were looking for me, about then, and still are, from not so long ago. So it was better for all of you that you not know. Not for sure."

She nodded and pulled back a little, her voice soft and thick as she continued with, "There's truth in that. I think Kieran knows…"

"You didn't tell him?"

She shook her head. "He's close with Colm and those lads."

That brought up my wariness. "*They* knew where I was?"

"No, no, I mean when I was told you were—were this cousin named Brennan comin', he rolled his eyes and said, *Cousin*. Like he didn't believe it."

That's when my brain caught up to me. Of course, Colm, Aidan and Jackie and them would know I wasn't dead. They'd snuck me into the Republic. Helped me heal. Prepared the papers for me. They might even have met Aunt Mari when she came over to ferry me to Houston. Since the Brits probably had rats in every layer of every part of the IRA, it's no real surprise they would have maintained as much silence as possible about my fate. So I doubted it was due to anything on their part that the British continued looking for me.

But what it *did* suggest to me was, the branches of the IRA were satisfied I'd done nothing to hurt the cause. At least, not deliberately. So they might be past wanting to wreak their own vengeance on me.

"That's still a worry," I murmured.

She nodded, again. "When you first disappeared, I did ask Colm if the IRA had put you in a grave. He tried so hard not to answer me without ever actually sayin' one way or the other, which gave me hope. So I wished and prayed and-and now you're here."

"You speak to Colm much?"

She shook her head. "Just now and again. But he's helped. Him and his mates. Helped a lot of us, in the Bogside. Whatever Ma needed, she got thanks to him."

"I'm glad to hear it." Maeve was still holding me, tight, so I asked, "How's it going with you?"

"Me?" She took in a long, deep breath then said, "It's just been me for so long and…and I-I was hopin'…prayin' more from the family would come. Then to be told I should expect a stranger to be here? Here! Now! At this time! Cousin or not, I told Mai to forget it, and I was not kind about it. But she said you were family and could help and…and it-it-it was all so damn confusin'. I'd so not wanted you in the house, I'd set you up with the Lowes, 'round the corner and hoped you'd understand but now I see what she was up to and..."

She dissolved into sobs, again.

"Shh-shh-shh." I rubbed her shoulders, saying, "It's bad, then?"

She nodded.

"Aunt Mari didn't help you any? Mairead, when she come?"

She wiped her eyes, still half-holding me. "No, no, no, Aunt Mari, God bless her—she stayed with Ma for hours a day. Talkin'. Eatin' together. That-that was so much a help. While she was here. Mai—she's off to havin' twins, again, so can barely fit up the stairs or down...and they'd be about due, now. Wouldn't they?"

"She was that far along?" I got a nod, in answer. "What about our uncles? Their families?"

"Uh—Uncle Michael came, from Sheffield, with his wife. Last month...no, February. But only for a day or two. Ma was not..." She huffed a laugh. "She was hard on them. Said she had no brothers, since they'd all abandoned her and so he left, early. Very sorry. But it was good to finally meet him, and we all had a good craic. Not one word from the others. He may have let them know how Ma felt about them."

"Rhuari not about?" No need to mention I knew anything about him or his situation.

"He and Bridie are up in Shantalow, now, so it's not easy. Though it is better for them, there. He's on with the Steelstown Primary and just lucked into a nice terrace home. There's talk of a full Irish school."

"I hear he's good with the Irish."

"Through Mairead, I'm sure...no, wait, he has a pen-pal in Houston. Do you know him?"

Oops. So I nodded. "He told you of him?"

"No, I learned through Mai. He talks more with her than me. I think because he's afraid I'll talk too much with Ma and set her off at him."

"Why'd she be off at him about anything? He's always so placid."

"She isn't, really. She's in pain and angry about it, so gets hard and cruel with her words. Just to lash out."

"I remember how that can be..."

"She set off at him a couple times, because he was here and

not his wife. Wantin' a woman to tend to her, not her own son. He never says a thing, but I know it hurts him. Doesn't help that Mai and Rhuari both agree with me, as does Aunt Mari. That sets off the worst in Ma when we bring it up..."

"Bring what up?"

"They've not told you?"

I merely shook my head.

She took in a deep breath. "There's a hospice in Dungiven. I want her to go there. And I don't want Kieran to know where she's gone till she's...she's..."

"Gone?" She nodded. "Maeve, what's this about?"

"Ma uses him to relay messages through PIRA's leaders, urgin' Eamonn to join in the hunger strike."

Fucking hell! "I thought it's just Bobby Sands and...and who was it? Francis Hughes?"

"Raymon McCreesh and Patsy Ohara, as well, now. Since more than a week, each. They've posted a list of those who'll follow, if it comes to that. She thinks Eamonn should add his name, and Kieran—he's so full of the glory of what it could mean. To have *a brother die for Mother Ireland*." She all but spit the words out. "He listens to her and she to him in this monstrous never-endin' roundabout and..."

"She listens to him? He's not fifteen."

"I know. I know. But he's runnin' around with Colm's pack of lads, and not all have Colm's cool head on their shoulders. The older ones fill Kieran's heart with stories and slogans and he passes them on to Ma as she feeds him tales about our great and glorious father's martyrdom. None of which I recognize. Which he then tells them, probably with even more exaggerations and-and they treat him like he's gold. At least Colm keeps him from flyin' too high. *He's* still got sense about him."

"The messages she's passing to Eamonn, are they through Colm?"

She shrugged. "I don't know. I don't think so. There's so many ways to slip them into the H Blocks. Even Father Jack's taken a few."

Of course. "He knows his way around, our Father Jack. I've seen him on the telly, a few times, talking to crowds or protesters or something or other. Leading demonstrations. He likes reporters asking him questions. Very well-spoken is he."

"Brendan...you have problems with him?"

I didn't want to answer that so asked, "How *is* Eamonn doing at the Maze?"

"Father Jack says he's well and good. Lost weight but not his mind. In fact, he continues to *increase his intellectual capabilities.* Through reading! As if he's taken Rhuari's way."

"Haven't you been to see him?"

"When I go he's always *on restriction from visits.*"

"But you're family."

"And Father Jack gets past them as his *spiritual advisor.* He's one of those who are sure that now the British hand is forced, they'll give in."

I snorted. "Not Thatcher. She's out to prove her balls're bigger than any man's." I didn't want to get into that, further, so I shifted to, "So Ma won't even think of the hospice? She'd have such excellent care."

"She's been slow in—I don't know how to say it—just in acceptin' what's happenin'."

I rolled my eyes. "That's our mother. Her reality is the only one that counts."

Maeve huffed a near laugh and patted me on the chest. "You're not wrong about that. But Father Jack finally got that part through to her. And he's workin' on Dungiven." Then she moved to take off her coat, saying, "I'll pop 'round the Lowes, after diner, to let them know it's no longer needed, then set you up in my room." She hung her coat on a hook by the door, next to a new mac.

"Why not my old room, with Kieran?"

"Because you're *a guest* and he's out and about, as usual, so no tellin' when he's comin'. Or goin'." Then she gave a vicious chuckle. "He thinks that's manly of him."

I chuckled then heard someone crossing the upper hall. I froze.

"Only me, Maeve," came a woman's voice, and Mrs. Haggerty appeared at the top of the steps, bright and happy and looking completely unchanged, her eyes locked on mine.

Christ, as I thought—of course someone would be with Ma while Maeve collected me from the airport. I should have asked who it was here before revealing myself. Now a cold sense of dread was filling every part of my being, for I knew how fast gossip flew in this town, and our Mrs. Haggerty, she was one of the fastest with it.

Shite.

Ghosting

Mrs. Haggerty reached the bottom step and stopped, her eyes still on me, wary and curious. "We heard ya come in, so I think yer Ma's lookin' for ya," she said.

I stepped forward and said in my best twang, "Hi, Ah'm Jeremy Lan-dau, from Yew-ston.

Maeve hopped in with, "His family's friends with Aunt Mari. He's come to stay a bit. Research a paper for university."

"My the-esis," I said, grinning big and wide.

"By the saints," said Mrs. Haggerty, "I thought I was seein' a ghost, Mr. Landau, for you're the very image of her second son. Well, almost. He was something of a simple, slender child and..."

I made myself chuckle and say, "That's what I he-yer, but me bein' Jewish..."

She laughed. "By the saints, a Jew-man in Derry! I hope you're not after that *crusher* food your people eat."

"Crusher?" Then it hit me. "Oh, *kosher*. No, ma'am, I really do like cheeseburgers too much."

She laughed even heartier as she reached for the mac. "He's a charmer, Maeve. Welcome to Derry, Mr. Landau."

"Just call me Jeremy," I said, kicking myself for not paying more attention to the damned coat.

"I do find it odd," she added, as I helped her into it, "you comin' to stay in this house at this time."

Maeve jumped in. "I should've mentioned it, Mrs. Haggerty, I know, but we didn't want to set Ma into a state and he-he-he won't be a burden."

"Oh, no ma'am. In fact, I'm helpin' every way ya'll need."

"He has medical trainin'."

"Well, isn't that kind of you?" Mrs. Haggerty said, then she turned to Maeve to say, "Now your mother and I had a good long craic so I think she's ready for pain pill and a decent rest. Bye to you both." Then she glanced me over and left.

That sense of dread would not leave. "She overheard us."

Maeve was smiling. "Bren, you could've told her who you were and why. She'd not give you away."

The hell not. "It's just the fewer who know, the better."

"I'm sorry. I should've said somethin'."

Well, what's done is done. "Ma still in the same room?"

She nodded. "I'm in there, too, which is why you're havin' my room. Sometimes she needs—she needs attention in the night, and that way I can hear her."

Oh. So the end was even closer than I thought. To my shame, I felt an odd sense of relief. "Have you ended nursing school altogether?"

She hesitated. "Sister Grace says this is good experience for me, once I return." Then she added with a forced laugh, "Or for when I have children. They can be almost as demandin'."

I had to chuckle. Then I took in a deep breath and looked up the stairs. Time to face the beast, as it were. Maeve jumped ahead of me, saying, "I'll lead you in."

So up the stairs we went, and I took it a bit slow so as to look over the same framed pieces on the walls as when I'd left. Dusted and well kept, and unmoved. And still not one of me. As if there ever had been many, really. Still, I'd have to say something about that, for a lack of photos can raise as much suspicion as there being too many of them.

Then we slipped down the same old passage to Ma's bedroom, in the front, and there was that creak just before the door. Then Maeve grew far too bright and cheerful.

"Ma, look who's come to see you!"

I walked in and caught the room in a glance—Maeve's roll-away bed against one wall, table piled high with medications and medical equipment I had a feeling I'd soon learn too much about, a couple of straight-back chairs, one of the two windows cracked for a bit of fresh air, and Ma's bed now a hospital type, its center cranked up for her legs and its back up for her to sit, with a small table next to it holding a portable extension of the phone.

And then I saw a skeleton staring at me with big, startled eyes above sunken cheeks, her skin as wrinkled as crepe paper and softly gray, her lips tight as ever. Her hands were all fingers and bones, and there was a smell about her like that of sour cheese.

"How'ya, Ma," I said, trying to keep my voice even.

"What're *you* doin' here?" she snapped. For all the rest of her having wasted to near nothing, her voice hadn't.

I reached for a chair, saying, "I heard you were ill so—"

"Did I say you could sit?" she snarled.

I froze, for a moment, damping down my anger, then left the chair where it was and turned back to her. "Do you want me to leave?"

She hesitated, then huffed and looked away. "Well, you-you-you're here. Go ahead. Take a seat."

I heard Maeve exhale behind me, soft and easy. "Are you doin' all right, Ma? Any pain?"

"Not so much." She took a deep breath and let it out, refusing to look at either of us. "Did you make enough of that juice, for a change?"

"I'll get you some. Bren, would you like a wee glass of lemonade, as well?"

With vodka, Valium, and a joint? Wouldn't mind a bit.

I just nodded and Maeve scurried from the room. I waited till I knew she was down the stairs then said, "So what's all this?"

She snorted a laugh. "I'm dyin', what d'you think?"

"So Maeve said. And Aunt Mari and Mairead and...and I'm also hearing you claim Da is not a Kinsella."

I hadn't meant to say that, but if she was going to be hard with me, I'd be hard right back.

Her glare cut into me, sharp and sudden. "Nobody said such a thing to you. Why would anybody tell you that?"

Her vehemence did make me question what Aunt Mari had said.

"Just something I heard," I said. "You know how gossip can be. All words, no substance."

She looked away and snorted, in answer.

I continued with, "You look better'n what I expected, and you've lost none of your voice."

Her cold black eyes shifted to me. "Hard as ever, ain't ya? Lookin' down on me, even in my illness."

"Those aren't soft words I'm hearing from you."

She huffed and settled back, a bit, then let her eyes give me a real once-over before she muttered, "You've filled in."

I shrugged. "Food in Texas is richer than here. And my job

called for me being physical."

"Mari tells me you work on cars."

I nodded. "For a while. Then in a bar. Fixed things on the side."

"Same as ever."

I nodded.

"You always were a creature of habit. Same things to do, over and over." She took a breath from a canister of oxygen and continued, "Like it with my sister, do ya?"

"As much as anywhere." At first.

"So you only come home to make sure I'd be gone soon."

Oh, Christ, my patience for this crap had long left me. So my voice dropped to a growl. "I don't recall you asking me to return. Quite the opposite."

"Never once did I say not to."

"Not to me. You didn't have nerve enough for that. You let Mairead and Aunt Mari help me figure it out."

She glared at me. "It's good you stayed there. You'd have only got more lads snatched by the peelers and the bloody Brits, with your ways. Our Eamonn's in Long Kesh, thanks to you."

Oh, for Christ's sake. "They're the H-Blocks, Ma. And it's called the Maze, now."

"What d'you mean? That's not the right name!"

"It is for the British. Or the Constables. Or Stormount. I don't care which."

She huffed. "How do you know to begin with?"

"I follow the news!"

I didn't like the way this was going, with my voice matching hers in sharpness, so I drew in a deep breath and added, "I-I-I'd once thought I might write our Eamonn, but I couldn't."

"And why not?"

That took me aback. "It's obvious. A letter with a Houston postmark? Wouldn't have taken a bloodhound for the British to track me down."

"Why would they do that? It's been—"

"It hasn't been that long since their last visit, Ma. They're still looking for me. Didn't Aunt Mari tell you? I even spoke with them, last time. Men from the FBI and MI-Five or Six or Forty-seven, or something. That last visit, I tried to convince them I wasn't this *Brendan* creature you so despise. I don't know how successful I was, except so far as I know they haven't returned. Yet. But give some thought to it, Ma. Sheltering an illegal lad? Especially who's considered a fugitive or whatever it is they think of me? Would you really want that sort of trouble for your only sister and her family? Your daughter and her family?"

She drew in a deep breath, through her oxygen mask then said, "There's...there's other ways, if you'd really wanted to contact him. You...um, you-you-you could've sent...sent your letters to Father Jack."

"You can't be serious."

"He could have brought them with him. He visits our Eamonn, now I can't. The only one who-who-who does right by him and—"

I cut her off with, "Maeve's tried to go."

"So she says."

That was unacceptable, so my voice grew sharp, again. "You dare call your own daughter a liar? When she's given up her life for you? You should be thanking her!"

"I'll not have the likes of you lecture me!"

"Somebody should, you ungrateful—"

I cut myself off when heard Maeve coming up the stairs, then held my breath, to regain control, and murmured, "Ma, I'm not here to argue."

"No, you're here to be your usual little self. Watchin'. Waitin'. Standin' aside as others do the hard work. Actin' simple while judgin' us fools and eejits not worthy of you."

Maeve entered and said, "Here's your juice, Ma."

"You went far enough for it," was Ma's reply.

Maeve said nothing, just handed me a glass holding what looked like water with a hint of a cloud in it. I eyed it, wary.

Maeve smiled. "It's boiled with the juice and slices of lemon, then cooled."

"Thanks, Maeve," I said. Took a sip—and it was like biting straight into a lemon. Without sugar. Lemonade? Oh, Aunt Mari would never have allowed this to be called that!

Never.

Ma took a gulp of it then said that was almost mewling, "Maeve, I-I-I think I will have my bed down and one of my pills. I've had too many visitors, today, and the discomfort's comin' on. I'm tired and want to sleep."

Maeve nodded, took a bottle off the table and handed her a tiny tablet. She swallowed it with another fair gulp of that lemon-water then gave her the glass. Maeve cranked the bed down as she settled herself in. Not another word was spoken, nor even a glance sent my way.

Maeve motioned for me to follow her downstairs. Then once we were in the kitchen, she said, "She is glad to see you."

"I suppose," I said. "She didn't once try to slap me."

"Bren..."

"It's Jeremy, Maeve. May as well get used to it. And have you any sugar? This *lemon water* is killing me behind the ears."

She huffed and set a bowl of cubes before me. I dropped in two and stirred them...and stirred them. The little bastards took their time dissolving.

"I-I'm sorry," Maeve finally said. "I should've prepared Ma before takin' you up. I thought that when she saw you, she'd be happy and then-then...open to thinkin' about-about..."

"Not your fault. And I will help as best I can. Do you get any assistance from National Health?"

"Nurses won't come here."

"Are there no Catholic ones in the area?"

She hesitated then said, "As you saw, many of the neighbor ladies come in and they and Ma have a good craic. While they do that I can tend to laundry and run out to get things and-and attend some peace meetings and just...sometimes just sit for a moment."

She leaned into the chair, seeming weary to the bone. "Rhuari does help as best he can. He's driven me to the Maze a couple times, and we don't say a word the whole way. There and return. And the silence is so lovely. He brings groceries. When they let him through. But they have the toddler and a new wain on the way, so he...so..."

She began to breathe heavy. Put her head in her hands.

Oh, Brendan, what a bastard you're being.

I went around and pulled her up into a hug, again. And she wept, again. I felt the proper devil for turning this all into something about me and Ma. It wasn't fair to my little sister. It wouldn't have hurt me a bit to be more decent—more adult than Ma, to be sure—for the little while she remained on this earth. I'd have the rest of my life to eat myself away over her hatefulness towards me.

It wasn't so very long before she patted me on the chest and pulled back, murmuring, "I'll be fine, now. Thanks."

She washed her face then took two beers from a cupboard, and we sat at the kitchen table. It seemed a bit more crowded than I recalled, then I was startled to finally realize there was a small washer and drier shoved in a corner, and without thinking I said, "We're upper class now, are we?"

We had a good long laugh, at that, Maeve and I.

Aunt Mari was still managing to deposit between fifty and sixty quid, each month, in Ma's account at the Union. Each time, she'd send a letter to let Maeve know how much to expect, so it could be allowed for. Maeve'd read them to Ma, then use the money for household expenses...and it was needed, for those lemons were priced dear.

"Is that what bought you the washer and drier?" I asked.

She nodded. "There's so much cleaning that needs done," she said. "I was usin' Mrs. Cowley's, but it was becoming so...well, difficult. So I got these second hand. Tur called some lads he knew, and they were a good price."

"Makes it easier for you."

She rolled her eyes. "Ma still complained about the cost for a week, but now she so loves the smell of fresh sheets, the only thing she can find to complain about is how I don't iron them."

"What? Who irons sheets? Ma never did that in her life."

"I know that. You know that. Everyone in the world might know that. But Mrs. Keogh once told her of readin' about it in some advice column, and Ma wonders at how selfish I am not to do the same for her."

"Christ, she gets her sheets changed daily and that's not enough?"

"Oh, Bren, you know as well as I, Ma's never happy unless she's got somethin' to complain about."

That brought a laugh from me, and I quickly saw that despite her being my junior by four years, Maeve was much more the adult, doing what needed to be done to care for the woman who gave her life, even in the face of her cutting comments. That it had worn her down to nothing wasn't touched upon, but I promised myself I'd not let my little sister see anything but care from me, again.

"It took me near a year to convince Ma to see a doctor for the pain," she said. "Even then, it wasn't till I found blood on the sheets as I washed them that I was able to make her go."

"What is it?"

"Cervical cancer. The operation was a week later. They brought in a specialist from Edinburgh. They were hopeful, but...but she did one round of chemo and refused any more. She won't do anything to fight it. I think she's ready to go."

I nodded. Took a sip of the beer. It tasted good, warm. I'd forgotten how much I preferred it to that ice cold crap served in America.

"I'll stay till the wake's done," I said, "I'm pushing it to be here that long, but..."

"Bren, I know you were caught in that bombin', in some way, but I-I-I don't really understand what happened. Takin' you all the way to Aunt Mari's? And stayin' there for so long? Without a word? And how could you not have been found out if the British wanted you, so much?"

"I told you, I was there as Brennan McGabbhinn," I sighed. "And I was in a coma, for six months. Aunt Mari had all the paperwork and everything, so it looked good and all the Brits could do was grumble about it. And when I came out of it, I-I-I was told...it was impressed on me that the changes had been made to protect us all." Including the lads who set the bomb.

Maeve let out a long sigh. "So you saw who did it..."

Saw Danny's look of horror and Colm so angry and the blinding light and sudden silence and the child's leg whispering closer and closer and fire and—

Shite, I punched my forehead with my fists. I should have said nothing. "I-I-I-It's all jumbled and I-I-I don't remember it, Maeve. I was near killed. And I'm telling you, my mind left me, for months. Months. But the Brits couldn't know that. Or wouldn't care. And by the time I was able to talk and think and respond in an intelligent way, it was set that I wasn't me, anymore.

"And that I wasn't allowed to come home. So I finally started up, again, in Houston and thought I'd stay."

"And cut us off, complete."

"I didn't." I did. "I-I-I got the impression the IRA was letting people think me in a grave. Hoping it would get back to the Army and-and-and I didn't want to ruin that. Mairead kept me up on the family, through her letters to Aunt Mari. And-and-and I was friends with Rhuari's pen-pal so learned much through him. They-they wrote each other in the Irish, and for some reason Rhuari could be more open with him. And that way, I didn't get you two...well, drag you, Rhuari and Kieran into the middle of my disaster. Then I-I-I just got into the habit of letting it go that way. You know how I can be..."

She nodded and drank more of the beer, and I could see Aunt Mari doing the same in this very chair not a month ago. Like she did back in Houston. A surrender, of sorts. I didn't want that for Maeve.

"Will you return to Aunt Mari's, then?" she finally said, her voice soft and kind.

"No. There's no place for me, there. Or here."

"Bren, I'm sure once you've explained how you saw nothing, the British'll leave you in peace."

"Over a bomb that killed several people?"

"Years ago. And I'm hearin' they want a way out. This war's been goin' on for so long, and at such a cost. They just want to end the sendin' of men here and wastin' money tryin' to stop what can't be stopped."

"They won't stop trying. That's what sent me to Houston in the first place."

"Ya shoulda stayed there."

I jolted around to see Kieran at the door. He was my height, same hair, wiry and had a mixture of Da's scowl and Ma's frown on his face. He'd be a fine-looking lad if he thought of smiling.

"Nice of you to show your face," Maeve snarled.

"I heard we had a visitor," Kieran snarled. "Didn't realize it was the traitor, returned. The lads'll love hearin' this."

That little fuck, calling me a traitor even as he knew nothing of what had happened? I rose, ready to lay hands on him, but Maeve's words cut through us both, like fists.

"Brendan is your brother, Kieran. He was not responsible for what happened to Eamonn, that was the British. Nor had he a thing to do with that bombin', which the Provos acknowledge."

He started to flare up but she cut him off with, "You don't have to believe me; ask Colm! You put more stead in his word than mine! It's only the British and RUC who do not. Brendan has kept himself hidden for more than eight years in order to protect us, to keep things from becoming worse, and has only come home, at great risk, to see our mother before she passes from this world. If you bounce about tellin' one and all he's here, *you* will be doin' the work of those who hate us. Wouldn't that make *you* the traitor, then?"

He drew himself up straight and angry, glaring at her, but Maeve did not even begin to back down. I sat back. Fighting a smile. Almost hoping he'd be fool enough to go against her. For I remembered how she'd been with idiot lads who'd toyed with her. I wondered if those boys still had scars.

Then I wondered if they were still alive.

"I asked you a question, Kieran."

He shifted his glare to me and grew huffy, as only a fourteen-year-old boy can be. "I won't share my room with him!"

Maeve sighed. "No fear in that, m'lord. My room'll need cleanin' and fresh sheets but..."

Then I remembered, "Maeve, what about the hutch? Is it still together?"

"In this weather?" she shot back. "I'd sooner his highness be out there. He already comes and goes as he pleases."

"It's cold, at night!" Kieran almost howled.

"I'll give you an extra blanket! Would that be acceptable to your high and mightiness?"

He glared at her then spun and stormed away.

Maeve huffed and sneered after him. "He'll be at Tommy Fields' for a day or two, till he grows weary of their mother's cookin'. That woman couldn't boil water without burnin' it."

"Maeve, I'd like to stay in the hutch. I have before."

She nodded, smiling softly. "When Eamonn'd bring Jackie and Aidan. God, those three together..."

"How're they doing?"

She hesitated then said, "Aidan was shot and killed, last year. Army check-post. Claimed he wouldn't stop his car. Two others died with him."

"Jesus, no one said a word..."

She nodded. "Haven't seen Jackie, since, and our Colm never mentions him. I know he's bein' sought by the Army. They came here once. Somehow knew he'd stayed in our home. Made a nice mess of things but found nothin'. Our claim for damages is still pendin'...and will be till the end of time, I'm sure."

Bloody hell, that gun. The pieces all over. I should do

something about it, before it's found out.

"No, Bren, take my room. You are more than a guest, here, and Kieran's nonsense is just that. And this way you're also more in the knowin' of how things are, with Ma. He'll get past his silly attitude, once Colm's had a talk with him."

"Are you telling Colm I'm here?"

"I'd say he already knows. I *will* let him know your name, while you're in country. I'll also let my friends in the Protestant World know we have a *visitor from America.* That he's come to see how the prospects for peace are growin', despite all those who push against it."

"Protestant friends?"

"The Peace Group I'm with. Try and find some way beyond the rancor and...and a meetin's set for Tuesday evening, in the Guildhall. That's the closest they'll come on this side of the Foyle. They're not happy with the hunger strikes." She chuckled. "And many are they who are not happy with us tryin' to find peace, right now. It's mad. Why not come with me? Introduce yourself around?" Then she added with a smirk, "It'll help *establish* you."

I chuckled, and despite my reservations, I agreed.

First Revelations

The next morning, I managed to convince Maeve to enjoy a nice, long leisurely bath. She'd already handled Ma's cleaning, which I'm sure I would not have been allowed to do, and from the look of hesitant pleasure on her face when I suggested it, I'm sure the morning's duties had been anything but pleasant, for the little washer was already in use, and it not yet seven.

So once I heard her slip into the tub, I took a few deep breaths, girded my loins, as the phrase goes, knocked at Ma's door and entered with her breakfast—a boiled egg with butter, no salt or pepper, and more of that hideous lemon water.

"Something to eat, Ma," whispered from me.

She glared at me, snarling, "Did I invite you in?"

"Do you want your morning meal or not?" I managed to ask, in a very bland voice.

She huffed and looked away, which I took for a *yes*.

"I need to speak with you," I continued, my voice far calmer than I felt. It helped my tight attitude that I was cranky from having slept on the divan. Maeve's and Keiran's sheets, both, were in dire need of a wash, so I'd wrapped myself in a blanket and let jet lag kick me into a near death-like slumber. Then woke with it still dark out and my neck and back pissed as hell at me as my head was pounding. I halfway wondered about snatching one of Ma's Percocets.

I set the bowl on a little tray with legs and placed it across Ma's lap. Then I added a spoon and wet napkin.

She ignored them and snapped, "You have nothing to say that I want to hear."

Of course. I brought a chair over.

She all but spat, "Brendan Kinsella, did I ask you to sit?"

I sat, anyway, saying, "I'm not Brendan; not while I'm in Derry."

That caught her attention. "What're you on about?"

"I'm Jeremy Landau. A friend of your sister's family, who's willing to help your daughter have a wee bit of a breather as he researches a paper he wants to write."

And now she was surprised. "What nonsense is this? Why would you be that?"

I sighed. "Stop it, Ma. You know as well as I, when I was taken across the water it was not by legal channels. The only way I can return is by the same method."

"But that...that was dealt with! And-and-and you were given another name and that's what everyone expects and..."

"No, while I'm here, my name is Jeremy. And to make it even better, I am Jewish, not Irish or Catholic. An additional layer of confusion to ward off the hounds. I tell you this because I think Mrs. Haggerty overhead Maeve and myself, downstairs, and she may think she knows who I really am. It's my hope you'll help cloud that in her mind."

"Why would I need to? She's a good—"

"She's someone who loves a good craic, and things will slip out. I'd like to minimize the possible damage."

"What damage could come from—"

"Jesus, I've already told you! The Brits still want to talk to me about that bombing. They may even believe I was involved in staging it."

"Oh, that's ridiculous. And it's been eight years. How could they even know you're still in this world?"

"I don't disagree, nor do I know what they think they can learn, but it's beside the point. They've been to Aunt Mari's more than once. If I'm arrested, it will be bad for the whole family, but so long as I'm able to claim I'm someone else, we might be fine till I'm gone."

She huffed and mumbled and glanced about in a fidgety way, then finally asked, "How long will you be here?"

I let an edge come to my voice. "How long do you think?"

She didn't flinch in the least, just leaned back and looked at the window. Her voice grew hollow. "So this is what's come back to me."

I sighed and could not help but ask, "If you didn't want me around anymore, then why didn't you just let them put me in a grave?"

That jolted her eyes back to me. "I-I don't know what you mean."

"I remember bits of what happened, Ma. In that house. Colm going to get you. The men fighting with you to put an end to me. You spent so much time hating on me, why bother saving me?"

"I...I never hated you..."

I almost laughed. "Jesus, Ma!"

"No!" She actually looked offended. "I hated how you looked down on me. And on your father. Always so superior and sneaky. Goin' your own way. Treatin' me like anything but your mother and disparagin' him."

"All the more reason to let them bury me—"

"You were still my child! My son...and...and then there was poor Danny, cryin', *It wasn't supposed to go, it wasn't supposed to go.* Colm frantic. And you broken and bleedin' and hysterical. And them idiot fools wantin' someone to take it out on instead of helpin' you lads! Bloody men, bloody stupid men, always doin' and never acceptin'. I should let those-those bastards blame you for their own incompetence? Let others take the blame?

"Eamon De Valera would never have allowed that. Nor would your father. My Eamonn. He was strong, once. A man, once. He did what was needed. Always. And our Eamonn is like him. You never were. Never could be, for all your sneakin' ways. Superior and condescendin'."

"So instead of killing me, you just killed who I was."

She grew still and cold, and a bit distant. Silent for near a full minute, lost in some memory or thought or something, I've no idea what, until a near-broken voice whispered from her with, "I had a son named Brendan once. I loved him, but he never loved me. Never loved any of us. Endin' him was needed to save him. Sendin' him away..."

She softly laughed. "Sendin' him away when he was runnin' away. Madness. All of it. But it was the only choice to be made. My sister and daughter the only ones willin' to back me. Not one of my bloody brothers would even respond. *Brothers.* More stupid men. But promises followed." Her eyes whipped at me, sharp as knives, again. "Promises he'd never return."

I coughed, more shaken than I'd care to admit. And angry. And hurt. I had to clasp my hands together to keep them from shaking.

It took me a moment to find my voice so I could say, "As I asked you, last night, would you prefer I leave? As I am...I am ostensibly no longer a relation to the family. And-and-and I now have papers saying I'm a citizen of the United States, so I can go anywhere. Do...do you send me off, again, or shall I stay? The choice is yours."

She looked at me as if I truly were a stranger. "Why did you send our Eamonn to Long Kesh?"

That was so startling a question, I coughed, twice, and all I could think to say was, "He's in the H-Blocks. The name was changed...to-to the Maze, years ago."

She seemed to sink into the bed. "And they'll never let him out, thanks to you."

"I-I-I had nothing to do with his arrest. I was gone months before they snatched him."

"No, it was..." Her voice trailed off and she looked at nothing before softly continuing, "I remember it bein' right after they took my child away. Poor little Brendan. So simple. Done nothin' wrong. Bastards wanted him dead 'cause he'd done nothin' wrong. No heart, those bastards. My poor Eamonn. What they told him to do and what they did when he did it and left him to hang so...so we had to..." And she was close to tears.

I coughed, again. This was beginning to worry me. Aunt Mari had been right about Ma's rambling but had been wrong that it made no sense. Even lost in her mind, she was revealing so much...and it almost made me feel sorry that I'd come.

Finally, she looked at me, confused. "Who are you? Why are you here?"

I coughed, then without a thought I replied in my Texas voice, "I'm Jeremy. A friend of the family. Come to stay for a bit. Talk with your daughter, Maeve, about the peace movement. Discuss how hopeful...and maybe even futile it is. I've also said I'd help her in exchange for a place to sleep. I have some medical background and she's pretty much stretched to her limit. Is that all right?"

She shifted her focus to the window. Dear God, how pitiful she looked at that moment. "I'm an old woman, dyin'. Have I the choice? So many dead. So many dyin'. Here we have Bobby Sands, the best of our lads, greatest in our cause, God bless him, starvin' himself in the name of Ireland and...and..."

Before I could stop myself I said, "And he'll die, as will more after him."

She was silent, for a moment, then nodded and murmured, "Yes, more will follow. There's a list. And our Eamonn will be one. Our Eamonn will join it."

And that angered me. "I'll be damned if he does."

Which jolted her. Brought her cutting eyes back to me, glittering cold with hate. "You already are, *Brendan*." She all but spit my name out. "Comin' here to meddle in things you know nothin' about, like a fool. A simple stupid fool."

I made myself rise from the chair, slowly. "I'm Jeremy while I'm here, Ma. Are we agreed on my staying?"

After a moment she grew distant and whispered, "*Jeremy*? You really should address me as Mrs. Kinsella." God, was her voice soft and kind. "Now run along. Mrs. Rafferty might be stopping by later, with the latest news, so leave me to my breakfast, before it's cold."

Which it already was, but I felt no need to say anything more. I just nodded and left. And stood still at the top of the stairs for I don't know how long, my brain frozen in place.

Coughing. Bloody fucking coughing. Wondering if I needed one of my pills.

Everything that had come out of Ma in those few moments— the anger, the hate, the confusion, the details and lack thereof— all of it tore through me in a wild mass of contradiction. This was the first time I'd heard her say she loved me. And acknowledge why she'd hated me. Why she'd criticized and compared me to others in ways meant to hurt me. Dismissed my abilities. Grown angry with me over little things. She was...she was...she was *insulted* at thinking I felt myself superior to her?

Had I felt myself superior? Is that how my dislike of her giving money to the church come across? And being put off by her mealy ways when dealing with the Housing Council? And my being more willing to work with Mairead for the family than her? And my anger at Da for his violence against us?

She held none of the same contempt for Eamonn as she did me, even though he had often worked around her. He was now the family hero, so I suppose her love for him was understandable. And Rhuari, he'd never gone against her like I had, and even left in a way she could almost accept instead of having to be spirited out of the country to protect the cause...and himself. I was beginning to feel the arsehole for not knowing or considering that had been my way...or had seemed like what I'd meant...and not trying to correct it.

If that makes sense.

Makes sense? Christ, nothing about our lives did, so why would that? And now with thoughts crashing to all points in my head? I'd have to give this time to settle so I could pick through it. Consider it, objectively.

It took Maeve coming out of the toilet, wrapped in a robe, hair still wet, to break me from my zombie-like attitude.

"Lose your way?" she asked, her voice tentative.

I nodded. "I remember this place being larger than it is."

"It's been fine for us. Remember the row we had about makin' over the hutch for Mairead and Tur?"

I chuckled, then said, "I want to stay out there. Be out of the house. I think it would make my being here more believable, should something happen. And should make Kieran happy."

"You think anything could?"

I shrugged. I already had a good idea of who and what he was, now. "On the nights you want leave, I'll sleep on the roll-away."

She sighed then patted my back. "Bath's yours, if you want."

I nodded, finally feeling the need for it, and headed downstairs for my duffel bag...and medications. My coughing had grown sharper and my heart was not happy. I had enough pills for three months. After that? Who knew?

The hutch was dusty and disheveled, with many of Eamonn's things still in it. Posters. Blacklight. Narrow bed. Cobwebs and dust. Saturday was taken up with a good bit of cleaning and two washes of all the sheets so I could have a well-made bed by nightfall. And by sweeping, scrubbing and putting unneeded items into boxes in Kieran's room, it was livable. I had to laugh at myself over that, remembering Ma's fanaticism over cleanliness, and now here I was close to the same.

Kieran was right; it did get bloody cold. The Tortoise stove Tur had found was still in place, so I tried to burn a bit of wood in it, but the exhaust piping had come undone and the sticks were damp so the hutch filled with smoke. Next morning, I fixed it up, cleaned it, and figured I'd buy coal for it instead of peat.

Sunday morning was bells through the town announcing services. Maeve made an excellent fry-up, and Kieran appeared just as she was doling it out, as if by appointment. Just cast a glare at me then fed himself with a fury that reminded some of our Eamonn, in his happy times.

I made no small talk. No need to encourage his animosity. Maeve, however, was chipper. Ma having a good night meant she did, as well.

Kieran cast her a wary look and asked in a softer voice than I'd expect from him, "No cries in the night?"

Maeve took a bite of blood pudding and shook her head. "She's been much easier, the last few days."

He nodded and turned his focus back to his breakfast, but he was now eating with more deliberation. I was about to ask him his feelings about Ma's coming end but the knocker sounded on the door.

Maeve glanced at her watch, frowning. "He's early." Then she popped up and went to the front door.

"Who is?" I asked, after her.

Kieran did not look up as he said, "Father Jack."

What!?

Father Jack?!

What the fuck?!

And here came the man, right behind Maeve as she said, "This is the American I told you of. Jeremy, meet Father Jack. He's our priest. Come to give Ma communion."

Oh, bloody hell, I was not ready for him. Still I managed to make myself rise, grin and shake his hand. "It's a play-sure." And did I lay on the Texas twang.

He smiled, looking almost the same as my last image of him. Just a touch of gray at his temples. He took note of the scars over my eye and my cheek. Scars from wounds he knew all about. So he fucking knew me from the first instant, and I would swear I almost caught a sense of glee in his eyes.

Still, he drew himself up a bit taller. "Jeremy," he said. "I didn't realize you were here."

Yeah, right, you bastard. Why else would you have come before breakfast is done?

But he was playing the game, in full, so I widened my smile and said, "I'm still gettin' settled i-in. Learnin' what needs doin' and all tha-yat."

"Yes, Maeve mentioned she was getting some additional help."

"In every way I can. My daddy's a doctor. Surgeon. I picked up a few things, off him." And I swear to God, Jeremy would have howled with laughter at how thick my twang was.

"That's good to hear," he said. "Our Maeve can use all the help you can give. Will you be here long?" His voice was so plain and surface in its rhythm.

"Not so very," I said. "Few weeks, maybe, then I'm off."

"That's good to know. Maeve, I'll need to leave, shortly, so do you mind if we go up to Bernadette's now?" That's when I noticed he had a small black valise in hand.

"Of course, father," she said, ignoring that half her breakfast was uneaten. "Kieran? You comin'?"

He shoved the last of his beans into his mouth and nodded, then followed her upstairs.

Father Jack cast me an almost amused smile as he said, "I would invite you, as well, Jeremy, but I understand you are not of our faith." And his tone held so much meaning, I almost laughed.

Instead, I grinned and shrugged. "Cain't help how you're born. But I can clean up, down here." Then added as my own little dig, "An' keep Maeve's breakfast warm, till you're done."

His expression did not change as he murmured, "That's very good of you." Then he went up to Ma's room.

I heard her greet him with, "Father, Father, did you know? I got a Jew-man in my house."

"Yes, I've met him, and he seems very pleasant."
She laughed.

Not a cackle but an honest laugh. A sound I hadn't heard in so many years, it jolted me. I don't know why. I hadn't missed it. Yet the sound of it still held me in place and I wished to hear more of it.

Which made no sense to me.

Then I heard the incantations for communion start and the responses from all three members of my family...and...and

The wish deepened. Washed through me in a soft silent passage that lingered in ways I never thought I would find pleasant. And it was thanks to bloody Father Jack.

For all that I disliked about the man, he had brought my

mother's professed faith to her and was treating her with kindness in her final days. For that, I had to give him respect and appreciation.

But I did not trust his intentions one damned bit.

Backgrounding

After Father Jack was gone, Kieran soon after him, and Maeve's breakfast finally eaten, I was shown Ma's routine. What pills to take and when, mainly. How to make that hideous lemon water. Bites of what she would eat and knowing what she would not. Maeve said she would take care of cleaning Ma, day or night, but sometimes I'd have to handle getting her a bedpan.

"It's kept under this heatin' pad," she said, as we stood before the table piled high with pills and ointments. Ma was asleep so our voices were soft. On a shelf above it I could see a curved basin covered by a small cloth. "It's on low, never off, because sometimes she cannot make it to the toilet in time, so this the next best option."

"But doesn't she have a...a bag or something?"

"Catheter, yes. But on occasion she will still need this, despite her constipation."

Oh, Christ. "Maeve, you've been handling this by yourself?"

She shrugged. "Work experience. I could be home care, by now. We need them in this area."

"And Kieran doesn't lift a finger?"

"He keeps Ma happy," she said, resigned. "That counts for more than you realize. Sometimes he's laughed her into takin' her pills when she doesn't want to. Eatin' some potato when she's off her feed. I begrudge him nothin', even if he is a little shite, at times."

"Understood. Sorry to have said it."

She looked at me, her eyes welling up. "Oh, Bren, it's so good havin' you here."

I smiled and touched my forehead to hers. She chuckled, and we left the room to go over the whole routine, again.

There was also the parade of various neighbor ladies and old friends—Mrs. Rafferty, Mrs. Keenan, Mrs. O'Faelan, Mrs. Quinn, and on and on—come to visit with Ma, each bringing a plate of something to eat. None of which Ma would touch. Of course, she received naught but sympathetic nods of gentle understanding, in response.

Maeve introduced me around as *the lad from America*. Some of these ladies I had known, while others were new. But all easily accepted who I claimed to be and we left it at that.

Except for Mrs. Haggerty, who loved to keep mentioning how much I looked like *poor wee Brendan*. I tried to avoid her. At least there were occasions when her son, Jimmy, and his sister's wains would be about to take her focus off me.

Monday, I went down to the *Derry Journal* to look through the massive volumes holding the old editions, starting with when Da was killed. They reported only what the RUC and Coroner said, at the time, but in even less detail. No pictures of him or my family as we grieved. One story did reference Aunt Mari coming from America to help with arrangements. And there was a photo of where he'd been found, which looked even more bleak than I'd imagined. Everything else was exactly as I remembered.

I deliberately avoided going anywhere near stories about the bombing. Dealing with Ma's stop-and-go hatefulness aimed at me was plenty enough to deal with.

For the life of me, I couldn't remember my parents' wedding date, nor did Maeve know. It must have been late 1949 or early 1950, going by Aunt Mari's comments, but I could find no wedding announcement for them, in the Journal. The clerk suggested I contact the registry of marriages for anything like that.

Which I did, but they had no record of a Kinsella being married in either year. I did that only for appearances' sake. I remembered Aunt Mari telling me my parents were married in Magherafelt and I was already planning to head there to look into what was on file.

It was already getting around that I was the American, so I was able to get through the checkpoints easily enough. More chit-chat about Texas, with some even wanted to ask about that bloody JR on Dallas. Knowing who'd shot him was serious cause for discussion, and they felt the explanation wanting. As I'd never watched the show, I had to fake a lot of what I told them. Like how I'd heard *Kristen was taking the fall for her real lover, which would be revealed in the next season*. That got the squaddies' chatter going, good, and kept their focus off me. It being told by a supposed Texan gave true weight to my words.

There was a pub close to the Journal that had a decent stew, so I had lunch there. I was offered more advice on what to add to my thesis than was needed and given stories that had absolutely nothing to do with what I claimed to be after. Though one ancient man named Joseph Perrin did make a great suggestion—in exchange for a pint.

"That bloody university in Coleraine," he grumbled. "They was nosin' about lookin' for stories we tell. Things we done. Families and histories and all that. Had tape recorders. Big bloody things. And notes. And were easy with their money, in the pubs. Many a man sore missed 'em, when they stopped."

"Did they come here?" I asked.

"All over. Here. Paddy's. McReady's. Casbah. Anyplace there's a lad in want of a drink an' willin' t' talk."

"People went along with that?"

"For a pint? They'd make Ireland the land of Vikings or sailed with the Spanish armada, if it'd get them a second or third fill. I think this one little cunt I knew of finally figured out he's wastin' his money an' hit over t' the Waterside. Then nothin' more. But they might have 'em writ out, you know."

"You remember his name?" I asked.

He shrugged. "Stephens or Patterson or somethin' of that nature. True Proddy."

I took a chance and asked, "I'm told the father of the family I'm staying with had lots of stories to tell."

The old boy chuckled. "Aye, I remember him. He was a hard one. Met a bad end. Sorrowful. It's what happens when ya talk too much."

What? "What do you mean?"

He was in the middle of a sip so looked at me, in question.

I shrugged and continued, "You said the man...Mr. Kinsella met a bad end 'cause he talked too much?"

"Him? No, him...he had a fine way with a tale. And friends. More'n anyone. What's the name of that one lad he was best mates with? Donnal? Danvers? Dermott. By the saints, those two had stories to tell. Ancient times. An' some about themselves. When was that? Twenty years past?"

"Fifteen," popped out of me before I could even think.

"Ya sure of that, are ya?"

"Uh, that's what I been told."

"Thought it was longer...but aye, that was about when the school was gettin' set up. All new, fancy equipment for them. Nothin' for Magee. Bloody Protestants. Selfish bastards."

Then he saw a friend come in, got me to buy him a pint to join his refill, and they talked about the Celebration Fleadh in ways that I did not recognize. British soldiers standing guard to make sure none of us left. Girls dancing jigs to rock bands who'd never come. Candy apples that made the entire Bogside sick when it was really just the gas and excitement of the battles. It was being completely rewritten.

I grew weary of it and told him I'd look into it the recordings when I had a chance, then headed home.

Rhuari dropped by with groceries, the next day, driving an eight-year-old Austin Maxi. He had grown taller than me and bulkier, with thick glasses to hide his sharp eyes behind, and it filled me with joy to see how well he looked. A Mrs. Carson was upstairs with Ma, at the time, so Maeve made an *official introduction* between us. In response, he took the glasses off, polished them, put them back on, looked at me, again, and shook my hand as he said, "Welcome."

He knew from the first second who I really was. The simple fact of his and Eldon's correspondence had told him of me. That put him well up in my estimation for so casually falling in line with the lies.

He hopped upstairs to visit with Ma, for a while. I heard both ladies greet him with warmth and kindness and was glad for him. He was only in for about half an hour, and the only real chatter was between my mother and the other lady. But he'd pop in with an occasional comment, and then when he was ready to go promised to bring Bridie and his wain next time.

Then as I walked him out to the car, I asked in my best Texas twang, "How long does it take you to get through all the checkpoints?" It was mainly because we were under Ma's window so might be heard, and also to lay a foundation with the neighbors that I was not of these parts.

He played along without a thought. "Add an hour or so, each way. I don't like Bridie to come; she's me wife. Made that mistake, once."

"What happened?"

"What happens with any young girl, especially one that's in her sixth month. But Maeve's better to tell you."

Then he left.

I went back inside and looked at the goods he'd brought, and wondered at the amount of them, making Maeve laugh.

"It's for tonight."

Crap, I'd forgotten about that, and I think it showed on my face, for Maeve cast a wicked grin at me and asked, "You're not thinkin' of backin' out, are ya?"

"I could stay here to take care of Ma..."

"Mrs. Haggerty and Mrs. Quinn are here for that. I'll make sure Ma's fed and clean and had her pills and injection, and then they'll have a good craic till we're home."

"It's down to a science with you, isn't it?"

"Out of necessity."

"I'm amazed you keep any of it straight in your head."

"I don't always. But you are comin', right, Bren...*Jeremy*?"

"Will Father Jack be there?"

She eyed me then said, "He sometimes is and sometimes isn't, and hasn't let me know about tonight."

So I shrugged a *yes*, smiling. She grinned.

I should have said no...and dear God, how I wish I had.

Hopes

We had to go through two checkpoints to get to the hall, and I quickly saw why Rhuari kept Bridie away from them. At Butchers Gate, every half-attractive woman was subjected to what the soldiers may have intended as flirting but was no less than the verbal abuse you might hurl at a prostitute. I saw two girls who couldn't have been sixteen, yet, walk away in tears as a pair of old women in the queue shook their heads in disgust.

When it came to Maeve's and my turn, I played up the foreigner aspect, which caught a couple of them off-guard.

"American, are ya?" a Sergeant asked me as he looked at Jeremy's passport. Apparently, the squaddies didn't bother sharing information with each other about anomalies, like me.

A private looked over his shoulder, fascinated. "Lan-de-ow? What name's 'at?"

"Some kind o' French..." the sergeant chuckled.

I fought back laughing at them. "Jewish."

"French-Jew in Londonderry. Who'd o' thought it?"

There was a bit more back-and-forth like this as others dug into the sacks of food and drink to check for bombs and weapons. They also found my backpack held an ungodly number of wrapped egg salad and onion sandwiches, bricks of cheese already sliced, apples, and snippets of toast, olives, crackers and cookies. Maeve snuck sandwiches, some cans of orange crush and a box of cookies to the squaddies as the Sergeant accepted a couple of my Marlboros as a *toll charge* to ignore her.

"Christ, Maeve," I said, then reminded myself of who I was and continued in a twang, "is it like this at every checkpoint?"

"Oh, that was nothin'," she said, leading me down Magazine Street to Castle. "You should hear how they are after there's been a rough demonstration. Today's must have been easy."

We headed down Shipquay towards another checkpoint, and

everywhere you looked you could see shops that had been burned out or smashed. Those that were open had meagre wares, but people seemed not to mind. The street had a fair number of shoppers on it.

We crossed the road to the Guildhall then entered to head through a hall to a smaller room in the back. Chairs had been set around for the meeting, with a couple tables against the wall for food and drink to be laid out, and one at the head for the meeting's leaders. It all looked a bit small but in good order.

A number of people were already there, mostly women in their thirties to their sixties but with a few men of pensioner age. All dressed neatly but still with a shabby air about them. The only one I recognized was Mrs. O'Canainn, but she seemed not to know me in any way.

It's sad, but the only ones I saw who were under the age of thirty were a couple of burly lads at the door, keeping watch for any who'd make trouble. They were being tended to by their girls or wives, who without a word followed Maeve into the room like hungry puppies. The moment we set the groceries down, they built flimsy paper plates of sandwiches and crisps—CHIPS, Jeremy! Keep your head straight. Then they took them to their lads to nibble from...which I'm sure they did when they weren't nibbling the girls' necks.

Posters extolling peace had been set up on rickety tripods. None of the *Brits out, Red Hand,* or *IRA Forever* variety allowed here; just useless pleas for Bobby Sands—as in, *Don't let him die.*

Maeve had told me he was standing for Parliament in a by-election, on Thursday, as Frank McGuire had died of a heart attack. It seemed they honestly believed that were Sands to be elected, Westminster would hear their prayers and put an end to the growing horror by accepting at least enough of the demands to cancel a need for his death and a second by-election. I hoped so but had my doubts.

She introduced me around, and aside from Mrs. O'Canainn, who did cast me a curious look now I was close to her, not one of these people had I ever known, except by name, thank God. It was just *Hi, nice to meet you,* and they were off to a corner to discuss the latest news of St. Bobby and his campaign.

I wandered about and took in more of the place, speaking observations into my tape recorder's microphone in my best

Texas. Mainly for appearances' sake, but also for the fact I'd never been in the building before and it was fascinating.

"The walls have wood half the way up," I said, "and it seems to have been refinished, with fresh paint above. The floor's been well-swept, and I think there was once carpet on it, but not now. The windows are arched and with simple translucent glass, almost like a church. Other windows in the building are stained glass and some show recent damage. The hall is a bit intimidating, even to someone like me."

An officious-looking gentleman entered to one side to watch it all with a huffy manner. I saw Maeve leave her group and stride over to greet him. He smiled at her, politely, but you could tell it was only thanks to good manners and not from genuine affection or interest.

More people showed up. Again, few had I met before so they had no trouble accepting me as *the American*. Though I did get a feeling they were more than a little leery of me. These came from Pennyburn and Springtown and Creggan and Shantalow. There was one from Brandywell whose son I'd once known and met her, but she did not even begin to recognize me.

The few from the Waterside, Altnagelvin and Tullyally, and that side of the Foyle were outnumbered four to one, and the looks they cast me were anything but welcoming. Jesus, but for what was supposed to be a hopeful gathering the mood was somber, at best. I think down deep they knew the outcome of the hunger strikes would not be good, and its aftermath worse.

The sandwiches, cookies, orange crush and ale were much appreciated, and someone had filled a bowl with punch to join it. As they began to take their seats, I maneuvered to where I was standing to the back, in a corner to the left of the door. I had more than a glance or two of wariness cast back at me and my tape recorder. It was still bright outside as two of the Protestant women, then Mrs. O'Canainn and another Catholic woman and Maeve took places at the table. Two seats were left empty.

Mrs. O'Canainn stood up behind the table and said, "I just received word of a bomb scare on the bridge, so that may explain a couple of absences. We'd best get started. If the last of us arrive in time, that's all well and good, but we need to be done and home by curfew."

There was gentle agreement all around, mixed with a couple

of groans from the Protestant few. Guess they'd have difficulty getting back to the Waterside.

So Maeve began with reading the minutes of the previous meeting. I had my tape recorder going, the mike pointed to the front, so wasn't really paying attention to the words. I could listen to them, later. I was more caught by the soft aura of surrender whispering over much of the audience.

Then that officious-looking gentleman, to whom I was never introduced and who never did tell me his name, came wandering up to me and tapped my cassette recorder.

"Amazing," he said, "how compact these things have become."

I managed to remember to use my twang as I asked, "Beg pardon?"

"So...you're our visitor," he said in a soft condescending tone.

I nodded and said, "I'm—"

He looked away and back over the crowd. "Come to watch us twist in the wind, have you?"

"I-I'm doin' research—"

"*Research.*" His voice dripped with disdain. "That's all anyone ever does, anymore, is *research things. Look into what's happened. Consider the options.* And let the world burn as they talk and talk and talk. But that's the Irish for you. They do love to talk." He turned a cold eye on me. "I understand you're housed with one of the leaders, up front."

That made me blink. That was a bit more information than I expected him to have. "I'm boardin' with some—"

"Rather sad," he said, ignoring me. "Mother's dying. Cancer or something. Father long dead. One of those Republican sorts." He turned back to the group. "Killed, as I recall. Some IRA patriot who got found out and done away with, or something."

Um...what? Da an IRA patriot? That shunted my irritation with the bastard aside. Because while I did not like this man, he seemed to know more about my family than I did, and I did not want him to stop talking.

"He was?" is all I asked.

He nodded, not really paying attention to me. "That's how those people are. Get a few drinks in them, they start bragging on themselves or telling stories of what they'd done. Little of which is true." He turned back to me and tapped on my tape recorder. "When I was at university, the machines we had were massive things. Supposedly portable but weighed a stone. And were reel-to-reel. These cassettes are much better. Easier."

"What school'd you go to?" I asked, soft and careful.

"Ulster. At Coleraine. In the second graduating class." He grew a bit distant. "A friend of mine wandered about recording things, back then. Stories. Songs. Meetings like this. Using that bloody...oh, what was it? Not a Nagra; that was later. Doesn't matter. He was killed by the IRA, few years back. Driving home. Left a wife and two children. Bloody papists."

I took in a deep breath, as soft and easy as I could. "There's been lots of that, over the years. Both sides."

He gave me a hard frown and said, "You're Jewish, aren't you?"

All I could manage to do was nod.

"Then you should understand the issue here," he continued, turning back to the crowd. "These bloody papists...they're just as hard to control as the bloody Palestinians. Running all over the world, killing in the name of peace. Disgraceful. Don't let them fool you with their claims of wanting love for all. They won't be happy till we're part of the bloody Republic and under the thumb of Rome."

"I-I-I don't understand. If you feel like this, why you lettin' them use this room for the meetin'?" And I was laying the Texas on a bit thick.

"If I had my choice, they wouldn't be here. Let them hold it in one of their bloody church halls. But it was thought using Guildhall was an acceptable compromise. Make it more likely people from the Waterside would show, as some have." Then a small smirk crossed his lips. "It'll be interesting to see how many show, next time."

And the tone of his voice told me exactly why he believed that.

He turned back to me. "Have *you* had any difficulty, staying in the Bogside?"

I shook my head. "Everybody's been real nice."

"Because they know you're American. They wouldn't want any bad publicity from you being hurt. Even if you are a Jew, bloody NORAID might make a fuss. Just take care. You can't trust these bloody bastards."

Then without another word, he slipped out of the room.

And I? Jesus, God, I felt as if I'd just been molested.

But oh, was it ever illuminating to hear the truest version of Protestant hate, direct from the horse's mouth. Like what I'd seen in part of that paper read by Billy Corrie's uncle. Of course, my tape recorder was still going. And while my hope was that it caught some of the committee's talk, I had a feeling that man's voice had drowned out much of what was being said.

And to be honest, would be far more interesting to dig through.

Like my Da being part of the IRA, when he'd done nothing at all for them when we lived on Nailors Row. I told myself he was merely conflating all Catholics into that one situation, but it seemed a bit too specific for me to brush aside. Perhaps I should start paying more attention to the craic going on around the town.

I tried to focus on what Maeve was saying—something about a caravan of cars or hiring a bus and going to the Maze to demonstrate their solidarity with Bobby, after the election. Hold signs reading *Give Peace a Chance* and *Working Together Makes Us Stronger* and the like. All very nice, but not one of the Protestants seemed interested in joining on the journey and only a couple of the Catholic crew truly seemed up for it.

Give peace a chance. Lovely thought, but it hadn't kept John Lennon from being shot, and—

Father Jack rushed past me to enter the room, removing his coat as he went. His complete focus was on the front table.

It should have been no surprise to me that he would show up; he was always in the middle of everything. It's just, I wanted nothing to do with him, yet. Something was telling me he was accepting my charade only because he had some plan in mind, to mess with me. I know it sounds paranoid, but as said before—I did not trust him a bit. So I should not have come with Maeve. I crushed deeper into a shadow and snuck along the wall to work my way out into the hall before he could see me.

I slipped outside and fired up a Marlboro. To my surprise, my hand was shaking so it took two matches to light up and then three good drags for me to even start to calm down. Christ, what I would have given for one of my emergency joints, just then.

I noticed a couple of people looking at me, oddly, so I set to walking up Foyle, past the car park and bus depot. A couple of squaddies saw me but one had been the recipient of my smokes so tossed me a wave. I grinned and waved back, glad he was across the street and unable to see the state I was in.

I needed to take my mind off Father Jack, so I rewound the cassette, plugged my headphones into it and played back everything. Listened carefully, especially to his comment about Da being caught out as an IRA man, or something.

That preyed on me. Reminded me of what that guy in the pub had said. What was his name? Perrin? Talking about how people talked too much, and some lad was recording their stories?

Da's injuries had been severe, but we'd accepted the official story. What else could we have done? But now? Thinking back on what little I'd known and remembered, it seemed to me he'd been tortured before he was killed. That was why we had to have a closed casket. I mean, even then no one had believed it was just a fun little game out of control, but since he'd been a Catholic and those two mental defectives who'd murdered him were Protestant, the authorities had decided to ignore the details of his death and leave the bloody politics of it to others who might care.

I passed a fountain and came up on a small garden spot built of brick by a long white wall and sat down. Pulled out my note pad and began scribbling note after note in it, posing questions I had no way of finding out the answers to. Not with certainty.

What had happened to the two men who killed Da?
Had the place he was killed ever been found?
Were his killers part of the UVF?
Had Da ever actually been part of the IRA?
Had he done anything for the Republican cause to make those men want to kill him?
Was he mistaken for someone else?

A nice list, but something to keep in mind was, it could all just have been a precursor to the Shankill Butchers. An offshoot of the UVF who'd tortured and killed several Catholics for the fun of it, around Belfast...as well as a couple of Protestants they were not happy with.

And I had to remind myself, much of what both that man and Perrin had said was gossip colored by memories. Third hand? Fourth hand? One-hundred and ninety-seventh hand? Who knew? Not exactly reliable information.

I decided to return to the *Derry Journal* and look deeper into the articles about Da's death. See if anything more was said about his killers. Or if they had any stories about the university seeking spoken myths. Check with the university, itself, to find out if there ever was someone with a tape recorder traveling around the Bogside asking for stories. Which, now thinking about it, did seem a bit wild. Especially as Da's stories were massive messes of details tossed about like a salad.

I rose and finally noticed the white wall was actually a sculpture of interlocking blocks, about twice my height and nicely done. Sections of it were set closer to the road and flanked an entrance to a park on the other side of it, at each end of the wall. I noticed a plaque said it was City People sculpture. Another new aspect of Derry, but one of the few that made sense.

Unlike so much else in this town.

I headed back to the Guildhall with a plan of action. I noticed a couple people from the meeting coming out, so crushed my cigarette, thought about having another then realized I'd gone through half the pack, without thinking. That would not do; I hadn't brought all that many with me.

I didn't feel like heading inside so leaned against the wall by the entrance. Saw a bus for Shantalow across the way get boarded by a couple of the meeting folk then toddle on as others growled past.

It finally hit me that the City Hotel, which had been at Shipquay and Foyle, to my left, was gone. It was now that car park. God, there was going to be change in Derry, whether they wanted it or not, and—

"Here you are."

I turned to see Maeve at the door, my backpack in hand. "I thought you were taping us?"

"I got some," I said. "And my thoughts. I can write it out for you, if you want."

She chuckled. "With your handwriting?"

I had to give her that, and chuckle. "Ask Rhuari. He's got a good fist for writing and—"

"You've seen his handwriting?"

Fuck. It was Father Jack, come up behind me.

I turned to him and said, "Hey-there, Father, you made it to the meetin'."

He drew himself up a bit taller. "Jeremy," he said. "It was my understanding you would be assisting Maeve with some of Bernadette's care."

"Mrs. Haggerty's with her," said Maeve, a bit too quickly. "And Mrs. Quinn."

"Excellent." Then he turned to Maeve. "You can be certain,

the next meeting I will not be late."

"It was fine, Father," she said. "And maybe next time..."

"Yes, I was probably expecting too much of her. I'm sure Joanna will come in to speak, then." Said with his patented grin.

And I'm sure you'll make...sure...wait...

Joanna will come?

Joanna?

The name slammed into me.

Joanna!?

Joanna will come in to speak!?

I could see his lips moving but I couldn't make out what he was saying. Nor was he looking at me, which seemed deliberate, in manner.

My mind was exploding even as I told myself he had to mean someone else. Another Joanna. He must. Of course. That must be it. That had to be it. It's not an unusual name, and it was only a coincidence he was saying it now.

At my side.

Knowing who I was.

Knowing I had known her.

Knowing full well I could hear him?

He'd taken us to Dublin and...and...and...

He cast me a glance, his expression quiet but his eyes far too full of awareness. He was watching for my reaction to that name. Waiting for me to ask him...ask him—

The world went while and silent and a leg drifted down to land before me and the smoke whispered away and I saw the fire and saw her fighting to get free from it and...and...and...

I coughed. Fuck!

Somehow I made myself take my backpack from Maeve and slip it on, turning away from him. Coughed, again. Shit! That was not what I needed, just then.

But Joanna?

Joanna?

No, no, no, Bren, he knew another Joanna. That was all. That's what it had to be, what had to be, what had to be and—

He tapped me on the shoulder and I jolted around.

"Sorry, Jeremy," he said. "I didn't mean to startle you. It was a pleasure to see you, again, and I'll see you, Sunday."

"Sunday?" Did he think I'd be doing communion?

"When I come for communion with Bernadette."

I smiled. Of course. I managed to say, "Sure. Sure thing. See you then."

He smiled, clapped me on the shoulder then headed over to the car park.

I watched him go, my head still spinning and...

Oh, God, oh, God, oh, God, oh, God, oh, God, this can't be. This can't—

Maeve pulled at my jacket and said, "We need to go. You comin'?"

I finally noticed the lighter heft of my backpack and that her bags were rolled up under her arm. Used that to center myself.

"Is...is this all that's left?" I asked.

"That's what I kept back for our return. They seem to like my sandwiches."

I just nodded. This nothing moment was doing more to calm me down than any of my mental gymnastics. I was almost back to thinking I was just being silly. I mean, I'd seen Joanna die. I'd watched the fire grow closer and closer to her and been unable to help. So it was just a coincidence, in name. That's all. Father Jack had only forgotten about what that name meant to me. Slipped his mind, is all. That was it.

I strode along behind Maeve, meaning to say nothing but still wound up asking, "He-he mentioned a Joanna. Was that one of the ladies at the meeting?"

"Was gonna be. From the Waterside. He'd been talkin' to her about sharing her experiences and gone to pick her up but she wasn't feelin' up to it so stayed home."

"Oh?" Was all I could say, for a good long moment, then I managed, "Is she all right?"

She shrugged. "No idea. I don't know her. Father Jack called, yesterday; thought she might help us with our push for peace. Don't do much good if she won't talk."

Oh, God, oh, God, oh, God, I was crashing back into the madness and this couldn't be! It couldn't!

"Did...did Father Jack know I'd be at this meeting?"

"I told him you were comin'."

Oh, God, oh, God, oh, God...it couldn't be. It couldn't. It couldn't. Joanna was dead. I fucking knew she was dead. She'd died eight years ago.

She had.

Hadn't she?

Had she?

Well...I mean...how did I know? I hadn't actually *seen* her die.

What if she wasn't dead? All those years, what if she wasn't dead? And I was mucking about in Houston instead of going to her? What if she thought I was dead, when I was not? Or worse— that I'd abandoned her?

Oh, no...no...no...this couldn't be.

It-it-it couldn't...

But what if it was? And Father Jack had thought to bring us face to face, again, with no warning and...and...and why? Why would he do that? Why would he want to cause pain like that? Tear our realities apart?

Oh, Jesus fucking Christ...what kind of animal would do that to anyone?

*****

I was glad I'd chosen the hutch to stay in, because I did not sleep, that night. Didn't undress. Didn't bathe. Didn't even light up the stove. I smoked and drank down every last bottle of Maeve's ale and paced and pounded my head and relived those last horrible moments—

The whiteness enveloping me.

The silence.

The dancing flames.

Joanna caught and struggling.

Trying to get up but the pain so great I couldn't.

Danny grabbing me.

The fire nearing her.

Colm's face between her and me and-and-and—

Then nothing.

Nothing.

Over and over and over and over, trying to make sense of the madness careening through my brain.

It all came back to one thing.

I had not actually seen the flames touch her. For all these years I thought I had. I was so sure they had. That she had died. I remembered no one trying to help her. No one fighting to put out the fire. It made too fucking much sense that she had died.

I kept telling myself it had to be another girl of the same name, Father Jack referred to. That had to be the explanation. There could be no other. And I tried. Dear God, I tried to convince myself the name and his comments about some event were but a coincidence. I mean, hell, just a walk through the center of the city had shown me the destruction wrought by eight years of bombings and murders.

No, fifteen years. It was ongoing long before I left.

Before I was taken away.

Before I was made no one.

None of it did any good. I shifted to wondering if-if it was my Joanna he mentioned, did she think me dead, as well? Those rumors had been spread. But how would she have learned of it? And it was just one of the stories being told about me. There was also the one about me leaving on the earlier train, so not even being here...

No. If she'd heard that one, she'd know better.

And the one about me being taken into British custody. Would she think they'd have kept me in silence for eight full years? As vile as they could be, I couldn't see that happening.

Dear God, my brain gave me no rest, even after dawn broke and I heard Maeve puttering around in the kitchen.

I entered and she instantly saw I was of no good mind.

"What's wrong with you?" she asked.

I shrugged, half-laughed and only said, "Ghosts."

She eyed me but set the kettle to going and said, "Tea?"

I nodded and went to the toilet. It was finally time to release some of the ale I'd drunk...and give my brain a chance to settle before breakfast.

It was going to be a long, rough day so best prepare for it.

Reconfigured

Two hours later, I was at the door of *The Derry Journal*, waiting for it to open. As the clerk already knew me by sight, he let me in early and I went to the books holding the Fall months of 1972. I shifted into auto-pilot, set it on the table, then paged through to the edition closest to my catastrophe. Which came out two days after and was...was...

White-white silence everywhere and...

I jammed my pencil into the palm of my left hand to keep from crashing back into that moment. Kept it there. Drew blood. But I was able to force myself to focus on the fevered story about the bombing.

The pictures tore into me. Of Joanna's father's shop, neat and prosperous; of a burned out shell surrounded with smoking rubble; of William Randall and Emily Briscoe, the two children who'd died, both in their second year of public school; of a tired, older man I recognized as having been a tailor in the shop. Joanna had pointed him out as always smelling of camphor.

Photos of three dead.

Three dead?

Three...

Below were horrified remembrances of what had happened. The Rover parked. A blond boy walking away and down the street. The children racing from the sweets shop and bouncing against the Rover. It exploding. A woman clerk and two customers in the sweets shop getting hit by glass and debris. The same to a waitress at Marianne's.

Photos with the names of two men who were employees of the shop, badly injured.

And a breathless point by point telling of how Joanna was saved from sure death by the heroic actions of her father and two others, even as the fire scorched them, hideously. Her injuries were critical and doctors at Casualty in Altnagelvin were not hopeful.

The next edition's update told how father and daughter had been moved by helicopter to a burn unit in Belfast. It also noted that her Da was part of the UVF in a higher capacity. The UVF howled that the deaths of two children was proof the IRA was built of nothing but animals. As if they, themselves, had not committed similar atrocities. OIRA shot back they would never have targeted children. Then PIRA admitted the bombing but said it had gone off prematurely. Of course, no one believed they had the ability. To add to the confusion, the SDLP raised the possibility the UVF may have set up the bomb, themselves, to be done with Martin for being a troublemaker. It seemed he'd surreptitiously met with some men from the OIRA to try and slow the spiral into violence.

It all would have been comical had it not become so tragic. And it boiled down to one thing.

Joanna was alive.

She was burned.

She was broken.

But she was fucking alive!

Always had been!

It wasn't possible.

It couldn't be.

But there was her school photo as the purest verification.

I stared at that photo for close to half an hour. Unable to move. I'd not seen it, before. She'd never given me one of herself, nor I one to her. It was like we knew to keep careful in our love for each other and-and-and I hated that I didn't have one, now.

And hated myself for not thinking to check and verify that she was gone, now that I knew she wasn't. I'd been so sure she was since I was and, dear God, how stupid I felt. Stupid. So bloody fucking stupid.

It took the clerk coming over to ask, "You done with this one, then?" to break me out of my nothing state.

I just nodded, closed the book, and left.

And headed straight down to the bus depot. I had no idea which bus I needed to catch in order to cross near Joanna's street. Was it on Irish we'd gone? A clerk took pity on my Texas idiocy and told me how to get to Altnagelvin. I remembered the bus traveled to there after I'd escaped Charles trying to hurt me.

The excuse I gave the clerk, aside from being a foolish American, was I wanted to understand both sides of the Foyle and the great divide between them, for my paper. She looked at me like I was not of sound mind, and I have little doubt I didn't even begin to act like I had all my senses about me, but it helped. As had being willing to share my Marlboros with the squaddies at the checkpoints. That I managed to do this without seeming full on mad was a small miracle.

The bus meandered about and I recognized little as we passed. Entire buildings gone. Those still working huddled quiet and careful. Men standing close by, eyeing the bus as it passed. Then I saw the stop where Joanna, Angela, Louisa and I had got off, all those years ago. And where I'd jumped on, when Charles was chasing me. It was unchanged, so off I hopped and made myself walk up to the side street.

Unthinking.

Unfeeling.

I turned down it and strolled along, getting closer and closer to the next street that led to Joanna's cul-de-sac. Walking like an automaton past nice-looking but vaguely-tired homes...

Until I reached it.

And stopped. At the corner. I could see her house, down the end. Little changed from so many years ago. Twelve years, since last I'd seen it. God.

I slowly drifted down the walk, towards it. Closer and closer. As if drawn by a string. Aiming straight for the door, unable to stop—

Until a young couple came out and got into a newer Vauxhall. They looked well-off and nothing like Joanna or her parents, so I waved and called in my Texas twang, "'Scuse me, can I ask you a question?"

They both looked at me first with fear but then with curiosity as my accent hit them.

"Where you from?" the man asked. Shite, a Belfast accent.

"Oh, I'm visitin' from Texas. Friend of mine, down there, has family 'round this area and asked me to stop by and say hi, for him. Last name's Martin. You know which house they're in?"

"He didn't tell ya?"

"Well, yeah, I wrote it down on a piece of paper but I can't find it. I just remember the street name..."

"There's no Martins on this block," the woman said, her glare close to malevolent. Also Belfast.

"Oh. Maybe I don't have the street name right. Ya'll lived 'round here long?"

"Few year, only," the man said, not as skittish as the woman. "Dunno who was around before us."

"Wasn't no Martin," she snarled. "Of that I'm sure."

"What's an American doin' here, now?"

"Oh, just researchin' family. Sorry to have bothered you."

"What's your name?" the man asked.

"Everett Casterson," I said. "From San Antonio. Texas."

"Sorry we couldn't help ya, Ev'rett."

"It's all right. They been out of contact and it's been years. Probably moved. Sorry to have bothered you."

Then I headed away, and I could feel both their eyes on my back till I turned the corner.

It was harder returning to the Bogside, and I had to spend a fair bit of time chatting with the squaddies to settle any concerns. And thank God I had an extra box of Marlboros in my ruck—no, *back*pack. But in doing that, I got to hear their harsh comments about being in Derry—hell, in Northern Ireland.

Most of them hated Thatcher. New anti-union laws passed made many of them uncomfortable, as they were from union families. Thought she was out to kill the unions and give over to the rich Tories. Nor could they see why they were in the area facing down Catholics but not Protestants, as the latter were just as obnoxious to them.

Oh, and what they had to say about the stupidity of their superior officers. All in soft voices, sharing discontent with a man they knew would never turn on them. It was odd to hear comments that made it seem like they were oppressed by the situation when I'd always thought them our oppressors.

I recalled something that was said to me. By Scott? No, probably Jeremy. No, no, it was Everett, talking about a former president who'd just died. Seems the man had said something like, *If you give the poorest white man a reason to look down on somebody else, they'll let you pick their pockets. Or help you pick them.* Something like that; I hadn't been paying much attention. Now wish I had, because it seemed to fit this part of the world, perfectly.

I made it to the library not long before it closed and asked for any phone directories they had. The clerk huffed but gave me some and I looked in them, all. Found well over a dozen Martins in each, all on the Waterside. And not one on Joanna's street. I supposed I could go around asking at each of the ones' address, but that would cause too much suspicion to rise. No, I needed an actual location...or, at least, a street name. I still wrote every one of them down in my notebook.

Before I returned to the house, I stopped into an off-license and replenished Maeve's store of ale with bottles of Carling and cans of Bass...and saw the price of Marlboros, here. Christ, if I didn't want to go poor and needy, it might be best if I stopped smoking.

Then as I approached home, I smelled fish frying and suddenly realized I hadn't eaten all day. So in I rushed and said, "That smells like heaven."

Maeve cast me a glare and huffed. "So there you are. Gone the day and just in time to feed, like your brother."

I realized Kieran was seated at the table, glaring at me, so I smiled and set the cans and bottles I'd bought across from him. At least that brought a smile to their lips.

"You look better than you did, this morning."

I nodded then looked straight at Kieran and said, "I need to speak with Colm."

"Maybe he don't wanna talk with you," he shot back at me.

"Maybe you should ask him, first."

He bolted to his feet, snarling, "I'm off."

I shoved him back on his chair, to his shock, and snapped, "Stop it! I don't have the patience for this nonsense. Have your dinner, then in the next day or so just let Colm know I'd like to see him. When and wherever he wants."

"And if he says no?"

"He won't. We're old friends. Chinas."

"Chinas?"

"He'll know what I mean. I have questions for him, and he'll have questions for me, I'm sure. And he can spread the word as to the arrival of—"

"You think you can fool him into thinkin'—"

"I'm not trying to. He'll know that, even if you don't. So stop playing the maggot."

"What?"

He honestly did not know what I meant, so I said, "Being an idiot."

He huffed, but stayed sat, glaring at me and bloody pouting, like a baby. It was too strange. Then he grabbed a Carling and got back some of his obnoxious arrogance.

I sighed and turned to Maeve. "Have you enough for me, as well, or should I get takeaway from the Chinese?"

"There's plenty," she said, eyeing me. "What's goin' on with you?"

I just opened a can of Bass and took a sip. Damn, it was good.

"Is someone up with Ma?" I asked.

"Mrs. Haggerty's daughter, Aura. She sometimes stops by before her shift."

I nodded and headed upstairs. Time to face the lion.

And hope for an answer or two.

Aura was a round, happy young woman wearing her cleaning apron. I put on a huge grin and introduced myself in my best twang. Which made her giggle.

"Is that how everyone talks in Texas?" she asked.

"Pretty much. I'm just up to see if Mrs. Kinsella would like some of the haddock Maeve is frying up. Or maybe a baked potato with some butter? I noticed some in the fireplace, downstairs."

Like used to be.

Ma glared at me but kept her voice civil. "No, no fish, the smell's put me off. Potato would be fine. Small one. No butter. And some lemon water."

Aura rose, still giggling. "It's near time for me to be on-duty, so I'll drop in on ya, Saturday, if you're up."

"If I'm still here."

"Oh, don't be daft. Cheers." Then she brushed past me with a "Good to meet ya." And she was gone.

"How're you feelin'?" I asked Ma, keeping my twang.

She only shrugged. "I may want some of the Percocet." Then she saw the Bass and her eyes grew sharp. "Or maybe not. Just yet."

I offered her the can, without a thought. She took it with both hands. And had a sip. Barely wet her lips. Then she let out a mournful sigh and offered it back to me. "The taste is wrong. Like drinkin' tin. Awful."

"There's some Carling in a bottle."

"That's even worse."

"The medicine do that?"

She nodded. "Nothing tastes right. Even the lemon water's startin' to go off on me. How I used to love making fry-ups and feastin' on them. Blood pudding. Beans on toast. Even dinner from the chippy. Or pasta and sauce. Simple tea and toast burned over the fire. None of it's right, anymore."

I sat in the chair Aura'd been in. "What else'd you like to eat?"

"No matter. The less taste there is to it, the better."

"How about a potato mashed, with some cheese?"

She cast me a wary look. "Mashed?"

"Like creamed potatoes."

She shrugged. "I have to eat somethin', I suppose."

"I'll bring some up, shortly."

"I heard Kieran, downstairs," she murmured with a near smile. "Let him bring it. He'll have all the gossip of the day. Better news about the strikes. Things you wouldn't have access to, Jeremy."

Jeremy. And she was serious about calling me that. No hesitation.

"Mrs. Kinsella," I asked, carefully, "what do you remember about the bombin' Brendan was caught in?"

That took her aback. "Brendan? What's he to do with anything?"

I decided to keep playing. "Third child? Second son?"

She cut me off with a huff. "Runnin' away from home like a spoiled brat. He always was. No shock he got hurt. He knew nothin' of the world."

"I...I understand he was badly injured."

"Stupid men." She grew confused. "Was it a bomb did it? Did they tell me that? No. Yes, he was hurt and they wanted him dead and I had to stop them. Didn't care about any of the rest. Didn't even have a doctor for him till I made them. Bastards. It was my husband stopped 'em. My Eamonn."

What? "Your husband?"

She almost smiled. "My Eamonn stopped them. They knew not to cross him."

"Eamonn Kinsella?"

"That's him." Her face grew almost beatific. "Oh, how he was."

"What...what can you tell me about him?"

"My Eamonn. Always there for the cause. Bold and strong, he was. Beautiful man." And she sighed, almost angelic as—

She bounded up the stairs, hair still wet, and flew into his arms, and he was naked and grabbed her and—

"But...but enough said about that," Ma continued.

"Well, when did you get married?"

Her expression grew confused. Distant. "Married? Married to my Eamonn? Oh, he was such a fine man, back then. Tall. Strong shoulders. Mari was so jealous of me, havin' him. Belfast was such a city, back then. Even for us."

Belfast? "You weren't living in Derry, when you were married?"

She rubbed her eyes. "Of course we were. Twelve years we had. De Valera come to Derry. I showed him our Eamonn. First born and beautiful. Our Brendan, next to him? It was like a punishment."

I had to draw in a breath and grip the can with both hands to keep from saying anything, in answer.

"I wanted to go back to Belfast. Be away from Derry. But it was too late. Word was around." She looked at me, so lost and innocent in her expression. "What did you ask me, Jeremy?"

It took me a moment to answer. "When were you married?"

"Why? Why ask that? My Eamonn is dead. Fifteen years dead. Why do you want to know?"

"It...uh...it would be a nice detail to add to my paper."

She nodded, almost like she was saying, *Ah-ha.* "For your schoolin'. Tellin' tales. Are they good ones? My Eamonn used to tell tales. People sought him out to tell them. To sing. All the old songs. The old stories. He knew them all. Told them all, and so well. His face open. His eyes bright."

"He told a lot of them?"

She didn't seem to hear me. Her fingers began to dance at the air. "I met him as a dancer. On a stage. He would speak and people would stop to listen. His voice soft, almost like music. Three girls and I, we danced after him. Once his stories and songs was done. We all thought he was fine. So beautiful as he spoke."

"When was this? Were you at a fair? In Derry? Belfast?"

It was as if I wasn't speaking. "The nuns didn't like him. Thought him wicked for bein' in that home. Kept me away from him as much as they could. He laughed at them. What a lovely laugh he had. I joined him and listened so happily to him. The music of his voice. The loveliness of his touch. They wanted to send me to another home, when I was with my first."

She took my hand, with movements so delicate they were like

a whisper. "I was a good dancer. Especially at *Sean Nós*. Even after my second I could still do a fine *Céilí*, and did at a few fetes. It was the third one ruined it for me. Brendan."

She drifted back in her bed, as if in surrender.

"My poor little Brendan. He had no interest in bein' part of this world. So never was, truly. It was hard to believe he was mine. Was my Eamonn's. Many wondered, considerin' the start of our marriage. It's always on the woman for gossip such as that..."

She seemed to surround herself in silence, her eyes looking at something a thousand miles away. I kept my voice soft, so as not to bring her out of her memories. "What was the start of your marriage?"

She almost smiled. "A lovely wet Spring day. I wore a cloak, give me by Sister Luke, to hide within. Priest was there but wasn't him married us. It was a man behind a counter. Mari laughed at him. Said he reminded her of Scrooge. So silly. He cast her a stern look, to hush her. It only made her giggle, the more."

"Where did it take place?"

"Such beautiful, green country. Magherafelt. No one knew us, there. Sister Luke took pity and helped us. On the bus. Mari in a seat next to her. Us right behind. Quiet. All done so quiet. And I was glad for it.

"So happy, we were. Two rooms off the Falls Road. Lovely neighbors. Him doin' well at the docks and the fetes and Nationalist polling. With our wee Eamonn. Then our Mairead."

A cloud grew in her eyes. Crossing her face. Sadness with it, and more than a little confusion. "Then come all those near ones...before our Brendan..." She looked at her hands, and they were shivering. She clasped them together, almost in prayer, and looked at me. "Is there some lemon water? And my pill? Where is Maeve?"

I took in a deep breath and smiled, saying in my Texas tones, "In the kitchen, fixing dinner. Want me to fetch her?"

She seemed to finally see me and grew close to tears. "You're a sweet boy. Not like my Brendan. He was a cat and we were all dogs, to him. Where's Maeve?"

I rose, saying, "I'll get her for you."

"Some lemon water. It's no good, but it's all I can do."

I went downstairs and found Maeve portioning out the haddock. "She's asking for you," I said. "Wants that lemonade and a pill?"

She nodded. "She's in pain, then." She handed me the skillet. "Help yourself."

"I'll bring up a potato," I said.

"I do that!" Kieran snapped, bolting to his feet. He paused long enough to snarl, "Ma don't want you here."

I rolled my eyes and snarled back, "But I'm not here, am I?"

He sneered and bolted into the parlor.

I turned to Maeve, who was filling a glass of that hideous liquid, and said, "If she says any more about her wedding, please let me know."

"Why you askin' about that?" she said, not looking at me.

"Maeve, do you ever recall our parents celebrating their wedding anniversary? What day it was?

"No...but I was hardly old enough to notice, wasn't I. Have you asked Mairead or Aunt Mari?"

I shook my head and portioned some of the haddock on my plate then added peas and half a potato. "It's something I just wondered about. I can check with the registrar's office, I guess."

Kieran came into the kitchen with a potato wrapped in cloth. He plopped it on a plate, cut it into pieces with a knife then added a pat of butter before grabbing the glass of lemon water and bolting upstairs. I heard Ma joyously greet him as if he'd been gone for years instead of me.

Then she asked, "Who was that man just in here?"

Kieran's response? "Nobody, Ma."

After which they spoke in voices too low to be heard.

I sighed. "He's a trial for you, isn't he, Maeve?"

"As I said, he gets her to eat and take her other meds. But she's close to the point where that won't be needed."

I grimaced. "I haven't said anything about the hospice."

"No need. After communion last, Father Jack suggested it might be better she be allowed to die at home."

I nodded.

"Bren...Jeremy, why're you after knowin' when Ma and Da were wed?"

"Something she said that doesn't make sense. So I want to look into it. Tomorrow, I'm off to Magherafelt."

"Oh...when will you be back?" she asked as she sat down to eat, a Carling in hand.

"Just there and back. Check a few things—no, wait, tomorrow's the election. I'll have to go Friday. Will that work all right with you?"

She nodded. "I was hopin' to help with the pollin'."

"Go. I'll stay with Ma. Maybe get more out of her."

"Before she's gone?" Said without a trace of rancor.

I shrugged. "She's never been one to give much information over, but when she's lost in a haze of memory, it wanders out."

"Why're you askin' for all this?"

It took me a moment to respond. "You remember how she treated me, don't you?"

She had to nod, at that. "Holy Mary, that time she threw your plate on the floor, in a fit. And you eatin' the whole of it, anyway. I didn't know what to make of that. I'd no idea why she was in such a state, and thought you were quite mad."

I shrugged. "No argument. But Ma kept the floor clean, so I wasn't so worried."

She almost laughed, almost huffed in confusion, but then took a sip of the Carling.

I drifted, for a moment, remembering that morning and how stubborn I'd been, not to let her see she'd affected me in any way. It had made her wary of me, for a bit, at least. Then finally I said, "I just...I'd like to know her reason for all of it. She almost told me why, when I was up there. Almost. And she was never like that with Eamonn, or Mairead. You. Rhuari. It was only me she was always at. And I...I'd just like to know what I'd done to cause it. I mean, aside from being born. And I'd like the answer before she's buried."

"Sometimes things cannot be explained."

I nodded."This may be one of them, but I still want to try."

Redirected

The next day, Kieran was off the moment he'd had his breakfast and Maeve had scurried out soon after, once Ma was settled. And asleep. In fact, she slept through the morning into early afternoon. Woke for her pills, stared at the window and said nothing. Not one word more than absolutely necessary before drifting back to sleep.

I sat in the chair watching her breathe, soft and easy. Sometimes a little moan as she shifted position, but nothing more. I had a hundred questions I wanted to ask her, but never a chance for any. When she did fully wake, into the afternoon, it was to ask for some lemon water and Percocet. I got it, gave it to her, and tried to engage her in conversation, but she just lay back in the bed, closed her eyes and ignored me.

So there was little I could do other than study her face. The sharp angles. Skin drawn and colorless. Lips pulled tight. Still with her own teeth. I knew so many of the neighbor ladies, even back when I lived here, had dentures. But not Ma. Her fanaticism about being clean had included us brushing our teeth twice a day. We'd all had good teeth and well cared for. A funny thing to think.

It struck me that Da'd had teeth almost like a wolf. Which I'd never thought of, before. I could remember his face being long and easy to screw into fury, and how black his eyes could be. But I'd never thought about his teeth, till now. I didn't even know if I was remembering them right, but I was thinking his were curved slightly inward, with long sharp ones to each side that added to his sense of menace when he was ready to tear into you.

I hadn't liked any of Da's pictures. He always looked on the verge of anger in them. But obviously Ma had loved his look, the way she'd spoken of him. I wondered if I could find early photos of him in the papers, talking about his story-telling shows?

I counted back from Eamonn's birthdate and determined my parents must have been together August or September of 1949.

Making Ma sixteen and probably still living in the orphanage. But did they still call them that, then? And was it here, in Derry? I'd always thought it was, but her meanderings had them living in Belfast with the birth of Eamonn and Mairead. Of course, they must have been in Derry for De Valera's travel was to here. When was that? Spring...summer 1951? I'd have to find out.

So that gave me the timeframe to work within. August 1949 to March 1950 for Ma and Da to be married. Living in Belfast till at least the birth of Mairead, in March 1951.

I had all these noted in my pad and sectioned off as to what to ask when. There was still the *Derry Journal* to dig into, but also the city library and a jaunt to Magherafelt and finding out what home Ma had been in. That might be part of the wedding announcement.

I could also ask Mrs. Haggerty, since she'd lived by us on Nailors then moved to Lecky Road, off Westland, with her two— Aura and Jimmy, who were both years younger than me. She might have things to say about Da.

I have no answer as to why I needed to know all this. It's not as if I were still part of the family. But it felt as if what happened to Da meant something more than mere happenstance and might relate to my current situation. Mainly, as to why I was kept alive. And why Rhuari was given extra protection in Belfast. And us allowed special dispensation for our needs, by the IRA. And maybe even why the powers that be were still seeking me out. I may have been allowing my imagination to run too much, but it was like...I don't know...like trying to repair a clock or motor and some pieces were missing. I hated when that happened and could not abide letting it just pass. Everything had to fit.

There was no clock in Ma's room, nor did I have a watch, and it being bright out threw off my ability to know the time. So I had no idea how long I was at this. In fact, it wasn't till I heard Maeve bursting in that I wondered at the hour.

Ma was still sleeping...though I had the feeling she was only playing at it. As if to keep from speaking to me, or something, so I just went down to the kitchen.

Maeve had half a dozen bags on the table carrying all sorts of things, and when I went to look she snapped, "Do not touch!"

I jumped back.

"These are for the polling station, tonight," she said, "waitin' for the results, and please stay away; your meddlin' would only make things harder for me."

"As you will, Maeve. It's your house."

"For now. We'll see, after Ma's gone."

Oh, shite. "You think the committee'd toss you out?"

"Not straightaway. Probably not till the end of the year. But a brother and sister living in a three-bedroom house? When others are in greater need? It's selfish, on our part."

Oh. Well. "Where would you go?"

"Rhuari and Bridie have said we can stay with them. I'll be back in nursing school and able to help Bridie with the wains. Kieran, however, he'd be on the couch and that doesn't sit well, with him. He might stay at Tommy's. I'd rather he not, but as you can see, he's hardly one to listen.

"Oh, Br—Jeremy, can you stay with Ma tomorrow, as well? Some of us are goin' down to the Maze to celebrate for Bobby, and Mrs. Haggerty and O'Canainn will be with us."

Without thinking, I asked, "Is she the same Mrs. O'Canainn from up off Nailors?"

She nodded. "She's three houses over, now. And she'll drop off some of her stew and colcannon."

"God, do I remember the beauty of that."

"Extra enticement?"

"I'd have said yes, anyway. Ma's been avoiding my questions and it will give me more time with her."

"You really think you can make any sense of her ramblings?"

I shrugged. "You never know. But this research makes me seem even more legitimate, doesn't it?" Then one of my more brilliant ideas hit me. "Y'know, I'd like to see Eamonn."

She stopped and let her gaze grow distant. "I can't remember the last time I saw him. Christmas, maybe? He looked so thin. Tired. Hair down his shoulders and beard like a maniac. Father Jack took Mairead to see him, a couple months ago, but they wouldn't let her in. Used *her condition* as their excuse. With me, it's always just, *He's on restriction, today. Sorry.* Bloody idiots."

"Might be different for me," I said, far more upbeat than I felt. "*Not being related. From the States. For my research.*"

She took in a deep breath then unloaded a bag of potatoes into a basket. "Ask Father Jack to take you. He goes every Monday."

Oh, perfect. Father Jack in the middle of it, again. But maybe it would be good to go head-to-head with him, finally. Cut through his games and find out more about Joanna.

So I said, "Great. I'll ask him Sunday."

*****

Of course, St. Bobby won his election and the celebrations and demonstrations were great and glorious all over the North. On the Catholic side. On the Protestant, more words and attacks and blame laid against Catholics for everything that's ever gone wrong in the history of the world. Included was the pushback from the powers that be.

There was no going anywhere unless you were willing to wade through the chaos, and my focus was more on getting Ma to provide more information about her and my Da's history. Which was damn near impossible to do because her ear was plugged to the radio. Then when the count finally was declared, she was about nothing but the glory of a man in jail who was on hunger strike being made a member of Parliament.

Mrs. O'Canainn was good to her word, that Friday, and left a pot of her stew on the stove when she came by for Maeve. And to my shock, Ma actually had some of it for lunch. Just a few bites and a couple sips of my Carling, but during that moment she was open to sharing some of her memories. Not with me, but with this unknown Jewish lad.

"It's glorious what happens when you don't back down from them what hate us," she said at one point. "My Eamonn never did. To his sorrow. Bloody Unionists. So many coming at you. Only got their majority by thieving and thuggery."

"When was this?" I asked in my twang.

"All across the North. Always lies and thuggery, and my poor Eamonn tryin' so hard to do right. Bloody priests treatin' him like he's filth, and him doin' nothin' wrong." Then she cast a confused glance at me. "Who made this?" And she held up her cup of stew.

"Mrs. O'Canainn brought it by, this morning."

She nodded. "Good woman. Took care of my Brendan when I couldn't. I was so proud of him. My Mai told me all about it. He could have been like his Da, had he been willin'. Never backin' down. Never. But we were dogs to his cat, always. Standin' aside.

Watchin'. Judgin'. It's like he knew..."

"Knew what?"

"Couldn't dance anymore, after him. Something broke in me and I'd start to hurt and not keep straight and...my Eamonn still told stories, so beautifully. But the drink took him. That bastard took him on."

"Took him on?"

She didn't seem to hear me. "Had to leave. Had to go."

"Go where?"

She handed me the cup, half of her stew still in it, and looked around, her gaze distant. "So nice, now. It wasn't to start, but my Eamonn fixed that. And Mrs. Haggerty...such a friend, always. Always." She wrapped her arms around herself and began rubbing them. Then her eyes locked on me and she frowned. "Why did you come back? I didn't want you back. They promised you wouldn't come back. Why did you come back?"

I quietly said, "To watch you die."

Jesus, God, I hadn't meant to say that. But the words came out before I could even think of them, and I felt the deepest shame in myself over them. "I shouldn't have said that, Ma. I'm sorry."

She almost smiled and nodded. Her voice was thin. "Don't be. It's honest. It was never love we shared. Was it? Nor trust between mother and son."

I had no response to that, so just looked away.

Her voice grew weary and low. "I'll have a Percocet."

I handed her a pill and she swallowed it with some of my Carling. Which I knew was not proper, but I was in no mind to argue with her. Then she motioned for me to lower the bed, and I did, and she closed her eyes.

I sat there for at least another hour as she slept. Not looking at her. Just trying to figure out how to justify my comment, to myself. And I couldn't. Because she was right. It was the first truly honest thing I'd said to her.

And what did that say about me?

Chinas, Again?

Of course, there was not one hint from Thatcher that she might be open to compromise, now that Bobby was in Parliament. Which led to more demonstrations and more people dying from being shot with supposedly non-lethal rubber bullets. More stones slung from our side. More businesses destroyed. We were locked into a repeat cycle.

Maeve stayed out in the middle of it, leaving me to handle Ma the whole time, and I was rather ticked off. I wanted to wander through the morass of hate and joy and pride and despair, myself. See if I could find anything that might give me hope, again. But Ma had a couple of episodes where she needed a full cleaning, and oh, did she hate me being the one to do it.

Almost as much as I hated being the one.

But I got her body washed in full, by pretending she was Angus in need of a bath. Which wasn't quite accurate a way to put it, since he'd loved getting scrubbed and rubbed down while she screeched and cursed like a banshee. I was as wet as she was, by the time we were done, and had more than a few scratches on my arms and face. But I also had her sheets changed and the floor all but polished by the time Maeve came home.

She was much impressed.

I made her a grilled cheese and she devoured it like a field hand as she told me of her adventures.

"Tried to caravan to the Maze but that didn't happen. Couldn't even get our cars to the bridge. Waterloo was so full of noise and anger. The Diamond, too."

I noticed some scrapes on her chin and asked, "Does that need tending?"

She shook her head. "Some silly constable in full riot gear thought me a stupid girl, but found I don't take kindly to being shoved against a wall. I think I broke his jaw. I hope. Just managed to get away, but if they ever find out who I am it's Strand Road for me." Then she grabbed my arm, her eyes shining bright. "Is this how it felt, Bren. At the Battle of Bogside? This? This rush of joy and wonder?"

I only nodded, remembering how exhausted I'd also been. But the happiness had barely lasted for more than just the moment.

She giggled with delight, then finished her meal and ale, bathed and collapsed in her room.

Father Jack came by on Sunday for the small communion for Ma and Maeve, which I continued to stay away from. But Kieran came with him and let me know Colm was open to meeting with me.

"I couldn't believe it," he said. "All that's goin' on and he tells me, *Midnight, tonight*. I asked him where and all he'd say is, *Me China knows*. Makes no sense."

But it did. The Circle Fort in The Republic.

"Thanks," was all I said, then he shrugged and went upstairs to join Maeve and Ma.

When Father Jack came down, I stopped him at the door and asked, "Could I work out a way to visit Mrs. Kinsella's son in the Maze?"

He frowned at me. "Why would you want to?"

"I figured I might build my thesis 'round this family," I said, as innocent as I could. "There's been lots of stories and discussions 'bout people who had a family member killed, but that seems to be the only thing people remember about them. I think I'd like to work it up to where you see how the day-to-day grind of the Troubles affects everyone, including those who haven't lost someone they love."

He looked straight at me and said, "But they have lost someone."

He was about to say more but I cut him off with, "Their father, yes. But he was killed before these troubles started, as I understand. He had no connection to what's going on, now. Did he?" And I looked straight back at him.

He gave the slightest hesitation then said, "That's true, but there's a middle son who's no longer here."

I nodded. "And no one seems to know what happened to him. He just went off and never came back. It's almost like he wasn't wanted so was sent away."

"That is hardly the case."

"Mrs. Kinsella won't speak of him and gets angry when I raise any question."

"You should speak with Maeve and Rhuari. They would know more about him—"

"As would his older brother, Eamonn. Which is another reason I'd like to talk to him."

"I doubt it's possible, right now, what with the hunger strikes and unrest going on."

"Of course. Just thought I'd ask. Never hurts."

He eyed me for a moment then said, "True. I suppose I could enquire. My next visit is planned for tomorrow. It might be best if I discuss it with them, first, and bring you the following week."

"Will you be at the peace meeting on Tuesday?"

"Of course I will. I can let you know, then."

I forced my expression to remain non-descript as I asked, "What about this Joanna you mentioned. Will she be there?"

Now he gave me a wary eye. "It is my hope."

"That'd be great," I said. Smiling. "I can find out more about life here from her, too. The Protestant perspective."

Then he left, deep in thought.

Ma was quiet the rest of the day, even after Mrs. Carson showed up and shared her dinner with her. I guess I wore her out. I stayed down and spoke with Maeve...until a phone call came through from Mairead and I had to write out a quick note—*She thinks I came over as Brennan*—and show it to Maeve.

She rolled her eyes in irritation, and the chitchat on her side stayed plain and simple. Then she went up to Ma to switch it to the portable receiver. Fortunately, Ma had already taken some Percocet and wasn't exactly coherent in her ramblings.

Except for, "I'm so glad one of my girls is out of this. It's good we left Belfast. You growin' up in that horror? And then strangers comin' in to ask stupid questions they got no business knowin' and assaulting you. Your Da was not happy about it, no question there."

It jolted me and I wrote it down, quick. Again, it sounded like Ma was saying Mairead was born in Belfast. So that gave me a tighter window to look into when they moved to Derry and why. See if anything came up about Da during that time, but in the Belfast papers. So I should hop by the library to see if they had copies of the *Telegraph* or the *News Letter* from that time.

I went down to the bus depot and found out that I had to get to Burt, which was at the base of the hill that Grianan Aileach was on. But there was no bus service that late, on a Sunday, so walking it was.

And getting stopped by an RUC patrol once I was on Groarty Road. Me being *an idiot American* helped me minimize that issue.

"I wanted to see that there circle fort..."

The constable was flabbergasted. "It's in the Republic. I don't think there's access."

"Oh, I was told this road'd take me straight up to it. And there's still plenty of light left..."

Well, two more hours of full light and slow twilight to come. And I told them of a story I'd heard, that the circle fort was home to fairies who would come dancing in its center once it was full darkness just after midnight. I wanted to see if it was true. The constable questioning me was almost laughing at me, but I noticed the older man behind the wheel of their well-fortified tender wasn't.

So they drove me up to the border, to find the road had been blown up and barriers put across, however nothing else done to keep the two peoples apart. So I got out, promised the driver if I did catch a glimpse of the fairies I'd let him know, and headed straight up the narrow road.

I could feel them watching me, for the first ten minutes, till just before I reached the second turn to my left, where I'd need to turn down to curl around to the fort. I cast a glance back to see the constables were gone so headed down it.

This one was even more narrow than Groarty, or whatever its name was, in the Republic. I walked along. Passed an old shed I did not remember being there, before. Did kind of recall a fork in the road and followed to the right. Looked up through shrubs and trees...and then I saw the hint of it, atop the hill. I kept on. Followed the road around and got a better look after a curve atop a rise in the road.

If I knew Colm, he'd have someone watching for me to give him the signal I'd made it. And twilight would be at its apex when he arrived. At least, I hoped that's how it would work.

The shrubs along here were wilder than before, the grass more evident. I saw homes that seemed recently erected, here and there, no lights inside—

I looked around and saw it was a church with a playground and there were houses close by, all their windows dark—

I stopped to lean against a post, my breath short less from exertion than memory...though I had just topped another slow rise in the road. I looked to my right and could still make out the hump of the fort against the darkening sky. Black and cold and solid, with the last hints of sunlight caressing it, close to three-hundred meters up and—

Joanna stopped to take in the view, her breath quick and sharp against the biting cold—

And she took my hand.

She was walking with me. Trudging across the fields and closer and closer to the summit, her face bright and pure, and her smile as sweet and gentle, as always. She was my guide, and I trusted no one but her as she was and—

I continued on.

And then I was there. By my thoughts, a couple hours early. A weak iron grate lay across the low entrance. I pulled it away with no effort, so I suppose it was meant to keep out stray dogs. Too bad for them this one knew his way about it. I slipped inside and, despite my shaky legs, quickly climbed to the top tier and looked out over the dark, cold land.

The distant slivers of water were silvery blue, as before. Gleaming alive and indifferent under the vanishing sun and rising moon and gentle clouds. Plots of land carved into a patchwork of farms spread below, their differences barely visible. And there was silence...a silence so elegant, it was like music. The wind nipped at my cheeks to underscore it, and my breath danced away from me as if joyous about it all. Even jammed into my coat, my hands were cold and my feet were near frozen but I felt more alive than I had since the last time I was here. I wished I could stay here forever, and I thought, *Joanna would love to have seen this, again.*

Jesus God, this was how life should be lived—free and open and happy and unfettered by hate or anger or even histories cloaked in self-righteousness. This world cared nothing for our petty human squabbles; it merely fulfilled its meaning in ways no man could ever even begin to understand. I'd tasted this truth on my walk to Claudy so many years earlier and was reminded of it on every walk home from *The Colonel's* in the dead of night. This made it true, full and complete. I wanted never to leave and—

"Howya, me China," cut into my thoughts.

Colm was walking up the steps to join me. It wasn't full dark, yet. Had he been hiding, close by? Watching me come? Making sure I'd be alone?

I let him approach and as he held out his hand, I punched him.

Well...I tried to. He jolted back and I barely brushed against his chin. He spun me and grabbed me from behind but thanks to my years of sparring with Jeremy, I was able to twist away and swing at him, again.

And miss him, again.

But his one punch to my gut did not miss. In fact, it shut me down and dropped me to my knees.

"What th' fuck, Bren!?" he hissed. "You got me here to beat me?"

I managed to choke out, "Why didn't. You tell me?"

He crouched beside me, frowning. "Tell you what?"

I managed to croak, "Joanna's alive."

And that took the wind out of him. He sat on the stones and dirt, his back against the wall. I let myself do the same, just not as neatly. My gut still wanting to do things I did not want it to do.

"Eight years." I gulped. "Not one word. I thought her dead. Dead and...and...she's not."

He sighed. "How'd you find out?"

"Chatter at the...at the peace meeting. Joanna. Waterside. Going to talk about...talk about her horrors. But canceled. Looked in the Journal. From that time. She was saved."

"I'd hardly call it, that."

All I did was look at him, but my expression must have held the greatest betrayal, for he added, "She was burned, bad. Her Da, as well."

I just kept looking at him.

"She was never supposed to be there. We knew of a UVF meetin' to happen in her Da's shop. Its offices. The bomb was set to go durin' that. When she'd have been far away. Or maybe even off with you and...and I'm sorry for her."

I finally looked away, unable to think.

He continued with, "I knew how you felt about her. Knew how you could be. Listen to no one, not if you didn't want to. You'll never believe the shock I felt seein' you comin' down that

street. How angry some of the higher-ups were at you even bein'
there. But then we saw your passport. That letter and your ticket.
And I knew you were leavin' and just sayin' goodbye. That's why
I got your Ma, to help me keep you alive."

I nodded. "They wanted to end me."

I could sense Colm also nodding. "You were bad hurt, and
some thought you'd die, anyway. But your Ma stopped it."

"And my father?"

"Your father's long dead. How could he have anything to say
in it? It was your mother fought them back. To my surprise. I'd
seen how she hits you. How she can scream. But calm and quiet
she was, and a doctor was called in. And you were snuck into the
Republic to heal. And your Aunt collected you for the trip."

"And I was cut off. Disowned."

"Yes. You were leavin', so we carried it on. But the fuckin'
Brits kept lookin' for you. We've no idea how they knew it was
you there." He gave a long sigh. "They still got you down as bein'
in America, y'know. Suspect your aunt and uncle helped you in
some way, but have no proof."

He put a hand on my shoulder, continuing with, "Me China,
I knew you. I knew with no question, if you'd known she was
alive, you'd have gone to her. No matter what. And once you
showed up, what little cover we had would've collapsed. We'd all
have been in it. We didn't want that. Still don't want that. Neither
do you."

I was almost back to normal. "Is that all there was to it? You
thought the only way I could be controlled is...is if I were lied to?"

"When have you ever been controlled, in any other way?"

I didn't like being told that, but it made too much sense. So I
murmured, "Where is she?"

"I'm not tellin' you, except that she's not in Derry. None of
her family is." He shifted around to emphasize what he was saying
to me. "Bren, she would not want you to see her, as she now is.
That would kill her. Remember her as she was. Walk on. Be a man
about it. It's the most decent thing you can do for her. For all of
us."

Of course. It would be. Only I couldn't see me doing that. I'd
have to let her know I hadn't abandoned her. I couldn't let her
think I would have just left her. But no need to bring that up, right
now.

So I leaned back against the wall and asked, "Do you know anything about me Da?"

"No..." From the way he said it, I didn't believe it.

So I took in a deep breath and kept on. "Is there someone you can ask? Maybe who might have known him, in Belfast?"

"No. Why?" A bit more emphasis and acceptable, but still not to be completely believed.

"All I remember of him is his fists," I said.

Colm nodded. "The bruises on you..."

"Now I'm hearing he told stories at fetes. Was a master of it. People would come to listen to him. He made money at it. And he helped with polling for Nationalists, in Belfast, and it...and it confuses me. Everything since I've been back confuses me."

"But your Da's long buried and no one can say, now. Memories have this habit of cloudin' everything, and your worries about him should be put aside, as well. It's good enough you come back for your mother. Let that be all there is to it."

"You think I'll let that be?"

I didn't have to look at him to figure he'd really rolled his eyes at me. "No. You're too stubborn a little fuck. Always have been."

"Even with me Chinas?"

"Maybe not as bad, but..."

I nodded. "I'm sorry about Danny."

"Yeah."

"I thought him better than that, with his abilities."

"You can never be certain with a bomb."

"Were I ever to build one, it would not explode till its appointed time."

"I know."

We sat there in silence, for a while, until he said, "Are those all the questions you had for me? Those and a fist?"

I only nodded.

He rose to his feet and gave me a hand up.

"How were you able to twist away from me?" he asked. "No one has, before."

"Aikido. With a friend."

"Did you make good friends, in America?"

I nodded. "Almost as good as here."

He smiled. "Sorry, but you'll have to walk back. No

constables for a ride, this time."

Of course he'd know about that.

"I've walked it, before," I said. "And can't leave till after midnight. I promised I'd stay to see if the fairies come."

That made him laugh. "Well, if any are willing to show when one of us is around, it would be for you. You've always been touched by their magic dust."

I half-snorted. "Me Ma says I'm just simple."

He clapped me on the back, saying, "She knows better."

"You haven't asked what I'm going to do when she's gone. Why is that?"

"Because, me China, I know you. Without question, won't stay here. And you won't return to America. You'll wander the world. Somebody said...somebody...was it Jackie? He said, *The only thing that might anchor you is the love of a woman.*"

I nodded. "A woman who thinks me dead."

"No, no, it wasn't Jackie said that. It was Aidan. After we learned of you and Joanna. Eamonn had said you'd have made a good vagabond. That once you started movin', you'd never stop, and it was Aidan's response, in agreement."

"Not entirely true, back then."

"What about now?"

I shrugged.

"Whatever you do now, Bren, be careful. Things have changed."

"What hasn't?"

"You're still me China."

I finally managed a smile as I said, "And you're mine."

We shook hands, and he was off.

I stayed till long past midnight...

And not a single bloody fairy showed.

Foraging for Details

I went to the library the next morning, and it had The Belfast papers on microfiche. Which I could make copies from, if I wanted. I spent the day digging through both but found nothing with any connection to my parents. No wedding notice. Not even birth announcements for Mairead or Eamonn. I even checked under the name of Clark, from Aunt Mari's thoughts, and while there were a couple of those they were obviously not my parents, brother or sister.

Obviously, I'd have to do a serious interrogation of Ma to get any real information. Hopefully enough to sort the wheat from the chaff.

When I got home, Maeve was upstairs with Ma, and her voice sounded strained. As nothing was set out for dinner, I called up to her that I was off to get something from the chippy, nearby.

She sounded so relieved when she called back, "I'll have a two. Been that sort of day. And Keiran said he'd be over with a friend so..."

"I'll make sure there's plenty."

It's good she mentioned Keiran, because he brought two mates with him. Tommy Fields, who was taller, thinner, and had spooky eyes under his russet hair; and Claud McCarren, who reminded me so much of Paidrig I almost asked if they were related. They feasted well, but what was good about it is how three of them joined with Ma and got her to eat some fish as well as a chip or two, and a few sips of Fanta.

As Maeve was in a *Do not talk to me mood*, I sat up a bit, on the stairs, and listened as they regaled Ma with stories of their exploits against the British and joys of covering every spot they could with a spray of paint. Tommy had been hit by a rubber bullet during one recent protest and still bore the mark from him. It seems he showed it to Ma and she was well impressed.

Claude joked about being snatched down to Strand Road and being tossed out ten minutes after, since they thought him an idiot. Kieran laughed and told of when Ma and Rhuari had been snatched, some years back, and kept for days and tortured. Which I knew was nonsense, and even Ma laughed at him, but the lads swallowed it up and Ma did not actually contradict him.

The problem is, they wore Ma out and she was off to sleep without the Percocet. Which I guess was good, but meant I'd have to wait a couple more days, since I was off to Magherafelt, first thing, and would not miss the Peace meeting for anything, that night.

The morning bus drove through country so rich and alive and green, it was as if I'd gone to a different world. My walk to Claudy would have looked like this, had it been daylight. Peaceful. Gentle. Lambing season fairly well-over but still the little beasts danced about in some fields.

As they had when Joanna and I walked to the fort.

It's funny, but I could return to my memories and not be cut by them, now. The walk was just something I did, long ago. It was special, still, but no hurt came with it. No sorrow of what was lost. Just simple remembrance.

And a hope that once I connected with her again, we could retrace our steps.

I had to change busses in Tobemore, a scrunchy little country town, but still managed the full trip in little more than two hours. Found the registrar's office, and in my best drawl let them know I was looking up a family marriage for a friend. So the lady helped me.

I gave the range of dates, and she found a copy of the marriage license in a box stored on a shelf in a well-maintained shed.

And there it was.

Eamonn Patrick Kinsella, born 9 September 1930 in Belfast, married Bernadette Alyne Farrell, born 12 November 1932 in Londonderry, on Friday, 3 March 1950. Witnessed by Sister Luke of Good Shephard Home for Girls, Clondermot, and Father Llewellyn of Whiteabbey.

So Ma was seventeen when she married, not sixteen. And while I knew Clondermot as an area of Derry, I could recall no mention of an orphanage, there. I had to ask where Whiteabby was. She told me it's outside Belfast. There was nothing more in the way of an address, for either. Still, that gave me something.

When I got back to Derry, I slipped over to the *Journal* and looked into the two issues after the wedding, but there was no notice. So I hit the library half an hour before closing, to retrace through those dates but still could find no notice in either the *Telegraph* or *News Letter*. It was like they wanted no one to know.

Well, that could be ascribed to Ma carrying my brother, at the time, but it still seemed off.

Then as I was about to end my search, it being close to closing time, I happened to catch a glimpse of a short article in the Telegraph about a fete that was upcoming in Lisburn. At a Protestant Church. There would be games and music and dancing.

And a seanchaí by the name of Edward Clark.

The photo that accompanied it?

It was of my Da.

I made a copy then asked the librarian what a seanchaí was. She had to look it up. She huffed and grumbled that it was *time to shut the doors and what a trouble this was and Americans never think of others*...until she discovered it meant *a bearer of old lore*. And that those who were good at it were honored in kings' courts.

"Is it an Irish word?" she wondered aloud.

"I think so," I replied without really paying attention. "I know somebody who teaches the Irish, so I'll check with him."

"I'd like to know, if you find out. It's a lovely word. Almost like that Japanese one. What was it?"

"Sensei," I said, still not listening.

"A master. A teacher. Who tells stories of old. What a lovely thing to do."

I only nodded. I was still too caught up in the idea that my Da was considered one of those when all I could remember of his stories was how confused they were.

I made it to the Guildhall just after Maeve arrived with her usual bags of goods. She cast me a baleful glare as she snorted, "Nice of you to show up."

I shrugged it off and said, in my twang, "Did you know your father was considered a master storyteller?"

She frowned and cast her mind back. "I don't remember his stories. I barely remember him tellin' them to us. And even then, it was at my bedtime and I was asleep in the middle of them.

Rhuari might recall. He was always more attentive."

True about that. "Is Father Jack still comin'?"

"So far as I know. But I hear his visit with Eamonn did not go well. He's going to speak of it, later."

Later turned out to be him arriving halfway through the meeting, and without Joanna. Which, for some reason, did not surprise me.

"My apologies for my tardiness," he said. "I'm afraid my hope of having a young lady who'd experienced the horrors of this conflict in a most hideous way was misplaced. As was my car. It's currently in a ditch on its side. I will retrieve it, tomorrow. It seems her brother is quite volatile and...well, with the assistance of a few friends, impressed upon me the hopelessness of my plan."

The consensus was it was horrible how the poor father was treated. Even the few Protestants who'd returned from last week agreed. A couple of men, none of them Protestant, volunteered to assist in righting the car and getting it back to Derry, but Father Jack smiled them off.

"I've already spoken to Diarmaid McClosky and he will drive out in his truck with me, then bring it back to his shop."

"Want help?" popped out of me before I thought about it.

The entire room turned around to look at me in full-on wariness as Father Jack shook his head.

"No, Mr. *Landau,*" he said, emphasizing my name. "Thank you, but that would complicate matters far too much. It seems there is very little actual damage to the car, itself; just my pride in having it happen for misdirecting my hope that another person might assist in our endeavors. Diarmaid and I will be able to handle it, just fine."

Nothing more was said about it, but this did at least tell me Colm's belief that Joanna's family had moved away from the Waterside was true. Making finding her that much more difficult, since Father Jack was also, tacitly, telling me he'd not take me anywhere near her.

As for his meeting with Eamonn, he had been allowed exactly five minutes so had only prayed with him across a small table, unable to even hold his hand in communion. "They are becoming more difficult, the prison authorities, and demanding. Eamonn has been moved to a different block and is kept apart from the other prisoners, in isolation. It is telling on him. I do not believe he has been subjected to any actual torture that could be brought before the European Convention on Human Rights, but I am looking into that."

"Could it be considered sensory deprivation?" I asked.

Again, people turned around to glare at me as Father Jack locked his eyes on mine, not at all pleased, and said, "I have no idea. I am not privy to the actions taken by the guards and RUC. But it could be something to look into. Especially since other prisoners might also be suffering from greater ill-treatment than usual, thanks to the strike."

I said nothing more, feeling I'd already overstepped my bounds.

After the meeting, as I was packing the remains of the edibles into my backpack, Father Jack came up to me in his quiet, casual fashion.

"It was very kind of you to offer to help, Mr. Landau. I hope I didn't come across as dismissive of that when I refused you."

I gave him a shrug. "I know how politics can get." And I kept packing. Seemed there was more left over, this time.

"Yes, quite. To my surprise, despite the current attitude towards Eamonn Kinsella, when I spoke with prison authorities about you accompanying me, they were open to it. Next Monday."

I think my heart almost stopped, for a moment at hearing it. I made myself look at him. No change in expression from earlier. In fact, the only time I had ever seen him with a different expression on his face was when I asked him if he was happy Eamonn had been attacked at Burntollett Bridge. And that had been a sneak attack, on my part. I doubted I could achieve the same result, again.

"Are you still open to that?" he asked.

I smiled. "Very much."

"Excellent. I will collect you, next Monday, at eight a-m. It's but a two-hour drive, perhaps a bit more considering the checkpoints. You may bring in a pad and a pencil, nothing more, I'm afraid. And they will want to see your notes before you leave."

"That should work fine. Will your car be okay by then?"

He shrugged. "I have access to another, if necessary."

"Then it's a date."

He smiled and walked over to Maeve.

And I realized I'd been crushing a package of Lemon Puffs.

Which were now Lemon crumbles.

As for Joanna, his comments being the third refusal to assist in my approaching her, I was now even more determined to find some way to see her, again. But there was also a warning, deep inside me, suggesting maybe they were right. If she thought me dead and I appeared before her, I could see that being an issue. Same for if she thought I'd abandoned her. What excuse could I give that wouldn't be silly and childish?

But then I reminded myself—there had been no mention of a bombing victim being carried off by the possible bombers. Just that the suspects drove off in a hurry in a saloon that was found the next day, burned out on a side road and—

Oh, shite. What if all this time she thought...had believed I had helped set up her father to be killed? And I was just trying to get her away from the site before the bomb went off? What if that's what Colm and Father Jack really meant?

Oh, no, no, no, I couldn't have that. I couldn't let her believe me capable of such a thing, no matter the consequences. So I figured I'd work on Diarmaid to find out where they'd gone to get the car...and also find out how his Da had fared after I left.

And finally, I'd let Joanna know everything.

Everything.

And she would see. She would understand.

She would.

She had to.

She had to.

Wednesday morning, I gave a call to Magee College and asked if they ever had a program that recorded spoken Irish tales. It took me three different people to find one who had an idea of what I was talking about, and think that University College in Cork might have been working on something like that. They also thought the university at Coleraine might have once assisted. Sort of a gathering of Irish heritage.

I got a name, there, and called, and they said they'd had a program but it had been made redundant, years ago. I found out they'd be in their office till four so called Rhuari. He couldn't take me. Bridie was ill and being tended to by the midwife. Possibly a miscarriage, which made my heart sink. Ma had gone through those, and despite his stoicism I sensed he was barely keeping it together. So I wished them both well.

It turned out Jimmy Haggerty was off classes, that day, and had his father's estate car, so he agreed to give me a ride in exchange for a full tank of petrol. To which I agreed. We headed straight out with sandwiches whipped together by his mother and bottles of Fanta.

He was a clean, clear lad with careful clothing, a careful haircut, and even a careful smile. As we drove, he told me how he'd been shrugged off the University at Jordanstown and was studying at Magee. Had a girl he liked, there. Felt at home.

"Unlike at Queens," he said. "At Magee, not once do I hear someone calling me Taig or Papist. You know what a Taig is?"

I just nodded, thinking of when Billy Corrie had referred to me, Danny and Colm as such. Not a pleasant memory.

Of course, it took hours to get past the city's checkpoints, and that's even with me sharing my Marlboros. Everyone was too much on edge, so I think the real reason we had so little trouble was my American passport. Then came another two hours on the open road, and more checkpoints, here and there. But we finally got to the campus—one of those wide, open, modern sorts with some make-do buildings and a surface level of calm—and managed to find the man's office in one of the newer structures.

He was a bit nervous about Jimmy but made a show of being polite, for me, and I played the oblivious American to the hilt. His office was plain, functional and cluttered, as it should be, and he already had a reel-to-reel tape recorder set up on a nearby table, with a couple of extra reels sitting beside it.

"These are the only ones I could find," he said. "I think most were sent to UCC."

I held up my cassette player and asked, "You mind if I record one or two?"

He blinked and almost trembled, which Jimmy noticed. I caught him hiding a smirk.

Then the man said, "Just don't tell anyone it was me let you."

I only grinned and nodded.

Then he started it playing and—

The sound of Da's voice was a punch to my heart. Gentle and melodious, it was. Almost playful. I had to keep focused on the slow-turning reels, so as not to let that man know how overwhelmed I suddenly was at hearing my Da say...

There is a tale of how harpies came to live in the Cliffs of Moher. It dates from back in a time before the wondrous few went to the earth and the world still held magic.

There was a morning, as the sun rose strong and proud from the sea, when the Tuatha de Danaan appeared on the shores of the east. Those on the hills, who saw the soft low mist roll in over Cuan Dhún Dealgan, told of how these amazing people strolled up onto the land with a pride and power never seen before. Tall and fair, they were, like angels pure and fine, with the early sun and wind making their golden hair dance like fire.

They declared it their new home as more and more came off their elegant ships. It was soon noted their abilities were so advanced, those who had been living here a thousand years before thought them gods.

He who led them was come to be known as the Dagda, and his figure was perfection among men. Shoulders broad and strength beyond compare. Face well-formed. Eyes the color of the sky as his chin offered a beard that put the sun to shame. It was said his parents were the wind and the sea, and none were they who could dispute it.

His mate was Morriggan, whose beauty was the greatest ever beheld. Hair flaming bright as the sky at sunset. Eyes as green as grass. Skin like fresh milk. Her mastery of the world's mystical ways was without compare, and it was said all she had to do was think of where she wanted to be and she would materialize there.

Tara was their home, built with beauty and grace, and three daughters did their union bring forth. Each as lovely as their mother, and each just as happy to follow in her mystical ways. To witness the five of them together was to know none better could exist.

Of those who first lived on the land, the clan Ui Bruiun was the best. For millennia, they had built their compounds near dashing streams, tended to their goats and pigs, and toiled in their fields, growing the finest barley and wheat. Their hunters were beyond compare, and never in winter were they without food to eat or mead to drink.

They were led by one Larne Ui Bruiun in ways generous and honorable, and his son, Caoughin was being well-trained to follow. He was himself a fine young man. Dark, sturdy and strong. Well-thought of as a hunter. Which he well-knew.

So the two tribes lived in harmony and grace. Each well-mannered with the other. Thus it would have remained...

Until there was a day when the Dagda approached the Ui Bruiun compound to seek shelter from a storm. Propriety demanded his request be honored, so he was offered a room unto himself, with a fire blazing and more than enough food and drink.

Had he been satisfied with that, all would have been well. But the Dagda being a man, his eye roamed over the lovely lass who was attending him. Her name was Caera. Hair as black as a raven's wing. Skin soft and pure. Lips like red berries on the vine. And a manner quite joyous. She was betrothed to Caoughin and propriety dictated she remain unsullied.

But the Dagda worked his charm on her and brought her to his bed. Some say willingly; some say not. Whichever way it was, Caera wound up with child.

This was a major breech of etiquette. A poor repayment for the Ui Bruiun's kindness towards him. So the Dagda was banned from their compound, which soon extended to all Tuatha de

Danaan. And Caoughin, severely embarrassed, cruelly spurned poor Caera, bringing naught but distress to their clan.

But this was not the end. For when Morriggan learned of the liaison, she was caught in a fury. To have the Dagda mingle with a common girl of the earth was an insult to her. Then to learn she would bring a child of his into the world? That was unacceptable. Using her mystical ways and with the help of her daughters, she found and killed the lass. Her intent was to also kill the child within her, but a boy had already been birthed and was beyond her reach.

Infuriated, the Ui Bruiuns demanded retribution so as to avoid war. The Dagda, now shamed for his part in the travesty, ended his companionship with Morriggan and strode by foot across the width of Eire to wash his sins away in the waters beneath the Cliffs of Moher. His promise? To add greatness to the boy he had sired with Caera.

This mollified the anger of the Ui Bruiuns, but Morriggan was not to be put aside so easily. Through dark, black magic, she and her daughters formed the Dagda's sins into seven harpies and set them out to kill the child.

The beasts ravaged the land, feasting on any male youth they found. Great battles occurred between the clan and those monsters, and many widows were made. Even the Dagda joined with them, but he was as powerless as the Ui Bruiuns, against them. Year after year the fighting raged, with Caoughan at the fore, throughout, and slowly, slowly, one harpy after another was destroyed until but three were left.

Morriggan finally realized the horror she had unleashed and relented from her anger. Despite her powers, she could not force the harpies to cease their dances of death. The only path she could see that might convince them to pull back from their slaughters, was to promise they would survive. For they were as wearied and beaten down as the Ui Bruiuns.

They agreed to shelter in the caves of the Cliffs of Moher and come out only during storms to feed on fish in the sea. In exchange, once each hundred years, when a small, black globe crosses the sun, a lad of the Dagda's bloodline would be offered for them to feast upon. To seal the bond, the first to be sacrificed would be Caoughan Ui Bruiun. At Darian's Point on Inish Ciuin.

Willingly he went, almost desperately, for he was destroyed by guilt for how he had treated Caera. And as retribution for having brought the horror about, the Tuatha de Danaan were banished to live within the earth, to be known only as faeries and the little people, thus giving the surface solely to the Ui Bruiuns and the other clans.

Thus, was the pact sealed.

So do not go to the Cliffs in the midst of a storm. Or well into the night. For you might catch glimpses of harpies dancing in the rain and mist. But if you must, have a care they do not see you, for they will not tolerate such impudence, and will cast any who witness their dance into the surging waters, below.

And so it has been for three-thousand years. And so it continues even till this day.

It was mesmerizing. His voice musical, almost elegant to the point of soothing. The story complete. I could only remember bits of it from when he was drunk and lost in the telling, and even Rhuari had said it made little sense.

Jimmy found it fascinating to hear. "It's Maeve's Da?" he asked.

His voice broke my trance. I managed to keep my voice calm and cool as I said, "Yes. They said he told some lovely stories."

"All I heard was he's a drunken brute."

"He was." I turned to the professor. "I understand the person who recorded this was killed by the IRA?"

He nodded. "This and many others. It's really sad. No excuse, but he was Protestant so no excuse needed by those people." Then he tensed and cast a quick glance at Jimmy.

I noticed Jimmy starting to puff up so quickly asked, "You mentioned other recordings. Were they of this man?"

"Oh, there were some, I think, but this was the only good one that I know of. The others, the drunker he became, the wilder and more incoherent the stories were. Like claiming he'd helped free Ireland from the English. But the date listed as his birth made him far too young, for that. Another where he'd killed a man, which was nonsense, for he'd never been to prison. Still, the recordings brought some interest, for a bit. Then it died out and the Troubles began, and almost everything was shipped to UCC.

"I think only the better ones were transferred down. There were a few more boxes with reels in them, but none with this man's name on them. And I know some went missing. God knows where. Would you want to listen to them all, to see?"

I shook my head, still affected. "This was all I needed. I just wanted to have something to show he was good at tellin' stories."

"And this is quite a tale, isn't it? Our History department did a search for it and could find no reference to such a story, ever told before. Almost like he made it up."

"Maybe he did. He used to make a livin', tellin' stories."

"Did he?"

"Yes, he was known as a seanchaí."

"And I thought it was merely to cadge drinks."

I made myself chuckle. "That, too."

Then Jimmy and I headed back to the car—

To find it covered in manure scooped from nearby flower beds. Three rather beefy lads were just dusting themselves off when they saw us coming and took on their bully-boy attitudes.

"Well, here comes the Taigs," one started.

I cut him off by snarling in my strongest Texas, "What the hell y'all doin'?"

Suddenly, I saw three pair of eyes as round and shocked as possible.

"Wait, now," the biggest snapped, trying to bluff his way through. "Who the devil're you?"

"I rented this car to bring me down here," I snarled back in my best imitation of Todd. "Now I'm gonna have to pay to get it cleaned? Fixed? What the fuck?"

The middle-sized one stepped forward to ask, "Where you from?"

"Where the hell you think!? Texas! Goddammit, that shit fuckin' stinks! Where's a goddamn cop?"

That got all three of them to cringe and big-boy whined, "No, no, no, no, no, no, sir, we are so sorry. No need for the peelers. We'll clean it off. Just a bit o' dirt is all. Give us a moment, and it's done. That's all."

It was *an effort to hold myself back*, but I let them do what they said they'd do. They still had the buckets they'd used to carry the fertilizer so found a faucet and washed them out. A pair of groundskeepers happened by, so set up a hose as the boys washed the car down with soap they provided. All the time they were apologizing and I was continuing to huff and puff, even while answering all sorts of questions about Texas and NASA and that bloody JR for the grounds men.

Jimmy was smart enough to say nothing, but if looks could kill, there'd have been a slaughter.

A full hour later, the estate wagon was cleaner than it had been when I got in it, that morning. I still growled and spit, but I agreed not to call the cops on them and away we went, leaving behind some very wet, very dirty but also very relieved Protestant assholes.

As we drove, and between checkpoints, Jimmy finally vented nonstop about the idiots who'd trashed the car, as well as the professor. All of it basically boiled down to, "They refuse us access to good houses, education and jobs, then when we don't wind up as rich as they are call us lazy drunks and worthless. But when we do try to better ourselves, they attack us just for bein' in the area. Bloody two-faced bastards."

"It's like that all over, Jimmy," I finally said.

"Even in Houston?"

My back gave a twinge at that comment, and I took in a deep breath. "Yeah. Everywhere."

"Fuck. I was thinkin' of America, once I'm done at Uni."

"What're you taking?"

"Computers. Economics. I've found a couple exchange programs with Universities in Boston, New York. Got friends there. They like it."

"Then I'm sure you would, as well."

"It's a long way to go."

"Distance don't matter. Wherever you go, your past is with you."

"That's what me Ma says. I think I'd rather be in London. Work in The City."

"Get out of here?"

We were coming up on one of the rural checkpoints as he nodded. Soldiers with rifles at the ready, who'd happily shoot us both and blame us for having to do it. So all Jimmy had time to say was, "Yeah," before they were yelling, "Shut your motor!"

I already had my passport out and was deliberately firing up a Marlboro, which quickly caught their attention...

And jolted me at realizing how little time it had taken me to acclimate myself to these gestapo tactics.

Yeah, Jimmy, get the hell out of Derry.

Nevermore

I played the tape of Da's story the next time Rhuari dropped by with some groceries. Mrs. Kieffer was up with Ma so both he and Maeve could just sit and listen. Once it was done, they said nothing for a couple minutes.

Then Rhuari shook his head. "I remember the basic story, but Da only told it to us when he was drunk and he jumped all over. Hearing it now, in perfect order, like he's performing a show..." He shook his head some more, unable to find words to continue.

Maeve picked up the copy I'd made of the notice for Da's fete and eyed it.

"I don't really remember Da," said Maeve, "except as this big monster of a man who could be scary. I look at this photo and think he was once very fine lookin'."

"Probably was," I said. "Till the drink took over."

Maeve just sighed and finally asked, "Are you playin' it for Ma?"

Of course. Perhaps this would get her to talk about him, again. But first I needed to know...

"Did Ma ever talk about me not being here?"

Maeve grew still then said, "She was gone a fortnight, then. Not a word back from her. Mrs. Quinn kept watch over us. She said she had no idea what Ma was up to and insisted it was no business of ours.

"Eamonn came by a few times. Let us know all was fine."

Oh, did he? I'd never thought of him as knowing what had happened. To my shame, I half-wondered if he was the reason the British didn't think me dead. He'd never been able to keep a secret.

She continued with, "Ma was just helpin' out with somethin' but...but when Rhuari and I asked about you, he only said he thought you'd gone lookin' for work. I didn't believe it. I didn't think for a second you'd have left without sayin' goodbye. But you *were* gone. And when Ma returned, she refused to speak of you. Would just tell us, *For all I know, he's dead, and good riddance.*"

"Christ, Maeve."

She looked at me. "But you did leave without a word to us. Rhuari or me. Your clothes were gone. Your rucksack."

It took me a moment to say, "I'd have let you know where I was."

"It's not the same thing. Sneakin' off."

"I had to. So Ma couldn't stop me."

"Stop you? How?"

"Why would she want to?" Rhuari asked.

For that, I had no answer. Because, in truth, she wouldn't have. She'd have led a parade. All I could think to say was, "To be contrary against me. Whatever I wanted, she demanded I do the opposite."

"That's not true, Bren. She was often on your side."

"Never seemed that way. I'm sorry, but my only plan was to find work and let you know where I was. I didn't mean for it to seem like I was abandoning you."

"Like her brothers did her?" Maeve said. "Uncle Michael was so very sorry about..." She turned to Rhuari, thinking. "How did he put it?"

"*The way things transpired,*" he said, calmly. "And he's been the only one who showed any concern for Ma."

Maeve nodded. "Aunt Mari says the other six know but may have been put off by Ma's treatment of Uncle Michael."

I saw a smirk flash over Rhuari's face as he murmured, "Yes, that is a perfect excuse to ignore the dying."

I took in a deep breath and asked, "Are you two upset with me for what happened? How *things transpired* with me?"

"That bomb does make things different," said Maeve. "It's still confusin' and on the surface seems similar. And I was so very upset over the lack of...the honest lack of concern for what happened to you."

"That's how I knew you weren't dead," said Rhuari. "And it was proven to me when I was given contact with Eldon. Only you would have thought of that as something I'd want."

"That's why we never said word-one to Ma about it. I do

recall how angry she could be about you, at times."

Rhuari sighed. "But she was different, after you were gone."

Maeve nodded. "Not so harsh."

"Unhappy."

"Turned to helpin' Women's Auxiliary."

"And when Eamonn was snatched, making sure Father Jack kept an eye on his treatment, more than others."

Maeve nodded. "It was like he had been the only one arrested by the British. Only one held."

"But never a word about you, that I know of."

"Nor me."

I almost felt like I was floating as I said, "But...I-I-I'm here, now."

"That counts for somethin'," Maeve said, unsmiling. "I am almost caught up on me sleep."

Rhuari hesitated then leaned forward to say, "Bren, let me play this recording for Ma. Alone." I drew in a deep breath, but he quickly continued, "I think she'll be more open to hearing it, in and of itself. She fears judgment, from you."

"So she's said," I whispered. "She told you this, as well?"

"When she and I were taken down Strand road, she managed to whisper to me, *Buck up, don't let your brother think less of you, should he learn of this.* I knew she didn't mean Eamonn."

"But you were arrested long after I was gone."

"I know."

That seemed a bit backwards. But I sighed and said, "Do it. But don't tell me anything she says or how she acts. I'll ask her, later. And I'm going to play it for Eamonn, when I see him."

"Is that wise?" Maeve asked.

"No," I said. "But it is necessary."

*****

We settled into a casual routine, even as chaos seemed to build around us. Of course, now that St. Bobby had won his election, there were daily demonstrations throughout the North, all demanding Thatcher give in to the striker's demands. A gathering in the Diamond turned into a sit-in until the Brits and RUC rushed people off with cruel punches and words. I was to one side, watching,. One peeler came up to me, scowling, then saw my NASA cap on my head, blinked and turned around to find someone who could explain this to him. Moments later, tear gas and rubber bullets were in use, with only a few injuries, this time.

The push from the other side was just as hard, and bloody foolish, I might say. Had they started out letting Catholics have even half the rights we wanted, all of this death and chaos and destruction could well have been avoided. Instead, they became selfish, snarling hounds fighting over a bone that had long since been gnawed to nothing. It was pathetic.

Holy Week was proving to be anything but. Jokes on the news and in papers, made by Protestants about young men starving themselves for a cause. Angry sermons from Paisley and his ilk, who condemned the strikers and all Fenians to hell. He certainly loved to grandstand, the fat bastard. Claimed to be a man of god when his words were solely of the devil.

And on the other side were Catholic leaders all whining, *Can't we all just get along?* Sometimes even negotiating themselves down from all they wanted, in the face of Protestant intransigence. What good is it to try and find common ground with those who demand nothing less than capitulation. No changes allowed. Ever! NOTHING!

Christ, I missed having naught but the snippets on the news and in the Houston papers to fill me in instead of having to live the idiocy, in real time.

Of course, the news-mongers took the British Army's view that everything was the fault of the IRA while few fingers were pointed at Protestant paramilitaries, despite the UVF crushing everyone they could. I never saw a single word about how the Catholic and Protestant paramilitaries had worked with each other in divvying up Belfast and Derry. I know I shouldn't be sorry for that, since it had probably kept Rhuari alive while he worked at that off-license. There was also little about how normal life was where he lived now. Not just Shantalow but also Pennyburn. People's lives barely impacted by the chaos in the Bogside and Creggan.

I continued to do the clueless American thing, basically hiding in plain sight as I walked around taking photos of landmarks and buildings damaged...and the guard towers wrapped in barbed wire and spikes. I'd found an instamatic camera with the flip flash during one of my garbage runs—its flash wouldn't flip but took only a little to repair—so had a heyday with that. Even had one occasion where two peelers came up and asked me what I was doing, taking photos down by the surveillance tower near the Apprentice Boys' Hall. Once they heard my twang, they laughed and told me to take better care.

Dear God, how the Bogside had changed in the time I was gone. Whole neighborhoods vanished, replaced by blank strips of flats or just open grounds waiting for development. I got near lost a couple times, and only the Rossville Flats were able to lead me back home again.

I made a show of going to book shops and the library and Derry Journal to *do my research* at least once a day. I found decent copies of Bernadette Devlin's *Price of my Soul* and *The Battle of Bogside* by Russell Stetler as well as Willie Carson's photo journal, *Vanishing Derry*. I did the *stupid American thing* of going to a bank to cash a hundred-pound traveler's check, playing it so foolish the clerk felt the need to warn me about carrying too much cash on me.

Of course, it being Holy week, Diarmaid was never around McClosky's. He had a thin, snarly helper in desperate need of a bath, and who never spoke more than a yes or no, to me. Mostly the latter when I asked about where Father Jack's car had been retrieved. I caught a look at it in the work bay; a newer Ford Granada saloon—SEDAN, Brendan! In gray with black pinstripes. Scrapes along its passenger side and a good crack in the windshield. I had a feeling this would not be the car we'd be driving to the Maze, on Monday.

Rhuari played the tape of Da for Ma, but they spoke in voices so low I couldn't make out what they were saying. I regretted asking him not to share her comments with me. I tried a couple times to get her to talking, but she'd just whine off about pain and needing sleep, and I'd get nothing from her.

Easter Sunday, Father Jack come by for the usual communion, and this time Mrs. O'Canainn was with him. I didn't know what game he was playing, but he kept everything in line with me being Jeremy. After the ceremony and as Mrs. O'Canainn was putting on her coat he even mentioned, "Jeremy, have you been to Israel? Such a beautiful country, so vibrant and alive."

"It's been a while," I replied, careful to keep my tone casual and Texan. "Near eight years."

"Were you there during the Yom Kippur conflict?"

I nodded, keeping my look as sharp on him as his was on me.

"Did you see battle?"

"I don't like talkin' 'bout that."

"Of course not. War is not meant for sensitive souls."

I shot back with, "Wars're started by old men, who then send young men to die."

"Wasn't it Einstein who said that?"

"No, some guy named Hoover. Secretary of War, of course."

"Of course, and while you're paraphrasing, the sentiment is consistent."

"It's something I was told by a man I knew, when he got back from Vietnam."

"It's but one more bit of evidence showing armed conflict achieves little but death and destruction. Your experiences in Egypt, you friend's in Vietnam, for example. Death begets death and gives life no quarter."

In Egypt? Not the Golan Heights or Jerusalem? Son-of-a-bitch, he's been checking into me.

He leaned forward. Put his hand on my shoulder and said, "Jeremy, at Tuesday's meeting of the Peace Council, we're going to see if there is some way to help resolve the situation with Bobby Sands. See if we can get Prime Minster Thatcher to relent and allow a member of the Queen's Parliament to live." Then I swear to God he almost smirked as he added, "Your experiences in Israel may help us draft a letter to the Prime Minister that shows how what she is doing will achieve nothing but further violence and bloodshed."

So that's what this was all about. Try and corral me into revealing who I was to one and all. Because were I to let Jeremy's name be added to a letter to that bitch of a Prime Minister, that would put him up as someone to be noticed by the press. The bloody British press. Christ, would they cause trouble for him.

Why was he doing this to me? Why?

My head was swimming as I rose, saying, "I'm an American Jew, Father Jack. Working on my thesis and helping an old lady preparing to die. I really don't think it'd be right to inject myself into this conflict till after all that's done."

"Of course," he said. "I perfectly understand."

"Are we still on for tomorrow?"

"Tomorrow?"

"You were taking me to visit Eamonn Kinsella in the Maze?"

"Oh. Oh." He actually seemed taken aback. "Um, I'm not sure. I neglected to take into account it's a bank holiday, and security with have lesser staffing, available."

"But *you* can go?"

"It's a religious holiday, and I am his spiritual advisor."

"I don't mind just going along for the ride. I'd like to see this Maze. See what it's like. Even from the outside."

He eyed me for a good long minute then almost smiled. "Well, all we can do is ask. I'll see you at eight."

I just smiled and saw him and Mrs. O'Canainn out, knowing full well this was going to be a fun drive.

The Long Drive

I was up and ready when Father Jack drove up in a brand new Mercedes. Which I was not expecting. He stopped and hopped upstairs to give Ma a quick blessing, which even Maeve seemed to think was a bit much.

"He was just here, yesterday," she muttered. "Never done this before."

I was standing outside the open door so just shrugged.

Then she leaned against the frame and said, "If you do get to see our Eamonn, would you let him know I have tried to visit?"

"Doesn't Father Jack tell him?" And I was actually surprised she was asking me this.

She hesitated, heard him heading out of Ma's room and whispered, "I'd like it to come from you. Please?"

"Of course."

Then Father Jack was behind her, saying, "Shall we go?"

"Ready when you are," I smiled.

We were quiet as we maneuvered our way through the checkpoints to head across the bridge and out of the city. All I brought with me was the cassette recorder, tape of Da's story, and my pad and pencil. I'd dressed in light colors so it didn't seem as if I was trying to look like a priest, and I was also wearing a loose jacket against the morning chill. In its pockets were my passport, wallet with fifty pounds in it, my last two boxes of Marlboros—I'd have to switch back to Blues or pay the extortionate price charged at the newsagents'—and my black Bic lighter.

I also had one in green but felt that might be considered a bit too pro-Republican. Silly thing to worry about, I know, but with the Unionists, better to assume the worst so you're not surprised when it happens.

It wasn't a great day for driving. Gray and overcast, the road wet in spots, dry in others. But there was not a great deal of traffic and the land speeding past was pleasant.

"We're making good time," said Father Jack once we were approaching Foreglen. "There is normally a surprise checkpoint between Toome and Antrim, but your American cigarettes do seem to make a difference in the soldiers' attitudes, so that may prove to be a minimal delay."

"You mind if I smoke?" I asked.

"Not in this vehicle, please," he said, then added, "And, Brendan, do you truly need to continue this charade with only us in the car?"

I shrugged and dropped the Texas. "It's kept us safe enough at the checkpoints."

"True. I don't blame you for this pretense. In fact, I find the entire situation surprisingly daring, for you. I had never known you as one to take such chances."

"To visit my dying mother, one last time?"

"You know what I mean. And the impression I've received from both you and Bernadette is that there was little love lost, between the two of you."

I shrugged. "Things are different, now."

"Are they?"

"I am."

"Are you?"

"You noted it, yourself."

"Does that extend to you being more honest?"

"When have I not been, with you?"

"When I first saw you at Bernadette's bedside—"

"You knew who I was. The second you laid eyes on me. Was there need to address it, verbally?"

The change in his voice told me my answer did not sit well with him. "Your silences could be construed as misdirection."

To which he got my silence.

He nodded. "Have things happened, in America, to cause this shift in you?"

"Nothing more than as happened here."

He chuckled. "And your evasiveness could also be seen as dishonesty."

I focused on the passing fields as I said, "I choose with whom I will and will not share my world, and you use that to accuse me?"

He huffed. "That...um, that is not what I meant."

"Of course not."

"I am merely trying to understand the full situation. That you return to see your mother...well, that makes sense, despite the danger to yourself."

I looked at him. "What do you know of the danger to me?"

"I've been in contact with...with certain people and when they learned you had returned, they voiced their concern. They have a narrative constructed about you that was satisfying everyone and—"

"What narrative? That I was dead? Or that I'd abandoned my family without a word?"

He had to think about his response, for a moment. Finally, he drew in a deep breath and said, "It was never officially confirmed, but many people believed you were gone from this earth."

"What a lovely way of saying that I'd died. Thanks to the bomb, I'm sure."

"As I said." Spoken in a very deliberate tone of voice. "It was never confirmed one way or the other. But your continued silence did serve to give it substance."

"The British didn't believe that."

He nodded. "They had no physical body to verify your death, so left it as a question."

"And an injured lad showing up on my aunt's doorstep only added to their questions, didn't it?"

"Naturally. But that was handled."

"Was it? I didn't get that impression."

"Why not?"

"Six months back they were thinking it was me at my aunt's."

"Which makes it all the more surprising you suddenly appeared here as—"

"As an American Jew? With a well-used American passport? Are the British really that on top of things?"

He had to shrug. "Where did you get such a passport?"

So...that's what this was leading to.

"Stole it," I said, looking out at the passing countryside. "Jeremy's a mate, and people kept confusing us as brothers. Even more, with my hair lightened and this goatee. And he'd just got his new one. I doubt he'll ever miss the one it replaced."

"But the State Department cancels the old ones."

I chuckled. "There's ways around that."

"So you, effectively, decided to flip off the authorities. Brendan, what purpose do you have in doing this?"

"I need one?"

He sighed. "In this day and age, in this part of the world, sometimes you need a reason to cross the street."

That, I had to give him. "You didn't tell the prison officers who I am? That I'm related to Eamonn, did you?"

"Of course not. He's on a permanent restriction from such visits. But still...you may still be a person of interest, to the British..."

I had to give him that, too. "As Brendan."

"Well, I must admit you've played your role well, in the Bogside. And it's commendable you've come to visit your mother in her darkest hour. But to take so reckless a step, now, visiting your brother? Why would you do that?"

I took in a deep breath and let it out slow before saying, "I need to ask Eamonn something. I need to see into his eyes when he responds. And since I'll not be here much longer, this is the only way to do it."

"What is it you need to know?"

"Something you can't answer."

"Brendan..."

"You didn't come to Derry till near a year after Da died, so you don't have the answer. You can't."

"Is it really so important a question?"

I only nodded.

We drove in silence, for a bit, then he said, "You know, I have access to a great deal of information that you are not aware of."

"Obviously."

"And the guards still may not allow you to see him. As I said, you may only take in a pad and pencil."

I just nodded.

"They most certainly will not allow you to record anything he says, so you might best leave that cassette player in the car."

"I'm not recording him." I hesitated before continuing with, "I have a tape of our father telling one of his stories. I want to share it with him. The guards can listen, if they like. They can have me play it before. I don't mind. And me being an American, and happily giving them the contact from whom I got this tape, at

Ulster in Coleraine, I think they'd appreciate a break from the usual hatefulness, conspiratorial nonsense and anger they have to deal with, every day."

"I think you're being optimistic."

"You won't back me up?"

"I have nothing to do with their decision."

I smirked. "Meaning, you won't. Good to know."

"That is not what I said, Brendan."

"Your deflection did."

"I do not appreciate that comment. Your request puts me in a precarious position. As a man of God, I am required to maintain a level of honesty that is—"

My laughter cut him off. His glare was quite angry. "You mock me?"

"No, no, Father Jack. Whatever you say or do, it's with the purest honesty and most open heart. I know that."

"Then why are you still laughing?"

"It doesn't mean anything. Only that, everything you do has a very good reason for it, and apparently that stems from your position in the Church. In the eyes of most. But you've as much as told me you're also close to the Provos, and your good reasons for your good actions can easily align with them."

"That is absolute nonsense and I—"

"You kept watch over me, as I healed after that bomb. Helped my mother, sister and aunt spirit me away, probably with the backing of the church."

"That is a complete fabrication."

I just continued with, "Helped them keep me alive. An honorable goal, from which you made your choices. I have no quibble with you over any of what you've done for my family. What you do for my mother. For my brother."

"I get the impression you are not being completely honest with me, again."

"What more is there? Any other issues we might have had are long dead and buried. Aren't they? Is there need to exhume them?"

"Is your cold attitude due to my refusal to take you to see Joanna?"

He took long enough to bring that up. I'd been waiting. I knew he'd use that to try and mess with me. A knife to the heart that he could honestly claim was not meant to inflict damage. I'd happily have cut his throat with it.

But all I said was, "I understand she was badly hurt."

"She was. She and her father, both."

"So you have spoken with her. Does she think I had something to do with that bomb? Is that why you're trying to keep me away from her? To protect her?"

He focused on the road, his voice quiet but audible. "I remember how the two of you were, so many years ago. When we went to Dublin. It was obvious, even then, how deeply you loved her. It was sweet and pure and innocent. And so very dangerous for you both, with the growing divide between the sides. I had no idea what to do or say about it, so let it be. I now feel that may have been a mistake, on my part."

"There were others who butted in."

He nodded. "It's sad that love is so fragile, in a world such as this." His face grew much older and more weary than I'd ever seen. "I wanted...I want to protect the both of you, but most especially her. She thinks you died, and her memory of you is good. Is as pure as your love was, for her. If you come back from the grave, you will destroy that. Are you still so stubborn you will not consider that...well, that perhaps, your actions would be detrimental to your intention?"

Oh, the son of a bitch. And there it was. She thought me dead. She thought me dead.

He'd hit me hard, right in the heart. And were my ghost to rise and prove her wrong, there could still be no reconciliation.

"You're right," I said, my voice so soft and unsure. "I do love her. But you almost speak as if she didn't love me."

That brought a flash of a grimace to his face. "I don't know, one way or the other, because I do not really know her. Nor did I ask her. I can believe she felt the same, but in all honesty cannot claim it without question. But I do know you."

Still twisting the knife. For there was much he was not telling me. I could sense it in his hesitations and careful...his oh, so careful choices of word. My heart began pounding and I felt the beginning of a headache behind my eyes. I had some of my pills with me so slipped one under my tongue. He noticed, of course, but said nothing.

After a few moments, I felt calm enough to simply murmur,

"Dear God, sometimes I hate this fucking world."

He hesitated before sighing and saying, "There have been occasions when I would not have disagreed with you."

And we exchanged not a word the rest of the drive.

The Maze

We did wind up dealing with another checkpoint, and my Marlboros and twang did help make the passage smoother. I decided then and there the high price of replacing them would be worth the money.

Then we got to the prison...and dear God, once I saw it, I was put in mind of photos I'd seen of Nazi Germany's concentration camps. Long, blank, evil walls splashed with mud and topped by razor wire and observation points. It made me cold just to look at them.

We were directed to park across a road then walk in through the main gate, which I gathered from Father Jack's huffiness was not normal for him.

When he started on about it, one rather surly mug snarled, "Be glad we're lettin' your sort in, at all." Which softened the second he heard my twang and saw me (very deliberately) fire up a Marlboro, and that I *oh-so-very innocently* offered him and his mates one. "Bloody cowboy smokes," he murmured as he exhaled his first puff.

"We-yell," I said, "me bein' from Texas..."

And bam, we fell into another fucking discussion about that bloody TV show. Fortunately, by this point I'd talked about it so many times with the squaddies and RUC, I was able to sound somewhat intelligent about JR and his sneaking ways. And Bobby and Pam. And Ma Ewing. You'd never know I'd not seen a single solitary episode.

The surly mug even walked with us down to the visitors building, to keep talking about it and, I got a hint, to cadge another smoke. Which I offered. And got the sweetest damn smile in thanks.

We passed blank walls of dirty white brick. Observation posts lined with some kind of metal siding. CCTV in brutal evidence. Razor wire swirling everywhere, and a paved road that led to a dead end. Cold-eyed guards everywhere. And the smell...like sanitized shit. I kept my Marlboro close to my nose.

That cigarette also worked when the prison brass huffed and puffed about me tagging along with Father Jack. I'd not be allowed solo access to Eamonn; that was a given. But my *dumb American* act, along with playing Da's story for them over a couple of excellent smokes—which left my reservoir precariously low for the return—slipped me past the regulations into a big, blank, barren room of bland white walls with several tables, where we were told to sit in the center one. The place was so empty, even my breathing seemed to echo within it.

There were three guards—one at the door we'd been led through, one at a solid security entrance, and one to our side, under a banner of windows.

After what seemed like an hour, with no a word spoken between Father Jack and myself, the security door opened and in was led a wild-looking man. Hair flying. Beard down his chest. A clean, crisp uniform in direct contrast to the dirt on his arms and feet in slippers. He was manacled and hunched over, and his eyes focused on nothing. Not even Father Jack, after he was seated.

"Eamonn," said Father Jack, very softly, "you're looking well. Um, I've brought a visitor for you. A young man from America. He knows your aunt and cousins. Jeremy Landau is his name."

No reaction.

"He's staying with your family. Helping attend to your mother."

I popped in with, "Givin' your sister, Maeve, a bit of a break. Y'know, she's tried to come see you, but they won't let her in."

That got a flicker from him, towards me. Then he whispered, "Ma's dyin'."

"Yes, Eamonn," Father Jack said, gently. "She is."

"An' I'm here. Won' lemme see her."

"As I said, last time, I'm trying to work out a solution to that. Doing all that I can."

"Won' lemme see her. Me own dyin' mother. Bloody—"

"Eamonn." I cut him off. "Do you mind if I call you that?"

He looked closer at me and offered the barest shrug in answer. He finally seemed to be aware of me.

"I'm also workin' on a story 'bout your family," I continued, soft and easy. "Since I'm livin' with them."

"Why?" whispered from him.

"To...to show the human side of this tragedy. And...and I'm just wonderin' if you'd answer me a question."

That vague shrug, again.

"Were you born in Belfast or Derry?"

That brought a confused expression to his face. "What?" and his voice had some body to it, this time.

"The information I find is conflictin'. So I just wanted to ask you. Were you born in Derry, or Belfast?"

He looked hard at me. Wary. Unsure. "Who *are* you?"

I gave him my usual introductory spiel about that then added, "I'm good friends with your aunt and uncle, in Houston. Near neighbors. Known them all my life. And your cousins. Grew up together."

"Do I know you?" Awareness was growing in his eyes. "I think I know you..."

I didn't want that, so I said, "I have somethin' I'd like to share with you. Your father used to tell stories. Didn't he? Big, beautiful stories about the history of Ireland."

That shifted him to a near laugh. "Da tried. But too drunk."

"Well...then maybe this isn't him. Could you say, one way or the other?"

I pulled the player from the pocket of my jacket and hit play.

Eamonn slowly leaned closer, frowning. "What's this?"

"A recordin' of a man tellin' a story," I said. I felt Father Jack's eyes boring into me. I was going to get a serious third degree on the way home, but I needed to know, for certain. And I needed Eamonn to verify.

So the story began. And the shock and surprise and finally wonder that spread over my brother's face all but brought him back to life. Which made everything worth it.

Now I knew without question, it was our father's voice purring through the pathetic little speaker, soft, soft, rasping but audible. He heard it. And his expression grew gentle. He licked his lips and began to breathe deeply. His eyes filled with tears.

"That's me Da," he whispered. "God, how long's it been since I heard this story? And told this well? So well."

He swallowed. Almost wept. To hide it, he cocked his head

to listen more carefully to the words now drifting around him. He shifted his arms to on top of the table, in full view so the guard had no reason to come over. He kept his body still. After a moment, the smell of him whispered away and all I could see was Eamonn...our Eamonn on the verge of happiness.

"When was this made?" he asked.

"Early sixties, as I understand," I replied.

He almost frowned and shook his head. "Da was already well into drink, by then."

"I'm told this was recorded as he was havin' his first pint. There's other recordin's that do become more and more incoherent as he speaks. But for years, he was a teller of tales. A seanchaí."

He nodded. "Where did you find it?"

"The original's at Ulster University, in Coleraine. But I think it's also at the UDD, in Cork."

"Listen to his voice. So sharp and clear and in control. So loving to every word. So he's not dead. He still lives." He turned to me. "He still lives."

Then he froze. His eyes began burning into mine, filled with wariness and questions and uncertainty. I let the slightest of smiles come to my lips. And there it came. The final recognition in his eyes along with surprise and hope. His back straightened and a light seemed to return to him.

"He still lives," he whispered.

I barely suppressed a gasp of joy.

He hadn't known I was alive!

He hadn't been part of the deception.

He'd also thought me dead.

The relief that swept over me was so complete, I felt as if I were in a different world. He could not have been the source of the Army's suspicion that I was still alive. I'd been so afraid that he'd let it slip, like he had so many other things. But he hadn't.

I was fighting the surge of emotion as I said, "Yes. He lives on. In this." And I tapped the cassette.

He almost smiled then shifted his gaze to Father Jack, behind me. I dared not look back at the man.

"Thank you for bringin' him, father," he said, then he rose.

I heard the man rise, saying, "Eamonn, we still have much to...to..." He was not expecting this to end, just yet.

"I must go now."

He started for the guard then stopped and said to me, over his shoulder, "I was born in Derry. Never Belfast. Dunno why ya'd think that. It's what me Ma told me. It's on me school records. Everything. I was born in Derry. I'm a Derry man."

Then he walked away.

More Details

En route home, Father Jack insisted I explain my question to him. "How could you not know where your brother was born?" he snapped, irritated at how Eamonn had brushed him off.

"There's a lot I don't know about my own family," I replied. Such as when my mother and father wed. That they'd lived in Belfast. "I never knew Da was a professional teller of tales, and so well-done. Knowing for certain where Eamonn was born helps me learn more about it. Sort through what's true and which is mere gossip."

"But I could have asked him that and—"

"I wanted him to hear our Da's voice, as well. To me, it was his, but I only remember his drunkenness. And I wanted to make sure I was right."

"And that is all there was to it? This nothing of a reason?"

I gave him a cool look. "I haven't seen my brother in over eight years, Father. I'd hardly put that down as *nothing*."

"I went through a great deal of trouble to bring you here," he huffed. "To have you interfere with my normal business is unacceptable."

I made my voice as innocent as possible to ask, "What normal business?"

That made him hesitate. "We...we sit, Eamonn and I, and meditate on the teachings of Paul and Peter, when they also were in jail. And I comfort him in this time of need and...well..."

"Pass him messages from the powers that be?" I got no response from that. I stretched and held the tape recorder tighter. "Tell me, is Eamonn with PIRA, OIRA or some other offshoot?"

"Don't ask me that. I do not know, nor do I care to. It makes no difference, behind those walls."

Perhaps. I was well out of the politics between those two groups, and it would have made no difference to me which he belonged to. But that non-answer suggested that one, Father Jack knew which it was, and two, was in contact with both offshoots of the IRA. To no surprise.

So I just watched the passing countryside and ignored every other one of his questions. If he wouldn't be honest with me, I saw no reason to be open with him.

*****

I stayed away from the next day's peace meeting. Let all of the ladies attend, as if to show great force in numbers. Demonstrations were planned and over the week held along William Street and in Waterloo and the Diamond and such. More and more people from around the world joined in the call for Thatcher to give in. News moderators took sides to discuss the nature of negotiation, with one saying you should never compromise with terrorists while the other harped on the idea of human rights for all, even those incarcerated for promoting those rights. Both in their best pompous attitudes.

I finally learned from Maeve that Bridie had not miscarried, but was on bed rest, to be safe. "So we'll not be seein' Rhuari, for a bit, I'll need to find another way to get the lemons." She was cutting and squeezing them into a kettle of water. She sighed and shook her head. "The way he tends to her. Loves her..." Her voice drifted off.

I put an arm around her and said, "Like you tend to Ma. And you'll someone who tends to you, as well."

She hesitated then said, "But I...well, I-I-I'm not lookin' for one...for one like Rhuari, you know. You-you understand?"

Yes, I did. And I held her tighter. "Changes nothing that I said."

She turned to hug me. "I knew it. I knew I could tell you. You're the first person I've told."

I kissed her on the forehead. "That makes me very proud."

"Dear God, I'm so glad you're back."

"For now."

She looked at me. "No, forever."

Then she patted me on the chest and turned back to making that vile lemon water.

Of course, neighbor ladies and friends kept coming in and out with food and cakes, and interfering nonstop in my attempts to query Ma about what I'd learned.

I did happen to get Mrs. Haggerty talking when she was about to depart, one evening. Maeve was upstairs settling Ma for the night and the old woman was putting on her coat when I asked, "You know when the Kinsellas moved to Derry?"

"Oh, good heavens, that was years ago," she said. "Decades."

"Was it before Eamon De Valera came to visit?"

"Visit?" She huffed. "We lined the street to see the great man and he drove past without a look at us. In an open car that was older than I was. Not one care shown. Bernadette was with me, yes. I remember that. Eamonn in one arm; Mairead slung over her back. Barely had her eyes open. Eamonn...her Eamonn...he was in Belfast, that day, at a fete. I think De Valera was going to be driven to it. Maybe. Dear God...thirty years it's been..."

"Mrs. Kinsella said he blessed Eamonn."

Mrs. Haggerty laughed. "Must've been when he blew his nose as he drove by us at speed." Then she grew somber. "Blessed? Or cursed? Mrs. Keogh thought the latter. Poor woman upstairs started having miscarriages. Still births. Wasn't till her Brendan came that she started back to normal.

"That was a horrible time. Terrible. Her Eamonn, he'd been such a good man. Young but willing to do as needed. But then Brendan came along and he took to drink. So sad."

Then she left, without a good-bye.

I tried to listen in on some of the chatter when Ma was being visited by a couple of women she knew, but their voices would be so quick and alternating between loud and soft, it was hard to understand what they were saying. I recorded some, but it proved to be useless.

There came one afternoon with a lull in the incessant chatter, when Maeve was taking a nap, Kieran was out, and I caught Ma awake and seemingly alert. I slipped into the room as she was doing nothing but looking straight ahead.

"Mrs. Kinsella, you doin' all right?"

She looked at me with a near beatific expression. "Just havin' a chat with my Eamonn."

I froze. "He's here?"

"Sometimes. I know when my hour's come, he'll be the one sent for me."

What could I say but, "I'm sure he will. Um...I found a recordin' of one of the stories he used to tell."

"Which one?"

"The...the one about the Dagda and harpies and..."

She nodded and smiled. "In the Moher Cliffs. You're the one who found that?"

I nodded.

"My Rhuari played it for me. So lovely to hear. My Eamonn, he could have a room filled with people, children, mothers and fathers, chatterin' on. And within a minute he'd have cut their noise to nothin' with the smoothness of his voice. The beauty of his diction. The drama behind it.

"Oh, to listen to him," she murmured. "A voice like a cool stream in summer. Gentle and melodious. To hear that, you'd never know he had it in him."

"Storytelling is an art, and I understand some people thought him a master of it."

"He could have been. It wasn't his fault."

"Wasn't his fault?"

"Belfast was a mistake. It was lovely, but a mistake. But most of his work was there..."

"When did you move to Derry?"

"I've always lived in Derry. All my little ones were born here. I could never live anywhere else."

"Who was Edward Clark?"

She cast me a condescending look. "Oh, Jeremy, if you want to work for any Protestant in the North, you have to have a Protestant name. He did well, with that." A cloud passed over her. "Did well till he married. That bastard had no right to threaten us. None."

I was afraid to say anything because it might end her train of thought, but this was making no sense.

"Who threatened you?" I asked in as gentle a tone as I could.

"That bloody Bates, wantin' more and more and never satisfied. Never enough. He deserved it. But it killed Edward. No...no...it was that priest who killed Edward. That priest." Then she looked at me, a bit afraid. "You almost look like him...but you can't be. He wanted to but never could. My Eamonn stopped him. My Eamonn stopped any who tried to hurt his own.

"Poor Edward. He did well by us but could no more. And all

my Eamonn could do was turn to drink, in sorrow."

"I don't understand. What happened?"

She frowned and looked harder at me. Her words sharpened into knives. "Oh, Michael Farrell, you've a fine nerve showin' up here after abandonin' me to the bloody nuns. Get out! I've no brother like you. None of mine would be like you! Get out! OUT!"

She swung her claws at me and I stumbled back. She still caught my arm and brought out some blood, screaming, "Out! Out!"

I left.

To say I was shaken up would be an understatement. I was also very confused. Could that be yet another reason she hated me? I reminded her of men who'd abandoned her? Well...mixed with my cat-like attitude and her seeing herself as a dog.

Oh, God, I hated that analogy.

Ma's screaming had woke Maeve, who was at the top of the stairs.

"What's wrong?" she asked.

"I was talking to Ma and suddenly she called me Michael and came at me."

Maeve cast me a careful look and said, "You do have a vague resemblance to him. She must've just got confused." Then she noticed I was bleeding. "Oh...come in the bath. We'll wash that and I've some plasters for it."

I was still kind of shaken, so I went with her. Turned out they were just deep scratches and needed little tending to.

"Oh, Bren," she said as she worked, "the fit she tossed when Uncle Michael slipped into her room, and said hello. He *is* small and darkly fair, like you, just with more nose and less hair."

"Good for him," I chuckled, then said, "I need to hit the library before it closes. Is there anything you want me to bring back?"

"Could you do the chippy, for tonight's supper? I'm not up to cookin'."

"Two piece?"

She nodded.

And I was off. I made it there an hour before closing and went straight to the microfiche to pull up the Telegraph for June 1951. Scanned through its headlines then did July 1951. And halfway in I found it.

Shankill Man Beaten to Death. William Bates, a church curator, was beaten to death in a horrific attack. Police are seeking a man known as Edward Clark as a person of interest. It is believed he has taken the ferry to Stranraer so Scottish police have been notified.

Apparently, Bates was a member in good standing of the Loyalist League, and many suspected this to be a sectarian attack. But Clark was also thought to be a member of the Church of Ireland so that suggestion was cast aside. However, Bates' brother, Alfred, swore to track Clark down and handle justice himself.

A quick shift to the men who were accused of killing Da showed neither was named Bates, and both had already been released from prison. But could that explain why Da was killed? It wasn't a random attack but that these men had found out who *Edward Clark* was and targeted him?

I had no idea. It seemed too pat and easy. But it could explain the horrific damage done to my father, and I wouldn't be surprised if a little more digging would find there was a connection between his killers and Alfred Bates. A story in the next day's paper mentioned a Catholic priest had witnessed the incident and said he thought it was but a drunken brawl that was initiated by Mr. Bates. That Mr. Clark had only been defending himself. That both victims were considered C of I, that gave a lot of credence to the priest's statement.

The priest's name? Father Llewellyn.

Jesus Christ, now it was time to see if Father Demian had ever had a parish in Belfast. If so, that could tell me what Da meant by his comment about priests coming at you from nowhere. He hadn't been molested. He'd been saved from hanging.

Only Ma'd had two miscarriages after that. Did Da feel it was his punishment? Did he turn to drink and become the monster I knew from guilt over killing a man and what looked like some quiet blackmail that followed?

For God's sake, Brendan, shut up. You can work yourself into a wild state if you keep guessing about things that may or may not have happened. Wait till you've got more to go on, then freak out. Okay?

I huffed and puffed at myself but agreed.

Research first. Freakout later.

The next day, I dug back into the *Derry Journal* and found a story on Father Demian. He'd come to Derry from a parish outside Belfast. His first.

Whiteabbey.

Where Father Llewellyn was from.

Of course, I couldn't ask Father Demian if he'd ever used the name of Father Llewellyn. My only choice was to ask the diocese, which was out of the question...or Ma. Which could be just as problematic.

Still, that night, I was prepared to take over for Maeve so she could do her Peace meeting and I could enter the den of lions, again, but Mrs. Kieffer was already on board. She was even larger than before but otherwise no different. "Bernadette and I'll have a good craic, God bless her," she said, "so you two be off."

To say I did not want to go would be simplifying my feeling. I really wanted to talk with Ma. But all I said was, "I dunno. Won't I be in the way of people talkin'?"

"Father Jack thinks it'd be wonderful for you to be there," Maeve said. "He said there may even be some Protestant leaders come to see, and it would be good to show it's not just the likes of us pushin' to end this conflict without further loss of life. We can't start till seven, this time, so we'll have a bite to eat, first, then a good night out."

"Go along, Mr. Landau," Mrs. Kieffer urged. "Our Maeve could use an evening with friends, and I've much to discuss with Bernadette, God love her."

I was leery of putting Jeremy's name front and center, but I could probably work around that as long as I didn't sign on to anything. So I figured I'd have a go at Ma, tomorrow, grabbed my jacket, and was about to leave with Maeve when I stopped, spun and asked, "Mrs. Kieffer, how long've you known Mrs. Kinsella?"

She sighed as she put her tent of a coat on the rack. "It's been years. I met her when her first was born."

"In Derry?"

She nodded. "My sister was called in as midwife, last minute. He was coming out early, so I helped. Her husband was telling stories at St. Eugene's. Singing songs. Such a lovely voice."

And she took a moment to sigh over the memory. I was beginning to think Da had groupies.

She continued with, "She was here to help the dancers what preceded him. Of course, she couldn't dance, not in her condition, God bless her. Wasn't due for...what was it? A fortnight? But he come out easy, thanks to God. And now he's in jail. Oh, by the saints, it's been a hard life for her, and now this."

Well...at least that verified Eamonn's belief.

So off we went, this time with no bags of food.

"Since it's late, Father Jack's ordered food in from the Italian place, tonight," Maeve said, "and others are bringing extra."

"What Aunt Mari'd call potluck."

Maeve chuckled. "I'd have some of it, as well, but I won't have a chance to eat so..."

"I'm your dinner date."

She laughed and wrapped an arm around mine.

The night was growing fine so we got Chinese at the base of the Rossville Flats and sat on a bench to eat it. I made a show of using chopsticks for any and all to see, as they passed. Even soldiers in a PIG hooted some foul things at us, so I waved my Marlboro to them. I suppose to them it appeared we were on a date. It struck me I should have worn my NASA cap.

A soft mist was coming in, adding a sense of calm and reason to the area. I looked around at all the new housing and the still vacant lots piled with refuse and shook my head.

"Christ, were it not for these bloody flats behind us," I said, "I'd not know where I was."

"Best not get used to it," Maeve said. "There's more changes comin'. I've even heard rumors the council's thinking of tearin' down the Flats. Saying they were a mistake."

I chuckled. "These fine old buildings?"

"Where the lifts don't work half the time?" Maeve giggled. "And where the roofs give our side the high ground and ability to fight back?"

I nodded. "I remember that, for Sixty-nine. It's amazing the damn things weren't gutted." I looked around at them. "Does wee Eammon still live there with his mother?"

"She was the abandoned woman, right?"

I nodded. She took a bite then let herself finish eating it before she said, "Not for some years."

I looked at her. "What happened?"

"Wee Eammon run off. Took his things and just...vanished. No one knows where he's gone. Includin' his mother. She fell deep into the tranqs and OD'd, but she was found and now? Now she's in care."

"Christ."

"There's those say she drove him away with her clingin' ways."

"True, so I wouldn't have blamed him."

"Yes, the less said the better."

I nodded. It felt so normal sitting there in the evening chill. Our food growing cold. Our bottles of beer, as well. The first hint of twilight sneaking in with the mist, adding a layer of wonder to a city drab and afraid. Most shops were rolled closed. Cars were few on the street. As were people.

I sighed. "I love it like this."

Maeve finished her meal and set the container beside her. "Mai says it gets brutal hot in Houston."

I nodded. "Like the gates of hell, for months. I only grew to where I could tolerate it, nothing more."

"Did you never think of coming home?"

I shrugged and ate more of my noodles. "Now and again," I said as I chewed. The B-girls would have been horrified at my lack of manners. "But it was made clear to me that wasn't an option."

"Yet here you are."

"No, I'm not. I'm neither Brennan nor Jeremy...nor even Brendan, anymore. I'm nobody."

"Except to your family. Did you never miss us?"

It took me a moment to answer, "Something terrible."

"I wish there was some way we could settle this. End you bein' on the run."

"That'll never happen. The British don't think me dead. No body to prove my demise."

"I may still look into it," Maeve said in a voice that gave me no room for dispute.

"As you will. But could you wait until I'm gone? Just to be safe?"

She looked at me for a long moment then sighed. "I suppose another month or two won't matter, after so many years. I just hate for you to have to sneak away, again."

"Come on, Maeve, am I the only lad on the run?"

"No."

"And do you think that will ever change? Really?"

"I don't know. I hope and pray...but sometimes the reality is just too much and it's all I can do to get up in the mornin's and care for Ma."

"You've been a rock."

"I'd rather not be."

The last of my noodles were ice cold so I chucked the lot in the bin, along with Maeve's, and we started for the Guildhall. "Do you know where Kieran is, tonight?"

"Off with Tommy Fields, I'm sure. Some others I don't know. Wouldn't be surprised if they're hurlin' stones at Guildhall."

I chuckled. "Danny and his mates would do that. Get the peelers to chase them, for a lark."

She looked at me. "You still think of Danny?"

"Now and again. He's the one took me up to Grianan Aileach and...and..."

Joanna looked out over the whole of Ireland, wind blowing her hair. Her cheeks red as rubies, as were her lips. The hint of Spearmint around her. So beautiful and alive.

I realized we had stopped walking and I was leaning against the burned out wreckage of what had once been a shop with homes above it. Maeve was just looking at me, waiting.

I smiled at her. "Sorry to stop you. Sometimes the memories come at me from nowhere."

"You and Danny were good friends," she said, her voice soft and caring.

I just nodded.

"I...I...at the bomb, I know he keep you from being grabbed. Took you away."

Colm told her, I'm sure. I could think of nothing to say so just gave my usual shrug.

"He was horrified at what happened. Nearly broke him."

I looked closer at her. Saw eyes filled with pain and sadness. "How well did you know Danny?" whispered from me.

Her smile grew wistful. "Well enough. Held him as he wept." I just looked at her, so she continued, "He'd come to tell me you'd been taken away. He didn't know where, or if you'd return. Or if you were even alive, anymore. And he broke down."

"Why you? Telling you and not Ma or...or Rhuari?"

"We were friends." And her eyes dug deep into mine. "We understood each other, without words."

I nodded and said, "He was too broken a soul for this world to let exist."

"I have no argument against that. And I know it may be that what we're tryin' to achieve with the peace movement will come to naught. It looked so hopeful a few years ago...but now? Now we just have to keep tryin'. For the sake of Danny. And Eamonn. And you. And pray tomorrow will be better."

"You're a better man than I am, Gunga Din."

She blinked and near laughed, confused. "What the devil's that?"

"Just one of the books I read to keep meself occupied. It just means you're...you're this country's hope. That's all."

"I'd not go that far. I'm hardly the only one fightin' for peace, as you're about to see. Come along. *Jeremy.*"

"Yes, ma'am, I'm a-right here with ya."

She chuckled as we headed on to Butcher's Gate.

*****

We wound up at the same hall as before. Father Jack was already on site, holding court, when Maeve led me in. He saw me as we maneuvered to get past him and his acolytes, but there was no hesitation in his pontification over nothing.

Well...except to joyously murmur, "Welcome, Mr. Landau. I didn't think you would be here."

I just smiled at him.

A table by the wall was already piled high with boxes of take-away, cakes and drinks, including thermoses of coffee and tea. Maeve sat herself behind the table in front, so I took a cake, a cup of tea nicely watered down, and sat in a chair at the rear of the room. And tried to ignore what felt like a growing tension in the room.

What made this more uncomfortable was how several new people were here. Not only Protestants but several friends of my mother. Parents of boys I grew up with. Some of them cast me awkward glances, as if thinking they recognized me. Of course, I couldn't leave now; that would call even more attention to myself. So when anyone came up to me to talk, I'd put on my worst Texas accent, give them my public name and say, "I'm just here t' watch. Doin' research." They all seemed to accept it, though some were on the reluctant side.

A few more people arrived, as did some who'd stepped out for a smoke of something more than a cigarette, then Maeve called the meeting to order.

The first bit of business was to introduce me, once more, to one and all as the American who'd come to see *The Troubles* for himself. There were murmured words of wary greeting and I smiled in acknowledgement. Then Father Jack slipped in from a side door to sit next to Maeve; I hadn't realized he'd left the room. The two of them passed whispered words, and both seemed troubled.

It was soon revealed that negotiations with the British over St. Bobby were no longer existent. Maeve announced he was nearing death in the cause of freedom, so the focus shifted to him. Joining with other relative action committees and the National Anti-H Block Jail Committee to intensify the pressure on Westminster.

They also wondered how they could help his cause without seeming to agree to the harsh reactions of PIRA and OIRA while still condemning comments from the UDF and UVF and RUC and all the damn letters of the alphabet? The tone was hopeful. Positive. Forward thinking. Certain that a well-worded missive from them would turn the tide away from disaster. Yet there was still a vague aura of disbelief that he and four other young men, who'd proven willing to destroy themselves, had not yet brought a softening to the hard heart and head of Margaret Thatcher.

Their sister organizations held the same belief—that Thatcher had to give in or face condemnation of the world. *Don't let him die* was still the phrase to hold over her head. Of course, there would be more demonstrations, and all wanted them to be peaceful ones and hold violence to a minimum. This despite the British Army doing all it could to provoke a reaction, and each of the recent ones had veered closer and closer to the chaos of full-scale riots, as was to be expected by anyone with a brain. So the sanctimony of how it's better to deal with people as humans instead of react like animals continued to sound like mere words.

But underlying it all was a fear that if any of the hunger strikers died, chaos would engulf the North.

I kept silent, though it was a difficulty, and pretended to take notes on a pad. A few people who came in during the meeting noticed and cast me odd looks, but none said a word until one of the latest old biddies stood up to face me.

"Excuse me, sir," she said, her eyes shooting daggers, "but just who are you?"

Maeve leaned forward to say, "You missed my introduction, Mrs. Heaney. He's Jeremy Landau, an American here on University grant."

Father Jack barely hid an expression of amusement.

"Then what's he doin', taking notes of what we're sayin'?" Mrs. Heaney demanded, her voice quivering.

I closed my pad and stood up, using my best drawl.

"Sorry if I'm causin' trouble. I'm just doin' a thesis on similarities between the issue in Northern Ireland and issues in Israel, like durin' the Yom Kippur war and—"

"What does Ireland have to do with a bunch of Jews?" she snapped.

"Bloody fascist state's what they are," said another woman, who wasn't even forty, yet. "The way they treat Palestinians."

"It wasn't Jews who killed Palestinians in Munich," popped out of me before I could even think about it, "or hijacked airplanes or—"

"They're only oppressed people, like us, calling for someone to notice and—"

"Mrs. Connor!" Maeve stood, her face cold and calm. "Mr. Landau is a guest whom I invited to our gathering, and I ask that you treat him as such."

"Why did you bring him?" The old biddy's voice was tinged with fear. "How do you know who he is? He could be sent to spy on us and—"

"My AUNT in America!" Maeve roared with a softness that

startled me. "She knows him and backs him."

"And how do you know he's the one she backs? Did she send you a photo of him?"

Another woman rose, dressed in a worn cloth coat and jumbled hat. "Maeve, your aunt's been gone from here since she married—what? More than twenty-five years ago! And didn't she marry a Protestant sailor from America?"

"My uncle's Catholic," Maeve sighed.

"What's that to do with anything?" said Mrs. Heaney. "She's taken herself away from our part of the world and what have they done for us, since?"

The woman who'd supported the Palestinians snorted. "Shown they're not of us, any longer."

Father Jack rose, his voice quiet. "Ladies, we can squabble over this for many days, when it's hardly of importance. If this man says he's Jeremy Landau, then he's Jeremy Landau, who has nothing to do with this conflict. Who are we to say otherwise?"

And there was a quiet contempt behind his words that cut deep. Maeve cast him an unsettled look.

"But I will ask," he continued, "for everyone's peace of mind, that he excuse our outburst and wait for Maeve, outside, as we continue our meeting. I would hate for him to be subjected to any further acrimony over political beliefs that have no bearing on the matter at hand. Let us make our decisions without him watching over us and taking his notes."

Maeve was aghast. "Father Jack!"

"We have much left to do, Maeve, and this is a distraction we do not need." He looked straight at me. "We appreciate you coming, *Mr. Landau*, but if you don't mind..."

Maeve fought to find decent words to say as Father Jack studiously ignored her. Had the bastard insisted I come to this bloody meeting only so he could find some excuse to throw me out of it?

I managed to hide my anger, make myself shrug and nod and back to the door. "Sorry to have caused y'all so much trouble. Was never my intent."

Every eye in that joint watched me leave, more than a few were not unhappy I was going. I forced myself to saunter down the hall, as if unconcerned, and passed a couple more old hens, arriving late. They cast me wary glances as they trudged on to do their pitiful little bit to help end Ireland's suffering, as if anyone who truly could end it would actually do so or even care a damn one way or the other. The entire play was craven and childish beyond words.

I stood outside, for a moment, breathing in the chilly evening mist, my mind frozen. Still barely twilight, even though half eight. Houston would be in total darkness, by now, and I'd grown too accustomed to that warm and heavy atmosphere, which even in the dead of winter could turn smothering. Now my jacket and jumper were barely enough to keep me from shivering. At least it wasn't raining.

Well, the positive aspect of being kicked out of the meeting was...none would think me Brendan Kinsella, now. It would be spread far and wide that Jew had been put in his place, after daring to defend others of his kind. Sent packing, he was, by none other than the leaders of the troupe. I figured that would give me another month's cover...and at the rate Ma was going, she'd be in the ground by then and I'd be far gone.

But God, God, God, why did Father Jack do that to me?

I had no interest in returning home to deal with Ma's nastiness or Mrs. Kieffer's quiet nosiness, so I came back to myself enough to wander up Foyle. Headed for the City People Wall.

The air had become brisk to the point of biting, and my nose and cheeks felt it. But it was good that it accosted me and kept me from diving too deeply into the chaos of my soul.

I could see Maeve begging for some reason to believe all would be well, if not for herself for the sake of her nephews and nieces and all future children. She needed the hope that someday life would be good for them instead of more of the same evil and corruption, just as she needed to believe that she would be missed by the next bomb going off near her, and that neither Rhuari nor Kieran would be shot by a British Patrol spooked after coming under fire, nor be targeted by the UDA or UVF or whatever other letters they'd poached for themselves.

But Father Jack—he knew better. He knew without question the whole reason for the evils being perpetrated was nonsensical and would only hasten the spiral into catastrophe. He'd even let me know, tactically, that sometimes he believed none of this would end until all sides were so destroyed and the world around them so completely ruined, there was nothing left to fight over. Yet still he parroted weak words of reconciliation and cast contempt my way for not doing the same.

By this point I was on the fountain and sat on the bench and smiled at the thought of how they'd been *redeveloping* this side of Derry most of my life. And it would keep on. I believed the talk of tearing down the Rossville Flats and putting in more human scaled housing because it would mean nothing except fewer places for Catholics to live. To congregate. Spreading us out far and wide, claiming it's better housing for our kind...but really just another way to break us apart. Communities that once were would have to be rebuilt, if they could be. Even then, we wouldn't be left to live like humans. To do that you have to have hopes and dreams and promise of a future to look forward to. A life to seek. And none of that mattered to any but those who didn't have it. It was nothing but a chaotic rearranging of chairs on a sinking ship.

I heard some shouts and what could have been gunfire coming from down in Waterloo, followed by running feet. Like when Danny and his mates from Shantalow had run past that night, so long ago.

I carefully and casually rose to my feet and sauntered back towards Guildhall, figuring I'd sit on the front steps and smoke one of my last Marlboros and—

"Oi, me China!"

I turned without thinking.

An RUC squad car was whispering up Foyle to me.

And hanging his head out the window behind the driver, like a dog on a joy ride with its owner, was Billy fucking Corrie, fat, round, barely fitting that ugly black uniform, a wide grin on his snarl of a face.

Oh, Christ, that fucking toe-rag had eyed me and called to me in such a way as to prove, without question, I was anything but an American in Derry.

I was worse than fucked.

Discovery

"Did ya think I forgot ya?" Billy called out to me.
The thought to run flashed through my head, but it would only give them an excuse to shoot me in the back. So I stood there as they pulled to a halt next to me and two others piled out with Billy and—

They pulled the pillowcase over me and wrapped me in the blanket and tossed me in the back of the Galaxie 500 and I landed hard as they jumped back in the car, laughing and we squealed away and—

The biggest of them punched me in the gut, bringing stars to my eyes and near killing my ability to breathe. Billy snarled, "C'mon, Max," then he cuffed my hands behind me and shoved me in the back, and seconds later we were speeding past the Guildhall to Waterloo.

The driver turned left then right onto William and aimed the squad car into the darkness then curved right onto Little James then left onto Great James and left onto Francis, where we caught the edge of a mist whispering in. The headlights blasted through its tendrils, making it seem to toy with us as it swirled up and over and away from the car only to disappear into the night then dance around to do the same. It struck me as alive and real, like ghosts whispering up to greet me with a laughing awareness of what was next to come, for while these bastards may have been in uniform, they weren't taking me to an RUC jail or any army encampment.

Then a rag was tied over my eyes and we curled around onto Westmorland, maybe...and then another left, and finally I had no clue as to where we were. They were driving around to confuse me, and they were being so casual about it I had to fight to keep from shaking, for I half suspected I'd not return.

I wondered if this is what happened with my Da, fifteen years earlier. I wondered if he'd gone willingly or fought back and been restrained, as I was. But no, he was too powerful a man to be held down by a couple Proddies, even some as burly as Billy and one of his mates. Da'd probably been promised a pint at a friend's pub and gone along and been slipped something to calm him as they tied him, so by the time he knew trouble had overtaken him it was too late. But I also knew he'd never cried or begged, not once. It wasn't in him to do that. He'd have spit and screamed and called all of God's curses down on the bastards making sport of him, but he'd never have pleaded to be set free...and nor would I.

Not ever.

In fact, I said nothing as we drove and turned and drove some more. Not one word. Nor did they. Though I did cough. That fucking little hack I had that came without warning at the worst times, that sounded like I was under water and no doctor could figure out why. What I did manage to do was carefully maneuver Jeremy's passport out of my back pocket and slip it down over my ass, under my briefs. It was torture to do without being noticed, but I was getting it there and—

The driver hit the brakes.

"Fookin' shite, Tam!" snapped Billy.

"Sorry," Tam said, his voice with that flat Belfast sound. "Almost missed it." And we turned to the right, rode over rough ground and stopped in a place that stank of burned wood and dead animals. They piled out and yanked me from the car and I nearly laughed at how ridiculous it was to be going through this, again.

They frisked me, rough and quick. One hand grabbed me between the legs and almost felt the passport...but got distracted by my wallet and ripped it from my pants. All he found in it was money. I felt my note pad being yanked from my jacket pocket and heard it be tossed aside. Then I was half-carried over jumbles of what were probably fallen beams and bricks to be slammed into a chair. The blindfold fell off but before I could even think to adjust my eyes, a flashlight was shined into my face, blinding me.

"You sure this is him?" said Max.

"Looks American," said another voice.

"He answered me, didn't he?" Billy shot back.

I closed my eyes against the light and turned away. When I opened them, again, I could just make out we were in the middle of a building that had been burned. I looked up and could see open sky between charred beams and the remains of a ceiling. The stench was overpowering, so it must have happened recently. There was still something dead in the area, and rotting.

Someone grabbed my chin and yanked me back to facing the flashlight. Then one came up to me—a tall skinny job, with a long face and even longer nose to match his frame. His eyes were coal black and near to laughing under thin eyebrows and a long forehead. He sported a moustache that barely filled out to cover half the distance between his nostrils and lips. And his hands were lean and calloused and holding me in place with a sturdy grip.

"So—you're the lad was spirited off," he purred. It was Tam, of the Belfast accent. "How long you been in America? Seven years?"

"Eight, Tam," said Billy. "Christ, you an' the maths."

Another man came up behind the skinny bastard, and I could just make out his uniform was tight on him...and not from fat; this one was building up to be Mr. Universe, looked like. Beefy hands clasped each other and rested on one knee. A beefy neck sprung up from powerful shoulders and a face that reminded me of a chipmunk whose jowls were filled with nuts. His eyes were hard as diamonds and twice as sharp, and his grin would have sent chills through a dead man.

"So first you vanish and we don't know where," he said, and I realized this was Max. "Then suddenly you're back with us and we don't know how. Would you care to explain?"

Explain? Like bloody hell.

Max leaned forward. "We know you cut out just after a bomb near killed two members of the UVF, and did kill three civilians. It's my understanding you made certain the main victim was in place, then helped your mate position the bomb."

"I think he's the one fingered the man," Billy said.

"I suppose that's why the IRA got you out of this country so quick. Fortunately for us, it wasn't before you also fingered one of them for the murders."

"Stupid bloody Taig," snarled Slim.

"Too bad he's beyond our reach," said Tam.

"Yeah, well, that's death for you," said Billy. Speaking of a mate he'd once played with. Dear God, how sorry I was I'd ever defended him from Colm.

"We know you didn't finger Danny deliberately, Bren," said Billy. "As I understand it, you went off your nut at seeing the consequences of your actions, and he and another lad had to drag you from the scene. And there's witnesses who place that third lad there. So he's the one we're interested in. Who was he?"

He paused, as if I were ready to speak. As if I were fool enough not to understand this meant Danny was so deep into PIRA, three years they'd sought him out and he'd kept his distance. Till his own goal. What was more, so had Eamonn, for he was high enough in the force to know who was with Danny. Never mind about him not knowing I'd still been alive; he'd said nothing about Colm. While in Long Kesh and the Maze! Where they could be as vicious as they liked with no one to care. I suddenly found a new respect for him. A deeper love than I'd ever thought possible. That one little realization shifted my brother to absolute hero in my eyes, and I wanted him to be as proud of me as I was him. So I stayed silent.

Max looked at Billy and got a shrug, in answer.

"Tell you what, Bren," said Billy. "I'll make it easy for you. I think it was Colm with Danny."

What absolute horseshit. If they'd been able to connect Colm in any way, he'd already be at Her Majesty's pleasure for the rest of his life, but I knew that not to be the case.

He kept on with, "Let us know and we'll drive you straight home. Nothing more to it. Even share some of the reward with you. Just a thousand pounds, but enough to get you back out of the country and set up someplace safe. I remember how you loved your money, more'n a Jew. So what d'ya say? Be a good lad and help your country bring a criminal to justice."

I just kept looking at him, impassive.

That seemed to irritate him. He leaned closer. "Y'know, the Brits know you were livin' with your aunt and raisin' funds for the IRA. They been tryin' for years to get the Americans to turn you over. Now it seems under Reagan, they'll get their wish. Is that why you come back? Because a fellow Irishman was about to hand you up?

"The Brits'd love to know you're here. They'd like to see us bring you to Castlereagh for their own interrogation. Seventy miles from your family and friends. No visitation. No rights. And they don't need anything in the way of evidence to hold you. Is that what you'd prefer? Or maybe just tell us a name and we sneak you back out of the country."

My lips did not move. Tam shoved Billy aside and grabbed my chin then yanked my face around to look at him. "Answer him, ye bloody bastard!"

He was daring me to spit at him, daring me to give him an excuse to throw me 'cross the room. I did nothing. Didn't even look at him, just stared right through him into the blackness. He sneered and shoved my face away. I turned my eyes straight back to Billy, but now Max took his place, and he was impassive.

"Y'know, half the reason the IRA lads snuck you from the country was to keep the Provos from killing you for botching their action." How could he know that? "You had a price on your head for some years, till events took over and brushed it all aside. I wonder if it'll go back on, now that it looks like you're talking to us?"

When he got no answer, he casually continued with, "You'll talk to us. After a few hours here, we've yet to have someone refuse us info enough to convince OIRA and PIRA they've grassed on 'em. Hell, become supergrasses. A couple were carted off soon as we dropped them back in the Bogside."

"What was that one bastard's name? Sean? Seamus? Crazy ass from Shantalow."

What the fuck? Shane vanished long before any of these assholes were in the RUC. Everything they were saying to me was absolute bullshit. It was pathetic.

"Never saw 'em again, but those were stupid lads who made us work too hard for too little. Too little to help. You don't seem a stupid lad. Are you out to prove me wrong?"

Still I was silent. So Tam smacked me in the back of the head. A ring on his finger sent a sharp pain down the back of my neck. I closed my eyes, for a moment, but that was the only reaction they got from me.

"So—you're a hard case, is it? Living in a wild and open country and all the while dreaming of Mother Ireland. Makes me think all the more that you were over there, illegal, living with your aunt and uncle, raising money for a major terrorist organization to help them keep murdering innocent people. Once the British get zeroed in to where you were, they can make the proper complaints and ask charges to be filed for harboring a fugitive who's in the country illegally."

Yeah, yeah, yeah, keep repeating yourself, asswipe. As if my bastard Uncle hadn't already thought of that and made sure there was a good legal explanation in case the Americans got nosy. It helped that I'd already seen how the system of justice in America wanted nothing to do with any case that might prove difficult to win, or might cause the district attorney trouble with a large block of voters. Seems the stupid lad was him, not that it mattered; he was in control, so even being dumb as a brick of peat he'd get along all right in the RUC. They liked their lads to be idiots in jackboots. So I did nothing but look at him, nonstop.

It's funny, but now I knew my course was set, I'd stopped coughing. Now I knew I was geared for a roughing up, I relished it. Hell, I deserved it. I'd been unable to protect Joanna. I was even willing to accept she probably thought I'd helped target her Da. I'd been unable to protect Rocky from Matty or Evangelyne from the hatefulness of those bastards in Deer Park and my own anger. My last hope of redemption was to protect Colm from these lying weasels, for no matter what they did to me, should their hands reach him it would be a hundred times worse.

I think Max saw it in me and—

SMACK! He backhanded my face. Nearly sent me flying from the chair. I saw blood drip from my nose down to the dirty soot and vanish into it. I straightened myself, let the blood race down my chin to stain my shirt, then my jacket. But still I did nothing more than look at Max.

He smiled and circled me, slowly, deliberately, his eyes locked on mine. "You're not so much. You'll break easy; I can tell. The quiet ones always think they're strong through their silence, but they're only afraid. They're only waiting for the right time to speak. And you will speak."

He backhanded me, again. Ringing filled my ears as tears filled my eyes. I tasted blood in my mouth. It was hard to focus, but still...I said nothing. Just looked at him.

Again, he hit me. And again and again. I heard muffled noises that sounded as if he was speaking to me, but the ringing in my ears was too strong and the darkness too complete for me to be able to tell. I shook from the adrenalin running in my veins. Then I felt myself being lifted up by Tam and Billy and focused my eyes enough to see Max had a police baton in his hand, swinging it back and forth and back and forth and—

Whipped into my crotch.

I cried out, it was so sudden. Furious pain exploded not only in my groin but across my sides and behind my heart up my neck. I gulped in air. Tried to double over but Tam and Billy wouldn't let me. My arms were about out of their sockets, adding to the pain. But the ringing stopped and my eyes cleared and I looked up and saw naught but dark blank cloud above as I gasped and tried to breathe and let out soft little coughs that sounded more like hiccups.

They slammed me over a fallen beam. Crushed my face against charred bits of the collapsed ceiling. Spread my legs apart with their feet. And Max clipped me between the legs with the baton, again. Again, I cried out. Gasped at pain piling heavy atop the hurt I already felt.

Max walked around me. And though I couldn't see him well, I could hear the smile in his voice. Distant and cold. "Speak, Brendan, before I see to it you never have a chance at siring a child. Come on."

I shifted as much as I could, but Tam and Billy still held me down and used their legs to keep my legs locked apart. I could tell Billy was watching me as if I were some stranger and not a lad he'd been mates with for so many years, his expression impassive. He didn't care this was happening, the son-of-a-bitch, and it only made me the more stubborn.

I made myself remember him helping the men at Burntollet Bridge. Helping them prepare to attack Eamonn. He'd known Eamonn and known he was on the march and still helped them. Helped hurt others. People attacked for daring to want freedom and respect. The hate I'd felt for him then returned, in full, and kept me focused away from the hideous pain careening throughout my body.

It began to drizzle. I could feel the light caress, cold against my neck, and then Max grabbed my hair and pulled my head back so the rain whispered softly over my face, and he leaned in close to whisper, "We can stop it with one word from you. Tell us the third lad's name. First or last, doesn't matter. We have that? We'll get the rest. That's not much of a trade to stop this—"

He ran a hand up my thigh and gripped my crotch and squeezed and I screamed. My balls had been completely shattered so this was like pouring alcohol onto them. The slicing howling pain tore into my nerves. Sent rolling waves of torture down my legs and over my sides. Then he did it, again, and I nearly passed out from the screams in my body. I whimpered as I gulped in air. My heart was shivering from the pain. I thought for a moment I'd lose my supper, the churning in my stomach was so brutal. I could taste it in the back of my mouth. I fought it back. There is no way in God's hell I would give them the satisfaction of seeing me hurl...but Christ I'd have given anything to be able to cry.

Max shifted to smacking the baton against my sides, first the left, then the right, then the left, then the right, not hard but enough to take me to the point of incoherence when I heard someone croak, "I wasn't. Part. Of it."

Max leaned in, lying atop me like a lover. "I didn't hear you, lad. What was it you said?"

And Jesus Christ, that's when I realized it was me who'd spoken. And my voice whispered, again, "I. Wasn't. Part of it."

"How d'you mean?"

"Joanna. Martin. Met her at. At shop. Headed for tea. Tea. When bomb...bomb..."

I regained some control and cut my voice off.

"Lad, you can put it any way you want, so long as you give me the name of the third—"

"Dunno," I gulped at him. "Saw Danny. Surprised him. Turned. Saw car. Knew. Car. Kids fell. Against it. Don't remember. Anything. Else. Nothing else. Just...just..."

The white, white, white filling the world and a child's leg appearing from the smoke and haze, slowly, endlessly flipping end over end, its shoe and sock threatening to fly off until it landed before me and blood from its torn end sliced across my face and...

I collapsed into sobs. I had no control of myself. None. Just lay across that beam, my whole body shrieking at me and me bawling a river of tears from the depths of my soul and pain and nightmares. I gasped at my breath and fought to regain some sense of control, but I could find no way to end the flood. I just kept bawling.

Max raised off me. "That's a convenient story."

"But easy to check." That was Billy speaking. "I heard he was seein' a Protestant girl on the sly. Neighbor was tellin' me Ma, and if it was Joanna Martin, it's easy to verify."

"She the one that was burned?" said Tam.

Billy gave a slight grunt of agreement.

Then Tam continued, "That cunt was a traitor to her people?"

Control of the tears snapped over me as fury exploded within and I couldn't help myself but yank my leg away and slam my foot against Tam's knee before he could react, gasping, "You don't say that about her!"

Tam howled and Max gave me a series of rabbit punches in the side, nearly sending me into madness from the pain before I shifted into a zone where I couldn't think. In fact, I didn't have a coherent thought except that I'd got some of my own back as I drifted into darkness.

And hoped I was drifting into death.

Murderous

When I came back to my senses, I was lying in a heap on the filthy, ratty floor. I couldn't see much but the legs of that bloody chair and, in a corner, little red lights that would glow on and off. Like a devils' eyes. I closed my eyes at even the thought of trying to understand them. Every inch of my body ached, and I tasted vomit at the back of my throat. Smelled it. Oh fuck—I'd finally hurled and given those bastards the last bit of control over me, despite all my promises to myself. My hands were still cuffed and my fingers had a million needles dashing into their skin to torment me, while my balls were throbbing in ways I'd never known possible.

I heard a car door close. Were they being joined by more RUC? Was this a change of the torture shift? Or had they called the Brits over to take me off? Hold me up before the sympathetic press to show they'd caught another dangerous IRA snake, after years on the run? Or hide me till my injuries were healed and they could start over? I determined if they went at me, again, I'd force the issue. I couldn't continue with this. Not this.

Instead, Max appeared and lit a fag. I could just see him stop next to Billy and Tam. They huddled in a corner, smoking; the tips of their ciggies glowing pinpoints of red in the darkness. It looked like it was full night, out. The rain still whispered down, soft and easy. I could feel the hints of it on my cheek and wondered at how gentle and kind it was.

"I talked to Brooks," said Max, his voice low. But everything else was so calm and quiet, I could still make out the words. "He called a lady he knows and she told him way back then, there was talk a Catholic boy'd been seen around Joanna Martin."

"Cunt forgets where she come from," snapped Tam.

I hurt too much to call him out on it, again.

"Billy." It was Max talking. "You knew the fuckin' taig. What's your thoughts on it?"

"Shite, I dunno. We parted ways when I left the Fountain." Billy sighed then kept on with, "But he never was one to get caught up in the politics. We was just mates, had fun." He chuckled. "There was this one time, Sixty-eight I think, where we walked into the middle of a contest between some lads by Waterloo. A brick come close to hittin' us, from the Paddy side, so Bren picked it up and shied it back. I laughed and did the same with a stone that come our way, slingin' it at the Proddy bastard who'd shot it at us. We did that for a time. Him fightin' his side, me fightin' mine, till all come runnin' at us and we had to split. He snuck us into some old lady's flat and she fed us. Fuckin' fed us. Thanks to Bren."

"You ever see 'em together?" I didn't recognize that voice.

Billy hesitated then said, "I saw Bren get on a bus off Irish, and he was talkin' to this girl who had long blond hair. Very pretty. As the bus drove off, I saw them both run the back of it and sit together, but we wasn't mates anymore, so I can't say." He sighed. "Max, that bomb...I know he'd never do that to someone he cared for."

"You thinkin' the fookin' taig's tellin' the truth?" That was Tam speaking.

"If he is, what do we do?" Billy asked. "Take him in?"

"Hold him till his story checks out," Max replied. "Put a medic on him. He'll be healed well enough in a week's time, so after that—it's his word or ours."

"And who'll believe a fuckin' Taig?" Tam, again. He loved to use foul names on people, though I think this time it was half to see if I was awake and listening in. I just lay there, letting out the occasional whimper, and not deliberately doing so, I can swear that to you. But there was still far too much pain for me to keep my reactions back when it rolled over me.

"Hand him to the Brits," Billy added. "See if they still want him."

So that line of threats had been more bullshit. They had no idea what the Brits wanted or if they gave a damn about me, anymore. Fucking idiots.

"I *would* like to know how he got in the country," said the unknown voice. He was the one who seemed most on top of things.

"Away on. With a border like a fookin' sieve and half the

Republic helpin' 'em do it?"

"True." Max started over to me. Without thinking, I cringed. "He's back." He grabbed me by an arm and lifted me up, nearly dislocating my shoulder.

I all but spat at him, "Fuckin' shite, you gonna kill me, get it done with!" Don't know why I said that; I now knew they had no intention of doing it.

Max laughed. "Brendan, lad, you've nothing to fear from us. You've been more than helpful. Let's get you to a medic and have you checked over. Make sure you're all right. Feisty young fellow like yourself is far too prone to accidents. Gentlemen?"

Tam helped Max sling me over one shoulder to carry me, adding to the screaming of my gut.

"Motherfuckin' shits! Bastards!"

"Shut up, ye fookin' poofter!" Tam said, then added, "Y'know, Max, I heard our Brendan raised most his money by sellin' this." And he slapped my arse, barely missing the passport.

Somehow, I managed to give off a deep laugh and shoot back at him, "So that was your fuckin' tadger I felt. Against my leg when. When Max fondled me balls..."

BAM—I was flat on my back in the muck and Tam was punching me. Seems I may have said something a bit too true. Max kicked me, but Billy pushed him away and pulled Tam off before either of them got too many licks in. Only for sure, my nose was well-smashed.

They yanked me up and tossed me in the back of the car. Billy got in and shifted my head to lie against the other door. He removed my cuffs as Max got in front and Tam jumped behind the wheel.

I heard Billy whisper, "Stupid fuck. You stupid fuck."

I knew he meant me. So I whispered back, "This what. You do to. Your China?"

As we started driving, Max looked back at us. "What're you two on about?"

Billy glared at me then looked at him and said, "Our Brendan's learned a few new words—aimed at me."

Max grabbed my shirt and pulled me up to him. "Y'know, I think I'll let PIRA know you told us how you were snuck out of the country, and we're close to an arrest. See if we spook anyone into runnin'. Catch a few lads. And it'll all be your doin'." In the rearview mirror I could see Tam snickering. Max turned to him. "Head up the flyover. There's an army checkpoint, just past."

"Thought we was keepin' him," said Billy.

"Yeah," Tam said. "And the reward..."

"Bloody idiot," Max snapped, "never was one. Shite." He let me go and I fell back against the door as the car turned. "Put the bracelets back on him."

"But they're ours," Billy snapped. "Let the Army use theirs."

"So take 'em off when we hand him over!"

I saw we were driving down Lecky Road, passing ghosts of buildings that looked like a war zone in the mist. The street deserted. Not even cars parked on the side.

Then I realized my door was unlocked.

Billy grabbed my hand as we headed up the flyover. He started to put the handcuffs back on but I pulled my arm away and shook my head. "No," whispered from me.

"Don't be an arse," he snapped as he grabbed it back.

I could see the Long Tower's lights through the mist, soft and glowing, whispering closer and closer. We were moving fast.

Billy grabbed at me, again, and I twisted away and saw the stone wall along the road appear as Billy punched me in the side and I howled and kicked him in his fucking face then opened the door to let myself fall out. All without a conscious thought.

I hit the pavement and rolled like I had so many times when Jeremy tossed me. Slammed against the wall and bloody screamed from the pain...but it jolted me back to reality.

I heard the car screech to a halt, Billy yelling, "What the fuck, Bren! Are yous fuckin' mad?"

I used the wall to get to my feet and rolled over it to fall to a lower embankment and land flat on my back, and could have died from how much it fucking hurt. But somehow I managed to use a walkway railing to regain my feet and stagger around a small rise for St. Columba's lights, skidding over grass and pavement.

I heard the car roar up and skid to a halt, near by, its beams shining through the mist. Doors opened and their flat feet hit the pavement, so I scrambled to hide in a shadow behind a gravestone. I saw the forms of Billy and Max run around the church, the beams of flashlights preceding them. They were aimed for the front entrance.

I scrambled to my feet and stumbled up to the rear door of

the school. It was locked. I slapped my hand against it. Gasped, "Help. Help." No one came.

There was banging at the Church's front door. Sounded like it was also locked, meaning they'd be scouring the grounds in a moment, so I staggered around the church to a side wall and rolled over it to land in another graveyard. I found a stone to cower behind as Tam's voice joined the others.

"Have you found him?"

"Thought I heard hm over here."

"Bastard's vanished."

I pulled the passport from my briefs then slipped it into a jacket pocket. I had to clamp my teeth tight so as not to moan from the pain rolling through me. All I could hear was the voices of Billy, Max and Tam.

"This bloody mist doesn't help. Can't see well enough."

"Why the fuck'd you take off his restraints?"

"I told you—"

"Fuckin' idiot! Tam, go back the car. Call in a search team. Tell 'em we saw a wanted man, here. Ask for a warrant to search the buildings."

I was shaking like a mad dog. I swiped some condensation off the tombstone and wiped my face, and it helped so bloody much.

"That church is locked up tight."

"GO!"

The mist had turned into a fog so thick, I couldn't see the bottom of the hill I was on. But I knew it went to Lecky, under the flyover, so let myself slide down it, as easy as I could, soaking myself before I was halfway done. It was cold and felt good against my face and back and sides. But there, I found a ten foot drop to some pavement.

Despair threatened to overtake me. I thought for a moment of just lying there till it was all over. But my anger fought back and I crawled over the edge...and down I went. Jesus, you'd have thought I fell a hundred feet, it hurt so bloody much. I had to bite my fist to keep from screaming.

I knew I couldn't stay there, so I used the wall to steady myself as I rose...to find another short drop down to Lecky and under the flyover. Again, I let myself fall and it hurt like a bastard. But I was away from the church into an area of shadows, and I knew how to get home from here.

I don't know how I did it, but I somehow found the will to head for Clíodhna Place, making myself go as fast as I could and blessing that bloody fog every step of the way. It helped there was no traffic on the road and the peelers were focused on The Long Tower. I had to duck in a shadow when PIG roared up Lecky, for the flyover, but that was the only close call and it hardly counted. They couldn't have seen me unless I jumped straight in front of them.

I moved fast, then slow, then staggered, then felt like I was going backwards. My legs were mush. My back terrorized me. My head threatened to depart from my body. But somehow, what felt like a year later, I finally arrived at Clíodhna Place. I had to pound on the door to be let in. Mrs. Kieffer opened it and gasped at seeing me.

"Jeremy, lad—oh, by the saints, what happened to yous!?"

I shoved past her and into the back hall. She followed me.

"I thought you were with Maeve. Who did this to yous? Jeremy, stop. Let me have you taken to hospital. You've blood everywhere. Let me clean you up. Jeremy!"

I stopped at the door to the pantry and pulled at the top of its frame. I grunted in pain but worked at it and pulled, and it finally came loose.

"What're yous doing? Jeremy, talk to me. Tell me what happened? Let me see if I can find Maeve for yous, here!"

I reached into the slot above the door and found the packet was still there—a felt bag holding the barrel and recoil bits wrapped in greased wax paper. I put the frame back and staggered into the kitchen.

By this time, Mrs. Kieffer was in the sitting room, dialing the phone.

I dropped under the sink and pulled away the fake slat by the water pipe and found it still held the slide and stop, also wrapped in greasy wax paper along with the precision tools I'd need. I staggered to my feet and headed for the stairs. By this point, I was barely noticing the pain.

"Kathleen, is Maeve still in the Hall? Get her to the phone. Jeremy's here and he's terrible hurt. There's blood all over him."

Climbing up to Ma's room was ordeal in itself, but I managed and entered, not bothering to knock. She was under oxygen but still rose, startled, as I went straight to the window and dug under the sill.

She pulled the mask away from her face and snarled in gasps, "What the devil. Do you think. You're doin'?"

I found the groove and pulled at it, and part of the sill dropped down to reveal a hole in the wall. I dipped my hand in the hole and found the last bits—the pistol grip, magazine and sear. I stood and Ma finally saw the blood covering me, then I collapsed on one of the chairs and made myself assemble the Colt, tearing a few strips from the parts of my shirt that weren't bloody to wipe off the grease.

"What's this?" Ma demanded. "Young man, you answer me! What happened? What's all this blood from?"

"Jeremy," Mrs. Kieffer called from downstairs, "Maeve wants to speak with you. Come down. Let Mrs. Kinsella rest."

I snapped the last of the Colt together, tightened the screws and checked the mechanisms.

Ma saw what it was and snarled, "Did you let some bastard Loyalist trash knock you 'round and now you think you'll prove to them what a man you are by shootin' them? Are you that sort of coward? Your father didn't back down when one came at him."

Everything seemed to be in perfect order, even after years of being hidden away.

Maybe I do know how to do things right.

Ma continued, "You—you always were the simple one. The lad with dreams and hopes of. Of leavin' this all behind. Fool who always looked down on us. A Catholic girl wasn't good enough for your like. No, you had to go sniffin' after a girl from the other side. Thinkin' it'd carry you into. Their world. What did it accomplish? If you'd stayed with your own. Eamonn wouldn't be. In The Maze. Ready to starve himself to death. My sister wouldn't be having to. Explain why you were in America without the right papers."

That startled me. I looked at her, frowning or scowling, I couldn't say which.

"She called but an hour ago, tellin' me the FBI's been around, sayin' they knew it was you stayin' there. How could you let that happen?"

I hadn't. It was too quick. Too soon for anyone to have alerted them about me. Someone else had grassed on me or the gossip had burned through to the wrong people or something. I didn't know. At that moment, I didn't care.

Ma's full voice was returning. "Now Rhuari's hidin' from the family an' Kieran's taken your place to fight your fight. It's a shame to me that I bore a son so hateful of everything we stand for. Who didn't care his own father was killed by. By those bastard Orangemen, may God damn then all to hell. BRENDAN, ANSWER ME! What are you doing?!"

The pistol was set and in working order, so I staggered out of the room and down the stairs. Her voice trailed after me.

"Brendan, what are you doing? Come back here! Come back, right this minute! Brendan!"

Mrs. Kieffer was still on the phone and heard me coming, her face a mass of confusion. "Brendan? You're our Brendan?" She turned back to the phone. "Here he is, Maeve." Then she offered it to me but I brushed past her to the settee. I dropped to my knees, grunting in pain, then reached under, pulled off one of the joyces to the leg and found there was still half a box of .45 caliber bullets in its hollowed out center. They rattled in the cardboard.

Mrs. Kieffer gasped, "Oh, by the saints above, Maeve, he has a gun! Brendan, what're yous doin'? What the devil do yous think you're doin'?"

I looked at her, popped the clip, and despite my shaking managed to fill it with bullets and jam it back into the grip. Then I shoved the pistol into my pants, zipped up my jacket and stormed out the door. The last I heard of Mrs. Kieffer, she was crying into the phone, "He's headed 'round the walls, Maeve, an' he's got a loaded gun! He's got death in his eyes!"

She was fucking right about that.

Another Ghost

I half-walked-half-staggered down Lecky. I remembered there were steps past the flyover that would take me up to St. Columba's walk, around to where I could look across the road to see the back of Long Tower and have a stone wall for support. I knew Max, Tam and Billy would still be looking for me. I had only seven shots in the clip—I hadn't slipped one in the chamber—but that would be enough for those three. Especially me old China. Jeremy had shown me well how to fire a pistol and be accurate enough.

The streets were deserted, of course, there being a curfew and plenty of patrols running about, but the fog was like a cloak around me. A shelter. I'd hear the occasional Saracen or jeep approach and have plenty of time to find a place to hold in as it passed, but most of them seemed to keep back in the Bogside and down Cityside. My only real problem was walking.

My adrenalin was abating and every step was turning into pure torture from the shooting pains in my sides and between my legs. My balls were swollen and getting worse, and my briefs seemed only to be rubbing them in ways that caused me agony. I had to force myself to keep moving. Accompanying it all was a deep dull ache in the whole of my back, and with my nose being so brutalized I could breathe only through my mouth, my lungs began to fight for air from the exertion of my strides up the low hill. I began to feel dizzy. I stopped and looked around for a wall to support me as I let my lungs catch up to me and found my stomach threatening to spew whatever was left in it.

I finally noticed my hands shook from the pain and turmoil building up inside. The realization I'd just been snatched off the street, taken to some unknown location and tortured into giving up information, as though I were a criminal well known to all, was finally taking hold. That what I gave them meant nothing to anyone was beside the point. A sense of brutal shame swept over me mixed with a horrible understanding of just how easily it had happened and how powerless I'd been to do anything about it.

And how I'd been treated like nothing but a mad dog.

My mind exploded in a thousand directions as I tried to fight my way back into control. But the pain in my groin and body and face mixed into memories of what had been done to me in Deer Park and I felt madness taking over.

And welcomed it.

If only it would just end the screaming in my heart and head. End the pointless fury filling my soul. Show me a way back to a life I'd once hoped for and dreamed of, away from this diseased circle of hell.

I heard footsteps quick, soft and tender approach in the fog, muted by the thick, swirling mist. I pulled the Colt from my belt. If it was those bastards coming to look for me, what they'd find is a bullet in that thing they called their brain. And chuckled at the thought of it, stepping one bit closer to madness when—

Someone's arms wrapped around me, from behind, holding me tight yet easy and kind and whispered, "Oi, me China," into my right ear. "What's this? What's all this?"

A voice I'd not heard in years.

Thought I'd never hear, again.

Danny.

Danny Gallagher.

Danny fucking Gallagher!?

His arms guided me into a shadowy area, where I twisted around and looked back to see his face. He was smiling, eyes shining as he gently murmured, "Here, me China, what ya doin'?"

One hand shifted down to wrap around mine. The one that held the Colt. Slipped it away from me.

"That really what you want, Bren? Kill and be killed, like has been goin' on for a thousand years?"

I forgot to breathe. I could not find my voice.

It was him. Truly him. Our Danny. Shining and golden.

"Am I dead, Danny?" whispered from me. "You come for me?"

He chuckled. "You always were the daft one, Bren. But stormin' down the middle of a street with a pistol, for all to see? That's mad as a hatter."

I saw my blood was on his forearms. Would that happen, with

a ghost? I tried to speak but he put a finger to my lips and brought out a cloth to dab under my nose as—

Strips of cloth, knotted at one end and shoved into a bottle of petrol to make a firebomb. All through the battle. Beautiful arcs of fire and smoke trailing down off the tops of the Flats as we fought back the peelers and...and...

"They did you some damage," Danny murmured.

I could only nod, loving the coolness of the cloth.

"Do you know where it was?"

As the car drove and drove and me in the trunk...in the boot...as I followed it on my Montesa and seemed drawn by the journey to the very place and...and...

I sort of shrugged. I was finally feeling nothing but a dull ache, so was able to say, in gasps, "City. People. Wall. Caught me. Drove. All over. Left a bit. Right. Left. Burned building. Near Lecky. Smelled. Dead animal? Something. Nothing else. Low. Dark. Silent. No windows. No light. No ceiling. My notepad. Still there. Maybe wallet."

"Good. Good." He nodded, his eyes tender and caring. "They won't get to use that, again."

The cloth whispered across my forehead and it felt so cool and I was so at ease, I said, "Danny...you're my second ghost."

He smiled. An honest smile. First I'd seen from him since forever. "*Second* ghost?"

I tried to smile back. "Joanna...not dead...but..."

He nodded. "I am so sorry about her, Bren," he murmured. "We thought she'd be with you."

I almost laughed. "She was. A while. Now they won't even let me see her."

"I know. But you'll find a way, won't you? You're our Brendan. Our China. You always find a way."

I was near tears. "Danny, what happened with you. I should have been there. Helped you. With Father Devil. Been your real mate and backed you and...and..."

"Shh...shh...you are my best mate. The only one who really was. Who bothered to be. And what more could you have done?"

I sort of shrugged, then almost chuckled. "But you fixed the bastard..."

His smile widened. "Shot his balls off. And his tadger."

"Was it really an own goal that took you?"

He almost answered, but we heard a car approaching. Danny listened then put a finger to his lips. I turned to look in its direction and saw Jimmy Haggerty's father's estate car appear in the mist, lights off. It pulled to a halt beside me.

And out popped Maeve. "Brendan, what the devil d'you think you're doing?! Walkin' in the open with the RUC and army screamin' around?! And holdin' that pistol!?"

I looked down to see the Colt was still gripped by me.

And Danny was gone.

Nothing but shadows, silent and alive in the swirling fog.

She was furious. "What were you gonna do? Shoot up a checkpoint? Now? When we've got the world on our side? You'll hurt everything we're tryin' for and...and..."

She got close enough to have a clear view of my face. She couldn't help but gasp, "Oh, dear God, Bren."

"This. Just what. You can see." And I began to shake. No, quaked from the inside out. Jolting horrific tremors.

She took my arm. "You are in no condition to be anywhere. Not physically or mentally. Let me take you home."

She drew me close then cast a look over my shoulder. From the side of my eye, I think I saw her mouth *thank you*. I started to turn but she held my face and that's when even greater pain rolled in and I groaned. It was sharper. Larger. Down my legs and across my chest, wrapping around my spine and gripping me even tighter than before. I could breathe. Barely. I could stand. Barely. Tears filled my eyes and gasps escaped me mixed with whimpers of grief and confusion and simple physical hurt. At that moment, I didn't care what happened, if I lived or died. I couldn't think or move.

Maeve gently took the pistol from my hand then wrapped an arm around me and whispered, "Come along. It's okay. You'll be all right. I'll see to it that you're all right."

And like a child, I let her lead me over to the car.

Jimmy helped me lie in the back seat, then he returned us home and helped Maeve guide me onto the settee. My head was propped up with pillows as she called into the kitchen, "Mrs. Kieffer, hot water, soap and some rags, please."

She brought them in almost instantly, it seemed, as Maeve sat beside me on a stool.

"You'll need ice, as well," said the old woman and she ran

back into the kitchen.

"Tell me if it hurts too much." Then she washed my face, checking constantly to make sure she wasn't doing more damage than good. One eye was swollen shut, and now the other would not even open. My upper lip felt loose and sharp, so it had probably been split. My breathing was even harder to come by, and my heart was screaming, but every part of me was so throbbing with pain, I could barely pay attention to anything let alone form a word.

Mrs. Haggerty appeared with a towel, saying, "Here's more ice." When had she come in?

Maeve lay the towel over my groin then scooped the frozen cubes on top of my crotch. I groaned then gasped as the cold began to seep through.

"So he is our Brendan." It was herself, whispering. "Dear Jesus, I thought it was but he...you said...he..."

Maeve cast her a sharp glare to shut her up. I almost rose but she pushed me back, whispering, "Whist, whist," as she took another towel, wrapped ice in it and laid it across my nose. I cried out and—

An older man was kneeling by me, checking me with firm yet gentle hands. "He's had broken ribs, before. I think two are dislocated. I'll have to set them." He turned to my nose and smiled. "Look who's back from the dead. Hold still." He stuffed cotton up in my nose and I near screamed from the pain of it. "Hold still, lad! You've a fine nose and we want it back to the way it was. As much as possible. You'll still look like you've done some boxing."

Maeve sat next to him, cutting strips of adhesive and offering up more puffs of cotton. And in moments he'd taped a cone-like cup on my nose to protect it.

Then I realized I was in Kieran's room, on his bed, naked and covered only by a well-placed towel. An ice pack still sat on my crotch. I looked at the doctor, as best I could.

"Leave that there for the night," he said, as if reading my mind. "And use it when the swelling comes back. I'd avoid the Jockeys for a bit and just wander about in your pajamas. I've given you a tetanus shot and penicillin. Your teeth look good except for one canine that's a bit loose; you'll need to see a dentist for that, so no steaks or hard candy till then. I've sewn your lip back together, but you'll need to rebuild your moustache."

He rose and handed Maeve a bottle. "One every six hours for the next three days. Oh, and those pills of his you showed me? Make sure he has them available at all times. He'll know when to use them."

"Thanks, doctor," she said.

"You did well by him, Maeve," he replied. "You should consider becoming a physician."

"I...I'll think about it. Thanks, again."

She saw him out and the next thing I remember was Rhuari at my side. She whispered to him, "He has a few more things in the hutch. Would you bring those?"

Rhuari nodded and slipped out.

"But Kieran..." whispered from me.

"If his majesty comes in, he can sleep in the bloody thing, tonight, or on the divan. You are stayin' in here, where I can keep a better eye on you."

Then she re-set the ice on my groin, saying, "We've already brought most of your things up." Then she headed out as Rhuari came in with the last of my clothing.

"I left your checks in here," he said as he held up two rolls of socks, then added, "Welcome home."

Oh, aye...welcome home. That's when my mind returned to me and I could see the hideous truth of it.

By all rights I should have been dead, just then. Had Maeve not found me, I'd have killed at least one of the bastards then been shot down and broadcast to the world as yet another Irish terrorist out to wreak havoc on the poor soldiers and constables doing naught but their best to protect one and all against the evils of the papist hoards. With a new clearness to my mind, I could now see how futile that would have been, and I could also see how logic and consideration of the consequences hadn't been a part of my existence at that moment. I was a wounded animal, trapped like that cat by those dogs, and I was set to spin into uncontrolled madness to protect myself, even while knowing it would save me from nothing. The lessons I'd learned in Houston had been tossed aside like a mere scrap of paper and I'd planned to do exactly the opposite of Jeremy's counsel. It was stupid. Stupid. And I felt the part of an utter fool for having nearly done it.

But logic had made a tentative return and brought to me the

awareness that it would be best if I slip away. Maybe go to Canada or Australia and keep apart from this evil. It would be better for all concerned. I'm obviously unable to deal with the situation as it currently stands. Soon as I could move, now, I could slip across the border and disappear into the Republic. Live in Dublin or Galway and just work and complete my life quietly and without care and—

The clanging of trash bin lids signaled a warning.

Jesus, here we go. The British army was now on the hunt.

For me.

On the Run

My first thought at hearing the approaching roar of Saracens? They've exhausted their search of Long Tower and are now going to scour the Bogside for this dangerous madman.

It was early morning light, out. The doctor's pills had taken enough effect so I could crawl from the bed and pull on a pair of pajama bottoms and a shirt. My passport was on the table by my tin of pills and the rolls of checks in socks.

And my wallet!

How did that get here? I'd have sworn Max tossed it aside. Of course, the money was gone, but still—

The vehicles screeched to a halt in front of my house. No time for thinking, Brendan. Get away from here.

I grabbed the checks and stuffed them into my jacket pockets and staggered for the stairs. I had no idea where my boots were but hoped I'd find them by the settee.

Maeve bolted from Ma's room, grabbed me by the arm and yanked me back down to it, saying, "You'll never escape them. Come here."

Ma was awake and as angry as ever, but she looked at me and pointed to the wall next to her, whispering, "Under my bed. There's a space."

I didn't hesitate but forced myself to crawl over her and slip down the narrow slot between her bed and the wall to find there was just room enough to crawl into. My back was pressed to the crank of her bed and a spring dug into my hip and I was beginning to hurt, again, but there was a panel of wood that ran the length of the bed, so unless they moved it away from the wall, they'd not see me.

The pistol dropped down on me and I grabbed it off the floor as Maeve snarled, "Don't try it! I removed the bullets."

I heard pounding on the door and Maeve crying, "Hang on,

for God's sake!" as she rushed from the room.

More pounding and the sound of splintering wood and Maeve snarling, "Stop it, you bloody bastards! I'm here to open it!" Hinges creaked and she continued, "I'm filin' a claim for this! Breakin' my door without givin' me the chance to..."

"We have a warrant for Brendan Kinsella," snarled a British voice.

"I don't understand," Maeve cried as several boots stormed in. "Please, be quiet! My mother's ill!"

"Collins, Stanley, you check the back," snapped the British voice. "Worrell, Edwards, you're upstairs."

I heard two men lumber up the staircase and burst into the room. Ma screamed at them, "You bloody animals! I'm sick, in here, and you blunder about like bloody bulls in a shop! What the devil do you think you're doing? I'll file a complaint! This is against the rules of engagement and—"

"Sharrup, ye feckin' 'ag," snapped one of them and I felt my blood boil at the bastard. "Sor, we got not'in' but a sick awl bitch!"

"Worrell, watch your language! Check the other rooms."

"What're you lookin' for?" came Maeve's voice.

"Sit down, sit DOWN!" snapped the British voice. "Now, are you related to a man named Brendan Kinsella?"

"What d'you want with him?"

"Answer me!"

"He's my brother, and what of it?"

"When was the last time you saw him?"

"It's been years! For all I know he's dead!"

"He's been with you at some peace gatherings and—"

"You don't mean Jeremy?"

"Jeremy?"

"Jeremy Landau," Maeve said in her best withering tone. Christ, she sounded so much like Ma at that instant, I thought she'd somehow got out of bed and gone downstairs. "He's an American Jew, NOT Irish, not a part of him."

I wasn't happy about her telling them all of this, after Ma's revelation someone had notified the FBI about me, but it had to be done to handle things, in the moment, and might give me time to get off away from this place and back to being Brennan McGabbhinn.

If I still had access to my duffel bag.

"Nothin' in the back rooms, sir," someone called.

Downstairs I heard, "We found some men's clothes in that hutch." A normal British accent. "It's been made into living quarters, quite illegally."

"I want to see them. You upstairs, come down!"

I heard them clumping down the stairs.

"Those are Mr. Landau's things!" Maeve screamed.

"So where is this *Mr. Landau*?" snarled the British voice.

"He's on the evenin' bus for Galway and Cliffs of Moher and—"

"'Merican labels on 'em, sor."

"Did you find anything else?"

"This empty rucksack, nothing else. The bed in the hutch has been slept in."

"I just haven't made it," snapped Maeve. "Sheets still need washin' and—"

"Sit down!"

"But these are Mr. Landau's things!"

"Why is he staying with you?"

"My mother's sister lives in Houston. He knows her oldest son. He's put up with us while here and—"

"Nothin' more, sor," came a new voice.

"Big sack's got 'is dainties," another snarled. Meaning my duffel bag with briefs, socks and under shirts.

"What about the upstairs?"

"Washroom's cl'ar. All rohms chicked awt. Nair a sigh o' 'im."

"Maeve, are you all right?" It was Mrs. Haggerty's voice.

"Keep outside," snapped the British voice.

"I'm a friend of the family, and I'll come in if I please!" Mrs. Haggerty snapped right back at him.

Then Mrs. Fitzgerald's voice cried, "We're watchin' yous!"

"I got a Polaroid!" cried another woman. Mrs. Carson?

"This is a sick lady's home, God love her!" *That* was Mrs. Kieffer.

I have to say, I never thought I'd be happy for the day a bunch of old hens would come pecking about in someone else's business, but they changed the tenor of British voice's snarls.

He gave a great sigh and said, "Leave all that. Outside. Miss Kinsella, I'm going to check on the information you gave me."

"Do it," snapped Maeve. "And if you *do* find my brother in this country, you bring him to me and I'll show you what true punishment is. His mother's upstairs, dyin' of the cancer, puttin' up with bloody animals like you stormin' through her house for no good reason and he's off hidin' somewheres? He can't come see her? You bring him to me and he'll find more than the back of my hand to his face, he will!"

Her voice headed outside and other women's voices chimed in with catcalls and rude comments, even after I heard their Saracens start up and drive away. The hens had pecked the British Lion to near death, it seemed, and I nearly lost myself and laughed about it.

The voices lowered to self-congratulatory laughter and murmurs so I began the slow, painful process of slipping out from under the bed. First, I peeked up over the side to find Ma looking at me in question. "Brendan, what is this about?"

I forced myself to climb out and over Ma, asking, "Was that crawl space worked up for Kieran?"

Ma hesitated then shook her head. "The...the one who had this bed before me. She has...had sons. Wanted." Then her eyes flared. "Sons who came to see her, no matter the danger."

"I'm sure *she* welcomed them," I snarled back.

Then Maeve came up the stairs, dressed in her robe.

"Did ya hear it?" she said, and never had she sounded more proud.

"Every word," I replied, out of breath. "You're a wonder."

"Just because I want the war to end doesn't mean I can't handle the bastards in the meantime."

"Brendan Kinsella, you tell me what this is about!" Ma's voice was tight with anger.

My face was showing serious bruises, now, so I looked straight at her, pointed to them and my nose, and said, "What you see. Here. Is me...*interrogated* by three constables. Last night. They want to know who helped Danny plant that bomb. They knew Danny's name; they know I know the other."

"What makes them think you know?" Maeve asked.

"They know I was there," I said, still looking at Ma. "You know full well they know, don't ya, Ma? Isn't that why they arrested you and Rhuari, after? Trying to locate me?"

Ma looked at me as if she didn't know me.

Maeve asked me, "If they're still lookin' for you, then they're still lookin' for that name. Right?"

I nodded.

Ma finally turned away. "Maeve, I—I'm after some lemon water and I need a Percocet."

"Aye, Ma," she murmured, almost absent. I only heard her leave because my eyes were still focused on Ma.

Who would not look at me.

She fucking would not look at me.

A grin crosses my lips, and I know it looked cruel. It was aided and abetted by the return of all that growling pain.

"Maeve's story has enough truth in it to keep them confused for a day or two, but they will return. It's best I leave, soon as I can."

She seemed not to hear me. I finally left the room and met Maeve as she came back up with water for Ma's medication.

"Get word to Colm," I said. "I need to meet him, again."

"Bren—"

"He'll know where. Tell him it has to be now."

"No! You're in no condition to go anywhere."

"I could cross the border. Heal there like I—"

"You'd never make it. I'm hearin' the border's tighter than it's ever been."

"They'll come back—"

"And you won't be here. Mrs. Lowe's still got that extra bed. We'll move you there, shortly. Them checkin' the busses will take time, with the demonstrations and near riots goin' on, and the information'll still have to go through their channels. Stay with herself, through tomorrow or the next day, then we'll move you to another place. You need time to heal. Time for Kieran to get word to Colm, and him to let us know if he can even meet you, let alone when or where."

I leaned against the wall, weak and beginning to shiver. My awkward movements were catching up to me...and the dull ache I'd managed, thanks to the pills, was getting sharper. I knew every word Maeve had said was far too true to ignore, any longer. So I nodded.

"You know this world better than I," I said. "I'll take your word for it."

Her eyes welled with tears. "It's never going to end, is it?

This war'll take the lot of you."

I could say nothing to that but return to bed. I felt weak and my hands were shaking, again. Whether I liked it or not, she was right; were I to fall faint out in the open, I'd be snatched up in no time and unable to do a thing to stop them dragging information from me. So all I could do was wait and see what would happen.

Which I did for the next week. At Mrs. Lowe's for two days.

Then came a couple days with Mrs. Haggerty. Got to know Aura's wains—Daria and Liam—and have a conversation or two with Jimmy.

Then I was with a family named Lynch.

Then...early in the morning of the 5th of May...Bobby Sands died.

And as expected, the North exploded into flame.

Return to the Past of Today

I moved back to Ma's home. As they'd already searched there, twice, now, seeking a lad from a case eight years old, I was fair certain I'd be low on the list of importance. For the moment. I still kept to my old room, listening to the news grow more and more hideous. People burned out of house in the Ardoyne. Murders on both sides of the divide. Soldiers and constables killed. Bombings. Protests and riots and the drifting stench of charred wood and CS gas in the air. Gunshots and screams of anger and pain and sirens wailing. It was the seventh ring of hell.

I hoped Madame Thatcher was pleased with the bloodshed she'd ordered, and the Protestant class with choosing to destroy their world rather than share it.

Then Francis Hughes died, and it grew to near insanity.

I felt completely useless and so bloody depressed, there were hours I'd little more than look out the window at passing clouds or gleaming stars, not daring to let a thought enter my head.

My duffel bag had been well-rifled, but the inside pocket was untouched. So that was good. I could, for a bit, become Brennan McGabbhinn to get across the border. I'd already removed my goatee, so I cut off just the red highlights still in my hair, letting the mass of curls keep growing, and that would be close to my photo in it.

Kieran slept in the hutch, and judging from the smoke drifting from its exhaust pipe he'd worked out how to use the heater. Maeve brought my meals up as she tended to Ma, who said not another word to me. Not that I cared. Her ramblings were now filled more with anger at everything in her life, myself included, while I could make no sense of what she was saying. She'd start a sentence about her Eamonn, then eight words in it's about our Eamonn in the Maze, then five words along it's about her hateful brothers and then the housing authority and Sister Luke and a full word salad of disconnected thoughts, words and meaning.

The fact is, further investigation into who my family was seemed ridiculous, just then, for there was nothing I could face thinking about. The one positive was that I had...with the exception of an occasional twinge...pretty much healed.

Finally, Kieran brought word that Colm would meet me.

"He said not to cross at Groarty but there's another spot you should be able to," he told me. "He said you'd know it."

I nodded, even though I really wasn't sure.

Then he said, "I'll go with you."

"No," shot out of me. "One man might make it, all right. Two? The paras would notice, and I'm hearing too much about shoot to kill orders going out."

"But are *you* well enough to make it?" he snapped.

I almost laughed. "Do you care?"

For the first time since he'd been around me, I caught a whiff of hesitation in him. "Colm...he'll hold me responsible if you don't show."

I had to roll my eyes at that. "He's not that much a fool. Would you draw me a bath?"

"Bren..."

"Dammit, Kieran, you need to be here for Ma!" I took in a deep breath to steady myself then added, "Lately, you're the only one can get her to eat or...or take her medicine. Pills for the pain. If you get snatched, you think she'll do it for me?"

Another hesitation, then he glanced down the hall at the door to her room. It was closed. For the first time, I saw fear in his face, and his voice close to broken. "Some-some-sometimes even I can't. It's like she wants the hurt. Welcomes it. Thinks she deserves it, and won't let me do a thing for her till-till it's too much for her and she starts to weep and she-she-she still smiles through it. Christ, Bren..."

He was shaking, and I finally realized he was far more aware than I'd given him credit for. That he understood she'd soon be gone. I felt ashamed of my attitude towards him.

"Kieran, she's just afraid of becoming addicted," I softly murmured. "To the pain pills."

He looked at me, incredulous. "What? Does she think the need for them will follow her into the next world?"

"With Ma? Who can say?"

He huffed a near chuckle. "Right. Right. I-I'll get the bath started. How's it to be?"

"Hot, please."

"As you wish, *madame*."

"Aw, bugger off."

He winked and slipped from the room.

Well...I might have regained my brother.

Once bathed, I still needed to move careful to fully dress, but I was mobile, again. While in the tub, I removed the plaster and cone from my nose. It hurt like a bastard but it wouldn't do for me to be out looking like that. The bruising was near gone, but my eye was still on the purple and yellow side. Couldn't be helped. I arranged my hair as best I could to partly hide it and put on my NASA cap to hold it in place, giving me at least a little bit of cover for it.

As it began to finally grow dark, Maeve fed me a massive fry-up. "It'll keep you all night, if need be," she said, her voice deliberate in its evenness. Kieran was there and fed, as well, his eyes never leaving me. He seemed caught between nervousness and uncertainty.

When it was finally dark, I was about to head out the front door but Kieran stopped me.

"This way," he said, and led me into the back yard. "Over the fence."

"That's into the Donnelly's..."

"Herself is expecting you. Colm thinks they may have men hidden about, watching for you, so over and out."

"They don't watch for you?"

"I'm not public enemy number one, am I?"

He offered me a leg up, so I took it, carefully straddled the fence so my balls were protected and smiled at Kieran.

"You're the lad," I said.

As I was about to shift off the fence, he stopped me with, "Bren." I looked down at him. "The other night, I saw Rhuari. Told him what you'd done. Almost did. He wasn't surprised, not a bit. Told me how you fought back the peelers when they stormed our house. Up Nailors. How you-you protected Mairead and Maeve and him and me and...and I didn't remember it. Didn't really know of it. Why didn't anyone tell me? Why didn't *you* ever tell me this?"

"I'm surprised the old cows didn't fill you in."

"People weren't speaking of you, at all. Like you were dead."

I almost laughed. "I guess that made me one of those *And enough said about him* sorts."

Kieran gave me half a shrug.

I shook my head. "That's why I never said much to anyone. The less people know about you, the less they can hurt you with it."

He nodded and looked away. "It's well past ten. Dark as it's gonna get. Colm said he's there after one."

"He'd be better to wait till two. I can't exactly leg it, can I?"

I dropped off the fence...and barely kept from crying out in pain at the sudden jolt.

Mrs. Donnelly saw me through her kitchen window, opened her rear door and turned away. I crept through without a word, passing her husband as he focused on the telly.

I kept to the side lanes and back ways leading to Groarty Road. Sometimes I'd hear a PIG or a Saracen roar close but they never came within sight. The sky was a cloudless chill, but the choppers were few and far between. Apparently, since Raymon McCreesh and Patsy O'Hara were fading towards death in the name of Mother Ireland, while the bitch, Thatcher, dismissed them as if they were little more than vermin to be exterminated—well, no one wanted to waste resources on chasing a ghost until they had to. And Maeve's story, backed up by her neighbors, had given them an excuse to pause. I truly think that's the only reason I was able to slip away and make it clear to the border without being found out.

Why Colm thought I knew of another spot in this area to cross at was beyond my knowledge. I'd only ever taken the Groarty route there and come back at the Buncrana Road crossing.

Still, I cut down Maple to a gate, slipped past it and aimed straight across rolling green fields to the border. Had to keep a watch for cow manure and puddles of God knows what muck, but I reached a thicket of trees and a small brook. I jumped across, landing half in mud that nearly sucked off my boot, but still managed to scramble up the side even though it tore at my aching ribs and added to the vicious pain in my sides. I had to sit in a bush and not move for ten minutes before everything stopped hurting enough for me to rise, again, then I crept across the meadow to the nearest fence. I crawled over it to this narrow, muddy, rutted lane, held for a bit to catch my breath and headed straight up the road.

Now the moon was out in full so there was more light than I wished for, but it mattered not. I was in The Republic, and none of the bastards tightening their grip on Derry could get to me— not legally, anyhow. Sure they could always just jump the border and grab me, have me down in The Maze before anyone knew better. But I figured I'd make it a hell of a time for them if they tried, and it would be ten times worse if Paras were caught on this side of the border.

I reached the Irish side of Groarty and turned to my right, heading down to the side road I'd gone up the last time I came. The stars were out in full...as full as they could be in the minimal darkness...but I still welcomed them. My companions, always.

I had to stop more than once as I walked, but it mattered little. If I knew Colm, he'd have someone watching for me to give him the signal I'd made it. And darkness would be at its apex when he arrived.

I hoped that's how it would work. I wanted to be there before him. I wanted to see how he came up—if by car or by foot or any other mode of transportation. If he came alone or had more with him. And if more were with him, if he'd approach me on his own or have his *backup right there*, as the phrase goes. Considering how I greeted him, the last time, I'd make no complaint, no matter how it worked.

The simple act of walking was hell on my side and groin, thanks to the up and down of the road. I stumbled a few times but never actually fell, despite my headlong push, and soon my adrenalin was up so that I didn't really feel the pain.

The shrubs along here were wilder than before, the grass more evident. I saw homes that seemed recently erected, but no lights inside and—

I looked around and saw it was a playground and there were houses close by, all their windows dark and—

I stopped to lean against a post, my breath short less from exertion than memory...though I had just topped a slow rise in the road. I looked to my left and could just make out the hump of the hill against the starlit sky. Black and cold and solid, with a small round extension to it, the hint of moonlight caressing it.

I worked my way through the shrubs and over the wire fence

mingled in them, and started across an open field towards the hill. In the back of my mind I'd come to the determination it was close to three-hundred meters up...well over 900 feet and—

Joanna stopped to take in the view, her breath quick and sharp against the biting cold—

And she took my hand.

She was walking with me. Trudging across the fields and closer and closer to the summit, her face whole and pure, and her smile as sweet and gentle, as always. She was my guide, and I trusted no one but her as she was and...

And then I was there. That weak iron grate lay across the low entrance. I pulled it away, slipped inside and, despite my shaky legs, quickly climbed to the top tier and looked out over the dark, cold land.

The distant slivers of water were silvery blue, as before. Gleaming alive and indifferent under the moonlight and tender clouds. The plots of land carved into a patchwork of farms spread below, their differences barely visible. The silence was elegant. The wind nipped at my cheeks and my breath danced away from me as if nervous about it all. Even jammed into my jacket, my hands were cold and my feet were near frozen but my ribs and balls barely ached. I wished I could stay here forever, and I thought, *Joanna would love to have seen this, again.*

This was how life should be lived—free and open and happy and unfettered by hate or anger or histories cloaked in self-righteousness. The world I saw here cared nothing for our petty human squabbles; it merely fulfilled its meaning in ways no man could ever even begin to understand. I'd tasted this truth on my walk to Claudy so many years earlier and was reminded of it on every walk home from *The Colonel's* in the dead of night. This made it true, full and complete. I wanted never to leave.

I have no idea how long I was there before I caught the shine of a car's headlights down the hill and leaned atop the wall to watch them peek around the hillocks and shrubs as the vehicle approached. Then the lights were gone, but I could still hear the car's engine...and it was a car, not a truck—or lorry, if you prefer, now. It stopped down the lane that led from the road to the fort and I heard a car door slam—and then just barely heard another close.

Colm was not alone.

I took my hands from my pockets and slipped them into my coat and under my arms, to warm them better. I'd not have him greet me and me having icy fingers, whether he wore gloves or not. Then I saw him stride up the path, and even in his parka he looked trim and casual. How had I not noticed that the last time?

Because he'd surprised you, from behind. Come up wary, and for good reason. Now he's trusting you...as much as he can.

I waved to show him I was here. He returned it and slipped out of sight under the fort. Moments later, he was climbing up to me.

"Bren," he said, offering his hand, no glove.

I took it like old friends do and smiled. "Colm, thanks for coming."

"No fist this time, eh?"

"I was an idiot."

"Can't say it's all on you." He put his glove back on his hand as he looked about. "Y'know, I hadn't been up here in years, till the other day. Not since I found the pack of yous paralytic on pot and whiskey. God, the memories. Good times."

I nodded, recalling me lying flat on the ground laughing at the stars and Danny having the last true smile I ever saw on him.

Colm waited for me to speak, but first I had to return to now, so I had nothing to say just then.

He finally took in a deep breath and said, "I've heard—the story is, you were interrogated."

Still I said nothing, just looked out over the silvery daggers of the distant lough. Apparently, I would have to prove myself to his people, as well.

"In a hidden place," he continued.

The baton slammed up between my legs and Tam punched me on the ground and I wept and...and—

I bolted to walk the top tier. Around I went, hands back under my arms, my eyes solely on the uneven rocks packed into the wall. I strode fast and didn't stop till I neared Colm, again. I did not look at him; didn't need to. I just nodded.

"What did they want to know?"

My voice was a whisper. "Who was helping Danny. That day."

"What'd you tell them?"

"Don't you already know?"

"The stories I hear are conflicted."

I turned my eyes on the daggers of the lough and whispered, "I told them all I could see was—was—"

The flames danced, danced up to Joanna and she struggled to escape them but they laughed at her and whispered closer and closer and her golden hair whipped about in the smoke and fire and someone was screaming and—

I must have spoken some of the memory because Colm's voice shook a bit. "Christ, Bren, I didn't realize you actually saw all of that. We just thought the bomb'd sent you off your head and—"

My voice had no emotion. "There was a child's leg in front of me. Did you notice that? Still had its shoe and sock on. I think it was a girl's, but it might have been a boy. I don't remember one way or the other."

He was silent for a respectful moment. "Bren..."

"I said nothing about you," I murmured. "I told them—all I could see was—was—"

The leg flew through the air and whipped blood against me as it landed on the pavement and then the smoke parted and—

Colm gripped my shoulder and I realized I was close to toppling over, again. I hadn't been so raw since those first days at Aunt Mari's. He leaned me against the wall, his voice cool and calm.

"The peelers're claimin' they know who else was there but are bein' cagey with it. Their actions suggest they're lyin'. They aren't seekin' me. Anyone specific, really. None of our grasses have heard question one, other than the usual shite. They just keep hopin' to stampede our side into makin' a stupid move."

I nodded. "Even Billy thought I was telling the truth."

"Billy Corrie?" I nodded. "He helped them torture you!?"

"He never laid a finger on me. It was one named Max..."

"Harris. Yeah, he's a right bastard."

"Maeve should've let me end him." My words snapped out like angry flashes of a whip.

"You'd never have got near him. Still..."

I looked at him, confused. "*Still*? What d'you mean?"

He pulled off his parka's hood and looked straight at me, and his eyes were black as coal. "If you'd died, the autopsy would have revealed what happened to you. And we could've used that, now, against the bloody bastard. You're not the first he's done this to. Add it to the lads dyin' and Thatcher's stupid commentaries and the one shot dead by a plastic bullet, the world would have joined us in condemnin' the Brits and the Prods and—"

I laughed at him, startling him into silence. "You think the world fucking cares? You think anybody gives a tinker's damn what happens to a group of Paddies in a place nobody even knows? Fucking shite, Colm, I give you more credit than that!"

If my words angered him or shocked him or upset him in any way, I couldn't tell. He just looked out over the vista to murmur, "You think we're tossin' our lives away over nothin'?"

"I...I think you're too optimistic about what the world will do, over this situation. Any situation like this."

He nodded. Stayed silent a bit longer.

"Bren," he whispered, finally, "your words about people and their actions...or lack of them...they may ring true, but not for all men. Many hate and care about nought but themselves, but so do many the opposite. And to believe in that...to believe that one *can* believe in somethin'...is not naïve. It's human and so much more important than anything else you can imagine."

I rolled my eyes. "You sound like Father Jack."

"He's a good man."

"Does he not mind you killing people?"

It took him a moment to answer. "He understands that ours are surgical strikes aimed at hate in a way that gains people's notice. There are some on our side who've gone too far and now kill for the sake of killin'. For the pleasure of it. Them we stop."

I shook my head, understanding. "So it wasn't an own goal that got Danny."

He snapped around to glare at me. "I don't know that and neither do you! And trust me when I tell you, that is not my way. Nor any of mine." But the sharpness in his words betrayed him.

So Danny had been killed by his own because his anger had overcome his humanity and that was the only way to truly stop him.

The knowledge was not a surprise to me, but I actually sagged a bit, in sorrow. It was naught but a ghost I'd seen the other night. My own inner voice taking form in a way that would stop me on the path to destruction. A wounded creature's imaginings brought forth merely to keep it alive. Of course. Somewhere, deep within, I'd seen the futility of what I was trying to do and stopped myself.

Didn't know I was that clever.

Colm's voice grew almost tender as he said, "Now you must keep in mind...it wasn't the sons and fathers and brothers of those men who hurt you; it was the bastards, themselves, who laid hands on you. They're the animals you refer to and, like rabid dogs, I agree they should be put down to end their sickness, and to show others there will be consequences for such vile actions. I'm glad me China didn't go wrong."

I had to smile. "To be honest, it was not for want of trying."

He patted me on the back. "You off to the states, once your Ma's...your Ma's settled?"

I shook my head. "They'll never let me back in. I'm stuck here or the Republic. Maybe I should stay here..."

"I could look into that. We have places..."

I sighed. "No. Ma's near gone. I'll not abandon her, now. Not like others have done."

He nodded. "I can send some scratch your way..."

"I'm fine for that."

He chuckled. "You would be. Maybe I should ask you to handle our finances. You could convince a penny it's a pound," he said. He was silent for a long moment before adding, "Brendan...why did you ask to meet with me, again?"

"I don't know." And I honestly didn't. It seemed to be the thing that needed doing but I couldn't remember why. Had I thought of asking to join with PIRA, through him? Had I changed my mind? Or was it simply...

"It's just...when my mother's gone, I'm gone. Never returning. But I'm remembering...Jackie asked if I would tell our stories to people. Keep their thoughts aware of us. Raise money for us. I didn't really understand what he meant...except to just tell people what's happening in a part of the world no one cares about. But it's more than that, now. It's...it's to keep us alive in a world that barely knows we exist."

I looked at him. "Me Da used to tell stories, before drink took him. Told them well. I've heard him."

He nodded. He knew. From Father Jack, most likely...but maybe from Eamonn. Who could tell?

I continued with, "What's happening here is horrible. It's

dogs fighting over a bone tossed our way by those who've stripped the meat from it. They take from us then laugh at us for being taken, and that needs to be told. But done in a way that people will listen and think, and not merely sigh and shake their heads and say, *Oh, how awful*, then go about their business. It needs to be told in a way that will involve them. That's what I will try to do."

Colm seemed confused by my little speech. "But how would that help? How would you even begin?"

I shrugged. "I haven't worked out the details, yet, but you know me. Once I start trying to fix something, I don't stop until it's done."

"True, that." He sighed.

"I'll just need a way to contact you, as I go."

He turned away from me, nodding. "I can look into that."

"No hurry. Maeve will always know where I am. Even if it's Shanghai or Buenos Aires. I've a mate who knows Chinese. Maybe I'll learn some to speak with him. Or Spanish." I laughed. "The world is my marlie, now."

"What?" he laughed. "Jesus, but you're a daft one, Kinsella."

"As many have said."

He removed his glove and patted my now frozen cheek. I smiled at him. Not another word passed between us as he put back his glove, pulled up his hood and danced down the steps to cross the courtyard and vanish into the night. Out of respect, I sat where I was till he'd been gone ten minutes. Then I slowly, painfully made my way back to Derry, intending to plan, think, and put into practice what I'd said I would do.

But reality had her own ideas about that.

The next night, Maeve came running to my room. Ma was in serious distress and had need of a doctor. She'd tried to call for an ambulance but none could come with any speed. I rushed over to Mrs. Haggerty's and returned with her to find Ma was breathing rough murmurs of pain and her hands were catching at the air. Her eyes focused on nothing.

As Mrs. Haggerty soothed Ma's ramblings and murmurs, Jimmy brought up his father's estate car. Maeve covered the back with pillows and cushions from the couch then I carried Ma downstairs, her breath harsher and her eyes more glazed. She weighed nothing, fortunately for my injuries, and said even less, her eyes locked on me with an expression I couldn't tell was hate, fear, love or confusion. The harsh scent of urine whispered then Maeve said, "Bren wait, the catheter's come out."

"You going to put it in, now?" I shot back as, with Jimmy's help, we settled her into the back. Maeve stayed with her and I climbed in the passenger seat. Kieran had already alerted our side, so their lads waved us past. But not three blocks later we hit a Brit checkpoint and had to stop.

"Lights off! Lights off!"

Four Paras, two with rifles cocked and each with an attitude on his sleeve, inched up to Jimmy's door. This big doughy bastard with ginger hair with a thick Burr snapped, "Papers," at Jimmy.

He handed them over, then Ginger glared at me. "And yours."

I handed him my Jeremy passport. He glanced at them all.

"Where ye off t'?"

"Altnagelvin," Jimmy said. "This woman needs urgent care."

A black Para looked in the back to see Ma wheezing and Maeve comforting her. "Ol' lady back 'ere, sir," he snotted in some Eastender dialect.

Ginger looked in and said, "Search 'em all."

I near exploded. "You out of your goddamn mind?! This woman's old and sick and—"

The third Para yanked open my door and dragged me out. He slung me against a nearby wall. More Paras joined him, each as ready to use his weapon on me as the next. "Against the wall! Spread your legs! Do it. DO IT! NOW!"

I did it. And they rough-handed me in every way they could, just daring me to try something so they could claim another IRA terrorist killed. It took everything I had in me to keep from crying out with pain when they slammed into some still tender areas. Then I looked to my right and saw Jimmy in the same position. Blood coursed down his face and he had this look of shock to him. Beyond him, I noticed someone peek out a window and pop back in their home.

Behind me, I heard Maeve begging, "Please, can't you see she's ill. We can't get a doctor here. We just want to take her to hospital. Please, hurry. No, you can't move her!"

"Shut the fek up," and it was Ginger's voice saying it.

I heard Ma whimper, aloud, and Maeve scream, "Careful!" And to my shock, I had to dig my fingers into the bricks of the building to keep from exploding into a rage that would've got us all killed.

"They're clear, sir." This time it was the black Para talking, referring to Jimmy and myself. Then I glanced about and noticed more people gathering at doorways and advancing on the checkpoint, like the forms of demons drawing near in the bare morning light. The Paras began to look nervous.

I heard another man approach and say, "Ross, what the devil's going on, here?" His voice was more educated, more aware than the others'.

Ginger answered, "Just a search, sir. These Paddies—"

"Why is this woman on the ground?"

"Please, sir, it's my mother," said Maeve, all but crying. "She's got the cancer and she's having difficulties and we're tryin' to get her to hospital."

"Sir, Paddies use all sorts of ruses to sneak weapons past and—"

"And have you found any?"

"No, sir."

"Then help put this woman back in the car and let these people get on their way, before you get another incident started." I heard him approach me and stop. "Whose passport is this?"

"One on th' left, sir."

He approached me and said, "You may stand down."

I pushed myself away from the wall and turned to face him. He was a captain, young as me and taller, his hair sandy, face freckled and eyes clear, and he seemed genuinely perturbed.

"Is your name Jeremy Landau?"

I shifted into my best imitation of Uncle Sean and said, "It sure is. And I want to talk to someone in the American Consulate."

"You'll need to ring Belfast for that. Why is there blood on your passport?"

"This ain't my first time at a checkpoint."

That brought a sharp glance from him. "Do you know these people?"

I hesitated, trying to figure out some story to tell, then Jimmy jumped in with, "He's lodgin' with us, sir. Friend of my aunt's, in Houston. She asked us—"

"Be quiet." His eyes never left mine. "You were about to say?"

"It's for school. I'm doin' my Master's in warfare and Aunt Mari—" Oh, shite, I couldn't refer to her as that! "Well, she's like my aunt, we're so close. Ever since my momma died."

"But you've been here for some time—"

"I stayed in Burt for a bit, to look at that ring fort. Uh...Gy-anana an Ail-leek?" I deliberately mangled the name.

"You've no entry or exit stamp to the Republic."

Jimmy piped in, "Should be, sir. I took him over and he caught the bus back."

"Well, from Gal-way," I said. "I took a couple days down there to see the Cliffs of Moher."

"All ready, sir." It was Ginger, again. I glared at him and he glared right back. The Captain waved him off.

"Landau—that's a French name, isn't it?"

What the hell? "Jewish."

"Why would a Jew want to know about *The Troubles* here?"

I snarled a smile. "You been to Israel, lately? Comparin' the two makes for interestin' conversations."

He smiled back and nodded. "I've no doubt." He looked at

Jimmy. "Are you able to drive? I can have a corpsman tend to you."

"I can drive," I said. "I lived in Hong Kong for a while."

Captain saw the entry and exit stamps for the place and nodded. "Ross, you know where Altnagelvin is, right?"

"Yes, sir."

"You and a couple of men lead them there, post haste. I apologize for the difficulties, gentlemen, but times being as they are, one must take all precautions."

He returned my passport to me. I hit over to the driver's side and Jimmy made his way into the passenger side. A jeep pulled out in front of us and we followed it towards the Craigavon Bridge.

As we drove, Jimmy leaned back and whispered to me, "He don't believe you, the Captain. That's why we got an escort."

To be honest, I hadn't given it a moment's consideration till that moment, but deep within I knew he was right. So I nodded.

"Is your passport stolen?" he continued.

"*Borrowed.*" Jimmy cast me an eye, just as we whipped onto the bridge. I noticed the Gallaher's Cigarettes sign was gone, and I thought of all the Blues I'd smoked. Guess I'd be going back to them.

Jimmy sighed. "Then he'll contact your state department for verification. Does this Landau fella look at all like you?"

"Almost twins...if I gained a foot, maybe."

"Shite. When we're at hospital, call Siobhan." He dipped a bit of paper in his own blood and wrote the number on the back of my left hand. "She's me cousin. Tell her all that's happened."

"I'm sorry for this, Jimmy."

"Sorry for what? I thought you were who you claimed. I'd not seen this Jeremy lad, before."

"Won't matter."

"Yes, it will. I've relatives in Newcastle. Siobhan's to call them if I'm snatched, and they're to call their solicitor, and he's brother to a member of Parliament. I won't be much troubled."

"You'll beat the Brits at their own game, you will."

"It's nice to think so," he sighed then added, "but you..."

I nodded and we said not another word till we rolled up to A&E.

Nurses and doctors swarmed out to meet us. Seemed the

Captain had rung ahead to inform them. They took Ma over and carted her to Urgent Care along with Maeve while I called Jimmy's cousin then stayed with him to see he was tended to. He needed but three sutures to close the wound. An hour later, a bright happy lass named Kelly was dropped off from out of nowhere to see Jimmy got home well enough.

Jimmy was hesitant to leave me and Maeve. "We can wait."

"No, Jimmy. Go. We'll grab a taxi once Ma's settled in."

Kelly nudged his arm and nodded at me. I don't recall her saying word one in my direction. She led Jimmy away...and I was left alone.

And I luxuriated in it.

I noticed it was now approaching dawn and I was feeling the need of breakfast. I strolled over to the café, had a fry-up and tea, then bought a cheese sandwich for Maeve with an honest lemonade drink and went looking for her.

After five nurses sent me wrong (two of them deliberately, I'm sure), I found Ma and Maeve in a dormitory room, curtains rolled up to hide them. Ma was on oxygen and an IV, with monitors connected to keep track of her heart and other vital signs. I noticed the catheter had been re-established and what fluid was in it was a hideous brown. She looked asleep, her skin drawn even tighter across her face, her mouth open and all her teeth revealed, more dead than living, already. Maeve sat beside her in a hard wood chair.

I brushed her arm with the lemonade bottle and offered her both it and the sandwich. She shook her head, no, then thought better and accepted both. She opened the bottle and sipped some. I waited. She finally rose and led me outside the curtains.

As she opened the sandwich, she said, "Time's come." I only nodded. It was hardly a surprise. "Doctors say she's into renal failure. Soon she'll be in coma...and then..."

Her eyes filled with tears and her voice whispered into silence. I held her close.

"Have you made arrangements?" I asked, suddenly realizing I'd never bothered to even wonder about it, before. As if doing so would mean Ma's death would come sooner, and I'd feel guilty about it happening. Silly thing to think, but there it is.

Maeve nodded. "I'll ring Rhuari to come. He can get hold of Father Jack—"

"Don't. The Brits won't let them come over—"

"They will, for this. The British aren't horrible people, Bren—"

"You can say that, after what just happened?"

She pulled back and looked at me, as if I were a stranger. Pulled off a bite of the sandwich and nibbled on it. "I'll be back directly. Thanks for the sammie and drink. And I'll send up a priest."

She wandered off, seeking a phone. I stood there, watching her go, and I noticed this curious absence of feeling within me. Maeve was fighting to keep herself in control as our mother lay dying. A woman who'd been one of the reasons so many years of our lives were hell. A woman who'd sliced anyone to bits if they disagreed with her in any way. A woman who'd brutalized not only me with her words, since I came here, but also Maeve. A woman who'd been more than cruel in her existence. Maeve was devastated that soon she'd be gone from our world. And I felt nothing about it. Not one single solitary emotion.

It was odd, just standing there, unconcerned one way or the other how things went. And I knew when Ma finally did die, there'd be no change in my emotion. Oh, it wasn't a conscious knowing; just the intellectual idea that death was coming and the person it called upon laid no claim to my heart or soul in any way, any longer. My love for the woman...love that lasted even after she'd disowned me...now it was as dead as my Da, now I knew it was lies she'd been feeding us, for years. Lies to hide something our Da had done. Her sole concern had been to help and protect him, even when he was at his worst.

Well, my sole feeling was for the pain Maeve, Mairead, Rhuari, Kieran and Eamonn would feel at her crossing the river into the unknowable world. And I swore to myself I would never let my brothers and sisters know whatever truth I was still able to learn about our Da, so they—

A groan cut into my reverie. I slipped back to Ma's bed to find her awake and looking about. The oxygen mask kept her from being able to speak, so she whimpered and her hands clawed vaguely at the air. I took her right one, so cold and frail, and sat beside her.

"It's all right, Ma. It's Brendan. I'm here."

She didn't look at me. Just said a word over and over and

over. Had Da come for her? I couldn't make it out so leaned closer. Lifted the mask a hair and heard, "Priest. Priest. Priest."

I felt a soft wave of cold filter through me. Death was here but my father was not, and she wanted a chance to make her last confession. I wondered if my sister would send the priest first or call Rhuari.

"Maeve's gone for one," I said, not knowing if Ma could hear me. "She'll be back soon."

She kept saying it. "Priest. Priest. Priest." Over and over, her eyes dancing about the room, her free hand still clawing at the air as if trying to keep death away. She had the look of fear about her. Terror in the quiver of her voice. I think she knew no one would come to absolve her of her sins. Were I to bolt down to the chapel and find one of the holy fathers sitting in a pew waiting for me and drag him back at a full run, I'd not make it in time. The little light in her eyes was already fading. Her voice growing softer. Her hands shaking with fright.

I realized I'd worn my dark blue shirt, so removed my jacket, rolled down my sleeves and buttoned them, buttoned the shirt up to the collar and pulled the neck of my white under-shirt up so it could be seen above it. Then I found Maeve's rosary and took both Ma's hands and kissed them and said in a lowered voice, "I'm here, Mrs. Kinsella."

Her shaking softened. Her eyes shifted to me, still unfocused but aimed at mine. She almost seemed to smile. "Father? Father? I'm dyin', Father." She drew me closer. Her voice a whisper. "Bless me...Father...for I have sinned. It's been...it's been...so many years since...my last confession."

After all those years at mass? Truly?

"God be with you, my child. What do you wish to tell me?"

"I need to...to be rid...hate in my heart, Father. There's so...so much hate in my heart."

"Release it, then," I whispered. I'd no idea if I was doing this right. I hadn't been to confession since I was twelve, and even then it had been a cold affair with Father Jack. Was I supposed to do an act of contrition? Was a Hail Mary sufficient for this? "God will know you have...have cast it aside."

"So much hate, Father. My son...so much hate."

I held my breath. Which son was she referring to? Surely not me?

"Do you hate your own child?"

"Made him. Prisoner. My hate. He's dyin'." Eamonn, preparing to starve himself to death. I was actually relieved. "Make him stop. Please, Father. Make him stop. Not right. But I...I put him there. Not right. Make him stop."

I went cold. Felt my stomach churn. She knew what she'd been pushing Eamonn to do was wrong and I couldn't believe it. My mother admitting to a mistake? What could I say but, "I will."

"Make him stop. See the truth. He's the one...the one...the one most important. Poor little thing. Never wanted to. To be of this world. I made it hell for him...stupid of me...so wrong..."

Fucking hell, or was she talking about...about me? "What did you do to him that's so wrong?" whispered from my heart.

Her hands were slowing and drifting closer to her breast. "Didn't...didn't understand...him. Didn't want him. He knew. And didn't want me. My Eamonn knew. So angry. So hurt. He knew. Poor little thing. So much better than us. And knew he was. He knew. Both of us. We knew. Near cut us apart."

Every word was like the twist of a knife in my chest.

"I loved him. Hated him. Loved him. Never knew him. Nor my Eamonn. Him either. Tell him, father. Please."

"I-I-I'll see to it."

"Promise me, father."

"I...I'm sure he already knows. Sleep well, my child."

She seemed to relax. Took hold of the rosary—no, gripped it and rubbed one of the beads with her thumb and whispered, "Hail Mary...full of grace...the Lord is with thee. Blessed art...art thou amongst women...and blessed is the fruit of...of thy womb, Jesus. Holy Mary, mother of God, pray for us sinners, now...at the hour of our death."

I'd never heard my mother repeat the rosary, before, and the feelings it brought me were terrifying. Anger. Guilt. Sorrow. Love. Shame. Disbelief. And all I could do was just sit there. Watch her hands move slower and slower. Watch her lips whisper lighter and lighter. Let her ease into her sleep as if she were at one with the angels. The rosary was tangled in her fingers when she finally ceased to move. I waited a moment, looking at her. She could have been napping, nothing more. Then I hit the call button for the floor nurse.

A stout woman came floating up to check Ma. "She's into

coma, now," she finally said, and called for a doctor.

Maeve appeared behind her, disbelief on her face. I rose and took her into my arms and held her as she wet my shoulder with her tears.

The priest she'd called for never showed.

Kieran was not to be reached, of course, but Rhuari soon arrived to be with us as we held watch over her slow drift into death. He walked in without a rush, his eyes red from weeping. Father Jack was with him; apparently, it was he who got him through the checkpoints and brought him across the river, and he stayed to administer the full and correct rites.

Ten hours later, she was declared gone.

And I felt the last of my soul go with her.

I walked away from Altnagelvin into a growling darkness. The clouds were low and threatened rain. The wind was soft but still had bite to it. There was a curfew, but my bed was the other side of the Foyle and I'd already done my last vile deed for the day. So I set off walking.

You see, after Father Jack finished Ma's last rites, and as Maeve and Rhuari knelt by her bedside to pray, I took him aside and quietly asked, "When will you visit with Eamonn?"

"I'll see to it he's informed—"

"When?" I snapped, cutting him off. I had no patience for his excessive words.

He eyed me, more than a little irritated. "Immediately, for something like this but—"

"When you see him, tell him his mother said she does not want him to join in the hunger strike."

"I'm not going to tell him—"

Again, I cut him off. "Ma told me as she lay there dying that it was a mistake. That she did not want him to be part of it, and that he should back away."

"Brendan, it is sin to lie about something so vital—"

"I'm not lying," and it was an effort for me to keep my voice low enough so the others couldn't hear. "You will tell him that it is his mother's dying wish that he not do this."

He gave a sharp sigh. "You're concerned over nothing. He's only in the queue. Not even in the top twelve on the list, so—"

"Tell him, anyway." And I forced each word out like a near hiss.

He gave his cool, condescending look then started to move away. "We'll see."

I grabbed him by the arm and said, "Father Jack, do as I say or I will destroy you and everything people believe about you."

And I knew the second part of my threat was all he truly cared about.

He spun on me, furious, and growled, "You have the nerve to say that to me? A man of God who—?"

I nearly spat out, "How's Father Demian doing?"

"What?"

"I hear he was shot. Not killed, merely castrated by a couple bullets. Some would say justice was served."

The look on his face became one of the purest anger. "What does he have to do with this?"

"Right, I should refer to him by Danny Gallagher's pet name, Father Devil. I know what he did to Danny, and God knows how many other lads he could get his hands on."

He barely kept himself in control, his voice a low, vicious growl. "You are referencing something about which you know nothing!" And suddenly I noticed his light brogue was non-existent.

I smiled. "I also hear you were instrumental in getting him transferred to Nottingham. How many lads did he molest there?" The anger in his face shifted to sharp wariness. I went in for the kill. "That's quite a little game you priests have—do something wrong, say *Oops, sorry, I shouldn't have done that*, and all you get is moved to another parish where you can start fresh and new, once again a *man of God* with no one knowing the better till you do wrong, again. It wouldn't take much to reveal Father Devil's evil, and how many times he's been moved, and how neatly the church has kept it hidden. And all because you won't give my brother a message from his dying mother. Is that the right thing to do, *Father* Jack? Where's that milk of human kindness you so love to talk about?"

He stepped back from me. Leaned himself against the wall, for support. Licked his lips a couple of times. He was trying desperately to figure some way around my brutally blunt threats. I kept my focus on him, as hard and cold as I could, but out of the corner of my eye, I noticed Maeve looking at us, a frown on her worn face. She'd be over in a minute and I wanted this settled before she got to us.

Father Jack took in a deep breath and whispered, "What makes you think he'll believe me?"

"Because he wants to, now he knows of his father and of me,"

I snarled back. "And I mean it—if Eamonn joins with the strikers and he dies, I will send your soul to hell on earth. Do you understand me?"

He straightened himself and looked me up and down, his mask back on. Disdain flashed across his eyes. "And to think I thought you the weak one."

I had to laugh at that. "This is how strength operates?"

"What're you on about, Bren?" Maeve had come up behind me.

I gave her my saddest smile and said, "Father Jack's going to convince Eamonn not to join with the hunger strike."

He hesitated then nodded.

Maeve shook her head. "Thanks, Father Jack, but you won't need to, not with two lads dead and the world complainin'."

It took all I had to keep from rolling my eyes at her. Ah, Maeve, still lost in dreams and hopes and prayers. And I felt it only best to let her keep to them.

It's not so hard to take the appearance of a man still willing to believe. A man who'd seen his mother's love and thought we all had it. I'd seen Rhuari's wife with their Angela and hoped all children were cared for as such. Hers was a decent soul, and despite all my wariness of God and the church, I whispered a prayer of thanks that she and he had found each other and hoped that they'd come through this time unscathed—at least, as unscathed as one can in a world gone mad.

I wrapped a hand around Maeve's neck and pulled her to me, forehead to forehead, then I'd bid farewell to the others, given Ma a peck on the forehead and strolled away. Once outside the place, I didn't even look for a taxi but just set off down the road. The little aches and pains I still managed to feel were of no consequence.

The streets this side were clean and neat, the hint of money about them. Not a lot of it, just enough to live like men instead of dogs. It was brutally obvious how much of the *reconstruction* financing London was pouring in would go to this side of the river. Already there were more new homes here, trailing terraces with neat front yards, gabled roofs and multi-paned windows, looking comfortable and warm, meant to house those fleeing the Cityside. More were to be built to replace the neighborhoods torn down in Bogside *for health and humanitarian reasons*...and to disrupt those of the IRA who worked from there. As if roaches couldn't move from one house to the next. I noticed no broken glass or torn up bricks or stones lying in the gutter. If there had been, the council'd have them all swept up. No paper drifted past. In fact, there was nothing to indicate human habitation anywhere I went. No cars moving. No passersby. No lights in the windows. Just silence and the vague hint of burning wood carried on the breeze. It was as if no one lived here, at all.

I strolled along the slow curve of Irish Street, still wondering at my lack of tears over Ma. What she'd said about me, not knowing it was to me, made no sense and my mind simply circled it, in wariness. In fact, I've no recollection of any emotional connection, whatsoever. Nor of any thought. I remember the bare sting of windy gusts on my cheeks. And my hands being warm in my jacket pockets, even though it was barely enough to protect me. And the scent of ale wafting from the courtyard behind a closed pub. And the sound of an army chopper flying past— rushing in the direction of the Bogside, it sounded like, though I didn't look up to see for sure. A flock of birds gushed from one tree to the next, thinking me a predator of theirs as I passed down Fountain, steep and close with houses and finally cars parked by. Turning at Spencer to head for the bridge.

The River is wide at this point but then curls tight until it reaches Lough Foyle. It drifted silent, no boats upon it. No gulls floated past, but then they wouldn't, it being long after their bedtime. An occasional fish would take a happy leap from the water, as if in joy at how for that moment only it was safe to do so and not wind up someone's dinner.

It was odd, crossing the bridge and no cars being on it. Nothing at all. It was odder to see the city center across the bridge and no lights being on save a few on the streets and the glow of bonfires on the far side of the Walls. But that's what happens after a riot; everyone huddles in their homes, curtains drawn against the evil of the night and children put early to bed. Cars locked in their garages and none but the *forces of good* out to protect against those with evil intent. Had the night been clear, I'd have seen to heaven and all her stars for sure. Maybe caught an image of God weeping, in their glistening pinpoints. If he still was capable of tears.

Headed over to Altnegelvin, there'd been a checkpoint at the base of the bridge. Now it was gone, and I did not understand why. Still, this way I'd be back to Bogside within the hour as—

A vehicle roared onto it when I was halfway across, headlights blaring. It aimed straight for me, and I could tell from the sound it was a Saracen. Which meant it had some Brits in it. They'd probably been told by the passing chopper a lone wolf was running wild in the streets, and they'd split away from a hidden group of Paras to take it out before it spread its rabies to the rest of the world. I just smiled and kept walking, a man without a care on God's Earth.

The Saracen screamed to a stop in front of me. Two Paras piled out from the back, rifles at the ready. Another popped out from the passenger door, pistol in hand. All three weapons were trained upon me.

"You," yelled the pistol holder in some Geordie mangle of speech, "'gainst th' side o' th' bridge!"

The paras didn't give me a chance to do a thing; they grabbed me, spun me around and slapped my hands on the railing. Then they rough-handed me in the usual way as I continued my best imitation of Jeremy's twang, "Whoa, whoa, what the hell's goin' on here?" Again, it would never have passed muster in Houston, but for these bastards it was fine enough. And then I heard, "Mr. Landau," and I froze.

It was that bloody little captain's voice.

"Here you go, sir," said Pistol, who I could now see was a sergeant. He'd taken my passport and now offered it over.

I looked around, forced a smile and said, "Hey, there."

"You remember me," said the little fuck. "How kind of you."

"I remember anybody who helps me."

"Perhaps you could help me. We're having some difficulties concerning your passport."

Bugger. "What you mean? You got it, right there."

"Yes, but something about it isn't right." He held it up and shined a torch on it, as if trying to look through it.

"What you talkin' about? It's valid for another two months and I'm headed back in a week and—"

"Oh, no question. But I wanted to double-check something, to make certain I wasn't remembering incorrectly, but I was correct—this passport was issued to a man who's now twenty-seven, and you appear to be five years younger."

"So?"

"So that on top of your foray into the Republic of Ireland for which you have no visible proof you've even been into that country, and the fact that you're staying with a family of known IRA sympathizers, it got me to wondering, why would a Jew want to be anywhere near Northern Ireland?"

"'At's 'cause 'e ain't a Jew, Cap'n," snarled this weasel of a grunt. "They all got names like Stein or Berg or some Jew crap like that."

I let some of my snarl into my voice as I shot at him, "Hey, you got a problem with me bein' Jewish, boy!? I'll file a complaint with the State Department—"

"Stop it." Captain's voice cracked like a whip. I made a show of holding back the rest of my comment. He came over to me, his sneer probably two removes from taking me down to The Strand. I had my eyes drop to the pavement instead of stare back at him. I didn't want to make this too hard for me.

"So, why *are* you here?" he all but snarled.

"I told you, I'm doin' my masters on—"

"Warfare in Northern Ireland. So you said. Which university?"

"Rice. They actually give a damn 'bout the reality of what's goin' on over here, not like U of H who only care 'bout football and oil and—"

I was pushing the chatter, and I think he caught a glimmer of that, for his eyes narrowed just a hint but then his lips fought to widen into a smile. And I relaxed. Maybe he was buying it, for now.

"You came through here some hours ago," he said.

"No kiddin'. I thought I'd get a ride back to the Bogside but..."

"But? Where *are* the people you were with?"

"Back at...at the hospital," I said, barely remembering to use the article like Americans do. "That old lady died."

That made him back up, a bit. "Too bad. But why are you walking?"

"Got no choice. I looked for a cab but couldn't find any, and there ain't been no busses runnin'. So it's shanks' mare."

I got a real glimmer of confusion from Captain at that phrase. *"Shanks' mare?"*

"Walkin'. It's a term my gran'momma used, back in Dallas."

"Texas?" It was the weasel of a para speaking, this time.

Christ! "Yeah," I said back. "You been there?"

"Naw, but I watch the Telly. That bloody JR's a right bastard."

The Captain was casting me a hard eye, still, but it was less certain. Then he smiled. "You know, there's one way to prove you're really Jewish."

"How's that? Want me to quote somethin' from the Talmud?"

He shook his head. "Wylie—arm lock."

The Geordie wrapped an arm around my neck and yanked me back, choking me. I jerked and tried to call out, but I could barely even get a decent breath. Then the Captain grabbed my jeans and pulled at the button.

I kicked at him, not even thinking about what I was doing.

"Get his legs!" he snarled.

Two other Paras each grabbed an ankle and held me in place and the captain yanked my jeans down my hips and pulled down the top of my briefs to show them what they wanted to see. The two paras shined their flashlights on it—

And the Captain jolted and blushed.

And for the first time in my life, I was happy for the problem that took my foreskin.

"Bloody 'ell," said someone, "'e is a fookin' Jew. Bloody 'ell!"

Then they released me. I didn't have to fake shaking, I was so furious at the casual violation they'd just perpetrated. Hell, I couldn't have controlled myself if I'd wanted to. I yanked my briefs and jeans back up and pulled myself back together as the Captain backed away.

"I—I'm so very sorry, Mr. Landau," he said. "This—this makes it rather obvious you're no Irishman. What were you here for, again?"

I tucked in my shirt, and coughed, and said, "I-I-I'm writin' 'bout how—how the conflict here's really 'bout class warfare."

"What shite." It came from the Geordie.

"Very good, sir," said Captain. "It's not safe for you to be out at this time, Mr. Landau. Hop in the back; we'll take you home. Where is it?"

I glared at him. "I don't know the house number, but it's down by those high-rise apartment buildin's. Near Waterloo."

"It'll be easy to find; there's little to that area now."

They led me to the back of the Saracen and *helped me* inside. I wasn't wild about being carted back in it, but I had a feeling the Captain still had his doubts and wanted more verification.

How the hell soldiers can ride in those damned things and still have any sort of decent temper is well beyond the realm of understanding. We bumped over rocks and potholes and gravel and bricks and curbs as if the driver was drunk, and sitting on that hard shelf that claimed to be a seat hurt my arse so badly, I'd have told them anything to make it stop. But stop it did, for they took me straight to Ma's, without even a thought.

We piled out and Captain and his Geordie knocked on the door, but I said, "No, this is that old lady's home. I'm couple doors down."

They marched me straight up to the Haggerty's rang the bell and the Mrs. answered, in her robe. I piped up with, "Hey, there, Mrs. Haggerty, I got a ride and—"

"Be quiet!" Captain snapped. He turned to her and asked, "Do you know who this is?"

For a moment she looked between me and him and I began to think she's about to make a muck of it, but then she huffed and said, "What sort of game're yous playin'? Come in, Mr. Landau. Leave these bastards to themselves. I've tea in the pot, hot and waitin' for you."

"So he is staying here?" said Captain. "Isn't this house a maisonette?"

"And what if it is? Is that any concern of yours? Am I not allowed to offer hospitality to whomever I want?"

He shrugged, but then he gave me a hard look. "So we can contact you here, Mr. Landau? Should we have any further questions?" I shrugged an okay and he saluted. "Sorry to have troubled you, madam." Then he backed over to the Saracen.

Mrs. Haggerty led me in and sat me on the couch, loudly saying, "Stand over here by the fire, sir. Take some of the cold off you," as she glanced upstairs.

Daria appeared on the landing to whisper, "He's still there, Ma."

She nodded. "So, Jeremy, have y' had anything to eat, lad?"

"A sandwich at the hospital," I said, just as loud.

"I'll do you up a fine breakfast, then. Won't be but a moment. Then you'll have to tell me all about your adventure."

"Mrs. Haggerty, I oughta let you know—Mrs. Kinsella died."

She cast a sharp, sudden, pain-filled glance at me. Then she crossed herself and whispered, "God rest her soul, and those of the dead. It's not an easy life she had." She took in a deep breath and murmured, "I'll bring you some tea." Then she headed for the kitchen.

I made a show of sitting in the worn chair before the fire, so the Captain would see me if he glanced in through the window. It was all for naught; I heard the Saracen start up and drive away.

Then Jimmy came down the stairs in his pajamas, the bandage gone, and joined me as Daria scurried into the kitchen.

"There's men outside, watchin' the place. I think they were waitin' for them to arrive before they left."

I nodded. It made sense. I was too much of an anomaly to be let go so easily. They'd now be checking with Washington on my passport, to be certain they weren't about to cause an international incident with my arrest.

"Is there a way out?" I asked. "In back?"

Jimmy shook his head. "You're marked, *Jeremy*."

"Then I need to get a message to Colm O'Faelan. Is there a way for that, without troubling Maeve or Kieran?" He nodded. "Let him know where I am? What's happened?"

"What good'll that do?"

"I've no idea how to get around this. Maybe he has a suggestion."

Jimmy eyed me, wary, then said, "I'm off to university, shortly. I'll do it, then."

"You're a good man, Jimmy."

He smiled and shook his head, in wonder. "You are full of shite."

Then his mother brought in piping hot cups of tea and we sat by the fire, and each of us kept to his own thoughts.

No More Lies

A bit later, I was seated at the kitchen table with Daria while Mrs. Haggerty was out borrowing a couple of eggs; Jimmy had been served the last. The girl, her little brother and mother, Aura, were staying with herself as her father set up a new life in Galway. The three of them in one room. So much like the old houses had been.

"Me Da's on with the university," she told me, proudly. "We're gonna have a house, and a dog. He'll fetch us, soon as it's settled, and Ma may not even need to work."

"Sounds great," I'd said, hoping it was true.

She was handling our morning tea in a very proper manner, I must say. Across from us sat little brother, Liam, fascinated with us to the point of total silence...as was the feral cat at the back door, lapping up his morning milk. Why Mrs. Haggerty gave it to him was beyond me; he was hardly a beauty nor had he a genial temperament. But in truth, I was glad she was doing it; he reminded me too much of that tom nearly caught by that pack of dogs, and perhaps this taste of milk would help him if something similar happened.

"White or dark?" Daria asked with deep seriousness, now the cups were set up.

She was exceedingly pleased I'd stopped pacing to join her. Stopped looking out at the gray morning mist as if I could see anything past the back of the house behind this one. Jimmy had left for university an hour ago, and now it was well after seven. I was desperate for some kind of word. But finally I had to acknowledge my nervousness was achieving nothing...so I forced myself to take a few breaths and join her.

"White, please," I said.

"Milk first or after?"

"After," I replied.

"Sweet?" she continued in the same manner as she poured.

"Lightly so," I smiled.

She put in half a teaspoon. Less than I was used to, but suddenly I was so enjoying the innocence of the moment, I didn't care. It was long past time when the Paras or RUC would normally come busting in to arrest me. They liked to do that by five in the morning, or six, if they felt like sleeping in. All to cause as much disruption as possible. Now it was full light out with no fog, and I was still here, wearing naught but my sturdiest jeans and a flannel shirt, socks on but no boots, and playing homemaker with a girl who so reminded me of Maeve, you'd have thought we'd gone back in time.

Christ, the mornings I'd sat at our table as a boy, quietly letting Maeve feed me tea made from leaves well-used, already, and bites of near-burned bread to act as biscuits. Even after Ma had been done with our porridge and we'd, yet again, had not quite enough to make our bellies happy. How old would I have been? Nine? Ten? And already aware of the limitations of the adults in the world.

I think then's when I got to where I preferred my tea light and on the weak side. More like warm flavored milk. Aunt Mari'd told me she'd tried to give me coffee, the first days I was there, but I wouldn't take it. Then Mai had told her of my preference, so had brought me tea. That, I'd accept from her. Then I would absently hold the cup under my face like it was gold, sipping it, lightly. With that, I would then nibble on bites of toast covered in jam or melted cheese or peanut butter, and that's how I was fed, to start.

"Not enough to keep a sparrow alive," she'd told me, "but it was better than nothing. And as you grew to trust me, I was able to put more on your plate."

"You think I didn't trust you?" I'd asked.

"For want of a better word, Bren. You would shrink away from any who approached you, except Dr. Gilbert. He's the first who got you to drink some tea for us. But then he's always been good with children."

I'd found it funny at the time, me being sixteen and my own man. I thought. I remembered none of it, but it sounded true.

Daria offered me neatly-toasted bread with butter and jam off an unchipped plate—my, but weren't we doing well?—and I took half a piece so she and Liam could enjoy the three left. Then I sipped, and the tea was strong enough to pull out your teeth if it so chose, but a taste of the jam settled it on my tongue. So I said, "Thank you; it's lovely."

It was just us there, right then; Mrs. Haggerty had planned to do a fry-up but had only one egg left, and now I'm sure she was having a quick chat with Mrs. Kelly. I was just hoping I'd be fed before Colm sent word as to what I was to do.

I guess it was time for me to wander off. Get away from the North. And keep wandering. I'd never had much of a plan for my life. Just work and marry and grow some wains of my own and treat them better than Da and Ma had treated us. True, it wasn't a very ambitious goal for myself, but it had pleased me to aim for it. I'd long accepted I was never the type who'd cure cancer or write great books or even stand for office.

When Father Jack had been having his talks with me and reminding me over and over that I was not living up to my potential...that I should strive harder...he'd given no thought to what I wanted. As if it were some duty to become better than I dreamed of being, so as to make him happy. Such ideas made little sense to me and were at odds with the notion of self-determination we all supposedly have. Apparently that was only if you did what those who considered themselves your betters decided you should do. I'd found far too often they were little better than myself.

So my focus had been on my own path, with disregard for the opinions of people like Father Jack, who had assigned me to the little box of weakling and simple and coward. I hadn't cared, for if things had not gone so horribly wrong with Joanna, one day I'd have asked her to marry me. To live with me in a whole new world away from these biting, clawing, vicious beasts who claimed to be men. And I saw nothing wrong with that being all there was to me.

Of course, that was if she'd agreed to do so. She did have ambitions. Once had. Now? Now, I knew nothing of her, for she was no longer an honest part of my dream; more like wishful thinking.

And a pain that would not be salved.

I absently touched the tattoo of her name. Could almost swear I felt it under my sleeve. I'd done nothing like it for Vangie, for fear that would jinx us. And look at what good that did.

I sighed, finally accepting the reality that there is no corner of the world safe from the howling, selfish, mad dogs of self-righteousness. People with dreams like mine were little more than meat for them to gnaw upon and feed to the just-as-vicious young they were breeding and—

Pounding on the door jolted me. Liam jumped, terrified, but Daria instantly turned to him and said, "Now Liam, don't be such a baby. It's just the Paras come lookin' and they'll be gone again, shortly."

Liam huffed and glared at me with accusation, and it cut into me. A child of six comforting a child of three, and both knowing what a knock at the door meant. It was not right. It was perfect evil. And all because of me. So I smiled at them, in comfort, and quickly rose.

"It's all right," I said, grinning to hide the sinking of my heart. "I'll take it."

As I strode down the hall to the door, another pounding began so I called, "Hold on, hold on," in my best twang. That voice gave the Haggertys at least a little cover against knowing who I truly was.

I opened the door just as a stocky Para was about to use his battering ram, so I slipped into to Todd's attitude and snapped, "What the hell's wrong with you? I said I's comin'!"

I thought for a second he was going to ram my head instead of the door, but another man stepped forward, one I'd not seen before.

"Are you Jeremy Landau?" he said, another true Brit.

Oh, shite. "That's me."

"Let me see your passport."

Already I could see the forms of women and children whispering up, despite the mist. And I could see the hate in their eyes. I started to get a strong feeling of ugliness, so I handed it over without hesitation. I knew that's the last time I'd have possession it. Right now my one concern was to minimize the Haggertys' troubles.

"I'd invite you in," I said, keeping the twang, "but this ain't my place so—"

"No need. You'll come with us."

"Wait, Mrs. Haggerty's not home an' her gran'kids're here, so I gotta wait till she gets back and—"

"What's this?" It was herself bolting from the house two doors down, a cloth holding eggs in one hand, and Mrs. Kelly right behind her and just as angry. "Mr. Landau, what's this?"

"It's nothin', Mizz Haggerty," I said. "These gentlemen just want me to go clear somethin'—"

"You bloody Brit bastards," she snarled, "he's an American. Just because you think you can treat us like dogs don't mean you can the whole world!"

"By the saints," someone added, "he's American?!"

"The fuckin' English!"

"Arrogant bastards, all!"

More women and children were coming out. I grew more and more nervous. I'd once wondered if this was another method of pushing back against the Paras—surround them with loud angry females to confuse the issue and dare them to raise their weapons. But this time even a quick look at how the squaddies fingered their triggers, and how too many already had the beginnings of wicked feral grins on their faces, showed me even a carton of Marlboros would do me no good. The riots of the last weeks had put them too much on edge to be willing to back down peacefully, even if it was to avoid an incident with a pack of women and children.

I couldn't allow it, not on my behalf, so I turned to Mrs. Haggerty and her mates and said, "Ladies, it's all right. Thanks. I don't mind goin' with 'em. I'll just call the 'Merican consulate from their office and get everything straightened out in two shakes of a lamb's tail. It'll be fine." I turned back to the man in charge with a smile, adding, "It's just a little misunderstandin', right? Don't want no trouble here."

I honestly couldn't tell if he was a commander or captain or just a top sergeant, but at least he was smart enough to look around at the noisy seething crowd, check his men's attitudes, hold his tongue and nod. He pointed to the closest of two Saracens and said, "In here," then begrudgingly added, "Please."

"Just lemme get my boots."

The look in his eyes shifted into a warning that I was not to do a damn thing more than what he'd asked, right now, no hesitation. So I shrugged and let two of the grunts lead me around to the back of the first beast, in tandem. The second I stepped from the house my socks were soaked through, and the mist was chillier than I'd expected so I much regretted not having my jacket or jumper. This was not going to be a pleasant ride.

A monster of a Para opened the rear door as three others kept close watch on me and the rest warily made for the second

Saracen, the women calling all of God's curses down on them and children as young as four maligning them.

But as I was about to get in I noticed movement from above, like an arm waving from behind a chimney, and looked up to see a single, dark, perfectly-shaped brick softly hurtle over the roof top to slowly, slowly, slowly curl up and then down, down, down, twisting and spinning like it weighed nothing as it whispered closer and closer, a thing of remarkable beauty and grace, floating in the air as if it were weightless, growing larger and larger—

Until it screamed of its danger and I gasped and turned away from it, thinking it might hit me. Instead, it slammed onto the bonnet of the Saracen behind me and ricocheted into the chest of a Para that was keeping watch on me.

He cried out and collapsed and his mates swung into full battle mode and the once-growling crowd of women burst apart like petals falling off an open rose in a sharp breeze as they scrambled back to their homes, dragging their children behind them as more bricks and stones came pelting down on the Brits.

And on me.

I was clipped in the back and hit full on my left hand as I scurried away from the Saracens to find a place of safety and saw the Paras taking cover behind the vehicles and a corner house, rifles prepped ready to fire and aiming, and I cried out, "They got real bullets!"

No hint of Texas in my voice then.

So the Brit commander grabbed me and slammed me into a doorway, snarling, "Right, you're from bloody America."

I couldn't help but burst into laughter at the comical anger in his face. He punched me with his pistol, cutting open my left eye, yet still I laughed. It was insane—the chaos a few rocks can bring and the stupidity of the anger of these bastards against those they occupied and the futility of it all in the face of the world's disinterest and the fact that Ma was dead and would never get to see any of this finally crush the spirit of those who lived here and no one would learn the lessons of the place because we were now a template on how to fight back against the oppressor and none of them could see how it never really worked, and this stupid bastard thought he could beat me into ending my laughter when it was beyond my control.

All of it.

All of it.

I heard gunfire from the Paras' rifles and laughed even harder as I choked out, "Ya stupid bloody bastards, you're shootin' at ghosts!"

More stones and a petrol bomb were the response, as was more gunfire. One Para's uniform leg caught the flames and his mates yanked him into the front Saracen to put it out, then the commander grabbed the collar of my shirt and dragged me in after them, his men scrambling in with us. The sounds of the stones clattering against the armor was deafening and the beast rocked as if ready to charge against its tormentors. The driver looked around, saw the rear doors being pulled closed so slammed into gear and the Saracen jerked forward. That's when I heard even more curses being sent the way of the Brits by the voices of men and boys and women, muffled by the armor and thick glass and lids covering the front windows, mingling with the hail of bricks and bottles and sticks and clubs being smashed against the sides.

I could see none of it for lying on the floor, the post of the driver's seat jammed against my neck and shoulder, the commander's pistol at the back of my head as if he'd caught me ferrying a bomb in my briefs. We jerked and stopped and jumped forward and sharply turned, the driver cursing louder than all other noises combined, until we'd broken free of the crowd and were on a straightaway of some sort. There was still the occasional stone cracking against the side or back or bonnet as people saw these monstrous vehicles storm past in complete disregard, but the Saracen's engine was now the main component of noise.

We turned and headed up the flyover then I heard us crossing over the Craigavon. Meaning we weren't going to the Strand Road Barracks. That gave my stomach a flip. Was I being ferried to an army base? Straight to the Maze? Then I remembered a reference made by Max to Castlereagh, the main interrogation center. I had only the slightest idea where it was, exactly, but by the turns and then the straightaway we were on, I knew where we were headed.

For Belfast.

Oh, dear God, the stories I'd heard about that place—some so horrible, even Amnesty International and the World Court had gotten involved. All to no avail. The British press and courts had shrugged them off, and in America it had warranted little more than a mention. But people made confessions there, and even with claims those confessions were made under torture they were convicted and sent to the H-Blocks and no one seemed willing to stop any of it. I couldn't even begin to understand why I'd be taken there unless it was for show—to prove that somehow I'd been an IRA operative in America so the world could shrug as my family was rooted up and all sent to jail for daring to care about me.

Oh, dear Jesus, this was not a path I'd ever thought I'd be on.

Before I could accept this in my own mind, the commander yanked me up to my knees, pistol still to the back of my head.

"Hands behind you," he snapped.

I wasn't given the chance to even think of complying. One of the Paras grabbed my wrists and slammed them together then handcuffed them, tight. I grunted from the sudden pain of it.

"Nothing to say?" the commander continued. "I thought you Irish bastards were full of words."

I was pulled up onto a seat, which was more uncomfortable than the bloody floor since a cylinder of some sort was pressing against my lower right back, and I just looked at him as he put his pistol away, a crude smirk on his rat face. The blood from the crack he'd given me was drying and tickling the skin of my cheek so I leaned back to scratch it against the side of a box sticking out from the wall next to me. He kicked my feet.

"Sit still, you fuckin' pug."

I smiled at him. It was meant to be a foul name for me, and when Everett had first called me that I'd almost taken offense. But then I'd grown to like the appellation, because he filled it with such affection, it had become a compliment of a sort. So even as the rat-bastard snarled it in derogatory fashion, I deliberately recalled the warmth in Everett's voice, and hoped he could be happy, in New York, and refused to let this son-of-a-bitch take that away from me.

Instead, I leaned my head into the corner of that box and wall and closed my eyes against the growing pounding in my head...and the growing fears in my gut. My hands tingled from the tightness of the bracelets. My arms ached from being held behind me. My throat was as dry as west Texas. The only thing that kept me from freaking, completely, was the understanding there was nothing I could do about this until we'd arrived wherever it was we were headed, so it would serve no purpose but to weaken me in their eyes. And give some British son-of-a-bitch the call to refer to me as a coward? I'd bloody stop breathing before I let that happen.

No, let's worry about it when we get there, Bren.

When we get there.

When we get there.

A Question

It was a long, hideous drive up hills and across open country, where the beast would speed up to nearly sixty, but then we'd pass through a town and slow to nothing, almost. Something I noticed was the first times that happened, rocks would fly at the Saracen— as was obvious by the sudden crash of noise against one side or the other—and my ears caught what I think was the din of dustbin lids clattering. You could barely hear them above the roar of the engine, but it was enough to make me listen harder and believe in it. Believe they were sending a message to me of solidarity. That gave me strength enough to endure the journey, even after we passed into territory controlled by *Loyalists* and the rocks and noises went softly into silence.

The drive continued forever—though by rights it probably was only an hour or so—until we took a sudden sharp turn and pulled to a halt. Through the driver's window I could just make out a gate framed by walls and barbed wired. Without a word, the barrier was lifted and we trundled in.

The back doors popped open and the Paras tumbled out, then I was dragged from within. A quick glance put reality to my deepest fears, for without question this was nowhere within the Maze Prison. They'd had no temporary caravan offices and the fortress-like attitude of the walls was far too indicative of a place that was trying to keep people out, not in. No, this could be nothing but an interrogation center.

This could be no place other than Castlereagh.

They dragged me into the nearest building and down a short, ugly corridor into a room—and I do mean dragged; I was not allowed to walk for that might have made me seem human. I was then slammed into a chair before a table, with two similar chairs opposite me and beyond them the one and only door.

My hands remained cuffed, behind me, in serious protest.

The room was blank, its walls not really white but of so sterile a color they might as well have been. A window with a glassy surface was perhaps three feet to my left; about six feet of open space was to my right. In one corner stood a guard in full armor—chest, helmet, belt with God knows how many different weapons on it, his rifle held ready. His eyes focused on me, wary, waiting for me to move wrong or give him any excuse to blast me in half.

I had no idea I was so dangerous.

I finally noticed a pair of long cameras in two different upper corners of the room, both aimed at the table. They did not move, did not even blink as they stared impassively at me. I wondered if they were even truly engaged, or if they were intended for show, only. Give a lad a sense of security enough to let his guard down, thinking they'd dare not hurt him with cameras recording it all. That might loosen his tongue just enough to make use of. I decided that they were recording, but that since the Army controlled this room it also controlled what happened in it and to any videotape that might be useful as evidence, so I'd be left with nothing to protect me.

Now I still was sore from my encounter with Billy and his mates—not too badly so, merely enough to notice when I moved wrong—so that brought to mind the question of if they intended to interrogate me in the same manner. But the floor was made of a single piece of linoleum that was well-worn, so any blood would stain it in ways that could not be got out, yet I saw no traces of that in it, right now. Perhaps they planned only to ask a few questions.

One can hope.

I coughed. That fuckin' bastard cough that I can't control when I'm scared and pops up at the worst of times. And I was fuckin' scared. Facing the impassivity of that room, it took everything I had in me to keep from screaming and begging and praying for deliverance. I'd begun to think that maybe Father Jack was right to assign me to the box of cowards. In truth, I had no illusions about myself. I recalled all too well how Max'd spent more time checking out my story than dragging it from me, which brought a wave of shame over me at my lack of will...and it mattered not that I'd given them nothing of use. Had I not had my history with Joanna to explain my actions, I'd have given names and dates and places and anything they bloody wanted from me, and never you mind they'd all be lies. A man will say anything he must to end that sort of torture. The thought of being put to that point, again, made me ill, for I could all too easily see the mere threat of physical harm making me weep and cower and hand Colm over to them along with Kieran.

Even Kieran.

Who had hated me. Well...who at least had looked down upon me, and him being ten years my junior. At least, I think he did. I wasn't so sure now. I won't say I'd ever seen contempt in his eyes when he glared at me, or even disappointment. It was more like he'd been in Father Jack's camp, thinking me typical of those who're willing to let others fight their fights for them.

Until he heard I'd been quiet during Max's interrogation.

Oh, Christ, I didn't want to lose that budding respect in him.

I coughed, again. Cleared my throat. Went back to my twang. "Could I have some water, please?"

The guard didn't even blink, just stood there like he was made of wires and plastic.

I coughed, again. Twice. It was coming harsher and I was threatening to shake, again, which was the last thing I wanted them to see. I took in some deep breaths and cried out, since I knew someone was behind that window and listening, at the very least, "Please, Ah just ne-ed a dri-ink of wah-ter. Shee-yit."

Nothing. Of course. Soften up the Papist. Act the part of a complete and bloody fool who'll never understand that when you treat a man like a dog his whole life, it does you no good to punish him for biting you in thanks for that treatment. The bastards. The fuckin' bastards. The stupid, fuckin'—

Whist. The door quietly opened, ending my mental tirade before it became verbal. Two men entered, neither in any uniform. One was older with half-grey hair and a long nose topping a moustache, his vested suit perfectly tailored; the other was closer to my age and Max's looks, and was subtly deferential to his mate, his suit obviously off a men's rack at Marks & Spencer. Neither of them had welcoming eyes as they sat in the chairs opposite me.

So...I was to be interviewed by the British, this time.

Tailored held a folio which he opened as he asked, "Is your name Brendan Kinsella?" His voice dripped with aristocratic condescension.

In my best, most obvious Texas, I snarled, "I wanna talk to

the 'Merican Consulate."

Tailored didn't blink as he said, "You're a citizen of the United Kingdom, not the United States. You have neither need nor warrant to contact them. Now answer the question."

He already knew the fuckin' answer so to hell with him. I took in a deep breath and looked away. And fucking coughed.

The younger one rolled his eyes and popped off in a more common style of British, "We know your passport's stolen—"

Tailored cleared his throat. The younger one grimaced.

That's when I noticed they both had this stick-up-your-arse type of bearing, so I decided they were both military—one an officer of high rank, probably a *Sir* or something, the other maybe a sergeant meant to be more of a bodyguard than actual participant in the questioning. And they were minimizing how they were soldiers of the Queen. So...this was going to be serious.

Christ.

Tailored looked back at me, his expression unchanged. "I suppose it matters not to inform you Jeremy Landau is currently being interrogated by the American Department of Justice. It seemed rather odd that a man so used to having his passport on him should not miss it for months."

Now, I don't claim to be all that smart or aware or even sure of myself, but for some reason the casual way in which he tossed me this information all but screamed to me he was lying. Knowing Jeremy as I did, if it was the FBI approaching him, he'd be damned sure his new passport would be in his right hand, his Uncle David at his left hand, and he had arranged access to his father's full influence. Considering how the man had attended to a number of Houston's elite, that would be massive. I also had a sense he'd extend it to Aunt Mari, should she need it, for she'd treated his son as if he were her own.

And suddenly my coughing stopped. It may seem stupid, but suddenly I knew they'd be all right. All my family would. For if Aunt Mari had even the slightest hint that I or any of them were being abused by the Brits, she'd roar louder than Thatcher could even dream of doing, and there'd be no complicit press to keep this story silent; not when the howls were coming from five thousand miles away.

And yes, I know it was a flimsy hope to grasp onto, but it served me well enough.

I looked at tailored and said in my normal voice, "I've had nothing to eat since dinner, last night, nor anything to drink since I was arrested. That violates laws put forth by the Geneva Convention and—"

"Is your name Brendan Kinsella?" The ice in his voice cut me off. The ice in his eyes nearly made me smile. It appeared that he was the impatient sort.

"That's an Irish Catholic name," I said, "and as one of your men saw last night, I've no Irish Catholic dick. So how could I even begin to be—?"

He sighed and referred to the folder. "At age twelve, you were circumcised at Altnagelvin to repair a congenital difficulty. Now answer the question."

Shite. "Well," I said, "I guess that's what happens when you get Protestant Sisters working with Protestant constables—a complete violation of doctor-patient privilege."

He nodded. "Then shall I assume from your unwillingness to give me a direct answer, what you mean is that you *are* Brendan Kinsella? Born five February, nineteen-and-fifty-six—?"

Now I rolled my eyes. "That's not what it fuckin' says."

He showed me the sheet of paper and sure enough, it had my date of birth as the fifth. I chuckled. "Then that's not me."

"Sir?" The younger one leaned forward. "My notes show he was born the second of February."

Tailored looked into his folder and nodded. "Ah, yes—you're right. Have this corrected." He casually handed the sheet to the younger one.

Suddenly I felt the proper fool because it seemed too much like they'd deliberately had the error made and got me to as much as verify who I was, all without lifting so much as a finger against me to do it.

Christ, I was a fucking idiot.

Tailored leaned forward. "Now that we know who you truly are, and you understand this, we've a few questions we'd like to ask. Simple questions, really, but vital to ending this spiral into death and destruction all around us, and in keeping your Aunt and Uncle from further legal issues."

"They didn't know who I was."

"Don't be ridiculous."

"I was brought over to them as Brennan McGabbhinn, a

cousin injured in a rather nasty accident and in need of special medical care, which I received."

"You expect us to accept your own aunt didn't know who you were?"

I shrugged. "She hadn't seen me since I was ten, and even then it was a sad affair, being me own Da's wake after his murder by Protestants. Also, there are no snaps of me to send her..."

"And why would the IRA arrange that for you?" said the lesser Brit. "A boy of sixteen who got caught sniffing after a Protestant girl?"

"I don't know who set it up or how," I snapped back. "I wasn't there. Mentally. Physically. Emotionally. I'm told what I had was a psychotic break...what was it? Akinetic amnesia, or something like that."

"Due in no small part to participating in the staging of a bomb that killed several innocents," said the suit, "two young children amongst them."

"The only part I had in that was I saw...I saw—"

The leg twisting and turning and drifting closer and closer to me and bouncing to the ground and blood from it splattering on me and...

"Answer me!" It was suit's voice, and I got the impression he'd asked me a question, but for the life of me I'd had no idea he'd even been talking.

"Come now, Kinsella!" he continued. "Do you honestly expect us to believe you just happened to be there at the same time Provos were initiating a major operation against a man suspected of being UVF? Considering what your father did?"

What my Da did? What the hell kind of nonsense was this?

I stopped looking at him...at anything, really. I hadn't the interest in it, to put it plain. Those two kids...playing—

Dancing around each other, squealing from joy as one tripped and fell against the Rover and white filled the world and...

Is this how you dig at someone? Pour salt into a wound that has yet to heal? Was he that sort of bastard, who thinks himself so superior in intellect and awareness, you are nothing more to him than a means to finding out whatever lies he wanted to have verified? To say I was off-balance would have been the fullest understatement of the ages. I could barely focus on his words. His supposed anger. He demands proof of that which could not be proven. It was some kind of circle he was talking in.

But what's odd is, it took away my fear of him.

I could now see any sort of conversation with this bastard would wind up giving away more than even I thought I knew, no matter how wrong it was, so silence and no eye contact appeared to be the best response.

He noticed. He slowly leaned closer, hands casually clasped. I could hear the smile in his words. "So you seem not to be interested in preventing other innocent people from suffering the same fate as Joanna Martin, a girl whom you claim to have cared for, very much. A Protestant girl, no less. Very pretty, as I understand—well, once upon a time. Some would say she's lucky to be alive. I don't share that opinion, myself, but each is allowed his own."

I didn't move, except to breathe. The bastard wasn't hitting me with anything I hadn't already used on myself. I wondered if he'd figured that, too, or if he truly thought he was shooting fresh daggers into my soul. All he was actually doing was telling me they'd questioned fucking Billy and got what they needed to hurt me, from him. The little shite.

I paid him no attention, except from the periphery of my eyes; the same for the younger one. My gaze stayed focused on a corner of the table, and I noticed it was rounded and smooth. Why I noticed that, I have no idea.

The vested one continued, "I understand you've tried to contact Miss Martin a number of times since returning to Londonderry. We'll have to see if that has occurred. I'm certain she's aware it's a criminal offense to consort with a known terrorist or IRA sympathizer. Of course, there's also the problem of harboring a member of the IRA, which your sister, brothers and mother will have to answer for."

Oh, Christ, he was a stupid man who thinks he's smart. Bugger. I closed my eyes. "My mother will answer for nothing."

"I think it's up to us to determine whether or not—"

I opened my eyes only to look at him. "She died."

I caught the first honest bit of hesitation in his manner. He leaned back and shifted to half-look at the younger one.

"Terrence?"

"Nothing in my file, sir. We...we knew she was ill..."

"It happened yesterday," I whispered, then snarled, "Perhaps your nurse contact at Altnagelvin was on her off-day, so the information hasn't been forwarded to you, yet."

In answer, Tailored gave me his coldest, most sterile glare then stood and strode from the room. The young one—Terrence—rose and kept the door open, saying, "Take him away."

A couple of constables came in to lift me to my feet, nearly yanking my arms from their sockets, and drag me down a hall to a series of blank cells. I was slammed into one, the cuffs were removed and I was pushed against the far wall. By the time I turned, they'd closed the door and locked it.

I jolted over to kick it and scream—croak, really, "I need some water! And I've had nothing to eat!"

No response.

Feeling began to return to my arms and hands and they tingled like mad, so I moved them about to speed up the circulation's return but it only seemed to make things worse. To get my mind off it, I paid more attention to the cell.

It was barely three meters square with a rubber block in one corner to serve as a mattress, and nothing else but a chamber pot. It stank of piss and shit and had no window; in the upper wall opposite the door was a vent that did nothing for circulation. The only light came from a single bulb in the ceiling, with a silence so complete, I could hear my blood coursing through my veins.

I collapsed on the mattress, wondering what next was in store, and found it loved to squeak. I figured it was a piece of foam covered by a rubber material that looked clean but was really quite sticky. I could almost feel it through my jeans.

My stomach began to protest. My head screamed at me. I felt nauseous. And don't think I hadn't noticed there'd been no official intake. Meaning there was no record I'd been brought here. I could lie on this bloody stretch of rubber for the rest of my life and no one would ever know. And they could do as the fucking wanted.

Fear of that last thought almost choked the breath from me, because I knew this had been much too easy a meeting with them. Far worse was sure to follow, but what it was I had no idea. Or how I'd fare under it.

For the first time, I was deeply regretting leaving Houston.

One Word

For hours, nothing happened except the light kept burning and burning and all sounds remained absent. I found myself humming melodies from my Houston albums just to fill the void, ending back on *The Banks of Claudy*...and smiling at the thoughts I'd had that night. Christ, was it only twelve years ago, last January? Holding a child's vision of what his life could be? Dreaming a child's dream that a girl I hadn't even met yet might become his partner in life? Hoping I could be the one who showed Eamonn and the rest of the People's Democracy how to avoid the trouble I'd seen coming?

All had proven to be impossible; once again, the world had seen to it that only hatred was allowed to flourish. Understanding and love were worthless in this existence, and my sad attempts at both had done little but lead me straight to this very cell. For I seemed not to learn from my disasters. I might have detoured here and grown a bit more aware there, but it's the end result that matters, isn't it?

And what was my end result? My love for two different girls had brought catastrophe to them both. My aunt and the B-girls now had questions about their love for my uncle. I'd helped put my brother in jail. And I'd lied to my mother as she lay dying. That last was a sin...but was it venal or mortal? I couldn't recall, it'd been so long since my catechism. But then, I had completely rejected the church.

It was here for the first time that I wondered—seriously wondered—if I had the nerve to just end it. I believed that might be the only way I could fully protect my family and mates from further damage. It's not like my passing would cause even a ripple in the meaning of time. Joanna was still dead to me. Vangie was pursuing another life in another part of the world, where I was not welcome. I'd achieved nothing on this earth but pain and heartbreak and would leave even less behind. At least it would cause embarrassment to the Brits to no end; Maeve and Aunt Mari would see to that.

Maybe.

The idea began to take on solid appeal. So how to do it? I'd come with neither belt nor shoes, but I could use my shirt as a noose. Do it quietly so they'd have no reason to come in till I was long passed. I looked about the room but could see nothing from which to hang myself; the fixture holding the light bulb was well out of reach. Same for the vent. And no handle on the door. Then I thought, I could just tie a sleeve tight around my throat and put a knot in it so I couldn't undo it before passing out...but I had no idea if that would work. Doesn't there need to be a lot of pressure on the throat to cut off the full flow of oxygen to your heart and lungs, and blood to your brain? Could doing it wrong merely leave me a mental defective?

Christ, wouldn't that be perfect? Wind up truly simple, like Ma'd always claimed.

Ma. My mother. Who'd loved me and hated me at the same time. And never said why. Except...the way I acted towards her? Was that all it was, really? I didn't know, not really. She'd been saying things that might also have applied to Eamonn.

And Da, attacking someone? That had happened so many times, it raised no question in my mind. Only it seemed Ma was referring to something other than anger from drink. It confused me far too much to even think I could make sense of it. And then again, why bother trying if all you plan to do is cut your own throat?

Could I do that? There was nothing sharp anywhere in the room upon which I could slice open my arms or throat...unless I was able to tear apart the chamber pot, but it was so solid, without some tool nothing was going to happen there. The studs on my jeans were metal. Could those be sharpened enough?

God, Brendan, don't be an idiot.

All right then, throat cutting is out of the question. What if I rammed my shirt down my throat to choke the life from me? It could become lodged in my esophagus and I could choke to death, that way. Even if I tried to vomit it out, it would only soak everything up and become more firmly in place. But how long would that take and would it cause much pain or me to—

The door whispered open and four guards came in.

"Up," said the first one.

I ignored him, so they grabbed me, one at each limb. I tried to kick them away, but they were more used to this than I was and held me down tightly enough to manacle my feet together, then they slapped a belt around my waist and shackled my hands to it, and me struggling wildly against them did nothing to stop them— hell, to even slow them down.

What was odd was, I said nothing through it all. Not one word against them or their mothers or their parentage or anything. All that escaped me were little grunts and gasps of pain as they held me in place and took complete control of me.

"Quiet one, in'nt he?"

"Fookin' Taig dunno how to speak."

"He's scared ya'll find out he loves your touch."

"Aye, that, look-it his arse move."

"Give it up, ye fookin' bastard!"

"Where ya think ya'll go if we don't get this on ya?"

"He knows what's comin'."

"Some playtime, eh? Ya'll like that, ya will."

"Wait'll ye see who's come to arsk ye questions, ye fook."

"I got me seat reserved to watch."

"I got the ale."

"We'll see how long ya hold ya tongue."

"Fookin' Taig."

"Papist scum."

They kept it up even as they dragged me back to that same interrogation room and slammed me into that same chair. But this time, the other two chairs were off in separate corners and the table was in the center of the room. And Terrence stood beside it, in camouflage trousers and t-shirt to match, thick shining boots on his feet. With him were two others dressed the same way, both of them fit and powerful, all of them with their eyes on me.

The guards left, probably to join their fellows in the room behind the mirror and drink beer and have a good craic about the stupid fucking Catholic bumbler about to be destroyed by those strong superior Brits. It'd be fun all the way around. Maybe someone would bring popcorn.

At that particular moment, I wished I'd eaten the shirt.

"Sorry to hear about your mother, Brendan," said Terrance.

"Looks like our information was a bit behind the curve. But then there's that American phrase, *Shite happens*, even to us. So—the wake's about to start. And the funeral's set for day after tomorrow. I know you're a good boy, Brendan, and you won't want to miss any of that, so why not just answer a few questions and let us send you on your way? Right?"

I just cast a glance at the cameras in the upper corners. They hadn't moved. He noticed.

"Don't rely on them for anything. They're ours. But you're a smart lad, ain't you? You already know that. Funny—but it's the smart ones who crack easiest. They think because they're smart, they can outfox us. But they can't."

Christ, did they all use the same playbook for their interrogations? The only difference I could find is, he had no baton on him that I could see.

"We can keep at this for as long as we want. So show me you really are smart, Brendan." He sat on the edge of the table, very friendly-like. "You know, we only need the answer to one question, really. Who was the other lad at that bombing with you and your brother?"

Colm sprang to mind but I didn't say it, because I also caught how he said it was Eamonn there. But it wasn't. No. No, this was a trick. Eamonn looked nothing like Danny or Colm. Terrence would know that wasn't true. And Danny was dead, so no one knew who the other lad was, but me.

So fucking Billy and his mates were right. The Brits were still on about that. Even after more than eight years. Why? Why did it still matter? Danny was well-punished. I'd seen his ghost. No question in my mind he was gone, and he'd have been the important one, wouldn't he? He's the one who'd built it. Surely they knew that. Of course, I'd shown him how to build a bomb. I hadn't meant to. Hadn't once thought of how my teachings would be used. But it had been me shown him the way to work electronic connections and that...and that had gotten people killed. Men. Children. Danny.

I hoped if I joined them in the next world they would forgive me.

Of course, I did not answer Terrence. I just sighed and looked at the floor. The bright linoleum looked even cleaner than before, as if it had been freshly washed and waxed, which for some reason unsettled me and—

Terrence took my chin and forced me to look at him.

"Didn't you hear me? Who was the other man with you and Danny Gallagher?" And there you go; he *was* trying to trick me. "Who was it set the bomb that blew up your girl? We know Danny-boy didn't act on his own; he was too young to be allowed such responsibility. Another man was seen with you both. We got a good description. Just need one last detail to verify it's the right man. So who was he? First name's all we want. We can take it from there." He waited then added, "Was it Colm O'Faelan?"

Ice shot into my heart and it took every bit of control in me to keep from freezing in place. So they knew Colm was there. No, suspected he was. Probably told that by Billy or Max or even Tam. And he wanted me to verify. I managed to let out a sigh of what could have seemed as sadness, but that didn't deter Terrence.

"You were mates with him, weren't you? Lads grown up together. Danny Gallagher, as well. Quite the electrician, I understand. Sad how psychotic he became at the end. I hear Colm is the one who saw to it he died by his own bomb. He probably decided the target for the bomb you saw."

Oh, thank God he was stupid enough to say that to me. It showed he knew nothing about Colm or Danny; he was just throwing possibilities at me in hopes of a reaction to latch onto. Some little giveaway that could let him reel me in like a fish on a hook. It helped to know this.

But to hide my sudden relief, I let my mind go. Not to complete nothingness. No, to the night I walked to Claudy. Instead of his voice, I focused on the soft lowing of cows and gentle bleats from sheep and the call of owls, so much so I don't think I even heard another word from him until he smacked the back of my head.

"Was it Barry Quincannon, then?" he snarled, thinking he was being threatening.

I'd no idea who that was, and I think it showed in my face. He nodded.

"Eugene Heaney?"

Danny's uncle? That man was no more capable of murder than Daria. Christ, I'd though *he* was aimed for the priesthood, with his ways. What the devil did this man think he was saying? It was nothing but nonsense to confuse me. Not even Paidrig would have responded to something so obvious.

He gripped my chin and kept up with more names, not one of which made any sense in regards to what he was asking. Each time his nails dug deeper into my skin. I thought of all the times Ma had done that to me, though on my arm or neck, mostly. Sometimes to the point of drawing blood. But I could tell he'd not cut me as deep. His nails were too closely trimmed for that. No, this was merely stage one in the destruction of my confidence.

I wondered what would be next. Thought of what Maeve wrote in her letter, of how Rhuari had been forced to stand upright for hours, facing a wall, his hands outstretched. How he'd been struck if he did not keep them up. How the Hague had called such actions a form of torture and the British snapped back at them so hard the great court cowered and whined, in response. Was that to be it for me? With no one to stop it or hold the bastards to account? I wondered if I could handle it as well as Rhuari, who'd been but fourteen, at the time.

And what of Kieran? Surely he'd been snatched, as well, and treated the same. And all he carried was disdain for it all, like he saw it for the royal game it was. Yet he was still out and free. Still seen as the lad by the powers that be. No hint of scandal to him.

I almost chuckled. I should have taken that into account when we first met at Ma's, last month. Should have understood his anger was probably his only defense against what had happened to him. His mates were the only ones who'd really understood, for they'd probably been through it, as well. I felt ashamed of myself for judging him so harshly, thanks to my near nothing of—

Terrence shoved me back hard enough to make the chair tip and let me fall to the floor. I landed hard on my side, jamming my shoulder and wrist against the belt and crying out, despite myself. I suppose he was angry I was paying him no attention. His mates picked me up and set me back in the chair, without a thought.

That bastard cough came back and I felt my stomach quiver, but I did not look at Terrence as he bent over to face me.

"Brendan, this is stupid. All we need is one name. One name and you can walk out of here. Go to your mother's wake. And her funeral. You're a good boy, Brendan; you'd want to do that. All good boys want to do that."

I still would not look at him.

"Are you afraid PIRA or INLA will find out you talked to us?

Is that why you're so quiet?"

Truth is, I hadn't thought about that as a complication. But I had heard that they would make people even suspected of informing disappear, and no one thought for a second they'd just gone on the run. So were there any indication I'd become a grass for the Brits, I'd probably follow suit. Straight into a grave. Like Shane. Meaning whether I spoke or didn't, the ending would be the same. So why worry about it?

"We can protect you, you know," Terrence kept on with. "We can fix it so they don't know you spoke to us. Or we can blame another person. We've got more than enough informants in the six counties. Blaming one of them'd be no trouble. 'Fact, it'd be worth it to get the bastard who helped you murder five people."

Five people? Only three had been killed at Joanna's father's place. No—wait—he's spouting wrong information, again, to get you to talk. He's all but saying, *Correct me; show me you're smarter than me; speak.* Like a fucking dog.

This was stupid. He and Tailored had already used this trick on me, once, so why be so obvious in using it, again? I just sighed and closed my eyes and—

SMACK! He slapped me off the chair! I landed on my stomach and grunted in pain. I gasped in air and my gut heaved from the sudden crush against the floor. His mates just grabbed me under my shoulders and sat me back in place.

"You're going to talk to me, Brendan," Terrence snarled, his voice deep and angry.

I felt blood trail from my nose and had the sense he'd reopened the cut on my face from the commander's pistol. I coughed, but this time from the pain in my gut and not from fear. I was too filled with adrenalin to now be afraid of him. Now I was ready to fight for my survival.

Or even for my death.

I think Terrence sensed this change in me. He stepped back and nodded, then he said in a voice that was too, too calm, "That was a stupid bloody thing for me to do, wasn't it? You Irish knock each other around all the time, so you probably like that sort of thing. Like your father—beating a man to death."

That caught me, and he noticed.

"We know all about that, too. In Belfast. Grant you, it's been thirty years, but memories are long. And enough details were shared with us to put it all together."

Thirty years? More lies to trick me...no. No, the timing *would* be right. If Ma was in Derry when Maeve arrived, that would have been just over thirty years ago. Jesus, Maeve was thirty? I hadn't even thought about it until—

He slammed the table, snarling. Broke into my mind. He'd been questioning me, and I'd actually not been hearing him. I had to do this mind-wander more often.

Only now his eyes were cold and cruel. Almost dead, as he straightened up and said in a voice that was as gentle as a fall breeze, "All right, Brendan. Your mates with the RUC already tried being physical with you, and got bollocks. So I won't waste my time with it."

He nodded to his mates and they yanked me up to lay me atop the table, face up, as he stepped out of the room. My head hung over one end, and my calves hung over the other. My ankle shackles were attached to the table in some way, so I had little range in which to move my legs.

Terrence came back in, a moment later, followed by some guards carrying two empty tubs and some pails of water. One tub was set on the floor, under my head, and the pails lined against the nearest wall. Then the guards left. I'd no idea what this devil was planning, but I knew it wouldn't be good, not from the evil kindliness in his eyes.

"All right, Brendan," he said in a voice as gentle and soothing as the devil's, "I'll give you one more chance. Who was the man with you and your mate? The man who helped you set the bomb that killed so many people? What was his name? All I need is his Christian name. I can find out everything else I want from that. So just tell me—what's his first name?"

I looked at the ceiling, beginning to shake, again. And I coughed. He nodded.

"Well," he sighed, "we've had a lot of success in loosening tongues with this method, and no fucking poof from the Red Cross need even know."

He lay a thick cloth over my face so I couldn't see. I heard a pail being lifted and felt his mates hold me down by my shoulders, each one also pressing against the side of my head to keep me from moving. Then water began spilling into the cloth.

I had no idea what the fuck they were doing. The water

choked me and I swallowed some. In truth it felt good on my throat, but it kept coming and coming and coming and I couldn't gulp it down and it went up my nose and into my lungs and I began to cough and fought to breathe and panic seized my heart as the water poured and poured and overwhelmed me like I was sinking under wave after wave after wave and I roared and began to fight like a madman—

And then the cloth was gone and I was choking and coughing and gasping in air and my head was bursting with a sudden piercing pain. Terrence grabbed me by the hair and slapped me two, three, four times to force me to focus on him and I could barely understand him as he snarled, "That was just a taste of it, Brendan. I can do this for hours and days. So give me his name."

I gulped in more air, deep and fast and...

I spit at him.

I fuckin' spit at him!

I don't know which of us was more surprised at me doing it, but he roared and slapped me another four or five times then jammed my head back and fitted the cloth over my face and began pouring the water onto it, again.

Thanks to the slaps, I'd not got a good breath in so I choked on the water, quick and hard. I fought to move my head. Fought to shake off the cloth. But his mates kept me immobile and all I could do was swallow more and more of it and let it fill my lungs and surround me in its evil cold unending cascades until my head felt ready to explode from the terror and my heart pounded like I was going mad and I tried to kick but couldn't and my hands wouldn't fucking move to let me push back up from under this hell and it kept on and on and on and on and I was sure I was dying and—

The cloth was whipped away, again. Terrence took me by the hair, again, and this time yanked me half off the table to face the floor and I vomited water into that other empty pail. It spewed from my nose as well as my mouth and I'd swear even came out my ears, there was so much of it. Then he shoved me back onto the table. I kept heaving and choking as he asked me questions that made no sense, like he was speaking another language, and I fought to get away from him but he kept yammering at me and asking me things and all I could do was shake my head until—

Suddenly, suddenly I heard him saying, oh so gently, his

voice echoing, "I have to wonder, Brendan, are you really that fuckin' stupid a bugger? We can end this, right now. All in exchange for one word, just one—the name of one man who's responsible for God knows how many deaths. You'd be doing mankind a favor by ending his reign of terror, Brendan. You're a good lad. You want to go to your mum's wake. And her funeral. You want all this terror to end. Help me end it, Brendan. Be the good lad I know you are."

To be honest, I couldn't have spoken then if I'd wanted to. That I was able to even understand him was a minor miracle to me. I was still retching from the water sloshing about in my lungs. I was coughing from my throat being so raw. I was bloody freezing from the cold air blasting in. My nose was screaming from the sudden influx of foreign liquids—not just water but acid from my stomach and God knows what else from within me. I was half afraid I was about to lose control of my bowels and I was shaking from the effort to just keep from screaming in fear.

"What's your answer, Brendan?" The question was so tender, I almost wept. Jesus Christ, but this man was truly a devil.

I looked away from him. My head was snapped back into position and the cloth laid over and I began to scream and scream and from someplace distant I heard laughter as the water began pouring and smothered me and filled me and I kicked and fought and choked and swallowed more and more and my heart shrieked in anger and terror and my legs flailed and—

Everything stopped.

I felt myself drift away from it all.

Peaceful and sad and easy.

I was dying.

I'd got my wish.

I was dying and it wasn't so horrible, drowning like this, no, not horrible at all as a gentle darkness enveloped me with tender caress and a grace so loving I welcomed it and—

Shattering noise woke me. Like a car wreck, shredded metal screeching to a halt against some barrier. I had no idea where I was. Could I be at home on the floor behind the settee? I'd wondered if I could hide there, once upon a time. Had I drifted to sleep and been dreaming it all? If so, next time I should have a blanket with me for I was fucking freezing and...and...

No. I was on the rubber mattress. My clothes wet and

clinging. Cold air blasting in. Hands and feet frozen. Heart still pounding. A dull throb in my head making it difficult to think. Christ, had I got so drunk I was arrested?

But my lungs ached horribly. Sharp pains exploded from my wrists and ankles if I tried to move. I looked at them. The shackles were gone but my skin was rubbed raw from me fighting against them. And then it all came crashing in.

It was no dream.

I wasn't dead.

I felt nothing about it. Not one emotion even approached my heart. It was just, *I'm still here*.

I lay flat on my back and slowly my mind rejoined my life. The light still burned in the ceiling, like an unforgiving sun, blistering through my eyes even when my lids were shut. Between the blades in my back was a sharp throb whispering over my spine. My thoughts—what thoughts I had—none seemed to be mine. My voice seemed to be another's.

Had I begun to talk? Was I speaking even now? I had no idea. I still could not make sense of where or how or even who I was at the moment. The four walls around me looked not at all familiar. The cold wet rubber under me behaved like a carpet hovering above the world.

I felt like it took hours for me to regain actual consciousness. True awareness. The throbbing in my head never ceased during this time, but did slowly become tolerable. I never stopped shivering, but it seemed to be more from the cold than anything more. Three more times the screeching crashing noise went past me door—past *my* door. The one way out. The one way to look for someone to come who could not come because no one knew where I was, of that I was sure. Even I was not sure of where I was.

Except I was.

I was.

I knew.

I knew.

A slat in the door snapped open and an eye bulged in to look about the room—then it pulled back and happily cried, "He's back!"

I assumed he meant me. Had I been somewhere and was not remembering? That would not be polite, not if I'd been with company. It's poor manners not to recall going places with people you know, or even those you don't.

The door opened and a man entered, followed by two more just like him. Triplets. I smiled and think I laughed. I might not have. I don't recall.

The first triplet nodded, smiling. "That's good," he said. "You're proud of yourself."

Then he kicked me. The brisk sharpness of it jolted me and everything crashed back into my mind. Castlereagh. The Saracen. Tailored. Terrence. The water. The fucking never-ending water.

It was Terrence who kicked me. He leaned in and snarled, "Think about everything we did, today, Brendan, and how we'll begin it all again, tomorrow. You'll speak to me. You'll talk to me. I swear by God before the next day is through, you'll think me your bloody father confessor, you fuckin' will."

Then he rose and gave me another kick in the back before he and his twins left.

More of it tomorrow and tomorrow and tomorrow and tomorrow. And I felt nothing. Like I was saying to myself, "I'll have the chicken fried steak every day this week and the next." It meant absolutely nothing.

Except...

My stomach boiled. And my cough returned. And I felt tears sting my eyes. I rolled over and my face pressed into the rubber.

I noticed my tears trailing over the plastic covering. I trailed a finger them. The covering squished in and around...and I felt a seam in the edge of it.

A seam sewn tight the length of the pallet.

Suddenly I knew—I wouldn't have to keep going. I knew how to end this, now. I knew what to do.

I made myself dig at that seam. Pick at it. Rub it and work at it and loosen the thread that held it. Took me hours. My whole body ached from the exertion. But slowly...slowly, I worked it open enough to see the foam rubber, inside it. I tore off a good chunk of it, and crushing it into my hand made me feel powerful, once more. Put me back in control of my destiny.

The next time they came, I'd have that sponge in my mouth. And I'd wait till they poured the water over me, again, and I'd swallow it and it would expand and lodge there and choke me and I'd be dead before they figured out how to keep me alive. They'd get nothing from me, not even enjoyment. They'd get nothing except my death.

The bastards would get only my death.

Hope

I didn't sleep, that night. I was given barely enough food to keep a toddler alive—a tiny bite of fried fish and some chips with a cup of water and two slices of hard bread. I'd wolfed them down, shaking from the hunger, and felt well enough for about half an hour before my gut began making itself known to me, again. So I'd lain down and tried to rest. But the light burned non-stop. And the icy cold would not stop. I got up to discover chilly air was coming in through that vent. And the floor was wetter than before, making it all the colder to touch. They were deliberately sending in both to keep me uncomfortable, since I had no blanket to protect me against it and only well-soaked socks on my feet. With water on the floor that bastard pallet would not dry out, so to lie on it was to make myself even more cold. If I did happen to finally drift off, those crashing noises kept jolting me awake. I finally realized it was a guard walking past and rattling his club inside a tin waste bin by the door.

I knew this was meant to help shatter me. What kept me from breaking down and letting my voice take over was that it would soon be done with. Permanent sleep would envelop me and I'd leave it to God to decide if I ever woke.

I finally stood up. If the bastards had no intention of letting me sleep, then I wouldn't even try. I looked at the four blank walls, the worthless things. Just something to enclose you. Something to make you think you were nested in a safe place. I rubbed my chilly fingers over one. Felt the harsh smoothness of the paint. Then without thinking, I bit into my thumb. Made it bleed. Used a bit of the wet sponge to dab it and write my name. I pressed it hard to keep it bleeding and then added a sentence to before my name— *Here was the murder of Brendan Kinsella.* It wasn't consistent in quality of line, but it got the point across, well enough. I chuckled.

I wrote more sentences elsewhere. Things like, *I had no joy in dying,* and *Is torture now legal in England?* and *Is innocence no longer a given?* Each took quite some time to do, and I had to tear off more bits of the pallet to do it. But by the time I heard the door latch pull, I'd covered the walls in my blood and felt a bit tipsy.

The guard who came in took one look at it and threw something at me, furious, then slammed back out. I realized it was a cup of porridge and two bites of bread, toasted and dry. There was a second cup that apparently had held some tea. Well, if he was so upset as to toss my breakfast at me in direct violation of every law there was, then I knew he'd soon be back, so I found that chunk of foam and slipped it into my cheek, then I picked up the porridge cup and swiped my one undamaged finger around it in to get the remains and licked it clean—

As the door slammed open, again.

I turned with my finger in my mouth to watch four guards roar in and slap that belt around my waist, again. I did not fight as they affixed my wrists to it and shackled my ankles. Somehow it felt unseemly for a man about to die to fight against those who were leading him to his death.

They were as verbal as ever, saying the same things as before, but I didn't listen. Didn't really hear them. Even when they hit me to make me look at them, I only smiled and drifted. I don't know why I was at such peace. It seemed to me I should be nervous or fearful about the coming finality of it—but the truth was, I'd been such a waste of life, such a disaster to all who knew me, it was better if I left this existence...and cared not if there would be another.

So off they dragged me, still cursing and hitting and laughing, and me not responding. It took an hour to get to the room, again, even though it was the same one as before. It seemed larger, this time, even though it hadn't changed a bit. Terrence was standing where he had, before, as were his twins.

"On the table," he said.

I was lifted onto it as if I were the weight of a feather and my legs were shackled to the table's and my head hung over the end. Terrence came about to look at me, upside down and so terribly, terribly serious. I smiled at him...and realized one of the guards was talking to him in some new nonsensical language. I felt weak and a thought hit me—how much blood does it take to write on four walls? Was that why I couldn't understand them? What if I'd lost too much to have this done to me, now? That wouldn't do. Wouldn't fit the plan.

Terrence grabbed my wrists and looked hard at my hands. Then he inspected each of my fingers. He glowered at me then rose to look at the guard closest to him.

"Has he been fed?"

More of the garbled talk whispered from the guard. I was feeling sleepy. Ready to drift into the never-ending darkness. Why wouldn't they just shut up and be done with it?

Then Terrence screamed, "You stupid fuckin' bastard, you think that's a help?! We put him through any questioning, right now, and he'll just pass out on us. We'd get bollocks from him! Take him back and fuckin' feed him, for fuck's sake! Stupid fuckin' Irish. Why the fuck're we here helping these stupid fuckin' bastards? GO ON!"

I floated up and drifted back down the hallway and into a new cell, one without my animal's trace on it and with a dry sponge foam mattress covered in the same fucking plastic. And air that was only tepid. An instant later, fresh porridge and bread and a boiled egg appeared at my side, with another cup of tea. But I couldn't move to get it. I was shaking too hard and my head would shriek daggers into my eyes if I tried to, anyway. So I just lay there and watched the blood slowly dry on my wrists and fingers.

Then Terrence came in, alone, seeming to be upset.

"What d'you mean he hasn't eaten? Aw, shite."

"Did ya read what he wrote in there?" It was another guard talking. Apparently he was back to using English.

"Of course I fuckin' did, you fuckin'—" Terrence cut himself off before he said the wrong thing. Then he knelt beside me...then shifted down to cross-legged...and made me look at him. His eyes were hurt. "Brendan, this does neither of us any good. So come along, lad. Eat something and we'll have a nice chat. No questions. No digging. C'mon, lad, just eat something."

I tried to turn away from him but the grip he had on my chin was too solid. Then he frowned and his fingers pressed against my cheek.

The cheek where I was holding the sponge foam.

He jumped on my chest and slapped me, over and over and over, and my heart was screaming and I couldn't breathe, and a guard rushed in but stayed back as Terrance forced open my mouth, shoved his hand into my cheek and pulled the foam out. Then he stood up, breathing hard and furious, and a feral smile crossed his lips. "You'll not get a second chance at this, you little bastard."

Then he yanked the mattress out from under me. I smacked my head on the floor, bringing sharp sudden stars to my eyes. I was beyond dizzy into floating madness and barely able to draw breath.

"What was it?" That guard was amazingly stupid.

"He sleeps without this, from now on. And I want him checked every five minutes."

"But we've got—"

"DO YOU FUCKIN' HEAR ME?" Apparently, Terrence was once a drill sergeant.

The guard got his back up. "I'll talk with my supervisor and—"

"No," Terrence sneered, "*I* will talk with him." Then he stormed from the room.

The guard looked down at me, shaking his head. "He's a right bastard, ain't he?"

I just turned away from him. I heard him leave.

I was shattered. It wasn't going to work. It fucking wasn't going to work. From now on, they'd check my mouth and all my clothing and I'd never have another chance to off myself. I'd even mucked that up. And soon they'd be back to start...to start that...the whole process...all over, again...

I started to cry. I kept it as quiet as I could, not wanting those bastards to know how close I was to breaking, even buried my face in my arms to silence my sobs. My heart still cursed me. My breath was minimal. I was shaking from within and my mind was all over the place.

Jesus God, I'd mucked everything up. I couldn't even get those devils to kill me. They'd come close once but they'd be more careful and never have another chance and this would go on and on and I knew I couldn't hold out against it unless...

Unless.

My heart wasn't so great. It had been fine while in the North...but could I force it to give out? Run around and jump and slam against walls? Would that work? That it hadn't given out, already, was almost a miracle. Or punishment.

What if I deliberately made myself mad? Could I just let my mind go? Could I do that? Was that my only choice, now? Drive my heart too far or do away with my sanity? I was now lucid enough to see I'd flirted with it, earlier.

The best suggestion was my heart. Maybe that was the way—the only way left to end this.

But how? How? Terrence slapping me had felt like it was beginning, but it hadn't. Not fully. What could I do beyond that to make it happen?

I had no time to answer. They came in and took me back to that room. Seems like Terrence thought I was faking my earlier weakness. I was slapped onto the table, but this time I kicked two of them—one in the side and one in the nuts—before they got me shackled down, and it took four of them to hold me, and when Terrence lay the cloth over my face I began to shriek incoherently but they held my head in place and the water poured over me and my screaming was replaced with choking coughs and sputters but for a shorter time, this time.

When the cloth was whipped off, Terrence slapped me and snarled, "What's his name, Brendan? What's his name? The man with you on that day?"

I just coughed and choked and gasped deep on the air as best I could till the cloth went over me, again, and we repeated everything and he slapped me more and asked the same fucking question, over and over and over till I lost control and wept and screamed and fought and spit and bellowed and I couldn't breathe and...and...and...

The whip sliced into my skin as the tree trunk dug into me and I cursed the bastards and their mothers and fathers and all the nations of the earth that allowed such creatures to walk amongst them and it cut deeper and deeper until I was on the ground and...

Max swung the baton up between my legs and I shrieked from the sudden pain and...

I watched the ants whisper back and forth along the black windowsill and followed their trek to the half-eaten sandwich that was now swarming with life and...

The car vanished into smoke and bits rained down about me as I tumbled back and rolled and skidded to a halt and looked around to watch a torn off leg land before my eyes and...

Joanna and I rode back from Dublin in Father Jack's car, me touching my shoulder every time she looked at me as if to say, "I'm yours," even though it brutally hurt me to do so and...

Joanna was trapped in the ruins and the fire was dancing up to her, dancing, dancing as she fought to get away and...

Danny yanked me to my feet but I fought him like a madman and someone was screaming and then...

She turned to look at me...Joanna...fire billowing behind her...making her hair fly wild and free and beautiful and she was accusing me and—

I found myself back in my new cell. The porridge and egg still where they'd been put. The now stone cold tea right beside them. A man in a suit was inspecting me. I was trembling—not from fear but from lack of control, for something about him was wrong and I was lying on the floor and cold and knew I hadn't eaten in at least a day and was shocked that I wasn't hungry, and—

It was Dr. Gilbert. Testing my arms and checking my wrists. Had they brought him all the way from Houston? But why would they do that? He was too old to...to—

"Sergeant Terrence," he snapped, "I don't know what sort of questioning you've been doing, but if you keep it up, I will be performing an autopsy on this lad, soon."

"Dunno what you mean, sir," Terrence replied. He was by the door, keeping wary watch along with his fit twins. "We were just at a table, talking, just like folk. Nothing more." And the twins shared a snicker. I even smiled at that one.

The doctor wasn't having it. "Is that how his clothing got wet—sitting around that table? Did you learn anything?"

"Just getting down to it, sir."

"I doubt that, very much. Look at the scars on his back." I realized my shirt had been pulled up, revealing the whip marks on me. "These are a few years old. This is not the first time you've had him in one of your interrogation centers."

Terrence scowled and stood at parade rest. "I have no idea how those got on him, sir. That's not what we do."

I choked out a laugh, making everyone look at me, and I gasped, "Riding crop. Arse. Hands there and..." And I let myself cough and cough and cough.

Terrence grew even stiffer, if that was possible, and snarled,

"I don't know what he's talking about, sir. We were just at the table asking him some questions and—"

The man rose, his face very irritated.

"Well, *sir*, might you consider the possibility that if you haven't got your answers by now, you won't because there might be nothing to get? Or do you prefer to question a corpse?"

"I think you're overstating it, there, sir."

"And when exactly did you gain your license to practice medicine!?" the man roared. "His blood pressure's astronomical. His pulse above one-forty. And that's at repose. I even hear an abnormality in his heart rhythm, but further testing would be necessary for that and—"

"Should we talk here, sir? In front of...of the patient?"

The doctor did not look back at me as he exited the room. Terrence cast me a brutal glare then he and the twins left.

I just lay there on the floor.

So maybe I'd die, anyway. My heart would do me the favor, after all. Wouldn't that be a kick in the nuts? Well, if that were the case...

I slowly rose, got the boiled egg and cup of tea and alternated between nibbling on one and sipping on the other. It wasn't till I'd finished the egg that hunger slammed into me and I wolfed down the toast covered in porridge. My stomach rebelled and threatened to send it all back up my throat, but by leaning against the wall and breathing slow and deep, I was able to regain control. Maybe I'd have a respite, now. I closed my eyes and the hell with the bloody light shining like the sun fixed in the ceiling and the blood crusting my wrists and fingers and—

The door slammed open and four guards came in.

Shite. Maybe no respite. Maybe that bloody egg, toast and porridge *were* to be my last meal. Well, I'd not make it easy for them.

"C'mon, up!"

I sat where I was. One of them clipped me on the neck with his baton then they pounced on me and dragged me to my feet. I kicked and snarled and refused to stand, so each one grabbed a limb and carried me from the cell, and twist and turn as I might, I could not get leverage enough to escape them. I don't recall saying a word as they did it; I think because I was afraid if I gave way to my voice I'd not be able to stop it once the water came, again. But that didn't keep me from spitting at them and grunting in fear and pain and exertion.

One was back to speaking to me in that garbled language, using words I felt I should know, none of them filtering into my mind's core; for all the willingness I had to understand him, he could have been spouting Chinese or Russian at me, like Jeremy and Vangie would to each other. I caught hints of red on one guard's face and thought, maybe it's blood, maybe I'd done that. And my grunts threatened to become laughter.

This time the corridor was endless, passing quickly in slow motion, staccato in movement, and I knew if it kept going one second longer I'd lose complete control and turn into a raving beast. That my own teeth hinted at the look of a dog only added to my feeling that I should bite and tear the flesh from these monsters and spit their blood in their faces, howling for joy. I may have snapped into one; I heard a yelp of pain but had no way to know from which of them it came or why, for suddenly we were at a door and I was being carried through and my grunts became screams and I was tossed in a bin and...

The hood covered my head, completely, and I was dropped into the trunk of a car and...

The lid closed and I was rolled away like a sack of potatoes and—

It stopped and the bin opened. I finally realized I was in the trunk of a car. The boot. Then I was grabbed and lifted and slung into the air and landed in dirt and grass, both moist and chilled.

I rolled over and scrambled back to be caught by a bush. I struggled with it. Heard someone's laughter, cold and derisive and harsh. A door slammed shut and the car drove away as I fought with that bush's branches till I was free of it, scraped and cut and dazed at the sudden lack of white enclosing me.

Then came the whisper of a breeze on my cheeks and the feel of a soft drizzle on my neck. My voice caught and sharp whimpers of confusion burst from me and I could see...I could see...

There were no walls around me. Just a wide roadway and fields of green with naught but trees and hedges hemming them in. No ceiling above me but low heavy clouds tumbling about in the chill air. I was on my hands and knees and the stones and twigs dug into them, even through my jeans. My shirt was still around my torso, but now sopping wet.

Wet cloth against me!?

No.

No!

NO!

I tore it off.

Let my torso be bare. I didn't care how cold I was. The cloth was gone. It was gone.

I sat back on my calves. Stretched my hands in front of me. My fingers were covered in mud. My wrists were red and raw. I turned my face and palms to the heavens to better feel the graceful touch of the whispering, whispering mist as I gasped in deep, sharp breaths full of—

Of freedom?

Freedom.

I felt no joy at this. No relief. Hell, I barely felt connected to any sort of emotion or reality. I just knew I was away from those rooms. Away from that cold cruel whiteness. Was this how a caged animal felt when released into the wild? Just away from that which imprisoned it? Safe in the openness that now surrounded it? Waiting, wondering if it was about to be caught, again?

That last thought jolted me. I needed some other space for my safety. I needed away from here, for this was too close to my captors. I fought my way to my feet and staggered across the road to cower behind a gathering of trees that gently rustled an offer of protection. I brushed my hand over their trunks in thanks. Felt the sharpness of their bark and reality of their dampness. Heard the shiver of their leaves reply they were glad to offer a moment's respite.

Beyond them was that open field, stretching forever. I hesitated. Looked around, wary. Saw nothing. Heard nothing. Sensed nothing in the way of a predator. My hands tingled. My heart pounded. My breath grew quick and shallow. Farther away was better than where I was, so I aimed straight for another thicket of trees at the far end of the field.

My eyes darted about as I stumbled and staggered, stones in the dirt digging into my nearly bare feet. I fell to my knees, twice...three times, once into a puddle of slopping mud, but forced myself to keep moving.

I reached the thicket to find a dashing brook growling past. The sight of it froze me to the spot. I could not even think of how to cross it without my jeans becoming soaked even more than they already were, and the thought of them sopping wet against my legs sent spasms of revulsion through me.

So I sat down.

And did not move for God only knows how long.

None of this made sense and the more I thought on it the less it did. I could not make myself even contemplate the reality of it. That bit of flowing water had slapped a fence up to my mind, and until the chaos in my head had begun to settle I could not even consider making a coherent thought let alone form a plan of action.

Shadows spit sounds at me. Birds and toads and insects of a nature I'd not heard in years. My mind danced back to my walk to Claudy and remembered nothing similar. Then walking to the fort with Joanna, and still nothing similar. Until a breeze slipped into a sharp chill wind to brush against me and I saw her face in the lowering light and smelled the mint on her breath and felt the bite of the cold air and echoes of birds settling for the night laughed into my ears.

I became aware enough to realize I was shaking, though from the chill and not fear or confusion, anymore. The brook's growls had become happy chirps of water slapping against the stones, as if to say, *What a pleasure it must be to finally listen to us. We will not harm you.* The scent of hearths burning peat or coal or wood surrounded me. My brain clicked hard enough to nudge me into thinking I needed to move along and find a way home before this new night took over, completely. There might be safety in the shadows surrounding me but there was no comfort...and that would grow worse as twilight took over the day.

I leaned forward and washed my hands and face in the icy water. Oh my God, how beautiful it was. How alive and real. Caressing my wounded fingers. Calming the ache in my eyes. Carrying my pain away with joyous movements. I near wept at the beauty of it.

Finally, I rose, slowly, like an old man waking from a long sleep. I worked the kinks from my legs and back, and wandered along the banks of the brook, instead. Why I did that instead of find some board or rocks to build a way across? I can only say it came from the need to keep moving, keep putting space between me and that hell where I'd been confined, and taking the time to work out such a simple task would have been too long in one location. Far, far too long.

I have no idea how long it took me to reach a road with a small bridge and sidewalk that crossed over the brook. I turned to follow along it. I still had no idea where I was or was going; all that mattered was the movement of my legs and the understanding that I was getting farther and farther away from danger.

I saw street signs as I passed but could not understand the language of them. Cars traveled along the road, forcing me to make myself stand still so as to control my staggering, or keep nice and normal in my walk so none would call the Paras down on me. I had a vague understanding that only socks were on my feet, but they were brown with dirt so might actually look like shoes. Then it hit me, I was shirtless. So no matter what I did I'd look wrong.

Oh. Well. May as well keep moving.

After perhaps a mile, a roadway sign approached and I stopped and stood before it until its scribbles took on some meaning. I was vaguely headed for Lisburn, it seemed, which was too southerly a direction for a return to Derry. Not that I was sure, but in the back of my head, now my brain was reconnecting to my reality, I was telling myself I should be passing through Antrim.

Antrim. The first leg of the People's Democracy walk of so many years ago. I laughed. It seemed I'd finally join Eamonn on his march, albeit twelve years late. I wondered what he'd say.

Of course, I had no money on me. Nor was it acceptable to hitchhike in this part of the world, especially when you're but half-dressed; that was sure to get me lifted, again, by Paras or the RUC. It had taken Eamonn and his group four days to walk it, and while they'd met obstructions aplenty along the way, he'd also been in top shape. Me, I still was weak, more dizzy than not, and too close to collapse to even think about how impossible it would be for me to make.

But what else to do? My hunger had vanished, as had my thirst, but they'd be back soon enough, and with a vengeance. I thought about calling Father Jack, collect, but considering our last meeting, I doubted he'd be willing to fetch me, so I hunkered down, headed in what I figured was a northerly direction and looked for a phone box to call Maeve, hoping she could ask Rhuari to fetch me.

I'd no idea how long I'd been kept in that horror or even what the time of day was; my only clue it might be late in the evening was the lack of steady traffic on the road. Had Ma's wake been held and her mass said and her been buried, yet? Who could say?

I happened onto a phone box not another mile up the road and slipped into it, picked up the phone and froze. I had no idea how to call collect in this country. I rang for the operator and hoped they could help me.

The second I heard a voice crisp and clean ask, "How may I help?" I decided to play up my stupidity.

"I'm sorry, ma'am," I said in my best twang, "but I'm lost and I got no money on me and I...I need to call somebody to come pick me up. Is there some way that I...well, that I can make a collect call and...?"

"What sort of call?"

"Collect. Uh...charge it to the other person's phone?"

"Oh, you want me to ring another party and have them accept the charges?"

"Yes, ma'am."

"I can do that for you. Where are you from?"

"Texas."

"God, you have lost your way."

"Yes, ma'am. I-I-I'm here for a funeral, for my aunt...and some cousins and I went out drinkin' and I got no idea where I am."

"What's your name?"

"Jeremy. Landau."

"Landau?"

"Yes, ma'am. My father's—he's French."

"Oh. The name of your aunt's family?"

"Kinsella. I got a cousin. Maeve Kinsella."

"Have you their phone number?" I rattled Ma's number off to her, like I was reading it off a slip of paper. There was a silence. "That's Londonderry. How is it you're in Belfast?"

Shite. "That's where I am? Ain't that a hundred miles away?"

"You did do some drinking."

"Oh, Ma'am, you got no idea." And my voice quivered as I said it...and not deliberately, believe me.

"Hang on."

The line clicked and went silent. For a moment I feared she'd cut me off but then I heard the double-ring pop through. And ring.

And Maeve's voice came on the line. "Hallo?"

"This is the operator calling. I've a trunk call from Jeremy Landau wishing to speak with Maeve Kinsella."

"Jeremy?!" Maeve's voice sounded near panicked. "Jeremy, where are you?"

"Excuse me, but will you accept the charges?"

"Yes, yes," Maeve all but shouted. "Jeremy, where are you?"

"I don't know," I said, keeping the twang in case the operator was listening in. "Bel-fay-ast, someplace. In a telephone bah—" Shite, I nearly said box, a sure giveaway. "Booth."

"Does it offer an address anywhere on the phone?"

I hadn't thought of that. I looked it over and noticed a tag on the side and wording at the bottom.

"Uh—Ravenhill Road?"

"That's near the city center!"

"In Bel-fay-ast?" I was starting to overplay the accent but couldn't help myself.

"Oh, Jeremy...and you're in a telephone box?"

"Yeah. Near a little field."

"Hang on." I heard Maeve softly repeat my words to someone then Rhuari's voice murmured back and Maeve came back on the line. "You're by a cricket pitch. Rhuari knows where it is. Stay there and he'll come to fetch you. It may be a bit."

"Well, it's that or shanks mare...uh...walkin'. I got no money on me. I'm real sorry 'bout this, Maeve. I'll pay for his puh—uh, gas." I bloody almost said petrol.

"Don't be daft. We're just glad you're all right."

We said our good-byes and I hung up and stepped out of the box. My heart was pounding and I was breathing hard, like I'd run half a mile, so I let myself slide down to the pavement and sit at the base of the phone box. The light was finally beginning to fade, so it'd be full twilight before Rhuari got here. If they'd let him out of Derry. But I decided not to worry about that and closed my eyes. Maeve had always been good for her word. I could rest here and let myself drift as I wished and let my plans be made on the morrow and that I'd—

"Howya, son?" jolted me awake.

Party Time

It was darker and two men—one older, one younger, both fat, scowling beasts—stood over me. Across the street was another tall lean bastard trying to decide if he wanted to join in on what looked like would be the night's festivities.

For some reason, I was sure they were Proddies out to protect their bit of the world from the dangerous Papist scum they'd fought so hard to keep in their place. Meaning they'd as soon kill me as spit at me, should I prove to be the enemy. And yet I wasn't the least bit scared of them. I felt nothing about them. I just smiled and nodded my head, and said, "It's all right, fellas—I'm just waitin' for my cousin."

"Fookin' hell, what kind of language is 'at?" It was the younger scowler speaking.

The older one frowned hard at me and leaned in to ask, "Where the fuck ya from?"

"Houston," I said, like a sigh, only I pronounced it *Eyu-ston*, like I'd heart Scott and Jeremy and even Everett say it.

"Station? In fookin' London?" It was the young scowler not believing me.

I squinted up at him. "What? No, Texas."

The lean one heard that and all but scrambled across the road. "Aw, fuck, Macky, he's from fuckin' NASA."

"Where the spaceships are?"

I blinked. "Uh, yeah—NASA's right by Houston."

"The divil; lad, what you doin' here?" said the older one.

"An' wit' no shirt or shoes." That popped out of the lean one.

"Funeral. My-my aunt died—an' we went out drinkin'—me an' my cousins—an' now they're comin' to pick me up. An' I got no idea where my boots are."

Old scowler squatted next to me, true concern in his eyes. "Son, you shouldn't be out here. It's dangerous for someone not known to us all."

"Ya sure you're not IRA and shaggin' on us?" asked young scowler.

"What? Oh—no, I don't think they let Jews in."

"You're a Jew? Comin' to an Irish wake?"

Oh, shit. "My...my daddy's Jewish."

"What's your mother, then?"

I took in a deep breath. "Dead."

Two more of the neighborhood watch strolled up, both carrying cudgels. "Howya, Pete, what's this?"

"Just a yank who's got himself lost."

"Looks like the ragged end of nothin'."

"He does."

"Got your papers on ya?"

I shook my head. My bet was these guys were probably UVF...but to be honest, I still did not understand how dangerous this all was for me—no, I just did not care.

"I had my passport," I said, "but I got no idea where it went. I come to like this."

Old scowler, Pete, sat on the pavement, beside me. "Listen, lad, this sounds like quite the story. Have you nothin' to prove who you are? Nothin' at all?" And he was almost tender in his questioning.

I shook my head. "I could tell you stories 'bout Texas, if you want."

"D'you work at NASA?" asked the lean one.

"No, I only been there, once. It's about twenty-five miles outside town and traffic's a bitch."

But I did tell them about my excursion to NASA with Everett, Jeremy and our crew from Mrs. Glendon's. That segued into the time Everett was caught in traffic during a rainstorm that flooded the freeway. I just made out like it happened to me, and how the only way I kept from being drowned was to climb onto my car's roof and jump across from one roof to the next to get to the side of the roadway.

The others were growing fascinated and I was feeling even more casual. Someone actually brought me a shirt to wear, and I thanked the heavens for it now being dark enough that they wouldn't notice the scars on my back or around my wrists. I left the sleeves loose to keep the injuries covered as much as I could.

Seems they weren't so unhappy about me being there, now it was shown I wasn't some wild animal come to burn them out of house and home. Like they'd done to the likes of me. They saw themselves as being under siege, again, like three hundred years ago, and they weren't liking it so were playing the victim as only a true oppressor can. I knew all this even as I spoke. Even as I told them of the characters in *The Colonel's*. Even as they noted local characters who matched the likes of Todd and Rocky and Lorraine. They were just people out having a fine time on a cool spring night, not monsters or beasts, so much like others I'd been around and seen.

The party was in full swing when an RUC tender drove up and stopped. One beefy constable leaned out the passenger window, confused.

"Howya, Pete," he said. "What's this?"

"Oh, we got us an American, here, tellin' us 'bout bars with funny people in 'em."

"An' ya should hear what he has to say about JR!"

Which made no sense, because I'd said nothing about anyone on *Dallas*.

"Oh, the rainstorms in Houston!"

"You give a shite 'bout that?" the constable shot back.

"It come down so hard, once, it turned the motorway into a river."

"Bollocks, Texas is desert."

Without thinking I popped off with, "That's just the western half; eastern half's like...like Florida."

The constable got out, irritated. "Bollocks! Me brother's in Texas and he goes on about how hot it is."

"What part?" I asked.

"San Antonio."

I nodded. "It gets hot there. He tell you 'bout the Riverwalk and...and he seen the Alamo, yet?"

"You been there?"

"Yeah. It's just a couple hundred miles from me."

Young scowler almost tried to smile. "A couple hundred miles'd put ya clear across Ireland."

The constable dropped to the pavement to sit cross-legged. "So what's it like? I been thinkin' of makin' a visit."

"Riverwalk's pretty. It's down off the street and there's good food and it's just—nice." As if I'd been there and wasn't repeating stories told me by Everett.

We kept on like that for hours, with me telling lies about Texas and myself as women brought out bottles of chilled beer. I was offered some but begged off *because of my stomach*. Pete jumped back to his flat to make me a concoction that would take the bite off the hangover. I drank it. Nearly gagged on it, and they all laughed, but they followed it up with bottles of Coke, which helped more. But what made it all worthwhile was the cheese sandwiches his missus offered me. Dear God, I was famished from the hunger.

Then someone tuned into a radio station playing the top forty and some couples swung into a dance while others shared stories of their own travels to London and Dublin and Galway and Spain, fuckin' Spain! Obviously, I was in a middle class neighborhood.

By the time Kieran drove up, the party had filled the entire block and was in near riot, and I was almost back to feeling human.

Of course, I noticed it was Kieran had come for me instead of Rhuari, and him not yet old enough to be legal driving. Not cool. And not a good sign.

Also, he wasn't old enough to read the area and see it would be all right to approach, thanks to the men and women and patrol car making merry around the phone box. In fact, he'd started backing away when I happened to see him and stood up and waved. He stopped and slowly edged the car over.

Well, there was no trouble at all, even though they knew he was from Derry and Catholic. They gave him directions on the best way to get out of town.

The best five ways.

Then they argued about which was better. He got fed and filled with drink, as well. Then finally it was time to be gone, before things grew too real, so I made a point of going around to the driver's door to get in and *stopping at why the steering wheel was on the wrong side of the car*. They all gained a great laugh from it and slapped me on the back and led me to the left side. That's when I offered to give them their shirt back but they said to keep it. A gift from Ireland.

When we finally drove me off, they were waving Kieran and myself a fond farewell.

He didn't look at me till we were on the A3 and well on our way, then he cast the wariest of glances. "What the fuck was that?"

I shrugged and said, "It was make nice with them or kill them all. Which would you have me do?"

"Christ, they could've turned on us at any time."

"They still will," I said, leaning back into the car. "Once those constables find out who I really am, they'll all be doubly pissed for the sport I made of them."

"How'd you wind up there, anyway?"

It took me a moment to say, "I was at Castlereagh."

His face went white. "Maeve was told you were in Strand Road."

"Maeve was told wrong."

His hands began to shake. "You—you've been there but four days. They could hold you for seven. Why'd they release you?"

I shrugged.

"Bren, people're gonna think you...they'll think since you were let go so quick..."

"They'll think I grassed on them."

He drove a moment, trying to figure out how to ask, "Did you?"

I looked away from him. "I don't know."

Stars

It took me little time to figure out we were not headed for Derry but were aimed south.

Aimed for The Republic.

I turned to Kieran and asked, "How'd you get out of Derry?"

"I didn't. Raymon McCreesh and Patsy O'Hara are near dead, so it's locked down with no one allowed in or out. Ma's wake was under surveillance, as was her funeral."

"Then she *is* buried."

"We tried to hold off, Bren. But we'd no idea how long you'd be held and Father Jack felt it best to be done with it. He preached a good one at her service—about the evils of the Brits and how they'd even prevent a lad from seeing his beloved mother off to the next world."

I couldn't help but snort at that one. "So you were there?"

"I snuck in."

"Where were you before?"

"I can't say."

"Who taught you how to drive?"

"Jesus, I've been boostin' cars since I was twelve."

"That's when I started working on them."

"I'm told you're good at it."

I nodded. "Was Eamonn allowed to be there?"

"Yeah. Under guard, but..."

"How did he look?"

"What?"

"When I saw him, his hair was wild and his beard long. And he hadn't bathed."

"He...uh, he looked good. Clean. Haircut and no beard. In a suit a size too big for him."

"PR."

"What's that?"

"If he looks good, it looks good for his jailers."

"Oh. Yeah, I can see that."

"Kieran...where you taking me?"

He hesitated. "To Colm. You wanted to see him..."

I knew what this meant. More questions...and a bullet if they didn't suit the questioners.

"I'd rather have a bath and a good shit before. Haven't had either...though they didn't feed me enough to shit out."

"They're expectin' us."

I sighed, smiled and leaned back in the car, grateful for the dark so I could rest my eyes. Who'd ever have thought night would be that sort of blessing?

*****

We drove up to a farm on the border, then Kieran hid the car in the barn. A signal appeared in the farmhouse and Kieran popped into a hole in the ground to sneak through a tunnel. I hesitated, flashing back to the rooms at Castlereagh and the long corridors, but Kieran looked up at me, wary, wondering if I was going to run. A sure sign of guilt, that. I made a show of stretching my back and legs, took a deep breath and forced myself to climb down the ladder...

Straight into a dark corridor with light only from Kieran's torch. It wasn't so very long a one but it was long enough so by the time he popped out, my shaking was out of control and I was near to panic.

Kieran looked down at me. "You afraid?"

I scrambled out of the hole. "The...the walls around me."

"You don't like tight places?"

I shook my head.

"Never knew."

"Not till...not till now..."

Then several men surrounded us, all dressed in black and wearing balaclavas. They motioned for us to follow them and headed for a small low building just the other side of a hill.

I stopped at seeing it. Fucking froze.

Kieran nudged me. "It's just in here."

"I won't go in," I said. All without a thought.

"C'mon, Brendan, Colm's waitin'."

"I won't go in a room. Not another room!"

"You that afraid? My big brother, scared to even so much as face his friends for what's gone on and—?"

"I'll face them out here! I'll not go inside!"

His mates grabbed me and tried to drag me into the building—

And I became a wild animal, screeching and kicking and clawing and biting until they let me drop to the ground. And I stayed there, flat on my back. The sky had cleared and I could see the stars cutting into the vague night. They were the only thing that calmed me.

Kieran glanced between the men, embarrassed, then snarled, "Be right back."

His mates continued to stand around me, as if on guard. I didn't need to look at them to see the confusion on their faces. It was cold, out, and the dirt was surely colder in their eyes, and I was hardly dressed for the weather, so what sort of fool would kick and bite to be let lie there except a madman. And it's best to let madmen be.

If only they knew how right they were.

Oh, dear God, just looking at the heavens—the bare darkness could not help but grow into the softest velvet, glistening with tiny diamonds. Watching. Silent. Heartbreaking in their beauty. Not in the least concerned with the stupidity of men. They'd existed a billion years before me and would exist a billion more after, and who was I to think my sad little seconds of life were of any true importance, next to them? They were the real alpha and omega. They were the true never-ending light. Not even God could own them, let alone man.

I cannot begin to describe the peace I found just looking at them. Watching them glimmer and shine and wonder at my fixation on them. At my feeling as one with them. Were I to die, I halfway thought I'd join with them to gaze down at other fools like myself, children too stupid to know anything of truth or love or belief. Would I weep as they sometimes do, the hints of their tears streaking across the sky for an instant? Would I watch innocents like Joanna and myself try to build a world between ourselves alone and question the assumption that such a thing was possible? Would I see the same hideous actions practiced in every corner of this pathetic little planet against men of black skin and yellow skin and brown skin and red skin as well as white? Would I even care enough to care?

I began to hope that I'd be left there to just lie until the light of day chased the stars around to the other side of the world. I needed no guards. The gentle stars wouldn't let me move, not so long as they had watch over me. Existence was meaningless aside from those tiny white dots in the near dark above me. I almost began to smile and—

Footsteps whispered up, careful, uncertain. I sensed someone squatting beside me then Colm's face drifted into my line of sight. Concern filled his eyes.

I half grimaced, half smiled and softly croaked, "Colm, please, you're blocking my view."

"What's this, Bren?" he asked, just as softly. "You plannin' to claim madness as your defense?"

Defense? Can a true state of being excuse anything? Can loss of your soul mean all is well? Can hate so vicious it rocks your very being be accepted as your punishment? It sounded to me like I'd been tried and convicted, all without a moment of explanation on my part. Not that I could offer any that would be believed. The whole point of this insipid little play was to ignore the facts and laugh at the truth and believe only the tales of idiots. Man's true fate.

I stared at Colm. "I will not go inside."

"Brendan, come along, you're playin' the part of a fool."

"Listen to what I say, Colm," and my voice had a true hiss behind it. "I will not go into any room. Ever. Do with me as you will, but you will do it in the open." I shifted my eyes back to the sky. Drew strength from the pinpoints of light so high above me. "You will do it under the stars. So they can bear witness."

"Then we'll drag you in." He started to rise.

I didn't move. Didn't even look at him as I snarled, "If you try, me China, I will rip your fucking heart out, do you fucking understand me?"

He stopped. Glared at me. "Listen to me, me *China*," and he all but spat the word out, "the only thing standin' between you and a bullet in the head, right now, is me."

Christ, he was so serious, so full of his own sense of meaning and grandeur and heroism, just like that fuckin' Brit commander—I had to laugh at him. "Then you better fucking move, lad," I choked out, "for there's some have decided I'm taking that bullet, whether I deserve it or not, so save yourself. Stand aside. I'm not worth the hell it'll bring you to back me." And I kept laughing, lost in the meaninglessness of it.

"Jesus Christ—what the fuck is this? I'm tryin' to keep you alive!" He was actually angry, which only made me laugh harder. He dropped to one knee and grabbed me by the hair and snarled, "Answer me one question—"

Oh, fuck—*one question? One word? One this or one that?* Jesus Christ, people, have some self-respect; go at least for a dozen.

"What did you tell them?"

I couldn't speak, I was still so choked with laughter, so he slapped me. Twice. I was just able to shake my head. His grip tightened in my hair.

"Don't tell me it was nothin'! They had you in there but four days, and now three of our lads've been lifted by the peelers. Your own brother near taken at your mother's funeral. So what the fuck did you tell them?"

I think he was planning to hit me, again, but I'd begun to regain control so he just released me and leaned back on his haunches to wait till I caught my breath, once more.

Finally, finally, I was able to whisper, "I...I don't know. What I told them. If I told them anything. Half the time I wasn't there. And the other half...tell me, Colm...how can you talk when you're drowning in a room without water?"

"Arra, talk sense!"

I just lay there exhausted, still breathing hard, and gazed back at the stars. "I lay like this. On a table. My face covered by a cloth. And I was drowned. Over and over and over. And just a cold dead ceiling to bear witness. What you do to me now is nothing. Nothing. Nothing compared to that. Just do it out here. No ceiling above me. Please."

Colm moved closer and gently turned my face to look at him. His eyes were wary. Uncertain.

"Brendan," he asked, "are you sayin' they used a water torture on you?" I couldn't find the words to answer him. It was all I could do to nod my head with the barest of moves. He looked up and around and snarled, "All of yous back away. Go over to the cars, now. NOW!"

They did so, all but Kieran. Colm beckoned to him then turned back to me and leaned in to whisper, "Brendan—Bren, me China, listen to me. Answer me." I could barely keep focused on anything, but I drew a deep breath and fought to smile at him. "That day the bomb went off—and you were caught by it—who else did you see, that day?"

What a stupid question. "You already know." I took another deep breath. "You...hit me. Then Ma hit me and you...you stopped her...dunno all of it. Don't remember all of it. My brain was a scramble."

"So I was at the house where you were taken. That I knew where you were."

What was he talking about? We'd already been over this. I just wanted to look back at the stars. They were the only thing I felt any kinship with, but he wouldn't fucking let go of my face, so I nodded. "Yeah, you were there. You and Danny. You brought Ma. Said you brought her. You were there. Danny was there. His eyes so big and scared and you hit me. And he was crying...crying...they wanted me dead...and Ma... You brought her. To fight with them. She stopped them, 'cause you brought her."

"Fought who, Bren? Tell me who she fought. Did you know any of *them*?"

"I dunno. Didn't see. Shadows. Ghosts. So many fucking ghosts."

He released my chin, his face lost in confusion.

Kieran's voice whispered, "But, Colm, if he saw some other men, there, could he have—?"

"Be quiet," came a harsh voice, I think from behind my head. Or top. It was a new one, and cold with cruelty and authority. I suppose he'd been listening in and...oh, of course. All these questions have been for his benefit. He continued, "He's actin'. Don't mean anything."

"It was Brits diggin' at him, this time," said another, "not some RUC poofs." Was the whole council out here, bearing witness to my interrogation? Oh, dear, that could be spooky.

"It's early days, still. Takes word time to permeate..."

"Not four days," Colm snapped.

"Depends," another voice asked, this one calmer and sounding more reasoned. All of them were above me, out of sight.

I almost chuckled. *If I can't see you, are you really there?*

"Look at the circumstances," said one.

"He's lyin'," another added. "He knew all the lads lifted."

"No," whispered Colm, "he knew Paidrig, only."

Oh, Christ, they'd taken Paidrig for this, now? Sweet simple Paidrig? Had I grassed on him?

Colm continued, "And he knew Robert only by seein' him drive me to the fort. Didn't know his name."

"But Robert's not one of us," snapped the harsh man.

"Yet they lifted him," said the calm voice. "So he could've told them he drove you—"

"Dammit, he knew *me*, not Robert!" Colm snapped. "Didn't even know his name, so how could he share it?" He came close to me, again. "Brendan, who else did the Brits want to know about?"

I didn't know. "Tell me who you want it to be and I'll agree."

"No, you have to tell me—what else did you know about?"

Emotions exploded through me and I careened close to weeping. "Colm, just you and Danny. Danny. Christ, I've seen nothing but ghosts since I come back. Ma. Joanna. Spirits indoors. Spirits outdoors. I-I-I don't know what I said! I don't know what I know!" I was flying close to hysterics.

"Spirits out doors?" It was the calm voice asking.

"What's he on about?"

"I tell ya, he's bloody faking madness; thinks it'll save him."

"Bren, get hold of yourself. Make some sense. Okay, you...you saw Danny the day of the bombing and..."

Why were they torturing me so? I could barely speak.

"He stopped me. Stopped me doing. Something stupid. Saw him. In the mist. Stopped me. It was Danny. Walking away. He's been to hell, our Danny. That fucking church sent him there. Father Jack. Bastard. Be careful with him."

"No need to fear there," said Colm in the kindest voice I'd ever heard in my life. "We know about him, now. Stupid man. Turnin' you over. But he doesn't know we know. So...he's the one you saw?"

Reading his missal in a nearby chair as I looked around and—

I shook my head. "Other house. White walls. He was reading."

"No, Bren, you said he was in the mist..."

"No." I somehow managed to shake my head, my voice a whisper, growling, "He didn't stop me. He's no ghost. But Danny. Our Danny. His eyes so hurt. So lost in pain. But he smiled. And he stopped me. And...and Maeve smiled at him. She saw him. Saw his ghost."

I felt Colm sit on the ground beside me. He leaned into my sight and I turned away. "Brendan...Brendan...you aren't sayin' you saw Danny the night Billy and his mates hurt you? You can't have..."

"I don't know, anymore! Please, Colm, just do what you must." I was losing my last shred of control and wanted only to sleep forever, please just let me sleep forever.

"Listen, me China," and his voice was so tender, I felt myself turn to look at him. "You talk of Danny. When did you see him last? Danny Gallagher? What did you mean by *his ghost*?"

"Didn't see much. Bare. In the fog."

"In the fog?"

I nodded, barely.

"What fog? When?"

I shrugged.

"Was it that day of the bomb?"

I sighed and managed to shake my head, *No*.

"Was it the day he and I fought? As boys?"

I almost growled as I shook my head, *No*.

"So you last saw him before you left?"

I shook my head.

"Not...not since you've been back?"

I drew in a deep breath...reminded myself it's Colm asking...and nodded.

Kieran popped in with, "He's talking to dead men?!"

Colm gave a sharp gesture with his hand. I think had Kieran been close enough, he'd have been struck by it. "This is your brother here," he growled, his voice more angry than I'd ever heard. "Do you understand me? Anything that's said here, he is your brother! Do. You. Understand?"

Kieran gave him a jerky nod of *yes*.

Colm leaned in closer. Held my face in his hands. "Bren, did Danny say anything to you? Or you to him?"

I sighed. Worked my right hand into the form of a gun, then surrounded it with my left hand. "Stop. Using. Place. Burned.

Place. Dead. Animal. Me. My pad. Wallet there." Then I put my left hand to my lips, all fingers touching, and shifted it around to where only my index finger lay against them before all my strength left me and my hand drifted down.

"That's how he got your...your..." Colm looked like he'd been punched in the belly. He leaned back, his face white and his voice cracked. "That's how Maeve got it back and...Jesus Christ, it was you told him of that place. That info. You gave it to him and you didn't say," he said.

This was fucking endless. "I don't know what I said," I said, tears taking me over, again. "Just get it done with! But do it out here. Please, Colm. I won't go in a room. I won't. I can't. I'll make you kill me, here!"

Colm released me and stood, slowly, but I gave him only the slightest of notice as I turned my eyes back to the stars. I heard him mutter, "Those bastards, those fuckin' bastards, mother-fuckin' bastards." It made no sense to me, not until he touched Kieran's shoulder and added, "Take care of him," and stormed away. I heard three other men go with him.

Then Kieran was seated on the ground beside me, his eyes wide and hurt. He put a hand on my heart and dug his fingers into my chest and his voice choked as he said, "Brendan—Bren, I'm so sorry. I am so sorry."

So he was the one designated to put an end to me. What had he to be sorry for? Weren't we all at one time or another?

I waited for the feel of the pistol. Waited for the crack of it as it sent a bullet into me. Hoped I'd join the stars. Hoped I'd be one of a cluster. I was so tired of being to myself and alone and wanting to be with those who cared for me. I felt a blanket pull over me, up to my chin. Felt something put under my head to support it.

And grew irritated. No need for these elaborate moves; it's not like I'll notice once I'm gone.

Then Colm strode back into my sight, shaking with anger. He knelt beside me and pulled me up. Held me in his arms almost like a lover would. As Jeremy once had. Like Vangie once had. As Joanna had that lovely day...walking to the fort and...and...

He brushed my hair back and I finally noticed he was near tears.

"Bren, they wanted us to think you grassed on us." His words spilled out. "They wanted us to think it was you told them about Paidrig and Robert, but if you'd told them anything of what you told me...about Danny...they'd be lookin' for him, thinkin' him still alive, but there's been nothin' about that. Anywhere. About me, they know who I am and might keep quiet hopin' to feed my paranoia and catch me on the run, but if they had even the thought Danny Gallagher was still alive, they'd be turnin' every household upside down till they found him. You...you told them nothin'."

His words made no sense. Was Danny alive? Had I not seen his ghost, but him? "I-I-I don't understand..."

"Listen, me China, it doesn't matter, because none of it was about me or the lads here. That's probably why they gave up on you. They decided you knew nothing. So the bastards sent you out to let us find you and hinted that you'd helped them. So we'd kill you. Just to give them somethin' to use in the press against us and hurt us more in the community and...and...but...but you're me China, Bren. You held firm. Dunno how you did, but you held firm. And I will never doubt you, again."

I tried to smile at him but think I only looked drunk.

He nodded to Kieran and said, "Help me get him to his feet."

I tried to push away. "I won't go in a room."

"You won't have to," said Colm. "But will you ride in the back of an estate car? With windows. Lyin' down."

Like the back of Lon's Oldsmobile. Big and curved windows and riding so soft down the road...no...no...

Or the estate car after Burntollet. Like the girl in the back?

Or Jimmy Haggerty's da's car...like Ma? His...his would be okay...

"Watching the stars pass," Colm kept whispering. "Will you let us take you someplace safe? So you can heal? Take as long as you need to heal?"

All this made no sense. "Aren't you gonna kill me?"

He just smiled and shook his head. Then Kieran took me under my right arm and I looked at him to see full and complete pride in his eyes for the first time since I'd been home. None of the disdain or disgust or dismissal or uncertainty I'd seen before. And I finally believed he meant it. For some reason, they were happy to be with me and ashamed no longer.

That definitely made no sense.

But I let them lead me to the back of an old Humber estate

car to lie in the back, and Kieran drove me to an empty house in the middle of Donegal...

Before I was taken to Aunt Mari's. White walls and thatched roof. Long and low. Peat burning in the hearth. A warm blanket over me as tender hands changed my dressings.

No...no, not in there...not, again...

But this time...instead it was a hothouse I was brought into, with glass for a ceiling, dirty but open to the sky. The stars just visible through the grime. And thick with plants and a perfume so rich it felt like a salve to my skin. There I was allowed to lie on a cot.

A rollaway, like Maeve's.

And just sleep. No dreams. Just a quiet resting darkness.

But my meals? Stews and cottage pies and full breakfasts and scones with clotted cream and gentle tea and Guinness...and, oh, that was, without question, pure heaven.

I made full use of it all until I could face four walls, again. Until I regained control of myself. But this time I didn't need six months to do it; I only needed six weeks. At which time I was ready for my new role in life.

Brendan Kinsella.

He'd been taken away from me.

But he is who I now am and always will be.

And I am so bloody proud of it.

Completion

I was kept in secret until the end of the hunger strike. I fixed cars, weapons, watches, whatever they needed...but no bombs. They asked...not Colm but another man...and my only word was, "No." He shrugged and that was that.

I also read the crap our leaders put out. Watched eight more young men die under hideous conditions in the hunger strike, each death sparking more rioting, death, and destruction. But each time a bit less fervent as it slowly became too damn bloody obvious how it would end. And sure enough, the families of the strikers saw the futility of it and began to intervene. So the strike was called off on the 3rd of October. Thatcher declared it *a major victory over criminals*.

To the public and press.

In reality, our political prisoners were now treated as such. All done very quietly, of course, so those ten dead had not completely died in vain. Unfortunately, no one truly cared to follow up on that aspect.

Instead, it was also obvious there would be years more of death, destruction and hate until we reached the point where the bloodletting had wearied us enough for both sides to want it ended, no matter what. Then, and only then, is there ever true compromise.

So now it was time for me to move on.

I was asked to tell what happened to me at Castlereagh, which I did before an official examiner. They said I may be called into court to support it, to which I shrugged. Nothing would ever be done; England had already proven that in 1978, against the European Court on Human Rights.

Colm had held onto my old passport, and Siobhan's solicitor mate suggested I should simply renew it, seeing as how the British wanted little to do with me after their torture. Granted, it was long expired, but she doubted there would be any real issue.

"You're an embarrassment," she'd said. "First, that they couldn't find you, and second that they can't really prove you ever left the UK. You will now be ignored. You'll probably have to deal with inland revenue over not having filed tax returns, if you want to maintain that you've been in-country the entire time, but I could look into it further, if you want."

"What's the benefit?" I asked.

"I doubt there would be a criminal case. Just fake some income, file returns for the last few years, pay back taxes and some penalties. But it makes your passport clear and you would then be eligible for National Health."

Meaning, I could get the medication I needed.

After a lot of thought and considering the possibilities with the fake passport Uncle Sean had provided, I asked her to go ahead. I returned my hair to its normal curly, and got my chin neatly shaved at the same barber's, then took new photos and gave them to her.

Now I had to see Maeve and Kieran with a proposition. When I put it forth to Colm, he backed me and quietly smiled.

"Danny Gallagher, *were he alive*, would have been of the same mind."

I returned his smile in agreement.

So it was arranged for us to meet at Rhuari's home in Shantalow. I slipped back into the North near Carnagarve with that trim cheerful Kelly as my minder. Two Army patrols missed catching us before we were collected by a passing van and dropped off a mile from where we needed to be.

The walk was easy in this area. Few patrols. Helicopters passed overhead, but they were obvious when approaching and simple to hide from. Then Kelly led me up to a row of nice two-story terrace houses, each neatly painted and with a little brick fence enclosing a patch of grass or gravel. They looked comfortable. Human.

Kieran opened the door when I knocked and it took him a moment to recognize me.

"Jesus, Bren...they made you a ginger?"

I don't know why they felt it important, but I was not one to argue, at that point. "For now," I shrugged as we entered. "It'll wash out."

Rhuari was halfway down the stairs, calling, "Maeve?"

She appeared from the kitchen, wiping her hands on a cloth.

"Naturally, you're just in time for supper," she said, smiling. Then she hugged me as if I'd been gone for twenty years. I hugged her back, just as much. "You've lost weight, Bren."

I shrugged. "The clothes're a size large. Deliberate."

She cast a glance at Kelly, who introduced herself, and she said, "We've a fine stew worked up with brown bread. Mrs. O'Canainn's recipe."

I grinned and said to my companion, "You're in for a feast."

Rhuari motioned to the toilet, saying, "Clean yourselves and join us at the table. Bridie'll be down in a moment. She's just settling the wains."

He nodded at Kelly as if he already knew her. I left it at that.

Bridie joined us a moment later—bright, bubbly, only up to his shoulder and nicely rounded, and so obviously in love with him, and he with her, she was the perfect compliment to my brother. I was near overwhelmed at how happy I was for them both, and that their son had been born well and good.

The meal was fine, especially since it was Bridie made the stew and bread. I loved my sister, but anything beyond a fry-up or fried fish was beyond her ability. We talked of nothing, despite how we'd not seen each other since I'd left the hospital after Ma's death, and I found I truly did like Bridie.

But then we were done and having another pot of tea...and it was time for business.

"Bren, I should tell you," Maeve said, "Kieran and me, we moved here, to Rhuari's."

I glanced at him, and he only looked back, impassive.

"Are you finishing your nursing?" I asked.

"Don't know yet."

"I say you should."

"There's much to think on and—"

"I also say..." and I had to take in a deep breath on this, "...Kieran should go to live with Mairead."

Kieran jumped to his feet, snarling, "What?"

"I spoke with her about it," I said. "You're now an orphan and but fifteen years of age. She's your sister, your oldest adult relative, who's available—"

Maeve huffed. "Brendan, I'm well of age."

"Hear me out," I snapped. "As an orphan, there are special provisions for bringing Kieran into Canada. Mairead and Tur are more than willing, and they have so much room in their house. So much..." I turned to Maeve, "I think you would be happy there, as well. There's an excellent nursing school not so very far from her home. You could finish there."

"While Eamonn is in the H-Blocks?" she huffed. "You want me to—to just leave him?"

"He'll be out, soon, according to his new barrister. He might even join you, in Toronto. We all think it best for you both. Give you a chance at a decent life."

Kieran snapped, "You think I'll run off like you did?"

"I didn't run," I said, looking him straight in the eye. "I was taken."

"You were leavin', Bren!"

"True. And I did not come back; I was building a life in Houston. It wasn't perfect, but it would've been one hell of a lot better than here. That's why I want you and Maeve to have a better go at a future."

"I couldn't play the part of a coward and—"

I shot my eyes hard into his but kept my voice calm as I said, "You will not speak to me, like this. I have earned some respect from you, so you will listen. You're not of age, Kieran. Eamonn agrees with me, and if you don't believe me, ask Colm. You will go to live in Toronto. Our sister will take care of you."

I turned to Maeve to add, "I cannot make you go; I can only hope you will. This way, I will know you're under the shelter of Tur and Mairead, so will have nothing to be concerned with."

Maeve grew very still. She finally understood what I was saying. Kieran also grew quiet and let himself sit.

"It's going to take all of you, isn't it?" She whispered.

"No," I said. "Not you or Kieran. And I will be in constant contact with you all. And...as I said, Eamonn may well be released before the year is out."

"Rhuari, did he speak with you about this?"

"No need to," he said. "It makes sense. I'll visit Eamonn, once a week, and he'll have here to stay, when he's released."

Maeve looked at me for a long moment then drew a deep breath. "Are the schools free in Canada?"

I shrugged. "Where are my things?"

"Mrs. Haggerty's."

"In my duffel bag you'll find traveler's checks wrapped in my socks. I have more than six-thousand pounds...which is well over twelve-thousand Canadian. Get them to me and I'll see to it Mairead gets at least ten-thousand of that. I think that will cover a lot of it. She'll help you with the rest, if need be, and you'll have a room to yourself and food a-plenty."

"When I have my certificate, I'll be returnin'."

"That will be by your choice. But may I offer something more? The way you cared for Ma, and for me when I was hurt, and I know you've cared for others when medical attention couldn't be had. You would be a fine doctor. It's been said by others. And you could do so much more good that way."

She blinked and concentrated on sipping her tea.

I turned my focus to Kieran. "You could help her become one, if you'd stop thinking only of yourself. They have good schools, and Tur can get you work. Perhaps you could even attend university."

"No, no..." said Keiran. "I won't go. I can't leave me mates."

"It's already decided," I shot back.

"What're you gonna do? Knock me out and cart me off?"

"Kieran, hush," said Maeve. "We'll discuss it later."

Kelly smiled and said, "I think we'll discus it, now." Then she dragged Kieran into the back yard.

Glancing out the kitchen window at the two of them, talking, I could almost see usual mix of fear, anger and condemnation in my brother...but it slowly gave way to no small amount of relief, as he accepted it.

So Rhuari called Mairead, and she spoke with Maeve to work out a timetable, and that was that. Of course, they had to get passports, but using the emergency process they came within four weeks.

A week later, once the money was transferred and plane tickets set up, Rhuari and Bridie drove Maeve and Kieran down to Dublin for the flight to Toronto. Both of them actually seemed excited about it, now. Mairead had already begun the process of making them legal, so I had no doubt they would be fine.

As for me? Despite what Maeve thought I was not willing to join with any of the alphabet crews, and I doubt they were hurt by my attitude. I had already been in contact with a passenger line in

Cobh and had a position lined up, once another man retired. Which would be the end of November. Once I left the North, I would not be back. My home was no longer my home. But I would keep in contact Colm and help raise funds to help those who'd been brutalized by the system as it currently stood.

As for Father Jack, one day he drove off and never came back. Where he went or what became of him, I did not care to know. He'd handed me over to Billy and his monsters, so maybe he'd gotten wind of our displeasure and just bolted. He was smart enough to.

The one thing I had left to do was drop by McClosky's and speak with Diarmaid...only it turned out McClosky's had shut down and he now worked for Nixon's. That was not expected. Still buying him a pint and couple pasties for lunch at a nearby pub got me the information I wanted.

"Yeah," he said. "Picked the Father's car up down near Ballymoney. Bloody trek, that. Took the church forever to pay, an' half the reason I lost the shop. Good thing me Da's not 'round t' see it."

"Can you show me exactly were?"

"Why?"

"I'll pay your expenses and your time. Hundred pounds?"

"An' petrol?"

I nodded.

"Your funeral."

I merely smiled and we headed straight out.

The Final Ghost

Diarmaid took me in an old Dodge Lorry breakdown truck, of all things. Half rusted to nothing, and with a nasty ride. I didn't remember this being Mr. McClosky's.

It took about an hour, dashing over hills and through valleys in a way that made the truck seem older than it was. Twilight was already beginning to grow, bringing its softness and peace to the gentle fields in every direction. Then before we reached Ballymoney, he turned onto a side lane and the shrubs and trees caught in the deepening darkness were giving birds a rest for the coming night...

As I walked to Claudy in no small measure of joy, hearing the bleating of sheep and soft call of cows settling down and—

"Th' car was there, on a side," he said.

We had rolled to a halt, probably not even a mile down that side road. I did not feel as if I were in this world, at the moment. It was too fine. Too close to magical, so I froze, looking straight ahead as the road continued into the growing darkness until—

"The bastards up there just let it roll down."

I was breathing quick and shallow as I looked to our right to see a thick wall of shrubs and a ditch...well, what could pass for a ditch. Meaning Father Jack's car had rolled down from my left.

To my left...

Somehow, I managed to turn and look.

There was a drive leading up a slow rise to a house and two other buildings. One side had more heaping shrubs while the other was open enough to see down to the main road. Someone was home, judging from the lights already on in the biggest building and smoke trailing from the chimney and—

"Need to fuel up, in Ballymoney," finally broke my concentration.

I nodded. Handed him ten twenty-pound notes, then got out

of the truck and said, "You can go, then."

"How ya gettin' back?"

I just waved him on.

He shrugged, used the drive to turn around and drove away.

I heard a door open at the house and hid behind the drive's shrubs. Two men came out, both tall, both fat, and one of them Charles. The other walked with a limp.

"Told ya, dad," Charles growled. "Just an idiot took a wrong turn."

"Ya should look around," was said in a raspy voice.

"Will ya give over? It was a bloody breakdown truck; lost is all. Nobody's comin' in one of those. Christ."

He stormed back into the house. His father slowly followed.

I hid there for maybe ten minutes, unable to decide what to do. A weird sense of fear and anticipation held me in place...but I could not have that...so I started up the drive. Crouching.

Not deliberately. More like I was programmed to that particular action. I went slow and kept tight to the bushy side and—

A dog barked from within the house, about halfway up.

I froze in place. Security lights flared on, nearly blinding me. After my eyes had settled, I noticed CCTV cameras at each corner of the house. And an alarm system set up. All screaming, *Stay Away*!!

That gave me two choices—go straight up to the door and introduce myself...or leave.

Instead, I sat on the icy ground, forgetting I was on a small rivulet that ran parallel to the shrubs till the cold water jolted me. But I did not rise. I stayed there. Watching that house. That main door. Waiting. Hoping. Remembering...

Escorting Joanna up to her home after the fleadh. And having a fine dinner—

Walking to the circle fort, that chilly day. Her golden hair dancing in the breeze. Lovely spearmint whispering around us. Just her and me, and I'd known it would be forever because she's risked all to see me and—

Driving back from Dublin, so many years ago, in Father Jack's car. Her in front, me in the back. Smiling as I touched the brand she had put on me. Father Jack driving.

I touched my shoulder where her name still cursed me. Still

held me. When I still had dreams. Simple dreams that would matter to no one but me and her.

Dreams.

Knowing our life could have been so lovely. A story told of how we, not only just us two but all people, we could have had a home like this in a world so peaceful and...and...

I finished work early, that day, for I wanted to be home and bathed in time for dinner. I'd pushed hard to be done, and the last client had picked up his car only moments before I closed the shop. If he hadn't made it, I'd have had to remain late, and that took time away from me that I did not wish to spare. Of course, it was Dr. Holleran and that bloody Anglia. Why he still drove the damn thing I'll never know. It was held together more by spit and wishes than by real mechanical knowledge. But some people grow to love their cars as much as they love their children. I never could do that, but I could still understand it.

Of course, he wanted to argue price. Again. "You'd sworn it would cost no more than twenty pounds, Brendan, and yet here this bill is for twenty-two and thirty. Where'd the extra cost come from?"

"I told you, I'd try to keep it at twenty, Dr. Holleran, but Parnell's is more expensive than Donaghey's, and they're the only ones had the part you needed. Here's the receipt."

"And yet you still charged ten pounds for putting it in, and it took you but twenty minutes."

"Plus a half hour on the phone calling about to junk yards asking if someone else had what was needed. If you had a newer car, sir, it'd be a lot easier."

"The car's perfectly fine. Here's your money, though I think it's just this side of robbery, I do."

I just shook my head and handed him his change. He got in, fussed about the car, checked everything and then drove off, the little beast spitting too much smoke out the exhaust for my taste, but that could be dealt with another time. I closed up the shop, locked everything down and headed off.

I had no car of my own, really needed none, but I was thinking more and more it might be good to have one. Gerald Haney was thinking of selling his Citroen 2CV now that it was near fifteen years old and rusting, but I could fix it up to where it would work fine, for me. I liked how they looked and rode far more than a Beetle or Mini, and the room in them was perfect for when I had to ferry a part back to the shop. So I hopped a bus and trundled on.

I lived on a street of simple terrace homes, each with its own little garden in front and a longer yard in back with a hutch. Nothing fancy, but I was of simple tastes. I liked having people around me I'd known for so long—Mrs. Kiernan and her cats, and Sandy Cowell with his wife and five wains, and Mr. and Mrs. Ross, the Scottish couple who lived two doors down because their retirement money went farther here than in Edinburgh.

My home was at the end, which gave us a bit more space, and was I proud to see how lovely it was kept as I approached. On this day, Joanna was in front, cutting some roses from a bush we had growing by the stoop. She saw me and waved and two heads popped up to scream, "Da!" then come running out the front gate. It wasn't for sweets in my pocket—I never carried those, for Joanna felt it was wrong to give children the idea their father is only worth greeting for what he had brung you. They'd race up to me because I'd fix their toys and listen to their stories and soothe their worries and understand how awful Ma was for not letting them go chasing about the cricket pitch near our home now it was almost time for supper.

A boy and a girl we had, with more wanted by us both. Eamonn, after my brother, not yet ten and already reading and doing mathematics better than I ever thought of doing at five years older than he. And Catherine, after Jo's mother, who loved to pretend she was a doctor repairing sicknesses in her dollies like I repaired engines in cars. Both bound for university, I could tell already, and didn't that make me prouder?

Of course, the Church was unhappy with me since I'd had them christened in both sides of the divide—at St. Agnes for my family and Christ Church for hers, and they were to be raised with the understanding they could choose either or neither as they wished, once they were of age, but until then they learned at one side this week and the other side the next. And I let them know that if one side criticized the other, they were to come to me so I could explain what fools such people were.

A kiss on Joanna's cheek, her lovely grin ear to ear at seeing me, and I could tell what that evening's dinner was to be—fish, of course, but baked in butter, lemon and herbs with carrots and green beans and freshly made rolls. She loved to cook more than simple meals, and even if the wains didn't always appreciate what was put before them, I loved every bite, no matter what.

Once I was washed and dinner was done, there'd be some time before the telly to laugh at the latest BBC comedy or some adaptation of yet another work by Dickens. Then the wains'd be up to bed and Joanna and I would share a pint—hers in a shandy, mine in a glass—and talk of her day. She taught at a nearby grammar school, where both of ours attended. We'd make plans for Saturday and she'd work out how well I was doing with the shop, which always seemed to bring in a bit more than enough to live on, so her salary was for putting aside and to be used for holiday. I'd talk to her about using the savings to buy Jerry's CV and do a travel around Donegal in it, with both wains. She'd point out the cost of insurance and registration and parking and the lot, but we'd find a way to make it work. There was also Eamonn coming by on Sunday to discuss opening a pull-in on the road connecting Derry and Belfast.

"There's talk of it being widened to a motorway, Bren," he'd said when first mentioned. "And to offer not only petrol but repairs, as well." He was always the one with plans...dreams as it were.

"I dunno, Eamonn," I'd replied. "I have me clients here, steady people, none of this fly-by stuff. We'd have to hire lads to do the work and I won't have just anybody."

"That'd be up to yourself, who was hired. It'd just need to be somebody from near Ballymaguigan."

"Will the road go through there?"

"Close enough."

"Have they actually allocated the money for this, in London?"

"They will."

That time-old phrase that made Joanna wild with anger. She was yet to be convinced, and Eamonn was up for trying once more to bring her into his way of thinking. Truth was, I wasn't so sure of it, myself. There wasn't so very much traffic between Derry and Belfast, since the majority of the economy was centered there instead of here, but it could mean something else was in the pipeline so I'd sent out queries to ask if any of my clients knew of anything coming up. So far, the word had been nothing.

Joanna was still against it and I was listening, no question, but I was also thinking, "If we did more than petrol and repairs, like in American truck stops, offering cooked meals as well as souvenirs and trinkets, it could prove good. But I'd go for a different location."

"Such as where?" she'd asked, curious.

"Toome. It's a nice town right by Lough Neagh and could bring in some of the tourist trade."

"Then why not Antrim?"

"Toome's prettier, and it's more the halfway mark."

She leaned on the table and sipped at her shandy, deep in thought, and the look of her lips touching the glass and the lightened ale drifting past them made my heart swell so, I felt it might burst. I was so lucky having her, and I knew it to the depth of my soul.

She glanced at me and my sudden emotion must have been obvious on my face, for she smiled and set the shandy down.

"Let's take the wains to Castlerock, tomorrow. Let them play on the beach. Let the sand scrub our thoughts. We could catch the train just after nine. Be there in less than an hour. I'll pack us a lunch, first thing. It'll be a nice treat for them, don't you think?"

I nodded, afraid to speak. She knew and caressed my face, and the touch of her elegant fingers brought me near to tears, I loved her so. She slipped her hand up to my ear and gently gripped its lobe to pull me close to her and we kissed. She tasted of the shandy with a hint still of the herbs from the fish and I pulled her closer. The back of her hand drifted down from my ear across my neck to tangle its fingers in my shirt and hold me even closer and I let my lips drift down her neck and nuzzled her breasts and she giggled in her deep, throaty way and whispered, "You sure you want another wain?" I chuckled in reply and picked her up and carried her to the couch and lay her on it and unbuttoned her blouse as she ran her hands up under my shirt and tugged at my jeans and I went mad with desire so left on her lacy bra and dove into the two mounds of pleasure encased by it and began to make love to her and—

The main door opened.

For an instant, I didn't know where I was. Or when. Full night had fallen, the sky clear and crisp and laughing with glittering beauty. No moon to dim it, yet.

Then the security lights went off and I saw a form framed in the warm glow from within the house.

Golden hair. Cropped short but still flowing lovely. Form slightly bent but still hers as she came out with a dog on a lead.

No, not a lead.

A harness.

With a handle.

And it was pulling at her, in my direction, softly growling.

"No, Baron, no. No woodchucks, tonight. I want you by me."

The dog settled at the sound of her voice.

It was her voice...but it wasn't. It was lower. Not as light and easy. And how she walked. Slightly bent over. Her left leg seeming as if it were more being dragged than used.

I knew she had been hurt. Damaged. Burned. But to what extent? I had to get closer. I had to see. I had to know if my fear of her having been more than crippled was founded in reality or paranoia. I edged up the drive to a more open area of the shrubbery and slowly crawled through them. Now covered in mud, and wet, through. I even felt a tear in my jeans, at the knee.

I didn't fool the dog with my soft movements. He looked straight at me and gave a low growl.

"I mean it, Baron," she said, her voice carrying a sharpness I'd never heard before. "If you can't behave, I'll take you inside."

The dog looked at her then back at me...but was quiet.

She was seated on a stone bench in a garden that was well tended. Late roses and cultured hedges. She wore a thick jumper and jeans, with slippers on her feet, and held a cup of what smelled like coffee.

Coffee? Not tea?

No spearmint?

There was a window opposite her, with just enough light filtering through to illuminate her face.

That is when I saw the scarring across her left cheek and eye. And her left hand was frozen in a crooked pose.

Baron was a guide dog. Did that mean she was blind, in full? I needed to know. I needed to understand.

I whispered, "Joanna."

The dog heard me and growled.

She heard me, as well, and stiffened, slightly. Turned to the sound of my voice. Frowning. Unsure. Showing the rest of her face.

Her right cheek was lovely as ever. Her lips untouched and—

I kissed her on the Ha'penny Bridge, asking "Is this too much," as I touched the tattoo and she kissed me back and scent of spearmint surrounded us and...

But both eyes were scarred over. She was blind. Could never see me, again. Never know me except by my voice and my touch.

I didn't care. That would be enough for me. I didn't care about anything else.

I needed her to understand, I didn't care about how she is, now, so long as she still loved me.

I didn't care about anything if she would still love me.

You seeing her like this would kill her.

That stopped me.

Then a side door snapped open, jolting me. I kept to the ground. Her mother, now larger and far more weary, appeared.

"Joanna, it's chilly out. Come inside. Supper's on, soon. Sit by the hearth. I'll bring you a book. The post brought a new one."

I watched Joanna hesitate, then rise and let Baron lead her to the door. But she stopped in the frame and almost looked around.

"Mum," she murmured, "do you believe in ghosts?"

"Don't be silly," was the woman's response. "I'll set the tape up and your ear phones so you don't disturb your Da. He's nodded off, again."

Joanna hesitated then continued inside. The dog cast one last warning growl at me before the door closed.

And was bolted.

And my world ended.

I rolled onto my back and looked at the stars. I could not move. I didn't care that I was wet and freezing. The stars were my friends and I needed them to comfort me. To explain to me why I hadn't stopped her. Told her I was alive. Held her, again. Let her know she and I could still become one, if she was willing.

You revealing yourself would kill her.

And I knew it would. Fuck Father Jack for being right.

Her world. It had been utterly destroyed, and even if we'd tried to rebuild it, nothing would have been the same.

There was too much existence between us.

All I could do now was tell our story.

And so the stars glistened. Silently mocking my childish dreams. I don't know how long I lay there before I was finally able to make myself rise, creep down to the lane and walk back to Ballymoney, freezing cold, my head and heart unavailable to me.

I caught the last bus to Derry. Rode past black hills and fields straining to be seen as clouds rolled in to hide those bloody fucking stars. The road ahead of us was barely visible, almost like we were headed nowhere.

Then we hit the edge of a fog. I say edge because we'd pass through moments of it then hit clear space then moments more, each one thicker than the one preceding it. The dark gray mist would flash over and vanish behind us, the headlights giving it an instant of life, and it seemed to me it was more alive now than I had ever been.

That mist was every plan I'd ever made silently whispering past. Swallowed by darkness. Having never truly existed. Soon to be burned away by the cruel morning sun.

It brought me to wonder—had I been born but ten miles to the west or north, would I have grown to see life in such a way? Would it have arranged itself in the form it did? Would I have found love and a future in a home of my own, and not been cast into darkness by this level of animalistic behavior? I like to think so, but truth be told, I can never know. I may well have wound up here, anyway...or worse. Who can say?

All I can say is, there comes a day where a man finally has to admit, if he's being honest with himself, that only those who refuse to know the evil of the world can still wonder at man's potential.

A story Jeremy once told me, came to mind...about the six nations living in Canaan. The land was rich and arable. Water abounded. So far as we knew, they existed in harmony with the world and their neighbors. We've found no stories to the contrary.

But then the Hebrews showed up and said they had to move. Said God had given the land to them. Claimed the six nations were not worthy of the earth they tilled, so they had to go elsewhere or be destroyed.

The six nations were offended by such a claim and refused to depart. So the Hebrews came roaring in and each was annihilated to the point of genocide...and everything was lost.

Everything.

Because one group of people decided *this land is ours and we don't care that you were here, first.* As it has been throughout history and always will be because—

Lights flared ahead of us and the bus slowed. I heard the distant growl of "Light's off! Lights off!" We pulled to a halt and soldiers stormed onto the bus, arms at the ready.

"Security stop," snarled one bulky bugger. "Papers!"

Then they checked each of us, in turn.

I offered mine up without hesitation, and they gave them the most perfunctory of glances. Nor was anyone searched or verbally harassed. It was just business as usual. *We're in control and you're not, so work with us, or else.*

A bit like Da's story with the Tuatha de Danaan and the Ui Bruiuns. And what the British had done in Ireland and the indigenous nations of America, India, Africa, and Australia.

I had to smirk. These soldiers were proof it continued to this day.

Some would call this attitude bleak. Claim it lacked understanding of man's capacity for great love and empathy. But in truth, man does not want to be different from the beasts, not really. The hope for such illusions is only in his heart, not his head, and one can achieve nothing without the other. It has always been so and always will be so, and all the belief in the world means little in the face of it. To claim mankind is a creature built of anything but animalistic selfishness is to fly in the face of reality.

I accept this, now, and understand it for what it truly is—the basis of human existence. Its destiny, if you will. I knew it was so when I saw the remains of Joanna. I knew it as I flew back to Derry to see my dying mother. I knew it when I so brutally separated myself from Evangelyne. I knew it as I was taken to Houston. I knew it as I left Jo at her father's shop, that horrible day. I knew it on Bloody Sunday and Internment and Burntollet and when my Da was killed. I couldn't see it, then, but deep within my soul, I knew...and I feared nothing as much as that knowledge making itself permanent within me.

Hopes. Wishes. Dreams. Prayers. Simple words filled with so much meaning to those who still held faith in their hearts. Each notion carrying a vague little promise that all will be well if only you just keep on. The tomorrows and tomorrows and tomorrows yet to come could still hold prospects of happiness and contentment. All you had to do is believe and there it would be.

Yet in truth, faith has never filled an empty belly. Ideals lead men to destroy their greatest creations and fear carries them into the depths of hell, and none would honestly, truthfully, have it any other way, despite all the lovely, lovely words one hears to the contrary.

So here it is, and willingly accepted. We are born. We live an existence of meaning to ourselves, alone. We die. All else is illusion. Now I saw this, now I acknowledged my life for what it truly is, I could admit to myself that it had turned out exactly as it must. For truth be told, this world is no haven for something as foolish as prayers, nor does it truly hold a place of safety for anything as childish as hopes and dreams.

And oh dear God, would that it were not so.

THE END

About this Author

Kyle Michel Sullivan used to write screenplays, but shifted to writing books that range from sunshine and light (*David Martin*) to cold and dark (*How To Rape A Straight Guy*, which has been banned more than once) to farcical and insane (*The Lyons' Den*) to mainstream romance (*The Alice '65*) to a tale of tragedy and redemption (*Bobby Carapisi)*. He has ventured into SF-Horror-Suspense with *The Beast in the Nothing Room*, done gay revenge in *Porno Manifesto* and worked up a vicious female revenge thriller in *Carli's Kills*, then taken Capitalism to its logical extreme in *Hunter*. He has also written murder mysteries (*Rape in Holding Cell 6, The Vanishing of Owen Taylor*, and *Underground Guy*).

Most of his novels are gay-oriented but not all. Many contain intense sexual content that fits the erotica category, but not all. Some are even romantic and tender. He's written what he's written, and each one of those books got him one step closer to this point.

He tries to build characters as vivid and real as possible and has a lot of fun doing it mixed with angst, anger, and amazement ... but that's the lot of a writer.

Other Books by This Author

General fiction
A Place of Safety-Derry
A Place of Safety-New World For Old
The Alice '65
The Vanishing of Owen Taylor
Bobby Carapisi
The Lyons' Den
David Martin

Adult Erotica
Blood Angel series - Léonidès (ebook only)
                    - The Prussian (ebook only)
Carli's Kills
Hunter
The Beast in the Nothing Room
Underground Guy
Rape in Holding Cell 6
Porno Manifesto
Curt (AKA: How to Rape a Straight Guy)